The Senior was behind them, unseen. "Come, my black friend, my pretty, great bug," he crooned. "Come see what I've brought you."

Yan felt Illyssa fumbling in her clothing. She palmed something small and yellow-brown and tossed it away with a flick of her wrist.

Behind them, a rising chatter of locust wings answered the Senior's exhortations. "I've brought you a witch, Son of Pharos," the Senior cooed above the rattle and scrape of chitinous appendages on the flagstones. The stink of dead flies and carrion was stronger than ever. Somewhere a bee droned melodically, a warm, earthy sound out of place beneath the red glare and alien machines. "A bee!" the Senior rasped desperately. "Kill it. He hates bees. Quickly now, before he—" The Senior's voice cut off in a rattle of chitin, a rising trill like a thousand crickets, and resumed as a shriek of inarticulate terror and pain.

By L. Warren Douglas
Published by Ballantine Books:

A PLAGUE OF CHANGE

And look for these other Del Rey Discoveries . . .
Because something new is always worth the risk!

DEMON DRUMS by Carol Severance
THE QUICKSILVER SCREEN by Don H. DeBrandt
CHILDREN OF THE EARTH by Catherine Wells
THE OUTSKIRTER'S SECRET by Rosemary Kirstein
MIND LIGHT by Margaret Davis
AMMONITE by Nicola Griffith
DANCER OF THE SIXTH by Michelle Shirey Crean
THE DRYLANDS by Mary Rosenblum
McLENDON'S SYNDROME by Robert Frezza
BRIGHT ISLANDS IN A DARK SEA by L. Warren Douglas

BRIGHT ISLANDS IN A DARK SEA

L. Warren Douglas

A Del Rey Book
BALLANTINE BOOKS • NEW YORK

A Del Rey Book
Published by Ballantine Books

Library of Congress Catalog Card Number: 93-90080

ISBN 0-345-38238-2

Manufactured in the United States of America

First Edition: July 1993

Dedication

You set me on a good course, Captain, and I will keep to it through whatever dark and heavy seas cross my bow. Someday we will meet again on one of those bright islands out there.

This one is dedicated to the late Arthur G. Folkringa, August 22, 1928–March 23, 1993, sailor and friend.

Appreciation

To Wm. Foster "Bud" Potts, for twenty-seven years of terrible advice and excellent technical assistance.

To Mlle. L. N. Rossignol, without whose persistence, patience, and perceptivity this book would never have come together. See the comma after patience, m'dear?

Prologue

Roke, a city on the Lannick Coast
Springtime, Year 3849, Common Reckoning

In a high corner tower of the second-largest cathedral in the known world, high-ranking churchmen watched in horror as the Son of God disintegrated before their very eyes. Now eight horrid creatures—clawed like crabs, black and glossy as crickets, big as sheepdogs, and as hungry as winter's wolves—prowled the corridors of Roke Cathedral.

Within days of their appearance, the monstrous apparitions dragged down and consumed several Church Militant guards, a scribe, and a Hand of the Order of Pharos. Later recovered, the drained husks of their prey lay unseemly light in their coffins. Were the voracious entities a plague sent by the dying god? Were they the god's murderers or avatars? Stupid, vicious, and deadly—should they be slain, endured, or worshiped?

Hernock Vann, the Senior of Roke, no longer having even the son of a god to turn to for counsel, ordered his carriage readied and called for a platoon of horse troops to escort him across the mountains and down to the Inland Sea. He ordered a ship to await him, to carry him to the city of Innis.

The Senior of Innis, Hernock's colleague, mentor, and boyhood friend, would surely advise him. Meantime, the black creatures were still confined to the tower, and showed no interest in its heavy oak doors or iron-bound gates. Convicts and stray dogs would suffice to maintain them in sated complacency, he hoped, until he learned what he should do.

CHAPTER ONE

"History has meant many things to people living and dead—and considering the span of this poor Earth's recorded past, six, seven, even eight thousand years, there are more lovers of the written word who are dead than living.

"Dead ones' words survive, as do their unwritten agendas. 'Those who do not study history are doomed to repeat it,' claimed one anonymous scrivener. 'History is written by winners,' claimed another. But if Earth long ago lost her own crucial battle, who wrote the histories we read, the tales we recount?"

Y.B., 3849 C.E., the Duchy of Wain

Yan Bando put down his pen. He was not a historian, not exactly. He studied the Mother of Wisdom, but only as an adjunct to his own true calling, the recently revived field of archaeology. Archaeology, unlike history, did not lie. Though incomplete and unclear, it was written in the soil. Its words were shards, ruins, and ancient spaceships, the bones of winners, losers, and those who never played the game.

Unlike the historians he studied, Yan was apolitical, and absolutely honest in his work; that was his first problem.

His mentor, the academician Lazko, was dead, his calcined bones mixed with the rubble of his house, the ashes of his books, and the slagged artifacts he had treasured, all now a vanishingly small paragraph in the book of the soil; that was Yan's second problem. There were others, of course, even before his current difficulties, but those were largely of a personal nature, and troubled no one but himself.

Yan rose and stretched, scratching his short beard. In the cramped fisherman's shed where he hid, he seemed large. He would have seemed it even in his father's great stone hall in the March of Musgone: muscles put on in his early training with broadswords and war axes had been augmented by years of shovel-wielding, wheelbarrow-pushing, stone-rolling research. Nobility, family, and war axes were things of the past, traded first for a dun robe and a scholar's cubicle within the walls of the university at Nahbor, and lately for dusty boots and a fugitive's dank hideaway; but his muscles endured.

Only this morning, in the university precinct of Nahbor, the two browncoat thugs who had slain Lazko had had good cause to regret Yan Bando's unscholarly musculature. In the early hours he had bought a sausage cake from a street vendor and, anticipating the sunrise rush of drays and oxcarts, had set out in darkness for Lazko's house. The iron gate to Wildrose Court made no protest as he entered. No lamps shone in the houses that walled the court, but a red glow lit Lazko's lower windows. Yan smelled smoke as he passed the long-dry fountain, and then saw wisps of it seeping from the roof shakes of the house. The old man's fallen asleep at his reading table, Yan thought, and his candle's caught something afire!

He rushed to the door, but some instinct drew him up short. The latch lifted at his touch, and the heavy oak panel swung aside to reveal a nightmare scene: Lazko was clearly dead, his head resting in a liverish puddle of thickening blood. Flames licked the far wall. Two men in brown priest's robes spun around as he entered. Their movements seemed leaden. The flames themselves danced unnaturally slowly, and the blood dripping from Lazko's writing table fell with less than expected speed.

Yan's personal demon took command of him, a kind of madness. He saw his surroundings with unnatural clarity and he reacted with inhuman speed, but to him, it was the world that had slowed. In the time it took to cross the room, his eyes and mind absorbed the missing volumes of notes on his and Lazko's joint research, the empty shelves where drawings had been stored, the pens and fragments of an inkpot strewn about. He saw the crushed ruin that was Lazko's skull, and his staring left eye—its punctured companion now a flaccid sac. He saw the oil pot in one brown-robed thug's hand, and the flaring pitch-pine splinter in his companion's.

Yan snatched the oil pot, cradling it in a broad palm even as his other hand plunged toward one priest's eyes. Gore splashed his fingers and his homespun sleeve. Whirling without waiting to see his opponent fall, he rammed the second priest with a shoulder and caught the burning splinter, crushing its flame. The oil pot sat unbroken, upright, though Yan had no memory of setting it down.

The second priest had no time to cherish memories when Yan's hands found his throat, his thick fingers nearly disappearing in overripe priestly flesh as he squeezed. Crushed, its structure and function destroyed, the throat was only a limp, fleshy tube holding head to shoulders. Yan shook his hands to free them. Fifteen seconds had elapsed since the door had swung open on well-greased pintles—less time than an emotion takes to form and flower, no time at all to feel the inevitable revulsion and shame he would feel when all was done.

Flames heated Yan's face. The notebooks! The thick, hide-bound tomes, their minuscule lettering cramped within narrow margins, were the essence of the old man's work and Yan's. They lay in an oil-soaked pile, licked by slow, lascivious flames. Most were already burned, but Yan salvaged four. Heavy as they were, he swung them beneath a curled forearm, damping their charred edges in his robe. He then reached into a smoking cabinet to withdraw a paper-wrapped packet, brushing embers and char aside with his bare fingers.

He recognized a long, twisted piece of metal: a souvenir of his excavations in Michan, a fragment of a wrecked ship of space. He saw blood on it, and Lazko's gray hairs. That corrosion-riddled shard had killed his mentor. It was the object that had started it all, the first discovery in a chain that led to this moment. He let it lie. Let the brownshirts sift the ashes for it.

The fire spread. Loft planks glowed and burning straw insulation sifted down; clothing smoldered. Yan reached down to close his mentor's staring eye. At the door, he pinched out the smolders in his own robe, feeling no pain though his fingers blackened.

Closing the door behind him, he walked swiftly but casually away. No alarm had been given. Minutes later, he stood in a shadowed alley, his chest heaving from exertion and emotion. His demon had departed unnoticed; now the world proceeded at a normal pace. Birds chirped beneath wood-shingled eaves and distant teamsters' cries awakened the city. Tears blurred his vision as he tore the blackened wrappings from the packet he'd taken and distributed dozens of one-ounce chips of soft gold—treasure from the wrecked spaceship—in the small pockets of his work robe. He grimaced in disgust: he had fouled his undergarments—his demon's inevitable sign. He left them there in the alley with the torn, charred wrapping paper.

When dawn first lightened his path, Lazko's ashes were cool and Yan was fifteen miles east of Nahbor. His black-smudged hands rested on a bag slung across his saddle. Their dark hair was burnt away, but the flames had not reddened his flesh. Ahead, the village of Wain nestled between rounded hills, and the waters of the Eastern Reach stretched beyond to the horizon. The sea was lead gray in the wan morning light, but as he rode down the easy slope, a sliver of sunlight broke through the clouds: a pale, pink reflection of the flames that still burned behind his eyes.

Stretching his muscles, Yan returned to his writing. It was not yet dark, and it would not do to wander about in Wain. He doubted that the Church's minions had picked up his trail in Nahbor, but a tall man on horseback was easily remembered, and the hierarchs would not assume their men had died in a fire of their own setting. He waited for darkness to obscure the waterfront, again picking up his pen and attempting to put the contradictions of "history" into perspective.

One version of history claimed that because humans were incapable of piloting ships that plied the stars, they were ready victims of alien races seeking serfs and laborers for their plantation worlds. Because humans went mad and died in the pilot seats of interstellar craft, because they were unable to cope with forces in the altered translight universe, the human race had been helpless when Earth was in turmoil. Melting ice caps and deforming continents had provided starfaring races with refugees, human cattle to fill their ships' holds. That was history as it was recorded in university archives.

Then there was history as the Church of Pharos told it: not of alien races, but of gods. The god Pharos lowered his golden ship to Earth not to save starving victims of climatic catastrophe, but Pharos' devout followers. He transported them not to barren planets as laborers or slaves, but to elysian worlds under distant suns, to Paradise.

Considering divergent realities, no wonder Church and University had been at odds for a millennium. Both, of course, had been winners for a while, but vocal ignorance outmatched silent knowledge, and the Church had grown while universities remained static and isolated, selling gadgets and expertise, soliciting only the best and brightest minds while the Church of Pharos proselytized among farmers and sailors, tanners, traders, and, most dangerously of all, kings.

A few years earlier, the large stone church in Wain had been only a log building where a handful of madmen howled and frothed and rolled their eyes, speaking in gibberish and calling out aloud to Pharos, their alien God. Townsmen had made demon signs at them or spat at their feet. Now men spoke softly of the Pharos Church, afraid of offending its members.

In truth, Yan reflected sadly, the Church had won its battle centuries earlier, and Lazko's death had occurred in a minor skirmish, a cleanup of resistance. Most universities had long since fallen, and brown-robed penitents howled "Pharos! Pharos!" in their halls. Nahbor, too, would fall. It was powerless to prevent the Church from inciting strikes and sabotage. Wild-eyed converts spit in the street when scholars passed, and most bright young men chose brown or crimson robes over the scholar's dun.

Tears blurred Yan's vision as he thought about Lazko. A much-younger Yan Bando had found the metal shard that killed him and had carried it first home, then to university, where it was eventually noticed by Lazko the antiquarian. The buried spaceship was excavated two short years later.

The hull, buried in six meters of silty peat, had been located with ancient instruments that marked the decay of elements. The discovery of a ship of space, any ship, in any condition, was momentous and controversial. The ship was of alien manufacture, and it had been wrecked on Earth. That alone was enough to provoke the Pharos priests—Gods did not have shipwrecks.

Churchmen had lurked about the excavation site, using their influence with suppliers and hired laborers to create shortages and work stoppages but hesitating short of outright violence. When the excavators pumped out the mire that filled the hull and saw what was within, the priests became entirely hostile.

Though the ship's metal had been badly corroded, the same acidic muck that attacked metals preserved wood and flesh. Expecting to discover strange, unearthly life-forms, the diggers found rude wooden pilot chairs with men in them—men as human as Yan, Lazko, or the Pharos priests themselves.

At that moment, archaeology collided with both versions of history. The evidence of the soil seemed clear: a ship of alien manufacture had been roughly modified for human use and, Yan was convinced, had been flown by them.

But what could he do about his discoveries now? Nothing. He had headed east to Wain because it was on the opposite coast from his father's estates, where he would surely be sought. Once he eluded any pursuers, he could head south, even to distant Burum. There were still other universities. Lazko had corresponded with Burumese scholars. Who knew? They might even have use for a digger of ancient things.

Somewhere behind the dark slim girl, the light of the world pushed piercing fingers into the earth. But here, an hour's walk into the depth of the Unending Cave, the only light was a single candle illuminating an old witch-woman's face. Seen by daylight, it would have been an ordinary face, wrinkled by sun and wind, gap-toothed as old mouths are, and surmounted by thinning gray hair like any crone's in the town. But here, in the earth's very gut, in the home of all secrets, it was a terrifying sight.

If I survive this, the girl reminded herself, I will be a witch, and I will fear her no more. She will be only an old woman. If I fail, it won't matter. I won't remember a thing.

"Outsiders call us witches, child," the crone murmured. "What are we?"

"We are children of a far star," the girl Illyssa recited in singsong. "Our minds entwine. Our thoughts reach out and speak with tongues of flame."

"High, green hills surround and hide us. What do we fear?"

"We fear black abominations, slavers and herders of men." The memorized words flowed. This was the easy part of her catechism; the real test would follow. "We fear the False Church, their tool," Illyssa continued, "priests who are their eyes and ears on Earth, and soldier-priests who hunt us for the black masters."

"We are hunted," the hag stated. "Are we wild pigs, then, or hares? Are we playthings or food?"

"We are star-wolves and raveners," the girl replied, her voice tremulous with the frightening impact of her words. "We are far-wanderers, dark-space rovers marooned on this isle. The black ones would use us as dogs in their harnesses, leaping and running their errands from star to star."

"What holds us here, planet-fallen?"

"The One Man was lost, and with him the Merging and Melding, keys to the stars. The Seed and the Flower do not breed true. The Ship lies beneath waters and the slavemasters circle above."

The old woman lit a dark cheroot from her single candle. "Enough, child. I am sure you can recite all the Responses word for word. But do you *understand*? Do you *believe*? Or are you no more than any village girl, a child of these mountains?"

"I am a child, Grandmother," the girl said in ritual singsong. "I am an unbeliever, unfit. Do with me what you will."

"Do you *want* to understand, to believe?" It was no ritual question.

Illyssa's eyes sparked with anger. "I want to know what is *real*," she said. "I want to believe what is *true*. If the Tales and Responses are history, I want to know that. If they're only madness of old women, I want to know *that*, too."

The hag sighed. "I can't show you ferosians, child. I cannot give you the True Flower to eat, either, and I can't take you through the corridors of the Ship. How will you *know*? What are you willing to risk for your assurances?"

The girl slipped back into singsong, unable or afraid to put her wishes into plain words. "I wish to eat the False Flower, and to speak with the minds of my ancestresses. Then I will believe. I have seen the simpleminded ones, now only wombs to birth and breasts to nurse, and I will risk becoming as they are."

The old woman responded with a sad, slow shake of her head. "Then risk it you shall. Have you said your farewells to your mother and father?"

"I have."

"Then we begin. When you emerge from this chamber, be you brood mare or witch, your parents' child will be no more."

CHAPTER TWO

Washington—(IPS)—The House of Representatives narrowly passed the New White House's favored antiemigration bill, which prohibits designated Nationally Valued Persons (NVPs) from boarding any non-government-owned spacecraft. Citing the recent departure of the entire faculty and many students of the Midland Technical Institute, ferried from the rooftops of the flooded campus to a waiting Faroseen ship, President Tuthill stated that "we cannot continue to permit the heart and brains of this nation to be excised, and still expect its body to function."

April 12, 2260, *International Weekly*, Geneva. From a facsimile in Volume I of Eustis Lazko's compendium.

West Wind's mast bobbed wildly as the young man descended to her deck, swinging a blue canvas sack ahead of him. It hit the smooth, bleached boards with a thump.

The boat's owner regarded him with wary neutrality. At first glance, the old fisherman thought, the lean, large-boned fellow looked out of place in ordinary traveler's clothing. His ice-blue eyes and narrow, distinctly northern nose hinted at noble birth among the foggy, heavily forested coastal bogs and islands. Omer mistrusted men of noble birth, especially those with thick wrists more suited to broadswords than teacups, with skin weathered to rich bronze, not pale. The times were unsettled. The only honest enemy was the sea. There were too many goings-on and intrigues for a man to let his guard down.

"Don't you remember me, Om?" the younger man asked.

The fisherman took another look. His yellow-gray bushy eyebrows rose in surprised recognition. "P'fesser!" he exclaimed.

"I never saw you so—no scholar's robe, no dirt on yer face. An' tha' beard, it ages you." He stretched out a leathery hand.

"You've only seen me in summer," Yan said. "I shave then, because of Michan's burrowing mites, but now that the digging's done, I'm like anyone else, I'm afraid." His faint smile faded. "At least I was."

"And what are you now?" the boatman asked. "You look to be well worn by the road."

Yan hesitated. How much did he dare tell? He'd picked the *West Wind* because Omer had worked for Lazko, ferrying supplies to the dig and artifacts back to Nahbor. But what did he really know about him? Eyes can't peer into a man's soul. "I've left the university on . . . on extended research. I go to New Roster. Will you take me there?"

"New Roster? Aya, it's a long sail. Nearly to th' other end a' the Reach."

"Will this be enough?" Yan held out copper and silver coins, a generous offer. "I must leave immediately."

"Aya, I'll take you there," Omer agreed. "And for that sum, you get meals, too. Is that all your gear, P'fesser? No crates or boxes? How can you do research wi'out your tools?"

Omer's words were casual, but Yan sensed falseness. I'm paranoid, he thought. He's only curious. The old man stared past him as if bidding the quaint, silvery wood buildings of Wain good-bye. "Well, then, cast off tha' line," he said gruffly. "Na—just toss it on th' dock. Now push us away." Yan pushed at a piling with a foot, unbalancing as the boat slipped sideways. He caught a tarred stay with one arm and a leg, then dangled over the water until he could get his other leg back on board. He barked his shin, and as he bent to rub it, he missed seeing what Omer had seen: a gaunt figure emerging between two shanties, robed and hooded in cloth the color of wet ashes, squinting at them over the low-angling sunlight that glared off the *West Wind*'s wake.

"Can I help with anything?" Yan asked.

"You paid your passage." The fisherman's words came from aft, over the cabin roof. "Help any more than that, and you'll be bruised all over." Yan grimaced at the hoarse laugh that followed. Shrugging, he climbed aft and settled against the mast to watch the shoreline recede.

The brown-robed priest scurried unhappily back to his waiting carriage. He would have to report that his quarry had escaped again. His driver, an acolyte and his current playmate, cringed and tightened his buttocks when he saw his superior's red, angry face. *He* would suffer the priest's rage. It already promised to be a most unpleasant day.

There was nothing productive for a landsman to do on a small boat rocking gently on nighttime swells. Observing Yan's fidgety unrest, the fisherman chided him. "It's a long few days to New Roster, Yan Bando. The sea's no place for a man who's na' at home wi' his own thoughts."

Did he know something was wrong? Had he sensed Yan's unease? The scholar was no accomplished dissembler, and he knew it. "I'm comfortable enough with my thoughts," he replied, smiling to cover his anxiety, "but only when I have a pen in my hand and paper before me."

"Aya. Always the p'fesser, eh? Then let's make a light for this airy study a' yours." He went below, returning with a contraption of glass and prisms. "A chart lamp. The glass magnifies the candle's light a bit."

Yan thanked him. What could he do now? He didn't want to bring out the notebooks. There were too many odd-looking pages of edge-punched paper spewed from the library's machines, and photocopies with letters too small and regular to have been written by human hands.

With considerable dexterity he fished new, creamy sheets from his bag, and using the hard book-covers within for a desk, he picked up his thoughts where he'd left them in Wain.

The metal fragment in Lazko's house had been the starting point of his trials, but the wreck itself was only one sad relic of a long trail of events that led further back in time. Philosophically, Yan suspected his troubles had begun when the first rudimentary cell divided in Earth's ancient seas; as an antiquarian, he was constrained to begin with the artifacts and events recorded in the books he'd saved from the fire.

By earthly standards of any age, the alien ship was enormous, thirty by two hundred meters of gray, pitted metal, like seven lengths of sewer pipe bolted together at the flanges. A conical trailing segment was tipped with a slender, pointed mast, and the leading end was a forty-meter sphere with a large depression in its forward surface. Four metal-mesh dragonfly wings a hundred meters long stretched from just behind the bulbous "head."

Yan, a careful observer, had noticed different degrees of pitting on adjacent sections, worn corners on pentagonal boltheads, and scarred lips on connecting flanges. He had deduced that the ship was no more than a conjoining of interchangeable modules: control, cargo, and drive. Hardly a "ship" of space, it was really a "train." Its odd pentagonal bolts and mixed four- and fivefold symmetries were clearly not of human design or manufacture.

Within, the leathery remains of a human crew were scattered on makeshift wooden couches in holds and hallways, their shriveled eyes still facing equally makeshift instrument panels. Colorful sheaths of corroded cable ran everywhere, secured to walls, floors, and ceilings with roughly welded staples and twists of wire. They ran through ventilation ducts, down hallways, in and out of once-airtight doors. Most of them originated within rudely cut openings in the vessel's gray metal and terminated at improvised crew stations, where branched tangles of colored wires ended in rough, hand-fabricated controls. In the forward control room, a huge machinelike pilot's seat made to enclose an unimaginably alien pilot stood abandoned, disconnected from the cable nerve net of the ship.

Imagine their surprise when those far-traveling men and women first gazed on the planet their ancestors had left long ago. No satellites had spun about them, no signals had greeted them. Below, no electric-bright city lights winked. Yan suspected the outlines of continents their slave ancestors might have recognized were changed beyond recognition. No polar ice caps would have glared. Could they have guessed how seas had risen, continents twisted and plunged, in the half millennium since their kind had left Earth as slaves of alien *ferosin*? Earth must have seemed void of intelligent life to them. Could their instruments have seen towns linked only by muddy tracks where mules and donkeys, oxen and barefoot men, shared the rutted ways?

How long did it take them to decide their course of action? Did they have fuel to return home to some far world? Would they have been welcome there? Only desperation could have forced them to land; their great ship was never intended to breach the atmosphere of a world. They had surely expected to have been met in orbit, but no one had come. No one had answered their signals. For all they could have known, they had been alone. It must have been a bitter dose, Yan thought, when they decided to take it. Once landed, they were trapped on a world so primitive that men had forgotten how to reach their own looming moon, had forgotten even that their ancestors had once stood on its surface. They could never again have seen the stars except as they winked from Earth's thick veil of air and cloud.

Perhaps they had hoped Earth's primitives could be taught the secrets they'd learned on some far world. Perhaps they'd intended it, but Yan knew it had not happened. The world would have been far different from the place of rude, dirty towns, of dusty roads and torchlit streets. That *he* knew.

There was a terrible inertia to ignorance. Without the scientific mind-set that linked cause and effect, without understanding hypothesis, proof, and disproof, Earth folk might have worshipped those ancient spacefarers or slain them as witches, but they would never have let them change the world.

Could anyone, ever? Archaeology gave Yan perspective across a vast span of time. He seemed to stand on a hilltop watching the river of eternity pass by, its roiled waters broad, its current determined. Historians stood on lesser rises than he, studying the courses of lesser tributaries, minor spans of space and time. A simple historian might not see the world-changing as such a daunting task.

But the courses of rivers, nations, and worlds *could* be changed. From Yan's high vantage individual cultures, eras, and histories seemed small and unimportant and, like the broadest river, the timestream had vulnerable stretches—meander loops where a narrow ditch could be dug. Shallow and narrow at first, the pent-up impetus of current would scour and widen it; time and history would soon follow the new course. Or tiny forces of frost, water and wind, spalling flakes of granite from crucial stones, could cause a landslide and block the widest streambed, diverting time and events into a new channel, a new history.

Presently, Yan Bando could only study the course of events. Changing it might not take much effort, but he didn't know those critical weak points any better than the old spacemen had. There were two kinds of knowledge involved: vast and tiny. Cutting the ditch, turning a meander straight to leave an oxbow lake bypassed by time, took map knowledge, vast in scope. One had to know where the stream was vulnerable. Catastrophic historic change—the landslide—demanded intimate familiarity with small, unlikely vulnerabilities: a king's momentary drunken lapse, a spy's mistaken observation, a nail, a horseshoe . . . Knowledge, sweeping and detailed. Which drunken moment? What distraction? What horse, what horseshoe?

Yan Bando, fugitive, was in no position to change anything, but he would still be able to supplement his knowledge with bits and pieces, to collect data and record them. Perhaps some wiser reader of his notes would find the key to change, and would turn humanity back into the channel that had almost led to the stars. The long diversion into dust, disease, and ignorance could yet end. Yan was determined to continue observing and scribbling, collecting a morsel here, a bit there, his small contribution to a future that might or might not be.

Wistfully, Yan toyed idly with the carved wooden object that hung from a thong about his neck.

"What's that?" The fisherman's harsh voice jarred him out of his gloomy reverie.

"Nothing much. A toy my father carved. A keepsake." He slipped its leather thong over his head and tossed the object up on deck. Omer caught it with a casual sweep of his hand. He held it further from his eyes than Yan might have; his eyes were used to staring at distant horizons, not examining artifacts close at hand. Carved from a single piece of soft pine, a wooden ball was confined in a delicate cylindrical cage. Links of chain were carved from the same piece. Flecks of azure and cerulean clung to the ball. The links, once gilded, were dull ocher.

Omer tilted the cage from side to side, watching the faded ball roll from end to end. "I had one of these," he mused. "Na' so small, though. They sell them in the markets a' Burum."

"The chain was longer, once. There was something on the other end, too. I don't remember what it was."

"Funny, the things we keep. I had a wooden chicken. The legs were gone, and . . ." His voice dropped off abruptly.

"What happened to it? I mean, did you lose it?"

The fisherman hesitated before answering. "Aya, I lost it," he admitted reluctantly. "I lost it in the fire that took my young son. I'd given it to him. I was at sea at the time."

"I'm sorry," Yan murmured.

The old man tossed the trinket back. It rattled, twisting in the air. "It was a long time ago." He shut his eyes against the sun high overhead. A long time? Yan thought. Some grief never fades. We just push it into untrammeled corners of our minds and step around it, most of the time. He slipped the thong back around his neck and tucked it beneath his robe.

The old woman bent over the small, limp form. She hesitated, afraid of what she might see. "Here, Illyssa," she said softly, "drink this. You'll feel better soon."

The girl stirred. The old one paled at the blankness of the girl's gaze. As the False Flower's murk faded, those glazed eyes brightened, and Illyssa's silence became full of questions.

"Yes, you survived the testing," she heard. "You are neither child nor brood beast now. What *have* you become?"

The girl's voice was faint and rasping. Her words didn't match her youthful face. "I am you, Grandmother. I am sister, aunt, mother, and mother's mother, to the beginning of our kind. I am Semal Gold-eye's lover, slave, and star flier. I am of Earth, then of Ararat, then of Earth again. I am that, and I am nothing. I am a tool in your grasp, begging to be used."

"You're still fresh from the spell of the False Flower, young witch. Your words and feelings are as much the Others' as your own. I won't accept commitment from you now." The old one drew back and sat on her wooden stool.

"I wish to give it," the girl stated flatly. "The Others have shown me much, but they fade. I speak for myself."

The crone shrugged, as if she'd heard such words before. How many young women had she heard them from? Illyssa wondered. "Then be used," she heard. "You may die. Do you fear that?"

"Everyone dies, yet we go on. I fear suffering, and my weakness to withstand it, but not death for good cause."

The old woman offered her a small cloth bag. "Then take this, and eat a pinch once each new moon. Then you may die when you wish it. The Others have shown you the way? You are ready?"

"I am ready," Illyssa said. "I am eager to be commanded and I await your direction."

"Then listen well. This is your task . . ."

CHAPTER THREE

We are faced with unpleasant facts. First, FTL navigation exceeds the capacity of the human brain. Second, synchronization precludes a team approach—words are not fast enough. Third, genetic, surgical and electro-mechanical augmentation have failed to circumvent facts one and two.

Faced with our failure to achieve human-controlled interstellar flight, the World Space Research Organization will shortly issue a final recommendation that affected member states accept ferosian offers to transport populations of afflicted areas to habitable worlds within the ferosian sphere of the galaxy.

From WSRO Chairman I.R. Devadutt's resignation speech, January 12, 2282. Nahbor University databank printout, Volume I of Eustis Lazko's compendium.

The light sailboat rode high in the water, dipping slightly behind each gentle swell. Omer tied off the tiller, adjusted the boom vang, and slacked the gaff keeper to his satisfaction. While the wind held, *West Wind* would sail herself. "I need sleep," he said. "Come dark, or if th' wind rises, pound on the hatch cover afore the mast. Food's in the ice chest aft." The companionway tambour snicked shut on his last words.

Yan stretched his legs. There were still a few hours until dusk, he observed, reaching for his bag. He took out one charred book, a record of events compiled from sources in the university library. Those events began seventeen hundred years earlier, with the first recorded landing of an alien vessel on Earth. Lazko's tight minuscule alternated with photocopies and printouts. Tabulating and sorting those articles, excerpts, and anecdotes, and statistics would have taken Yan years using edge-punched cards and beechwood dowels, but cultivating the interest of archivists with access to the university's computer databases had taken only weeks of Lazko's time. The books, Yan reflected regretfully, were Lazko's only legacy.

Yan read of alien landings and unsuccessful human attempts to pilot ships duplicating the aliens' own. The pages that followed, to the end of the volume, were accounts of further landings, names of alien ships, even descriptions of passengers taken on. The early entries were copies of news reports. Some described beautiful, livable planets promised to refugees from fairy-tale places like New Orleans, Kiev, Paris, and Tokyo. Later entries were terse: name of ship, date and place of arrival, candidates accepted, and departure. The cities named were less romantic: Pittsburgh, Indianapolis, and Baltimore. By Indianapolis, Lazko had written "Innis," and he had identified Baltimore as the Isle of Baltum. Of course, there were no current names for cities now beneath the Inland Sea.

The political and theological impact of that first volume had been apparent to Yan from the beginning. Having no use for simplistic gods or a Church built on hyperbole and deception, he viewed the Pharos cult's influence as a malign cancer that sapped the lifeblood of human society, draining its intellectual vigor into the Church's own sour pot. Religion and politics in this age, he reflected, are one and the same.

According to the Church, the Five Gods had once divided the universe among themselves, with Earth on the periphery of the realm of Pharos, neither the strongest nor weakest god. "Pharos," Yan had heard priests claim, "is a busy God who travels constantly about His vast domain, and Earth is the least of His possessions, hardly worthy of His notice." But even if He forgot Earth, they insisted, the four rapacious Others would not; Proon, Rath, Inoo, and Dumeen awaited Pharos' least moment of forgetfulness, ready to sweep in and destroy, to deny Him a portion of His Power, and only the brownskirts' continual noisy prayer kept His attention on the insignificant planet Earth.

Like all effective religions, the Church used both carrot and stick. Deep within Pharos' realm, sermons said, were worlds where souls of devout—and vocal—Earthly worshipers found refuge. Saintly humans might be taken to them still occupying mortal bodies, and might be given unspoiled worlds to populate with their seed, for the glorification of the God.

The Five Gods were mentioned in Lazko's compendium—but not as deities. Whatever they looked like, no matter how technologically advanced they were, and whether those names referred to their bearers' species, planet of origin, race, tribe, family, or even trading company, to Lazko and to Yan after him the *idumeen*, *tsrath*, *inouwa*, and *ferosin* were mortal beings, not gods.

How did that relate to Yan's problem? First, acidic soil covering the wrecked ship had preserved more detail than churchmen could tolerate. Even grains and seeds were preserved, and whether in storage sacks or crewmens' acid-tanned stomachs, the telltale seeds were not from Earthly crops. The crewmen had not been on Earth long enough to eat local food, or to use up what they'd brought from the stars, though they had not died in the wreckage of their ship upon landing. They had lived for hours or days until the ship's locks had been breached and the ship boarded.

The evidence of charred bodies and scarred walls was clear: crewmen had fought, with wrenches and kitchen knives, against fiery weapons that burned at a touch. Crew bodies lay where they had died. Pilots had burned in their makeshift wooden seats, probably while trying to get the ship aloft again, to no avail. Their murderers had then sunk the ship in the bog, at that time still an arm of the Inland Sea, using explosive charges at the hull's weakest points.

The unknown murders left no traces. Either they removed their own dead, or the attack had been so successful that there had been none. Who were they? Yan wondered. Had they been early followers of Pharos, incisively rewriting history even in that remote time, or had they been alien ferosin themselves, avenging the theft of their vessel?

The key lay in the stratification of the soils, the archaeological sequence. Yan gazed at a sketch he had drawn so long ago that it seemed like a different life entirely. At the bottom he had drawn crosshatches, labeled bedrock. Above were limy lake-bottom deposits and the wrecked ship. Higher still was a thin layer that contained human artifacts dated to 2600 C.E. Clearly, the ship had been sunk before the human trash had been deposited, at a time when seas still rose, when continents subsided, and when the known world had been a place of tiny, shifting principalities. Even then, ferosin visits had been a fact of Earthly existence for four or even five centuries. Enough time had passed for early ferosin "passengers" to have colonized and tamed new homeworlds, to have changed and mutated under new suns, and to have returned.

2900 C.E. was the accepted end of the Age of the Ferosin,

and the first reliable mention of the Church of Pharos occurred after 3100 C.E. following the Oma-Cansi wars, concurrent with the rise of the nation-states of Yan's time.

"I am drawn to an uncomfortable, even sinister, conclusion," Yan had written on the same page as the sketch. "The murderers of the human crew were not early followers of the Pharos cult who happened upon the ship. Whoever they were, they tracked it from afar and followed it to its resting place in remote Michan. I believe they did so not out of malice alone, but to protect some secret so important that it was worth extraordinary effort.

"Who were they?" he had written. "What was that secret?"

If there were answers to those questions, they would not be found in Wain or Nahbor, or in the ship that the churchmen had so laboriously reburied, stripped of undesirable evidence that humans had once been the equals of their gods. At any rate, Yan mused, he was a marked man. Perhaps someday the Church would forget him, but in the meantime, he had gold, good boots, and a deck underfoot.

The more he pondered, the more he became convinced there was more behind the Church's overreaction than he could fathom. Strikes and sabotage at the dig were the Pharos hounds' way, not fire and murder. What could it be? There were great libraries in the Church-held lands bordering the inland sea—Innis and Roke, with their cathedrals, cloisters, and archives, for example. Once his anonymity was assured, perhaps there he could find answers, and new questions as well.

In the broad marketplace of Roke a wizened old woman sold bees, fertilized queens of a new variety. Their production of rich honey would, she guaranteed, surpass local hives populated by offspring of captured wild queens. "Taste my honey, good-man," she cackled, exposing a crenelated grin.

"Aya, sweet thing," her potential customer joked, "an' I kin stick my finger in yer honey pot?"

"Buy my bees, y' randy fool, an' yer'll sell honey 'nuf t' buy the prettiest pot in Roke." The farmer, and scores of others before and after, bought oddly striped queens from the crone. Their hives ran rich with thick honey, and they prospered.

The hag, too, prospered for a year, then two, but at last, late in the winter of 3848, an oddness caught the attention of an Indic of the Order of Pharos, inquestor-minor to the Junior of an outlying town. For a year farmers of his district had bought queens, and never had the old woman left Roke to replenish her supply, nor did she keep hives of her own. Each morning she left her hovel behind the Geross chandlery with bees in her grass cage, and each evening she returned there.

The Indic planned to have her tortured to obtain first her explanation, then her confession of witchcraft, but as soon as he grasped her skinny arm, she smiled up at him, and died. In her shanty he found only bedding, a candlestick, a carved child's toy, and a wooden box containing half a hundred dead queen bees. An urchin stole the candlestick and a fishwife claimed the bedding while the Indic lunched in a nearby tavern. Upon his return, he tossed box and bees in a renderer's fire. He kept the toy, a blue-painted ball in a four-barred wooden cage, to give to his sister's boy—in return for a smile, or even a kiss.

CHAPTER FOUR

THIRD SPACESHIP LOST!!!

Luna—(Reuters)—An experimental spaceship with a ferosian-type "stardrive" destroyed itself moments after launch Thursday. The drive module was not at fault. "From drive engagement in lunar orbit to impact with a minor planet in the outer belt twenty-seven seconds later it performed flawlessly," said United Space Technology spokesman Marvin Ambler. "Course deviation in the last eight seconds of flight was pilot-instigated." Data from monitors along the flight path will confirm that human error caused the deviation that led to the fiery disaster, Ambler said.

Undated facsimile of a clipping in Nahbor University archives.

The day was hot and clear, the breezes light and steady. The boat kept a steady course, constantly adjusted by a wind vane attached to the tiller by cleverly rigged ropes and pulleys. There was nothing Yan needed to do, but the uneventful hours could not all be filled with reading. The sun was too bright, and the steady motion made him drowsy. Unbidden, stirred by his personal "demon's" recent, unwelcome appearance, his thoughts turned to his youth, to the first visit of his family's unique curse . . .

How many wan, rainy mornings had he spent huddled in a firelit corner of the old stone manse with cousins and sisters, passing little Enri from lap to lap while Gran'ma wove tales of adventure from the fibers of family history? The scariest stories were about madness, and Gran'ma saved those for the gloomiest, stormiest days. They were so alike that he had suspected

Gran'ma told the same one again and again, only changing people's names.

The madness. Like a water moccasin in the reeds, it hid in the Bando clan's blood, only raising its deadly head in the heat of battle. Battle, where all the stories began. They all ended with one naked man standing, holding a blood-slick axe, the madman's weapon of choice. As bloodied as his weapon, standing dead-eyed, exhausted, like a butcher among the day's slaughter—that was how Yan imagined the madman, amid stacked human carcasses, enemy meat. Madmen were not heroes, Gran'ma insisted, horror and disgust twisting her wrinkled face as if she'd stepped in something that reeked and steamed. Madness was madness, though the Bando clan sometimes reaped the benefit of it.

"The signs are always clear," she told the children. "A madman's wounds don't pain him, and his strength is like two men's. His eyes see everything at once, and he fouls himself not out of fear, but to lighten his burden, because he has lost his humanity and cares for naught but the next kill."

At the edge of the swamp, beyond the last plowed field, lay a pitiful cluster of untended graves, where his clan buried the remains of their afflicted. There were more tales in Gran'ma's repertoire than graves, so Yan assumed that those who survived their battle wounds had run off, not wishing to live in shame on the periphery of the community, shunned and alone.

Men of fighting age were old enough to have sired children, though, children to carry the trait which would curse their distant descendants. Thus Gran'ma's cautions: every male child was at risk because the clan was small and inbred. Puberty was the time madness took hold, but it might not reveal itself then—or ever, if the madman's life was peaceful. Gran'ma would frown when she said that, as if peaceful times were less blessing than failure, for without the heat of battle, the curse lay dormant, poisoning the blood of unborn generations.

As a youth, Yan had accepted the tales with tolerant amusement. After all, no family was without taint of some kind. Every landowning clan on the river had moldering bones to hide, or so *their* children implied, in hushed voices. With the pragmatism of youth, he said of madmen, "They always *won*, didn't they?" Later, he learned differently.

At thirteen, Yan had known the difference between "work" and "fun." Work was anything grown-ups wanted him to do. If they had *ordered* him to take his little brother Enri into the delta marshes beyond the overgrown graveyard in search of succulent bullfrogs, it would have been work, but since no one had commanded it, he supplied the family with meal after meal of delicate white frog meat. That day, both boys had carried frog spears, and Yan had slung a bolo from his belt for squirrels and such.

They filled their mesh bags by noon. "Put them in the pond to keep cool," he ordered his little brother. "I'll be along soon." Yan settled himself on a dry hummock in the shade of a bent old black willow. He dozed, but Enri's terrified cry awakened him. "If the brat's found another skunk," Yan panted, sprinting down the faint trail, "I'll bury him to his neck in muck, and leave him for the crows!"

Enri had found something larger than a skunk. When Yan burst into the clearing, he glimpsed the boy's red shirt in a slim ironwood tree that bent with his weight. Enri bobbed like a cork on a fishpole while beneath him a dark shape undulated. Yan saw Enri's little frog gig dangling loosely from the neck of . . . a fat, black bear. Before Yan could make up his mind what to do, Enri lost his grip on the smooth gray bark and fell.

Abruptly, something happened in Yan's head. The quiet swamp became noisy. He heard every faint birdsong, every twig that rattled in the listless breeze. He heard Enri's attenuated scream and the sodden squish of the bear as it turned toward the fallen boy. His mind worked with abnormal speed and clarity, cataloguing things he'd been unaware of: the weight of the frog spear in his hand, a breeze on the side of his face, the harsh rale of breath rushing out of the bear's nostrils, ever nearer. Even running headlong at the beast, he kept downwind, choosing his footing to avoid betraying twigs and noisy canary grass, counting his paces, measuring his decreasing distance from the bear; all that in the time it took the bear to turn around. Before the beast had time to react, Yan thrust his gig into a glaring eye and pulled Enri's spear from its neck.

"The stupid bear wanted my frogs," Enri explained. "He couldn't have them, I said. He got mad, so I killed him."

"You didn't kill him, Enri," Yan murmured halfheartedly, "and you should have left the frogs instead of angering him."

Enri sniffed the air, eyeing his brother curiously. "Hey, Yan! You smell like shit." He pointed an accusing finger and laughed shrilly. "You were scared! That dumb bear scared you! Yan shit his pay-unts," he chanted. "Yan shit his pay-unts!"

Yan grabbed Enri's shirt in both hands and lifted him until they were nose to nose. Enri's little feet flopped and dangled. "You stupid brat! I just saved your life." Enri's face turned red, but it was really the haze of anger in Yan's eyes.

"Put me down, or I'll tell everybody you shit your pants!" Enri threatened.

Yan dropped his brother, suddenly less afraid of the threat than of what he himself might do next. A killing lust still coursed his blood, and his heart hammered like a battle drum. "If you say one word about *any* of this, I'll tell Pa what you did, and he'll beat you until your butt bleeds. You know he will. And then *I'll* drag you down to the graveyard at night, and let Rath and Inoo eat you! Understand?"

Whether because of Yan's threat or his uncharacteristic anger, Enri wailed loudly. Pressing him, Yan made him promise to tell no one about the bear—or his own embarrassing release. He wiped snot from Enri's upper lip with his shirttail, then hugged him until he quieted. "Wait here, Enri," he said.

Behind a clump of willow brush, he removed his trousers and sloshed them in the water. He scrubbed himself first with leaves, then with wet sand. Now he knew why his mad ancestors had gone naked into battle.

The bear was by now deep in the swamp, nursing its wounded eye. Yan nursed wounds not of the flesh and mourned a loss not yet come—a loss beside which an eye, even two eyes, paled: his family, his home, and his eventual inheritance. He mourned, even as he made plans for the future that he knew would come. There was no doubt in his mind. No normal man moved or thought as fast as he had. No ordinary man countered bear claws and teeth with a flimsy frog gig and emerged unscratched. The demon of madness had saved Enri. And Yan had been wrong all along: madmen didn't win, they merely prevailed, and in prevailing lost all they held dear—as would he, when his own demon became known. So he made plans.

He could no longer inherit his father's station or sire heirs of his own. Even if Enri forgot what Yan had done today, there would be other dangers, other lapses, and his awful secret would come out. But there was still time to make changes. He could seek a career where violence was uncommon, where his secret could stay buried in the depths of mind and genes. He would become an academician. Not a priest—the priestly life might be serene, but Yan was too forthright to exchange one hypocrisy for another. Besides, he was attracted to pretty girls, not men or boys. What course of study would he pursue? History? The long-dead violence in books hurt no one.

Yes, a historian, he decided. I will begin at once. I'll slacken in the fencing yard, and fumble with the war axe, perhaps injure myself. Father will be disappointed, but he won't suspect. Not all eldest sons grow into proper heirs. Growth and manhood can change promising boys. It will take time to build my charade . . . if my demon gives me time. He sighed, and without raising his eyes from the ground turned toward home. Enri followed. Yan always knew what direction he faced, and even what time of day it was. He was never lost, not even in the dark caverns beneath the manse. Was that also his demon's gift?

Years later, Yan learned that Madness was no disease, no demon. Ancient books speculated that such enhanced perceptions and reactions were genetic survivals from a distant past when life went to the swift and clear-thinking. Even ordinary men and women demonstrated uncanny strength at times to lift wagons, beams, or stones from the bodies of loved ones. The trait was unusual, but hardly a curse. Enlightenment came too late for Yan Bando. No longer heir to his father's estates, no longer even a promising scholar at Nahbor University, he was a fugitive and—the ancient, ugly word grated harshly on his mind—a *berserker*.

Looking at his hands through narrowed eyelids, Yan was not surprised to see that no blisters had formed. Only the heavy gold, and spark holes in his robe, remained to prove that the previous night had really happened.

Supper was a cup of pale, vinegary wine, with white cheese and sweet onions on a slab of coarse yellow bread. After he ate, Yan went below. He pillowed his head on his sack and awoke only once, when the boat's motion changed so it no longer rolled him against the damp hull planks but centered him on the now-level bunk.

Tiny hot squares of sunlight piercing the hatch-grating awakened him. He struggled from sweaty, clinging bedclothes and climbed out of the muggy cabin. Omer was availing himself of the light breeze and munching an apple. "Breakfast," he said around his mouthful, indicating the cockpit with his thumb.

Yan found another apple and two filets of smoked fish in the ice chest. The salt and sweet tastes cleared away the last traces of sleep. "Where are we?" he asked.

"We came around King's Head a' dawn. Now we've a straight

run for New Roster if the wind holds. P'raps t'morrow, or the day after."

Yan looked away from the sun still high over the starboard rail and followed the scintillant wake with narrowed eyes. No other sails were in sight. He had not expected pursuit, but still, the empty horizon was reassuring. He could not predict how the fisherman would react. "Are you a religious man, Omer?" he asked, testing.

"I pay my tithe to the sea gods, P'fesser. In Pharos' ports, I bring my fee to the counting house, to keep the brownrobes' unlucky feet off my deck, but I don't 'spect I'll float off in the sky when I die—more'n' likely I'll just sink to the bottom. I'd prefer it." He gazed steadily at Yan. "You, now . . . what special interest do the priests have in you?"

Yan stiffened, at a loss for an answer. The old man saw, and responded. "Aya, that's it, isn't it? Tha' priest skulking on the docks *was* seeking you, wasn't he?"

"Where?" Yan blurted. "He saw us leave? He saw me?"

"P'raps. Sun in his eyes, though." Omer's eyes narrowed. "If you're in deep wi' th' browncoats, P'fesser, you'd be wise t' tell me outright. I won't chuck you over the rail, and it might save us trouble later."

"I suppose you're right," Yan admitted dubiously, "though I doubt they'll bother you, once I'm away."

Throughout that day, Yan recounted his experiences in some detail. Omer, having sailed supplies to the wreck site, had no trouble visualizing how Yan's work had upset the churchmen. He had seen the ancient wreck laid bare like the bones of some piscine behemoth, had seen its entrails of corroded pipes and ducting, its veins of still-bright insulated wires, its internal parasites, which had been large-brained bipeds.

Yan expressed curiosity that he had found no cables between control room and engines, and no intercom between pilot and crew. "Your mysterious murderers likely removed them," Omer suggested. He was more interested in the background material, the historic data and Yan's interpretation of it, than in wires and cables or the Pharos cult's discomfiture. Before long, Yan reluctantly opened his sack.

From then on, the old man was more than willing to show him the rudiments of boat handling, freeing himself to pore over Lazko's notes, methodically tracing line after line with a callused fingertip. Where, Yan wondered, watching him from the tiller, had a fisherman learned to read?

Occasionally, Omer questioned a particular word or place name, or burst out enthusiastically with revelations that surprised the younger man. "Aya, Yan! Those star children. The Moromen tell tales a' them!"

"Moromen?"

"They live beyond the western edge a' the Oman Empire. I've never been there—it's all dry land, even desert. No place for a sailor. But they get about. They send their young men to proselytize amid us eastern heathens."

"Well? What about them?"

"Wha . . . Oh! The star children. Moromen youths sacrifice an ear or a finger to their god—he's like the Old Christian one, I think. They do it to remember the Great Bolide, a meteor that crossed over their land way back when. The way they tell it, children born in the years after its passing were deformed—born wi'out arms or legs, or joined t'gether for life."

"The Great Bolide! When was that? Do you remember the year?"

"Not for a fact. A thousand years, they claim."

"I've read of it! It was seen all the way from the westernmost ocean to the Merkan lands north of Michan. 2884 was the date. Could that be it? Let's see . . . 3849 minus . . . yes! Nine hundred sixty-five years ago. That's no coincidence, either, I'm sure. The Bolide was indeed a ship of space."

"How's that?"

"The radiation. No natural meteor strews poisons that kill and maim unborn children. The engines of starships harness the sun's own fires, only they're not designed for use in a planet's atmosphere where their emanations can do harm."

"Then how did such ships land? These aliens—the ferosin, the ones the Church worships—don't seem to have killed people."

"When men built their own ships, those used only in space had fusion engines, sun engines. Others burned less-harmful fuels, and were used just for landing. The starships had another kind of engine, for far traveling. It's a measure of that crew's desperation—or their ignorance—that they'd use fusion engines to land their ship."

"And what desperation was that?" Omer wondered aloud. "What need was so vital they'd kill babes and poison the blood of generations? Do you know that, P'fesser?"

"I have suspicions," Yan replied, "but I'd rather not voice them yet."

Time passed in reading, sailing, and speculation. Omer took the first night watch, though it was too dark for reading. There was much for him to consider. The tales the young scholar told, and those his books implied, were of strange and surpassing interest. As a young fellow, Omer would have dropped everything to pursue such a quest—to look for ships that sailed the night sky. But now? He packed his pipe with moist tobacco, aware of the clumsiness of his fingers, his enlarged knuckles, his wrists far too bony for the thinning musculature that worked them.

Early the following morning land emerged to starboard. Omer said New Roster was just around the first headland—he pointed just south of the rising sun. "We sail this course another two, three hours, then follow the coast to the mouth of the Jensie River. We'll slip into port easy enough, if there's moonlight." He hesitated, pondering. "Yan?"

"Aya?"

"Nah—nothing. Just thinking aloud. I wish I had more time t' read those books a' yours, that's all."

Yan's thoughts during the dawn watch had paralleled Omer's. Lazko's death had just begun to sink in as fact instead of fragmented nightmare. Yan had stepped from his father's influence to Lazko's, and though he didn't consider himself helpless or dependent, he missed the guidance and companionship each man had provided in turn. Was he yearning for yet another mentor? Thinking of the coarse-spoken fisherman, he chuckled ruefully. His father was a mountainous man of commanding presence. Lazko had been erudite, thoughtfully elegant in speech and manner. His skin had been pink, his hands slender and unmarked. Omer was, by contrast with the other men, skinny, harsh, weathered, and callused. But the same penetrating intelligence and curiosity lit his eyes. Yan shrugged off such thoughts. Omer had his life on the Reach, and his boat.

When the sun was low and the glare was no longer forbidding, Yan shook his pen from its case and uncorked his ink bottle. "When I fled my father's house," he wrote, "driven by the demon Madness, new options opened before me. I never knew what discoveries lay beyond. I didn't plan my course. I changed tacks at the bidding of capricious winds. Again, I flee, with no plan or course. Will this flight lead to even more momentous discoveries? My mind is open, a lens where mysteries converge. I don't know what I will find, and I seek no particulars, only knowledge itself. Ancient spacemen long dead, alien star-travelers long departed, twisted histories, and a contorted present await me. Is there some focal point where all converge?"

The sun was four hours down when they entered the estuary of the Jensie River. Even by moonlight, Duke Harrum's capital was unprepossessing. Low buildings lined the wharves. Sagging roofs and crooked shingled walls huddled against dank winter winds that swept seasonally from the Bekwah forests across the Reach. The harbor was silty and shallow, and *West Wind* left a black trail in the duckweed-skinned water. At a public wharf near the harbor mouth, Omer paid a sleepy watchman for a creaking slip with rotten pilings. "No need for an inn tonight," he told Yan. "You can save your gold for when you really need it."

Yan stiffened at the mention of the gold, hidden, or so he'd thought, in his robe belowdeck. He edged toward the companionway to see if it was safe. Then, reconsidering, he raked Omer with his eyes, seeking telltale bulges in his rough clothing. "Easy, Yan," the old man murmured coolly, grasping his arm. "I didn't touch it. I pulled your robe over me t'sleep, and as t'was hard and heavy, I looked. But go below and count it." He shrugged. "Go ahead," he urged, his eyes opaque, revealing nothing. "You've no reason to trust me."

Yan peered closely into those eyes. The fisherman met his gaze steadily. Tension built moment by moment. Then Yan smiled wordlessly and slid the companionway tambour shut with a sharp clack. He removed its iron key and tossed it to Omer. "Is it too much to expect we can find a decent meal in this shantytown?"

CHAPTER FIVE

Valdosta, GA—(SPC)—The Georgia Royal Guard confirmed using tactical nuclear weapons to destroy seventeen bridges on the Suwanee and St. Mary's rivers. "We have stemmed the tide of armed refugees from the Florida peninsula," said Maj. Gen. Charles C. Maston. "Georgia will continue to take in the homeless as fast as they can be absorbed. Our checkpoints on [International Highways] 75 and 95 are still open."

Maston added that Farroshan spaceships had been sighted, saying, "I saw two of them coming down near Jacksonville myself." Estimating the capacity of each ship at 150,000 passengers, he said that at least that many had starved in Georgia refugee camps already, and that Farroshan ships were the only hope for the rest.

April 9, 2271, source unknown [L.]

Pushing back his greasy beechwood platter, Omer tilted his chair and placed both feet on the table edge. The tavern was quiet now that most of New Roster's drinkers had departed for their beds. He took a deep draft of dark amber beer and, balancing the mug on his knee, eyed Yan speculatively. "It's been a thousand years since the Bolide. Wha' d'you expect t' find?"

"I don't know," Yan admitted, "but I can't just hide in some backwater, waiting for priests to unearth me, growing old while I wait for *their* memories to fade. I won't be organizing digs, not with the Church alerted to me."

"Aya," Omer said, sighing. "It's a fair quest, Yan. I've half a mind to go with you. Pittsburg, Innis, Chatoo . . . I've been away from the Inland Sea ports a long time, now. But I'm tired, and drunk, and an old fool . . . perhaps tomorrow I can help you choose your route. I once knew those lands well."

Yan, too, was a bit drunk, and when they reached the *West Wind* he fell asleep in his clothing. Omer stayed topside. He remained on the dock long after Yan had fallen asleep, leaning on the peeled cedar railing, digging at a rotted board with his toe. His thoughts, clouded by drink, cleared as did the sky, cooled as did the night air. The boy's like a big, clumsy puppy, he mused. His notebooks and pipe dreams are one thing, but this journey is a bone that's just a bit too big for him. I wonder if he'll make it?

The auroras were particularly bright. Flaring curtains brushed the northern sky with luminous emerald and azure folds, trembling fringes of rose and mauve. Omer held pebbles picked up along the path, throwing them one by one into the stagnant water. Intersecting rings and arcs mirrored his thoughts, his life. It was impossible to say just which people and events that had rippled his own pond contributed to any particularly high peaking intersection, any rogue wave.

Tamas, he thought. My son. You'd be almost Yan's age now. Could you have survived the fires, the slaughter? Should I feel guilty I never sought out your grave? Tamas would be shorter than Yan, he thought. If his boy walked up to him, would something in his eye or his walk give him away, or would an old man just walk on by, never knowing?

He tossed his last pebble and pulled out his pipe in one motion. Stuffing the pipe with shredded black tobacco, he reached for a match with the other hand, an easy, long-practiced motion. The match's sulfurous flare momentarily overpowered everything except the moon, which peered from a thin translucent veil of mist. I'd be useful to him, he told himself. He's tough enough, but he's naive. Omer puffed several times on the gurgling pipe, but the fire hadn't caught. He spat a bitter slug of tobacco at the duckweed-skimmed water. His wife's face seemed to hang there in front of him; a trick of the moonlight, he told himself. I'll not hide from your memory any longer, Narah, my love. I want it back. I want to see the places you loved, to sail the waters you sailed with me when we were happy.

He lit another match, its bright, wavering glare deepening the grooves and fissures of his face. A wet, cool drop fell on his forearm. Another followed it, and together they ran down, dropping to the water below. For the first time in twelve years, he didn't blink back his tears, or wipe them secretly away.

* * *

"Breakfast, Yan!" Omer's harsh voice pierced the cabin staves. Yan swung his legs from the narrow bunk and sat with head in hands. He had drunk too much the night before, and he was paying for it. He clutched Omer's wrist through the open companionway and let himself he hauled up, swearing profusely, though without Omer's color or originality.

At the tavern, Omer forced him to down smoked eels, eggs, coarse sugary rolls, and kaf. Then, with only a mild headache and a vast lethargy, Yan settled in the blackened oak booth, looking sideways at the old sailor's weathered face. "Did you mean what you said?" he asked hesitantly. "About coming with me?"

"Aya, I suppose I did," Omer admitted with equal caution. "That's assuming an old man wouldn't hinder you. I haven't finished reading your books, yet, slow as I am." He steadfastly avoided Yan's gaze, instead staring intently into the sunlight diffusing through smoke-glazed windows.

"What about your boat?" Yan asked. Omer said he had relatives in New Roster who would rent it. Yan, less perceptive than he could have wished, pondered the old man's unease. Then he reached across the table to grasp Omer's shoulder. "I value your friendship, fresh as it is," he said with formal intonation. "For that reason alone, I'd want you to travel with me. But also, I've been cloistered too long, and I doubt I'd fare successfully in the strange lands southward. I'll pay for your assistance—I'm sure it will cost less than I'd lose by being cheated through inexperience. Can we talk about it?"

Omer's smile split his face with a score of wrinkles. "Aya, Yan. Now that we're agreed, let's haggle."

Noontime customers were drifting in by the time arrangements were completed, and their table bore new scratches, neat rows of tallies. Omer haggled well. Yan was to pay all expenses including weapons and clothing, and would leave a deposit with the local Seaman's Guild chaptermaster, too. If Omer didn't claim it within five years, it would go to his sister's children up the coast.

With pride and finances in order, both men walked with lightened steps, Omer to make his arrangements, and Yan to book their passage to Portage, the furthest town up the Jensie River. There they would board another barge for the trip down the Ganny River to Pittsburg. Since barges left New Roster on a daily schedule, they spent their final night on the *West Wind* and boarded the first barge in line just before dawn.

It was a square-prowed box, heavily made, with splined timbers and no internal structure—as much a raft as a true hull, Omer commented disparagingly. For the slow journey upriver, it would be towed by twelve yoke of oxen. Pole-pushers would keep the ungainly seventy-foot craft off the banks.

Neither man had much baggage or any weapons except knives. The gold was now concealed in wide leather belts beneath their oily sheepskin jackets, used ones purchased cheaply. Swords, Omer declared, would only have hinted that they had wealth to protect. He suggested that they sleep lightly and assume an air of inoffensive poverty. "Besides," he added enthusiastically, "in Pittsburg we can buy arms right from the finest smithies."

Barge travel, easy on the hearts of the old, offered little diversion for men accustomed to controlling their own progress. Of the twenty-odd passengers, a dozen started a rotating game with cards and dice that continued throughout the daylight hours in the shade of large wool bales stacked amidships. Omer played an occasional hand, neither winning nor losing much. When darkness fell, the game continued beneath the stern lantern.

During moonless hours they halted. The towline was guarded by a man ashore and another aboard. Otherwise, progress was steady, as fresh oxen were furnished from station houses along the route. By the end of the second day, they were forty miles upstream and it was time to change boats. The rapids ahead could be negotiated by barges, but that demanded daylight and skilled piloting. Instead, crew and passengers offloaded cargo onto waiting wagons which skirted the rapids by lanternlight. "Besides," the bargeman added cheerily, "after a night's work, you'll sleep all day tomorrow."

The eastern sky was barely aglow when the travelers boarded the upstream barge. Omer, used to hard labor, remained awake until after the noon meal. Yan, who had discovered new aches each waking moment, slept until cooking smells from the sand-filled firebox wafted aft to him, and after eating, slept again. Omer wished he could look at Yan's books, but that would have brought undue attention. Common travelers didn't read.

Every day about midmorning a downstream-bound barge was sighted and their own craft hastily made for the bank. Floating with the current, the other boat had no steerage way; polemen kept it going side-on to the current and fended it off occasional obstacles. When the morning juggernaut was past, oxen were goaded and the slow voyage upstream resumed. The children aboard, who watched it all, would return to less-interesting pastimes like hide-and-seek among the bales.

On the third morning, Yan observed a curious silence when the children rushed to the rail. Puzzled, he peered over the gunwale. Instead of crated ironware and scruffy passengers, the passing craft held russet-garbed soldiers with muskets stacked upright and swords in their laps. In the bow sat a man with beardless chin and short-cropped hair, his brown-and-maroon garment reminding Yan of the Pharos priests' robes.

"Mercenaries," Omer murmured. "Guards for a courier—the Church Militant brother."

"Church Militant?" Yan asked. "What's that?" Omer explained that priests in Michan and Wain were Brotherhood of Pharos missionaries. In the more urban southlands, on the Inland Sea, he would see the full spectrum of the Church of Pharos: scores of interlocking orders and sects, rankings like "Midis," "Indics," and "Hands." The Church Militant was a lay order of soldiers, retired from duty but still shaved and trimmed. "They can fight, though," Omer finished.

"Omer, were you a soldier once?"

"Why do you ask?" His voice was wary.

Yan had trusted Omer with his tale, and he felt that the older man had not responded in kind. He knew nothing of his companion's past. He had been aware for some time that Omer wore his Eastern Reach accent like a mask that slipped on occasion, revealing that the man behind it was more than he pretended to be. Omer's penetrating questions, and his grasp of new and unconventional ideas, gave him away to Yan, the scholar. His slurred speech and coarse manner hid an intelligent and educated mind.

"A wise man," Yan ventured, "accepts little that his eyes and ears tell him. There's much in the world that won't bear close scrutiny." He paused, peering. When Omer merely met his gaze, he went on. "For example, I am not what I portray to our fellow passengers, nor are you. The Church, too, has more faces than men suspect. Even the stars show little of their own nature, pinpoints of light that are warming hearths of worlds.

"So what of Omer-with-no-other-name? Who moves the puppet-fisherman's strings? Shall I guess?" Omer smiled as if challenging him, and tipped his water skin to refill his leather travel cup. "You're a seaman," Yan continued. "The salt water in your veins is no affectation. But you're no common fisherman. You've trod much larger decks, as an officer, perhaps."

Omer's eyes widened just a bit, Yan thought. "Interesting ideas y'have," he murmured. "Go on."

"What sort of officer? Not a merchant. You think more like a scholar than an accountant, but you have no scholar's reserve. You take risks. You decided to go on this ill-defined quest based on a smattering of fact and fancy, for no greater gain than a wage. You see the patterns that underlie Lazko's historic anecdotes and you act on them. Yours is a tactical—no, a strategic—mind. You were a naval officer, weren't you?"

"I surrender to your superior force, lad. I'm sure you've guessed I don't wear the name my mother gave me, either."

"I thought not. But why would a man hide his true name? Murder? Piracy? Not you. What's left is politics. Cansi? Demoyne? Who put a price on your head? Why?" Yan paused for Omer's answer, but the old man just shrugged. "The only hole shaped to your peg is Senloo, and the last Oman war. Were you a captain of a Senloo ship, or more?" Yan mimed a crone peering into a crystal sphere. "Clouds part," he intoned. "Sun rises. I see a man in blood-red and night-dark cloth piped with gold. I see one who wields fleets as another swings his axe."

Omer shook his head as if struck. "You're sharp, scholar. You even got the piping right. Aya. Senloo. I commanded the last fleet to disband when they burned our ports. You can fill in the rest."

Yan could. Even as a child he'd heard of the battles in the south, of the last great war between the sprawling Oman Empire and the city-states that had opposed it.

Cansi straddled the river like a jeweled bridle on the Empire's ambitions, while south and east of Cansi, the city-state of Senloo perched on the dissected loess bluffs of Land's End. When land-bound merchants gained ascendancy in Senloo, they had repudiated their own sea knights, the backbone of Senloo strength, and allied themselves with the Oman Empire.

Homeless, without logistic support, Senloo vessels were hunted down by the traitors. A few ships escaped to neutral ports and were sold to purchase new names for their crews. The usurpers in Senloo put prices on the heads of sea knights—especially the knights-admiral who had commanded—hoping to secure their estates by the deaths of the last legitimate owners.

"It ended twelve years ago," Yan commented. "How did you end up in Wain, as a fisherman?"

"Like most of us who survived th' bounty hunters, I took a new name, and never worked at a post higher than second officer, always on far-sailing vessels. We had meeting places and codes arranged, and still a few friends in one port or another. I worked Cansian ships for the most part, and prospered, but bounty hunters still sought me, and I had to kill more than one. I grew tired, so I came home."

"I thought Senloo was home."

"New Roster. I've family in a dozen towns on the Reach."

"Then how did you become a knight-admiral of Senloo?"

"I went south as a boy, and signed on a Senloo vessel by chance. There was risk in the far-trade, and I rose fast. I owned my vessel by my thirtieth year. When war began, I earned a fleet by my fortieth. The titles and landholdings that went with the knight-admiralcy meant nothing to any of us, though. They just guaranteed safe anchorages and warehouses. Our true homes were our decks. Honor meant far voyages, new ports opened. Some of us had factors as far away as the Kaffa Islands."

"Strange, but I never thought of the sea knights as traders. The histories dwell only on their battles."

"Aya. But battles make better tales, don't they? Nevertheless, merchants we were, though our ships were built to be converted from cargo hulls to warships in a week's time." He paused to sip his tepid water.

"At any rate," he continued, "when the Cansian trade palled, I sold my shares and came home. I bought *West Wind* from an uncle, and fished the Reach, with the odd hauling job thrown in. Didn't mind it a bit. I figured I was getting old."

"But the far-traveler still lives in you, doesn't he?"

"Aya, Yan. He lives." Omer raised his eyes to the clear summer sky. "I've caught a glimpse of still-further shores, beyond my dreams."

That night was their last on the Jensie River. At dusk, the barge tied up at Portage, seventy miles from New Roster, a few days' walk if the way had been smooth and dry.

Most passengers went to the town's lone tavern, but Yan and Omer, after a quick meal of bread and meat, departed on the last coach to the far end of the portage, on the Ganny River headwaters, to find berths on a boat downstream to Pittsburg.

Luck changed their plans. A light galley was at dockside, and they arranged passage. It promised to be a quick two hundred miles. The trip would be nonstop, since the Ganny was wide and unobstructed for most of its length. No money changed hands; Yan and Omer agreed to pull oars for two shifts, four hours each. Yan doubted his ability to perform the unfamiliar task, but the officer and Omer agreed that he had the physique for it. Anyway, they assured him, if he mistimed his strokes, the overseer's padded lash would help him get back in rhythm. Yan thought neither man's jokes funny.

The officer tossed him a pair of well-worn gloves with double palms, then went aft to greet his paying passengers. When those came aboard, Yan and Omer took their seats quickly. The passengers were seven brown-robed priests. "I've seldom seen so many high-ranking brownshirts traveling together," Omer commented. "I wonder what's stirred them up?"

"I don't know," Yan whispered back, "but I'm not looking forward to a day and a night in their company." But whatever the priests' errand, Yan knew it didn't concern him. He and Omer had traveled continuously, and no word could have preceded them. The barges had been slow, but roads along the Jensie were impassable this time of the year. Besides, he and his notebooks had probably diminished in importance to the churchmen of Nahbor even as his distance increased. Still, he was anxious to be under way.

At first glimmer of the rising moon they shoved off. Yan was surprised by the ease of pulling the oar through the water. He was even more surprised when, in perfect time with the rowers' pace, the overseer gave him a half-dozen strokes of the lash, accented with instructions delivered in rhythm: "It's *not* enough to *move* the oar, you *lazy* cur. Now *pull* the damn stick *hard* and earn your *pay*." Yan pulled after that, his mind occupied with both raging thoughts of vengeance and wonder at how the man could tell who was—or was not—pulling his weight.

When shift was called he stumbled onto the catwalk, and no thought persisted long. Four hours of fitful sleep did little for his burning muscles or his disposition. With his first pull on the oar, he moaned aloud at the agony in his back and arms, and swore softly until the lash's touch reminded him that speechmaking was neither expected nor desired. From then on he saved his breath for rowing, and though the rest of the voyage seemed to stretch forever ahead of him, when he shipped his oar at a bustling, well-lit Pittsburg dock, he marveled at the speed of the trip.

Dawn was still a figment in the eastern sky. He had never traveled so far in such a short time. Omer, who had survived his own stint in good condition, found a rooming house with hot baths every day until noon. Yan slept until dragged from his bed and pointed toward the tub. Omer had already bathed and made use of the house's masseuse, whose skill he recommended to Yan.

After a half hour's soak in a long tub with three other bathers, Yan's muscles were restored to a semblance of normality, and the masseuse completed the process. Feeling lightheaded but entirely well, he ate boiled eggs, mutton, and beets, and then he and Omer prepared to seek a smithy to buy weapons.

They struggled to lift a heavy maple armoire enough to slide Yan's canvas sack beneath its raised floor. It would take more than a cursory examination of the room to find it, and a lone burglar would not be able to budge the massive cabinet.

The Unending Cave was six days behind in the east. Those Others the young witch had met there had told her of this land called Tenzie, whose populous cities and great universities once welcomed her kind. Later, mysterious unquenchable fires had burned witches, merchants, scholars, cattle, and wild things with equal abandon, leaving the land itself sere and dead. But that was long ago. Now Tenzie lived again, though brown-robed priests blinded and burned witches with singular glee lacking even in Roke and Innis, where the church Seniors dwelt.

"Brownshirts may burn my corpse," the girl murmured to herself, "but I will be shed of it before they strike their fire." Then she chided herself for buying trouble. To the caravan she traveled with, she was only a bride traveling to the house of her husband-to-be, and they sheltered her as was the custom. On good roads, she rode in a carriage with curtains drawn. On rough trails she walked beside the wagonmaster, hooded and veiled even in the heat of day. He considered her a proper bride, not one of the lowland sluts whose bared faces belonged to any man with an eye in his head.

She did seem a proper bride, with her false baggage trunk full of rag-wrapped stones—soon to be abandoned with her present identity—and her small dowry chest, oddly slotted and baffled as if it held a small pet. The chest never left her side, and it was considered bad form indeed for strangers to express interest. What treasure did it contain? The caraveneers, proper Tenzian men, never asked.

Ahead, gleaming between brown grassy hills, was the northern arm of the Inland Sea. There she would sail for Innis, where her new master purportedly awaited her. "My husband, the Church," she mused, "who will receive this dowry of quiet death." Aboard ship, safe behind a locked cabin door, she opened the small container for the first time in many days.

CHAPTER SIX

> The tales of Witchery abounding in these hills all demonstrate Unnatural Command of all four Elements, but the Witches themselves seem most enamored of Fire. The folk of Old Smithy remember well the great Fire, only two generations aback, that started when a Witch-Child conjured Fire between her fingers . . .
>
> *Handwritten copy of a narrative by Inman Bune, ca. 3780* C.E.

Omer pulled his cloak tight. It was chilly, and rain threatened. "Inman Bune was a charlatan himself, Yan," he said as they walked. "And the fire trick's done with refined naphtha and a hair-fine loop of platinum wire."

"Aya, I know. Most of the accounts Lazko collected are like Bune's—old folks and dodderers who 'remember' what they want to, if someone's there to listen."

"Like your historians, then?"

Yan grinned. "Exactly so."

"I don't know what Lazko wanted with all those old witch tales, anyway," Omer mused. "Are they just stuff you grabbed from the fire? They don't have anything to do with spaceships."

"I'm not sure. Lazko collected them for some reason. He was fascinated with anything out of the ordinary, but it's less the tales themselves than the fact they exist at all that intrigues me. Something out of the ordinary has gone on in those mountains for centuries, and the constancy of the witch tales convinces me there's truth behind them, if we could only see it."

"How can you do that?" Omer asked. "I mean, you can't just wander, holding a 'witch wanted' sign."

"Why not?" Yan responded facetiously. "I don't have any better plan right now. Once I reach the Mountain Freeholds, where the tales converge, I'll keep eyes and ears open. Something will turn up. At least it always has."

Most of ancient Pittsburg was crumbled and gone. Stories and pictures had given Yan a false impression of a town snuggled among towering ruins of an earlier age, where skeletal steel scaffolds reached for low-slung, coal-dusty clouds. But such structures had long since been torn down. The value of a steel beam as raw material for tools exceeded the utility value of any building it supported. Modern Pittsburg was unusual only for its size: a hundred thousand people either worked in its smithies or labored to feed, clothe, and entertain those who did. Wood vied with stone along the once-broad streets, filling them with low dwellings and shops seldom more than three stories high.

Their destination was a timbered structure reaching two stories above its tallest neighbors. The center of existence for a hundred men and their families, the smithy was a busy place, nothing like the one-man shops of lesser towns. Tall flues like dark fingers balanced clouds of ocher coal smoke on their tips. The day was overcast, so the effluvium tumbled across the rooftops, and the air stank of sulfur. A soot-covered youngster greeted them in the forecourt and led them past roaring forges to a showroom.

The owner's effusive manner was out of proportion to their short acquaintance and humble clothing. Yan surmised that such behavior was typical of these city folk, who lacked the reserve of northerners. Their host expansively indicated their choices: all four walls were hung with tools and weapons.

Yan was overwhelmed with the variety of edged and projectile arms, some quite ornate, but Omer was unimpressed. "This is a fine display, Master Helder. I'm sure your hoes and adzes are th' pride of many a farmer and carpenter, but there must be other blades, of unusual quality, which you'd not hang with the common store." Almost all trace of Omer's usual slurring was gone; ignoring the differences in timbre between his voice and the smith's, Yan thought their speech was identical.

"A man of perception," the smith replied. "Yes, I maintain a collection of fine, unusual weapons. Follow me." A doorway opened to a windowless storeroom where the smith lit a fatty candle. High shelves stacked with pine boxes filled every niche. Their host slid one box out, opening it with exaggerated care. He unrolled soft, oiled-leather wrappings from two swords and held the box close to the light.

Yan was surprised at the plain offerings. The sabers, as Omer called them, were an arm's length overall, with narrow, curved blades. Their grips were wire-wound over weighted hafts, with only simple perforated straps below the hilts. The blades were dull-colored, swirled with blue and brown, gleaming only on their fine-honed edges. Beside each was a scabbard of black brass. Omer selected a blade and weighed it in his hand. He flexed it and sighted its length to see if it had bent. Nodding, he sheathed it, and hung it from his belt. Yan hesitated. "Master Smith, I am forest-born, trained on broadswords and—"

"Ah, ser Northlander," the smith said, eyeing Yan's large frame, then reaching to a high shelf. "Axes are a specialty of this house. We ship them as far as the Dragon Isles, and supply royal houses in Michan and Bekwah, too." He opened this box with difficulty; it was heavier than the other.

When Yan saw its contents, he drew a sharp breath. The axe that gleamed within was mounted on a short haft. Its leading edge swept a full span from tip to tip and was opposed by a four-grooved spike of rectangular section. A ball-shod butt balanced steel with steel, all shining like moonlight on still water.

"The coating is chromium," the smith murmured, matching his speech to Yan's reverent gaze. "Examine it. It will not rust in water or blood, and only the honed edge needs to be oiled."

"A song sung in fine steel, indeed," Yan alliterated, quoting a childhood saga. In the courtyard, he tested its balance on a plank target, to the delight of boys and workers who watched it spin end-for-end and thud home in the same spot time and again. By the time spatters of rain drove Pittsburg's noxious smoke even closer to the ground, Yan was satisfied. He oiled the blade and wrapped it in its leather shroud, spurning the rawhide sheath.

"An axe is no gentleman's weapon," he said. "Once taken from its wrappings, it must remain bare in hand until no need for its naked edge remains." He sounded as if he were quoting someone. "My father," he explained to Omer, who was surprised and puzzled by the bitterness in his tone, by the ugly twist of his features. He had been surprised to witness Yan's skill with the weapon, too, knowing that the scholar's soft hands had not practiced with such a weight on an ash shaft in some time. He resolved to ask questions later, when the time was right.

Their next objective lay past the galley wharf and their inn. Great dark clouds scudded overhead, and gusts of wind indicated that the drizzle would soon become a downpour. They sought the main wharves at the confluence of the Ganny and Minong rivers. Passing the riverside barge docks, they recognized their galleymaster, surrounded by russet-clad soldiers and priests. "Let's not stop to chat," Yan said sarcastically. "Our hostel's ahead, and we can find a carriage." He hunched his shoulders. Near-horizontal gusts drove cold wetness through his clothing.

Rounding the last corner, they were a hundred yards from the rooming house when they stopped abruptly. Three Church soldiers stood by the door. A carriage waited at the intersection, and brown cowls hid its occupants' faces. Light seeped from beneath the balcony doors of their room on the inn's east side.

"They've na' forgotten you, lad," Omer whispered, "though how they tracked you here puzzles me. Could we ha' rowed their messengers here oursel's?" He gestured Yan to walk again, and they passed the inn as if they were ordinary pedestrians with business in the neighborhood. "We'll ha' a hard time leaving Pittsburg now," Omer continued. "They'll watch the wharves."

"There has to be a way," Yan breathed. "But we can't just leave, Om. The books are up there."

"They've probably found them already, Yan. We're best out a' here ere they ha' us, too."

"I can't leave them. They're all that's left of Lazko."

Omer peered toward the inn. He shrugged, resigned. "Then we'll ha' t' fight our way in . . . and out again. Tha' axe a' yours is going to be blooded sooner than you thought."

Yan clutched his bundle closer, his face pale in the wan light. He saw visions of naked warriors splashed with gore, mad eyes fixed on an unreal world where there was no pain, no fatigue . . . "I can't fight them," he hissed between clenched teeth. "We have to think of something else."

Omer, the old warrior, wondered at the contradictions Yan represented: such fear of danger in a man who'd just purchased a war axe, and who was damned good with it. This was unexpected. Had he misread his companion? He'd have sworn that Yan, for all his scholarly ways, was no coward. Hadn't he slain two Church thugs already? So he claimed. He shrugged. Now was no time for questions. "A diversion, then," he suggested. "One of us can draw them off, but there may still be fighting. Will you . . . ?"

"The balcony is clear," Yan observed, ignoring the question. "I'll climb up there. How can we draw them away?"

"Leave that t' me," Omer murmured, already planning. "When you hear a commotion out front, you'll know when t' move."

Moments later, their simple plan complete, they parted, Omer to the front of the inn and Yan to the balcony side.

In the darkness of a deep entryway, his movements slow and hesitant with shame, Yan prepared for his ordeal. He would have to fight. He knew it. Diversion or not, the room would not be unguarded. He laid the axe aside and shook out of his sheepskin jacket. He removed shirt and worn boots, then let his coarse trousers fall. Already, his body was reacting to the imminent battle. His slowness of motion was relative. His thoughts raced. His bowels gurgled like methane bubbling from a raft pole in swamp muck, and he squatted naked in the darkened doorway, as far from his belongings as he could get.

Strapping his belt around his waist, he made a crude garment of the axe's wrap. Girding my loins for battle, he thought ruefully, fighting shame. That's what I'm doing. He picked up the weapon, and waited for minutes that seemed an eternity.

Shouts and a protesting whinny broke the silence. Iron-shod hooves clattered on rough cobbles. It had begun. A shadow fell across the balcony and a russet-clad soldier emerged. Unable to see what went on, he withdrew. Had he left the room? Yan sprinted for the balcony, bare feet flying over cold stones, the bruising impacts unheeded. In a single motion he thrust the axe between his bare thighs and leapt for the loggia's lip, then pulled himself up. Hanging one-handed, he swept his weapon overhead and felt its spike bite wood. Thunder and the patter of fat raindrops buried the noise. He flung a knee over the low rail, his eyes flashing in spilled lamplight from within, adjusting instantly to the glare. A jerk of his corded, blood-engorged arm pulled his weapon free.

The hallway door on the far side of the room was just swinging shut. A raking glance showed him that the room was empty. The armoire door hung on broken hinges and clothing was strewn about, but the heavy cabinet was unmoved. He tilted it up in one easy motion and swept the bag of books out with a foot, making no noise but the swish of canvas on polished tile. He let the armoire down again just as silently.

The hallway door opened. He realized his error. In his augmented state, goaded by his demon, it seemed that the soldier had been gone an eon, but in truth he had only moved a step beyond when Yan entered the room, and had heard some slight noise and turned around at once.

Yan tossed the sack onto the balcony. Noise no longer mattered as he turned to face his enemy. Comprehension flooded the soldier's face when he saw Yan's nakedness and the evil sweep of his axe. Wide-eyed fear crawled across his features. Yan had time to set the axe firmly in his grip and to adjust his stance for a single well-planned killing blow. Emotionless, he pondered the terror in his opponent's eyes and considered turning his blow mercifully aside. But no one knew of his demon yet. If this man went free, in minutes or hours the Church would know what they faced in Yan, and their next blow would come in stealth and darkness—an assassin's poisoned arrow or a flurry of crossbow bolts from windows around some small, confined square.

Yan let his arm continue on course. He felt the impact of steel on flesh and bone as resistance to his motion, no more noticeable than a leafy branch, and saw the man's head split like a winter squash under a cleaver. He spun toward the balcony.

Later, he remembered nothing of his return to the shadowed doorway, of donning his clothing, or of the stink of his feces pooling there. When he met Omer at their rendezvous, his axe was wiped clean of gore, and his breathing and heartbeat were no heavier than normal, considering that he had run several hundred yards. "No trouble at all," he lied to the fisherman as they slipped away from the turmoil behind them.

The carriage was overturned down the street, and soldiers were pulling enraged priests from the uppermost side door. "Did you do that?" Yan asked, steering talk from himself.

"I spooked the horses," Omer admitted, "but I didn't stay to watch when armed mercenaries came out of the inn." He eyed Yan quizzically, but withheld questions, and made no comment about the telltale spatters of red-brown blood on his right hand. Nor did he attempt to cajole the younger man from the black despair that enveloped him.

Let him think my silence is shame for my cowardice, Yan decided bitterly. I let an old man take the greater risk, stealing a carriage full of high churchmen right in front of their bodyguards' pikes. I merely retrieved a bag of books from an empty room. Better he believe that than know what I truly am.

"We'll scout the wharves," Omer said, breaking Yan's silence. "There's a score a' ways out a' any town, and they can't have men to watch each one. Besides, howe'er they've followed you, they can only know where you've been, not where you're going. They can't know that until they see us board a ship."

Nearing the juncture of the two rivers, they saw no unusual activity, no troops or churchmen. The rain had passed and the air was silvery clear, the sky a white, featureless ceiling, clear and blue-green low in the west. The tall masts of two oceangoing vessels loomed over river craft and low roofs. On a small square facing the wharf, a shed's outside tables proclaimed it a tavern. Crossing the flagged court, they made for an unoccupied table and, seated with Yan's sack beneath his bench, they blended with the sailors and stevedores. "Who's going to identify us?" Omer speculated. "There are hundreds, even thousands, like us."

One drink later, Omer rose and ambled toward the smaller of the ships. Judging by her waterline, she was the more nearly loaded, and probably ready to sail. He passed out of Yan's sight as a chain shed intervened.

Another half hour passed; another drink went down Yan's throat, and another still. The sun hung low beneath drifts of carmine and vermilion clouds. Yan strained to peer through the forest of wooden masts for Omer. To relieve his eyes, he turned toward the buildings fronting the square, and saw movement in the upper-story window of a coal dealer's office. Had he seen a flash of crimson on a brown sleeve? Low-angled sunlight, and deep shadow within, made identification uncertain, and brown clothing was common. Then a vagrant ray glanced redly off the sleeve of a chain-mail shirt, and he was sure.

He glanced back to the ships again, afraid to take his eyes from the window for long, but concerned that his attention might be noticed, too. Omer approached. "Sit over there and don't look at me," Yan hissed. "Up over the coal dealer's. Two men—and one's a soldier. They're watching the wharf."

Omer ordered a mug of spring-chilled cider and waited until the waiter retreated before speaking. "I expected as much. Browncoats ha' been asking questions, the ship captain says. But there's good news, too—I've paid our passage t' Innis. We sail tonight on the tide, with a full moon and no stops until Dan, a seacoast port. Our vessel's out a' Cansi, and her master's a Christer, wi' no love a' the Star Church. If we're aboard when she sails, we're free men. I'll walk back aboard, being expected. Spies'll pay me little mind, but you and tha' bag . . ."

"I'll pay the tavern boy to deliver it for me after dark, in a cider keg, and I'll promise him an extra coin from you when it arrives. Have a line over the stern for me. I can swim."

Omer nodded, rising. Yan watched him leave. A churchman

and a red-clad mercenary approached him from behind a high-piled dray. Omer gestured widely and shook his head, then spat on the ground. The priest raised a hand to strike him, then thought better of it. In his other hand he held a small black lacquer box that he swept through the air about Omer, as if brushing away invisible cobwebs, while gesticulating to his companion, who made as if to block Omer's path. The fisherman put a hand on the hilt of his sword, and with the other hand motioned toward the ship, where several armed sailors watched everything. With a shrug for his master, the mercenary allowed Omer to pass.

Yan went into the tavern, carrying his sack in front of him to shield it from view. He instructed the tavern boy and paid him, then was shown to a rear entrance. A gate by the outhouse opened to a narrow space between buildings. Yan pushed through burdock and thistles, emerging on a side street whose sheds lined the water's edge. Moments later, he was knee-deep in the garbage-fouled water of the Minong. He made his way between pilings and green-coated barges, working his way toward the Ganny side and the tall ships' moorings. A clatter of heavy-soled boots on the planks above stopped him short. Hugging a piling, he peered upward, but saw only that two pairs of feet blocked the light between the boards.

"There's been no sign of two such men," he heard one voice say. "If I had a price on *my* head, I'd run for the woods."

"God's voice spoke when the old man passed," the other protested.

"Is that what I heard?" the first one shot back. "I thought you had a cicada in that box." His voice dripped scorn.

"Do not mock Pharos, soldier. The God speaks in many ways—but it may have been a fluke. I know little of these things; I was only given this magic device today. Anyway, it's unlikely that fugitives would choose *this* ship. It's bound for Innis."

"May I ask why, Brother Ardrus? I know nothing of the men we search for, not even their crimes, let alone motivations."

"Their offenses are unimportant, now, Corporal. They killed a scholar and burned his house to hide the deed. What is important is that we recover the things they took from the house before it burned. The Church must have them back."

"The task seems hopeless," the first voice said. "I don't know what they have taken. How can I help find it? And we can't search every house in Pittsburg, nor every fisherman's scow."

"Not so. They carry gold consecrated to Pharos. It bears his Sign, and if they approach this box I carry, the God's voice within will tell us the gold is nearby."

"As it spoke when the old sailor passed?" The corporal's tone mocked his companion. "No disrespect, Brother, but I see only a box, and heard only a clicking. Is a sacred relic in it?"

"It is a gift from the God. I move this lever so . . ." A noise penetrated Yan's hiding place, a rapid clicking, one click following so closely upon the last that they created a continuous tone that was indeed like the electric drone of a cicada. "Strange," the priest mused. "The clatter was less intense earlier. Perhaps I moved the lever too far." Shadow blocked the sunlight between boards as the box was set down.

"What is that circle of glass, Brother Ardrus?"

"When the pin within points just there, at that mark, then consecrated material is nearby. You will see that it falls just short of it now. I wonder why? Perhaps I should walk around with it, and see if the influence grows or fades."

Yan stiffened. Everything from the wreck had been slightly radioactive. Lazko, using ancient devices from the University cellars, had traced the source of the contamination to a leaking container, perhaps some sort of fuel. The gold was not dangerous, even close to his body, but it obviously registered on the scintillometer the browncoat had set down above him. The priest's footsteps thumped about. Yan considered letting his belt down into the water to mask the betraying emanations, but the guard was right above him. He didn't dare move.

"The sign is strongest here," the priest said when he returned. "Go beneath the wharf and see what causes it." Yan's stomach knotted. He was so near the ship, and safety. But he had no weapon, and there was no hiding place.

"What must I look for, Brother?"

"For anything, man. Anything unusual—a bag, a box, a man . . . anything. Now go. Find it."

Yan took a single gold piece from a belt pocket and wedged it conspicuously between a crossbeam and a plank. When the guard's drumming footfalls moved across the wharf, he pushed himself rapidly to the nearest barge and ducked underneath it, pulling himself beneath its flat oak keel. Straining to hold the breath in his lungs, he rose as slowly as he could on the far side of the barge. Then he listened, forcing himself to breathe quietly.

"Are you near it? What can you see?" Brother Ardrus called querulously. "Answer me, man!"

"Damn all priests," the corporal muttered. "That shit-packing faggot isn't wearing chain mail. *He* should be down here himself." Already, the soldier imagined, rust was reddening his chain shirt and staining his padded undergarment. Who would have to spend off-duty hours wire-brushing and scrubbing? Who would pay for the new undershirt he'd have to buy before the next inspection? "I'm right below you, Brother. I don't see anything." He glared angrily up at the planks. Right there, in the priest's shadow, something glittered. The corporal reached upward, then withdrew his hand, smiling broadly. Tonight he would come back. He wouldn't complain about getting wet a second time—the lovely yellow gold was worth a month's pay. How had it lodged there? Had the fugitives, fleeing this way, dropped it? Without doubt, the chip of gold was the source of whatever the devil box scented. "May I come up now?" he pleaded. "There's nothing here at all. Perhaps the relic box is at fault. Your murderers are surely miles away by now."

"Perhaps you're right. At any rate, the dials didn't move all the way around. It may mean nothing."

Yan peered around a barge and saw the corporal backing toward the wharf's edge, his eyes fixed on the spot where the gold lodged, memorizing it for his return. He climbed from the water. Yan waited until he heard two pairs of footfalls on the cobbles beyond, one crisp, one sodden, before he retrieved the gold and replaced it in his belt, laughing. The corporal would have wet feet again, and for nothing. Yan felt sorry for him, and almost considered leaving the gold. But no. The corporal would sell the gold, and priests would acquire it, confirming Yan's presence in Pittsburg beyond doubt. Better the soldier found no wealth, and maintained a bitter, self-protective silence.

Yan waited for dusk before swimming to the stern of the loaded vessel. *Pride of Cansi* was carved on the lower transom. A heavy rope hung there, pulled away from the ship by a small current. He waited until darkness before he climbed it. He was so tired by then that he would have fallen back in the river with a resounding, betraying splash if the rope had not been pulled from above. Waiting hands grasped him and pulled him aboard.

Yan told Omer about the gold and its betraying emanations. The two of them emptied their belts into a cloth sack, which Omer took below and sunk in the foul-smelling, opaque water of the bilge. In their cabin they changed to shipboard garb, drill trousers and shirts. "Where's my sack?" Yan asked anxiously, looking around. "The captain's safe," Omer reassured him. "The governor a' Pittsburg himself couldn't warrant a search there."

"When can I have it back?"

"We'll stay below until *Pride*'s well away from the wharf. The captain's quarters are forward over the deck so you'll have to get your sack later. But we can reach the galley without going above—there's kaf heating. I s'pect you could use some, about now."

Because *Pride of Cansi* was moored with her bow toward shore, it was necessary to warp her stern-first into the main stream, where current could swing her around. The coal-fired steam tug that pulled her was a rare sight in any port, but one of two in Pittsburg. Yan watched the strange machine through a porthole. As he listened to the deep chuff of the engine, his eyes followed its greasy black smoke upward. He wished he had paper to sketch the tug at work, to record the way power was transferred from firebox and fat boiler, through pistons hidden below the open gunwale, to shaft and screw beneath the roiled waters of its stern.

Once in position for downstream passage, *Pride* still was not independent. Strong southwesterly winds funneling up the channel threatened to drive her onto the rocky shores. There was no room to sail, so *Pride* would be towed downstream. For Yan, that was an unsurpassed opportunity. Recovering his pens, he persuaded an officer to let him visit the tug, a short, easy row for the two crewmen who took him across, as the tug had only to maintain steerageway, a speed slightly greater than the current. He spent several hours aboard the *River Ox*, as the tug was affectionately called. By lamplight, he sketched its workings and made copious notes as the enginemen explained things to him. He was less than content with their exposition; the engineers had no real concept of why the complex system of pipes, valves, and linkages worked. They knew only rules for operating it, specifications for repairing it. Yan had experienced their cultural blindness before. Few folk saw relationships between parts, and fewer cared. That, he thought, is why we live like primitives. The machines of the ancients were products of engineers who combined many techniques in one, folk who asked not only *why*, but *why not?*

After the rowboat returned Yan to the *Pride*, it took on a passenger: the river pilot, who by law and custom remained on the *Pride* from Pittsburg to the estuary where the channel widened, would return to the city on the tug. Once Yan was aboard the *Pride* again, the ship's motion changed abruptly as the towrope was cast off. She was free now, and under sail.

The slender young witch peered into the murk. From offshore at night, Innis gave no hint of the festering evil she knew lay at its core. The dim lights scattered over its rounded hills were further apart than those of villages seen as the ship passed up the bay, and no brighter. The Cathedral towers were lost in darkness. Nevertheless, dread gripped her stomach and her heart pounded against her ribs. The ship would dock at first light.

Nervously she fingered the latches of her dower chest. She glanced at her cabin door, reassuring herself it was bolted, then unlocked the box and reached within. As soft, gentle touches brushed her fingers, a muted hum filled the close confines of the cabin and an odor of mildew and honey wafted out. She smiled, reassured. Her tiny charges were well. Her mission was, as yet, on its proper course. *This bridal gift will be delivered*, she vowed, thinking how the fate of worlds would be changed.

CHAPTER SEVEN

Taken from their sky-born lovers,
Southward borne on warming winds,
Into bondage all were traded
To the black-skinned lords of Burum.

Grief took some, but broken pledges
Were forgiven by the sisters;
Pale upon their death-beds lying,
None begrudged their easy passing.

Anon, a score become a dozen
Pleasure-slaves for Burum's kings;
Pledges kept, they bore dark children
Named in secret for the lost ones.

Sons were torn from mothers' bosoms,
Sacred names were never given;
Gelded by their jealous fathers,
None knew of their precious burden.

Excerpted from "The Women's Song," from *Folktales of the Bamian Highlands*, Chapter VII, "Cryptic Tales & Nonsense-songs."

"Yan?" Omer looked up from the book on the messroom table.

"Yes?" Yan, too, had an open volume before him. Both books, and several others about, were from the captain's library.

"I think I know the connection between those witch stories and your starship." He pushed the volume across the table.

"What? What is it?" The captain's books were geographic, relating to peoples and ports a Cansian ship might visit. Omer had pulled the book of folktales from the shelf on a whim—a whim that had paid off, from his smug smile. "It's a poem. It may even explain why your witches fly no more ships."

Yan read the passage. "Nonsense songs? Oh, I see. Another witch tale. He scanned the ten quatrains on the open pages and then peered at Omer. "I hate this kind of stuff. It's not poetry, just a rhythmic mnemonic. Sorry, Om. I don't understand. It's about slave women. Witches?"

"Aya, it's about a witch. Read verse six."

" 'Ilse, the third to bear the name,/Bore a daughter called Martina/To the Overlord of Burum,/Samel of the Golden Eye.' "

"You're th' scholar, Yan, so you tell me—who was Samel Gold-eye?"

"Samel . . . you mean Samool Gold-eye?"

"Th' same. Some call him Semal, too. No matter."

"He was a king of Burum, oh, about a thousand years ago."

"Aya," Omer agreed. "When—exactly."

"That's important? Let's see . . . around 2800? No, I don't remember . . . but from your evil look, I suppose you do." Even though Yan was getting used to Omer's teasing, he was annoyed to be led by the nose. Omer sensed his mood, and replied quickly.

"Aya, I do. Semal took th' throne a' Burum in 2890." Unable to resist, he asked Yan one more question. "An' who d' you think helped him gain his throne?"

"Damn it, Om. Stop playing guessing games. Who?" Yan thought he should be able to figure it out, but he was too annoyed. That, too, he suspected, was part of Omer's game.

"A cabal of witches, tha's who. Odd, eh? An' only six short years after th' Great Bolide?"

"Of course!" Yan exclaimed, his frustration forgotten. "You're the sailor. How long would it have taken them to reach Burum, say from somewhere in Hudsin or Nipigon?"

"A year, considering th' ships they had back then. Maybe two. Assuming they could speak th' tongue, an' pay passage."

"That's it, then! The 'witches' were starship passengers, I suppose, and the 'sky-born lovers' must have been the crew. The women were enslaved, likely by a shipmaster—they would have been foreign and naive—and later the crewmen found them, and bought their freedom with technological secrets, weapons . . ." Yan saw Omer shake his head. "What's wrong? What am I missing now?"

"Not just missing. Why complicate a simple tale? Where's it say their men came back?"

"It doesn't, but . . ."

"The *women* were witches, Yan. An' it wasn't weapons they gave Samel. It was magic."

"I didn't think you believed in fairy tales, Om." Yan sniffed scornfully.

"Tha' depends on what you mean. I don't hold with priestly mumbo jumbo, an' I know all th' tricks a' cards and dice, but still, some things can't be explained wi'out calling them magic."

"Such as?"

"Clairvoyants who see th' future; old women who can find water or sunken ships; people who speak wi'out words. Those are *real*, Yan. I've seen them."

Yan was not prepared to contradict such conviction. Besides, he thought, there were many such phenomena, all unexplained—but he balked at calling them "magic."

"Magic's anything y' can't explain wi' what you already know," Omer said. "Tha' could be mind reading or . . . or 'thermonuclear fusion.' See?"

Yan nodded thoughtfully. "So the 'witches' really had paranormal talents." He reread the verses. "I see now—that's the 'precious burden' in verse four, and the 'Gift of Seeing' in the eighth."

"Aya, you're right—as far as you go. Since you still don't see, I suppose I'll ha' t' show you. Let's go on deck."

Knowing Omer was determined to have his fun, to force Yan to discover for himself whatever the old sailor had already figured out, Yan rose after him and tramped up the companionway stair.

"Look around you, Yan. There's your 'magic.' " His sweeping gesture took in sails and rigging, masts, hatches, and the wheelhouse where the helmsman stood. Still, Yan was unenlightened. "Wha' would it take t' steer this vessel if there were no sheets t' trim the sails, and no wheel or *cables* running t' th' rudder?"

Then Yan understood. "The starship! The control cables didn't go anywhere. Then the *women*, the slaves, were the starship crew. That's it, isn't it?"

Omer nodded, grinning at Yan's pleasure. "I wondered early on, when you told me there was no way t' steer th' great iron hulk and no way for th' captain t' speak wi' his crew. When I started reading about those witches . . ."

"Telepathy," Yan said. "And pyro-something . . . control of *thermonuclear* fire." Omer noted with tolerant irony how easily Yan accepted the unexplained and unexplainable, once he could find a name for it—as long as the name was not "magic."

Yan held up the slim book of verses. He waved it at Omer. "Nonsense songs?" He smiled. "I suppose it would seem so, not knowing what we know. 'Sky-born lovers' . . . a starship's crew; and their menfolk, separated in slavery. You're right. This is a key. We even have names for them now: Ilse, Martina . . . incredible. Could there be a less likely place to discover this? They came south, were enslaved and separated, and ended up with Semal Gold-eye, the founder of the Burumian empire."

"I wonder what the Oath of Innis was?" Omer said.

"Look at the seventh verse," Yan suggested. "It was to keep their heritage alive, I think—to remember the past. That gives me hope. I wonder how much their descendants remember today?"

"If they're alive," Omer commented.

"I have no doubt of it now," Yan countered. "The Inman Bune account is less than a half-century old. His account and this tale are related. 'Witches' can't have survived all this time, then died out yesterday."

"Getting knocked up by Semal . . . that makes sense, too."

"It does?" Yan asked. "I must have missed something."

"Semal—or Samel, or Samool—was known to be a 'witch' who used 'magic' to establish his empire. So when the real 'witches' left, they took a bit of him along, in case it bred true. The poem shows that their 'secret' was genetic, not technological. I think they lost it with their men."

"That may be. They must have hoped Semal's 'talent' was the same as their own men's, then. That may explain why those piloting attempts failed, when we first got the star drive."

"What? Now I'm missing something."

"Genetics, Om. And history. The old WSRO, that oversaw the experiments, was part of a government whose philosophy was egalitarian. Dealing with many races of man, it considered all men equal in fact and under law. Men and women were 'equal,' too. They didn't consider that a crew had to have men *and* women, each with specific 'talents' not available to each other or to the population in general."

"Why not? I mean, I can understand their not believing in witchery—but anyone knows women are better at some things."

"It's culture. By comparison with them, we're rude and primitive, and we accept that sex is the great divider. But with their technology, men's and women's roles converged."

"All the more reason to have women piloting their ships, I'd think."

"That's not the point. They may have *had* women pilots, but they were indisposed to look for qualities that were *specific* to women—or to men. But where do you get the idea that they lost something vital? Don't the 'precious burdens' and 'precious sons' passages indicate that the men's talent *wasn't* lost?"

"Possibly. But I don't think the "Gift of Seeing," whatever it is, was what they lost. I think it was something else."

"Then they never did find it, or they wouldn't still be hiding in the mountains." Yan shook his head disconsolately. The poem, though seeming to confirm the reality of the witches, and thus the validity of his quest, also pointed to an uncomfortable conclusion: that the witches themselves could no longer pilot a starship, even if they had one. He said as much to Omer.

"Don't let that depress you," the older man said. "It may not be so. At any rate, did I sail the trade routes all those years just to see the happy faces of those who received my cargoes? Trade was only an excuse, something to pay the way. The voyage itself is the true reward."

"So you see how knowledge grows?" Yan asked later as he and Omer climbed into their bunks, swaying with the roll of waves from *Pride*'s forequarter. "Sometimes the key is no more than being open to all the facts and clues that abound. Think about it—I didn't know, when I bought passage on *West Wind*, that *you* would know about Moromen and the Great Bolide; you didn't know what you'd find in that little book of folktales, either, but if *you* didn't know what *I* had already known, from Lazko's books, then the 'Women's Tale' would have meant nothing to you."

"Knowledge is like a magnet, isn't it?" Omer mused.

"Exactly," Yan replied, "but only if you're open to it. That's what's wrong with people, with our world, today."

"Not enough openness?"

"Just so. That, and the inability to connect seemingly unrelated things—like steam engines and dynamos."

"Now you've lost me."

"Technology isn't discrete, but people today don't *look* for connections. There's no technological mind-set. A steam engine is just a way to power a tugboat, a dynamo is a child's toy for making sparks, and a radio is a magical device. You said the sea knights had radios, once."

"Bought from the Collegians of Oma. Sealed boxes that worked for a while, then died. We returned dead ones and bought new every year. They were expensive necessities, and when war broke out, we couldn't replace them."

"They 'died,' " Yan said, "when their batteries ran out of electricity. But a child's toy dynamo . . . those sparks are electricity, too. You might have been able to repower the radios with a few wires and a child's toy."

"I see," Omer said quietly. "One device makes it, another uses it. That's your connection."

"Yes, but that's not all. What does it take to spin a dynamo?"

"A hand on the crank?"

"A source of power, of motion. Like a steam engine. One steam engine could run a hundred dynamos and power as many radios. See? The connection *there* is mechanical, not electrical. Together, engine, dynamo, and radio, they are really one complex device."

"Nobody else thinks like that," Omer said. "Amazing. As long as we *separate* everything, we can't progress, right?"

Both men agreed that it was a sorry affair. Omer went so far as to speculate that some far place might even use wheels on children's pull-toys without ever discovering the oxcart or the chariot. A whole new way of thinking had to be taught in order to change the world. And as that was not something either of them could accomplish, they said no more of it.

Perhaps if the elusive witches retained enough bits and pieces of ancient technology, a start could be made on it, with help from the surviving colleges and universities. It's clear where we're going now, at least, Omer said to himself before he dozed. The greatest university left is at Nobi, in Burum, and beyond that . . . the Mountain Freeholds. No place for a sailor, but I suppose if the boy really wants to . . . It was late, and the ship's motion lulled him. Yan was already asleep.

From offshore, Dan was a sleazy collection of hovels and wharves, but the waters flowing sluggishly to the shore told a different story. Each stream branch of the delta carried distinctive stenches, like guild cards identifying the industries the channel served. Dense forest hid the town, but a sophisticated nose could seek out districts of papermakers, felters, beamers, and dyers—and practitioners of more noxious trades—by following the trickle whose particular odor declared their presence upstream. At the waterfront the streams converged beneath the wharves, and the composite stink, overlaid with the distinctive aroma of human nightsoil, created a palpable barrier for unaccustomed noses.

Halfway to shore, Yan and three others decided there could be little in Dan to tempt them closer. They ordered their rowers to turn back to the *Pride*, which awaited a consignment of hides and paper bound for Innis. The other pinnace, with businessmen aboard, continued shoreward.

"How can human noses inure themselves to that?" a merchant named Harf, or perhaps Haff, wondered once they regained the *Pride*. "My eyes were burning."

"A slaver's hold is less foul," a well-dressed fellow agreed. Yan wondered how he knew. Eyeing the rings constricting the fellow's fat fingers, Yan assumed his expertise was not gained from *residing* in such a hold. Revolted by the company he kept, he turned away quickly, just short of impoliteness, and returned to his cabin.

"What happened to you?" Omer asked upon seeing his scowl. "You look like you just found a turd in your soup."

"Close," Yan said, not amused. "That place is sickening. Is it all like this? Fanatic, murdering priests; slaves and slavers—a world of miserable ignoramuses?"

"I suppose Dan's worse than most," Omer replied matter-of-factly. "But don't let that prejudice you. There are pleasant towns, too."

"How did we sink so low?" Yan grumbled, ignoring Omer's words. "A thousand years ago we reached for the stars, but now the whole world has its head in the muck. And the knowledge to rise up again is still around—that's the worst of it. Nahbor hasn't scratched the surface of its accumulated lore. It's all in the databanks, as long as anyone's left who can access them, at least. But we're all still sweating, rowing, hauling, and shitting in our rivers, as if it's always been like this. Why?"

"Resources?" Omer suggested. "The old mines went deep. We don't have the metals or oil the ancients did. Even Pittsburg runs on secondhand steel, not ores."

"Even so, we could build a sewer—or a starship—if we cared to. What happened to the will to do it? Did the ferosin take it away with the refugees? Are we only the dregs of humanity here on Earth?"

Omer didn't answer him. Wherever the answers to his questions lay, they were far outside that small cabin on the *Pride of Cansi*.

The captain was late returning from Dan. The ship was to have sailed at moonrise, and the moon was well up already. Yan and Omer stood at the port rail, staring at the fog-dimmed lights of Dan a quarter-mile distant. "What's keeping him?" Yan wondered aloud. "Has he betrayed us? The Church would pay him well, I think."

"That's not his style," Omer reassured him. "A Cansian captain's richer than some kings. Such men don't mess in politics. Anyway, I hear a boat." The creak of leather-wrapped oar shafts drew near. Fog hanging close to the water made the boat appear as a dark patch on the water beneath them. A thin rope flew up, over the railing. Omer darted for it.

"You on deck! Tie off our line, and get Orzen here, now." It was the captain, his voice low and urgent. "Tell him 'Cansi's wall is breached' got that?"

"Aya, Captain," Omer said. Orzen was the mate. While Omer sought him, Yan tied the boat's painter off and helped the captain aboard. The boat was not one of *Pride*'s pinnaces, he noted, but smaller, with a low, unstayed mast. Four rowers climbed aboard. Six had gone ashore with the captain, so something was definitely wrong.

The squeal of beechwood sheaves shredded the nighttime quiet as furled sails dropped flat. Yan felt a dull shudder through the deck as sails filled with wind. "You there! Get forward to help on the capstan," he heard the mate order hoarsely. Yan jumped to obey. Something bad had happened in Dan.

Sailors pushed four-foot staves into the capstan hub. Omer grabbed two more from their rack and tossed one to Yan, ramming his home in an empty socket. Yan imitated him. The capstan was a huge rimless wheel, with a wrist-thick hawser snubbed around its nave and threaded forward through an iron-rimmed hole. "Push, you bastards," the mate called. "I want that anchor clear!" Yan was not sure how long it took to take up and coil fifty or sixty feet of heavy rope, but it seemed as if the anchor broke surface and was made fast in record time. The *Pride of Cansi* was under way.

The stiff motion of her deck hinted at well-filled sails and a reaching course—southwest, Yan thought. By the time he caught his breath, the ship had cleared the low headland west of Dan. He and Omer went sternward, consumed with curiosity about their sudden departure. Both men tacitly assumed it concerned them in some way.

They were right. As they mounted the short stair to the afterdeck, the captain motioned to them. "You two—join me below. I have questions, and I hope your answers will justify two dead crewmen." His words were ominous, but his mild tone reassured Yan.

"Aya, Captain," Omer assented. "Will we outrun our pursuers?" He gestured aft at sails following in *Pride*'s wake.

"They'll give up," the captain replied. "We've every scrap of sail on the poles. Besides, they're small craft, and no vessel can outsail its own length—as I'm sure you know."

"What does he mean?" Yan asked in a whisper.

"It's a fact of sailing," Omer replied. "If a small vessel can sail its own length, say twenty feet, in three seconds, then a hundred-foot vessel like this can sail a hundred feet in about the same time—all other things being equal. It means the universe, or the sea gods, won't allow us to be caught."

"That's all very interesting," Yan growled, "but it's not what I meant." But it was too late for Omer to reply; the captain's door stood before them. He gestured them to a pillowed bench beside the sweeping transom windows, beyond which they could see their pursuers diminishing with distance.

"Kaf will be brought," their host said. Yan was not sure whether he should feel relieved. Kaf, and a comfortable seat with the morning glare from the sea beyond in the captain's eyes instead of theirs, hardly presaged an unpleasant interrogation. They sat in silence until each had a steaming cup in hand.

"I am Haige," the captain said for Yan's benefit. "And you are Yan Bando, my most expensive passenger, ever."

"I don't understand, sir," Yan replied. "What have I done?" And how did the captain know his name?

"The *Pride* earns no fees with a hold full of air—and we took nothing aboard in Dan. The death-geld for two men's families . . . The bill for tonight will be the price of a ship, yet I have no accounting of *why* it must be paid. Enlighten me."

"If I understand you aright," Yan said cautiously, "we are to blame for an untoward departure and the loss of your crewmen. If you claim this, then it is so. I have no wish to impugn your honesty or your perceptions, but I'm ignorant of what transpired, and of our connection with it."

"Saving your responsibility for last, perhaps your companion can explain the value of safe harbors. Ser Knight? What price would a man of Senloo have placed upon them?"

Without a blink or a denial, Omer replied, smiling, "I compliment you, Captain. If you'll tell me how I revealed myself, I may owe my life to you yet another time." Then he turned to Yan. "The Cansian fleet fought battles and maintained costly blockades to establish its right to trade unmolested. Dan violated its treaty, and will pay heavily."

"Trade is the fleet's blood," the captain interjected. "No one profits from a blockade. But now, an example must be made."

"What will happen?" Yan asked.

"Dan will die," Haige said. "There'll be no killing, but in a year, there'll be no town, either. Even before our war fleet arrives, the foreign merchants and factors will be gone with their goods, and producers of leather and grain will have found other routes to the sea—through Innis, perhaps. Dan will be a swampy village at best, or gone entirely."

"But why?" Yan demanded. "And what could we have done to cause all this?"

"Yes," Omer added. "If we are to accept responsibility, then tell us what happened."

"Very well," Haige growled. "My men and I were taken before a Pharos hound, the Junior of Dan, who demanded the two of you. He described you unmistakably. Informed that my passengers are wards of Cansi while they tread my decks, he urged me to lure you ashore. I pretended to agree, with no further plan than to return to the ship, but the Junior became suspicious and refused me leave. He 'suggested' he would trade me for the two of you.

"The treaty was broken." He sighed. "We had to fight. Man for man, my crew proved superior to fat priests and elderly mercenaries. But that was then. I have questions now."

"Indeed. We'll answer them as best we can," Omer agreed, "but there is much that I myself don't understand."

"Begin thus," the captain said. "You claim the brownshirts pursue you for heretical acts, which are of no matter to me. The Junior claimed otherwise. I am inclined to believe you, but you said that your pursuers were left behind. Since no ships have passed us at sea, and only the *Pride* had put in at Dan, how was the Junior able to describe you? Convince me you have not lied."

"I can do that," Yan interjected, "but it will be necessary to start at the beginning and tell our whole tale." Omer agreed that nothing less would suffice. He himself wanted to hear Yan's explanation of the Junior's knowledge, which deeply troubled him.

The tale was hours in the telling, but was completed in one sitting, interrupted only for more cups of kaf and several visits to the sternwalk to relieve themselves over the rail. In conclusion, Yan described the ancient devices called radios, by which men could communicate over great distances. "I didn't see the radiation counter closely," he added, "but it was no simple thing cobbled together from old plans, nor was it a device of the ancients. It was shiny and new, yet well made. Events seem to prove they have radios as well—possibly also new and shiny."

"Then the Church indeed has an odd source of supply," the captain said. "Whether it is your University or some clever folk on a far shore, it concerns me. What other devices might they have? What weaponry? I cannot risk my ship by aiding you further. I cannot dock at Innis, with you aboard." As they departed, the captain added, "One more thing you might be wise to think upon—just what is so special about *you*, in Church eyes? What do they think you know *that you don't*?"

Yan had no answer, nor did Omer. The gold? But the Church had riches beyond imagining. Was it the notebooks, or, as Haige seemed to suggest, was there some bit of knowledge not remarkable in itself, something the Church wanted, or wanted suppressed? What could it be, to stir up such a termites' nest? Yan had to learn more in order to know, or to find out what he already might know. His life could depend on it.

Yes, knowledge was always the key, he reflected. Every datum gleaned made those already known clearer. He envisioned the accumulation of knowledge as a juggernaut, a snowball rolling down a hill, gathering momentum and mass. The nonsense song would have remained just that without Omer's insights, and those had in turn been stimulated by the notebooks, facts Yan had supplied. If I have enough data, Yan thought, then everything will come together in a great spasm of insight. If, that is, I live long enough to experience it.

Pride would go south. He and Omer would slip away, and enter the "holy" city of Innis unremarked. There, if anywhere, he might find out why the Church so doggedly pursued him.

With that understanding, perhaps he could find a way to remain free of the priests long enough to continue his quest for witches and ancient spaceships unmolested.

Innis. Witches or star pilots. The Oath of Innis, mentioned in the "Women's Song." Yes, the spoor seemed to go south to Bama and Burum, and to the Mountain Freeholds beyond, where witch tales and perhaps witches abounded, but it seemed that Innis had been a way station on the ancient starfarers' journey south. Had their captor sold them there, on Innis blocks? It was only appropriate that he, too, should go there, in their footsteps, so to speak.

The clangor of Innis never ceased. Day and night, the narrow streets were filled with folk, and their voices were magnified by overarching stone walls and trees. Even after several days, it still unnerved the mountain-village girl. The sky was never more than a narrow strip overhead. Each street led only into others, wider or narrower, just as crowded with busy, pushy people. And no paths led to meadows, copses, or spring-fed pools.

Worse than crowding and incessant noise were the brown-robed men—Pharos priests were everywhere. Almost every fourth person was an emaciated priest with cruel, cynical eyes, a fat, vapid one whose hungry glance skipped over her to focus on a street urchin, or worse, a small, plain one whose appetites could not be sated by food or flesh, only death and burning . . .

Fastidious or slovenly, everyone avoided the greasy-haired wench with the dirty bandage over her eye. Her pushcart reeked of day-old fish, not too far gone to be eaten by poorer folk. No one stayed close long enough to wonder about the cloth-draped wooden box half buried in her dull-scaled cargo.

She had canvassed the entire city in a matter of days, carefully considering each location before surreptitiously releasing her tiny creatures. Was there a garden beyond that wall, a rich man's courtyard with fountains to cool the air, columns and balustrades draped with early-blooming vines? Was it a rare vacant lot overgrown with vetch and clover, with clumps of abandoned, late-flowering lilacs? In such places she lingered, her practiced hands groping in her box to select one of her "pets," one lively, fat, and ready to fly. Now only two were left. Those she would keep for tomorrow, for the Cathedral's inner court. She had a way in. It was all arranged.

CHAPTER EIGHT

You pray to Pharos in your huts! You pray to him in your fields! I hear your prayers rise to the sky above, but does Pharos hear you singing on street corners and calling his name? No, I tell you. No! The Old Believers have a church, the black Moskers have a tower. What do you have? Pharos has told me what he wants from you. He has shown me the plan of his great Temple to be built here, on the very spot where I stand!

Attributed to Hekkor the Apostle. Prob. apocryphal [Y.B.]

The *Pride of Cansi* rolled gently in the dying swells as dusk overtook her. She seemed to stand motionless, though still under full sail. Occasionally, a folded scrap of yellow paper floated beneath her port rail. "That's the fourth little paper boat I've seen," Yan remarked. "What are they for?"

Omer tapped his red-clay pipe on the rail before answering. "The fellow in the bow calls 'mark,' an' the mate stands aft and computes the *Pride*'s speed. He'll know when we're south a' Innis, where you and I cast off on our own." He nodded toward the Dan harbor boat still trailing from the *Pride*'s stern. Fitted with a spritsail, it would be adequate for the northward run into Innis Bay. The *Pride* would sail directly on, heading far south to Tawnyo for a cargo of wool and grain.

Climbing into the small boat, Yan convinced himself he would have been wiser to forget Innis, to stay with the *Pride* and get as far from the Church and its murdering priests as he could. After a month in the south, they could surely find a ship heading east to Burum, and make their way overland to the witches' mountains. Instead, he was in a tiny boat on a moonless night, in the middle of an endless sea. Yet only in Innis could he dig out the priests' secrets and trace the fine thread that linked witches and spaceships, radios and scintillometers, to the murder of his mentor and the destruction of his career. The incident in Dan had shown that hiding was no option. He had to confront his enemies in their nest—or sneak into it, a rat in the woodwork—to find out what he needed to know for his own survival.

Despite darkness and anxiety, a low coast loomed gray and indistinct within a few hours, and Omer declared they were within Innis Bay. At sunup they entered a sluggish creek on the east shore. They buried the tainted gold beneath a streambed boulder. A cloud of silt momentarily marked their cache, then dissipated.

A beaten trail intersected the creek. They followed it to the outskirts of Innis where, on a small promontory, they found a cluster of unpainted clapboard fish-houses. One proved to be an inn of sorts, where they enjoyed a breakfast of water, coarse bread, and broiled fish left over from the proprietor's dinner. The jam pot was aswarm with fat honeybees with distinctive yellow bands across their abdomens—a new variety, less ferocious than most, and prolific producers of honey. The innkeeper demonstrated their docility by wiggling a fat, greasy finger among them, retrieving a gobbet of jam. Brushing two clinging insects away, he popped his finger into his mouth. Omer shrugged and followed suit with a wooden spoon, but Yan, fastidious, ate his bread dry.

From a window overlooking ramshackle docks Omer pointed to the bay's sharp westward curve. "Innis." The forest was a green cloak over the bay-head hills. The upper stories of tall buildings seemed no more than spattered lime specks on that verdant fabric. Yan was unimpressed.

Approaching the city, it was clear that Innis was no tree-covered ruin, but a bustling city of rain-washed limestone, well-shaded by massive oaks and upswept elms. Laid out on a grand scale, it must once have been a spacious and open town. Buildings oriented to gridded streets thrust many stories above the trees. Recent generations, responding less to grandiose concepts and ancient technology than to exigencies of horses and oxcarts, had filled wide avenues with moss-covered clapboard and shingle structures set haphazardly wherever a few square yards of ancient pavement remained free. Narrow paths threaded between them, so constricted that Yan and Omer had to turn sideways when they encountered citizens approaching. Omer drew upon memories of Innis as it had been years earlier to guide them to the city center.

The real center of Innis was the Cathedral, a four-cornered fortress with a central tower adjacent to a walled compound, a small city in its own right. Perspective, intervening structures, and the lay of the land hid it from their view at present. The old sailor claimed acquaintances in Innis: former crewmen now smugglers, slavers, even common thieves. Such trades, he explained dryly, far from being unwelcome in Innis, formed the basis of the city's prosperity. "We'll visit the slave market when we've rested," he declared. "I may find a familiar face."

When the sun stood overhead, they emerged on a broad, stone-paved esplanade overlooking a muddy stream. A single span of pockmarked dolomite crossed it, and on the far side stood a balconied edifice of similar stone, displaying a carved mug, bowl, and spoon over a wood-columned portico. A dozen streetside tables invited lunchtime customers. The narrow alleys of the outer town had been breezeless and humid, and Yan's eyes brightened at the sight of sweating pitchers of cool ale. They found an empty bench. "There's th' Cathedral tower," Omer said, pointing to a conical red-tile roof jutting above distant trees. "It's a mile from here, so you can guess how big it is." The tower loomed threateningly, a blood-red brooding place—the nest of his enemies, Yan reflected. Perhaps that same priest who had issued the orders for Lazko's death even now surveyed the town from some high balcony, perceiving Yan and Omer themselves as inconsequential insects among the busy throngs.

Yan shrugged away such thoughts. "Can your friends help us get in there?" he asked. "There must be records, and we could shorten our search for the 'witches' by examining them."

"Are you mad, Yan? That's the Church's stronghold. Why not peruse the libraries and archives about the city? Those are for scholars' use. Once inside the Cathedral you'd never get out."

"The texts and histories will tell me only what the Church wants people to believe," Yan said angrily. "In there, in their sanctum, they must keep factual accounts of their activities, if only to inform new hierarchs of what has truly gone before. Think, Om! We've speculated that there were other ships from offworld, human-controlled ones, if only because it's so unlikely that I'd have stumbled across the only one. There may be records of others they've destroyed . . . and perhaps of some they didn't.

Above all, there must be accounts of the alien ferosin and how the Church came to worship them."

"What's tha' t' us? Even if we find there were other ships . . . th' Church isn't about t' let you dig them up." The old sailor frowned. "What can you *do* wi' what you find out?"

Yan sighed. "I don't know. Once I thought . . . but that was long ago."

"What? What did you think?"

Yan's smile was self-deprecating. "Poking around the shipwreck, though I was old enough to know better, I told myself someday I'd find out how to fix the vessel, or to build . . . even a small one, a purely human one—" He shook his head. "Silly, isn't it? But still, no one will *ever* do it if the secrets are all hidden in Church vaults or in enigmatic witch songs, or still buried in the ground."

Omer returned his smile. "You're a scholarly pack rat, is all. Collecting baubles and bright little tidbits."

"I suppose so," Yan admitted. "I've always felt if I collected enough of them, they'd sort themselves out, and someday I wouldn't just *know*, I'd *understand*. It's a hard habit to break."

"Aya, but there's no harm in it. You could be a drunkard or a pederast . . . or a priest."

Yan shuddered at those alternatives.

Omer raised his shoulders in a shrug, and scratched his thin, grayed beard. "I'll ask around. But check th' libraries first. I'll do what I can, if only t' get us out of here sooner."

"Thanks, Om." Yan squeezed his forearm. "Shall we find a room for the night, or start sightseeing?"

"There are chambers above," Omer said. "We can lock up our duffel." He waved to their waiter. "Boy! Ha' you rooms above, and a safe place t' store our luggage?"

"Ay, ser. And cheap, if your coin's good silver."

Omer laid small Pittsburg coins on the table. The youth picked one up, flipped it expertly, and listened to it ring on the hard maple tabletop. "Three more like that for the night, I'd say."

"One more and a copper," Omer countered. After mild haggling, three silver coins changed hands, and they were shown to an airy room overlooking the esplanade. A sturdy oak closet would do to stow their belongings. Omer slipped a heavy padlock through the iron hasp, and they descended the stairs unencumbered except by light cloaks and daggers. The price of their room included hot baths, but those could wait. The walk would be hot and sweaty anyway.

* * *

Walking beneath the looming Cathedral compound walls, Yan tensed each time a brown-robed priest approached. He became inured to their ubiquitous presence when they took no notice of him except to avoid being jostled in the narrow ways. At worst, he reminded himself, it will be several weeks before they suspect we aren't still at sea.

The slave market was a broad streamside clearing amid shacks and palaces. Omer identified the tightly closed cloth tents and pavilions of slave dealers by their colors. In busier seasons they would be so numerous the city's alleys would seem broad and deserted by comparison. Expecting to see lovely, exotic women auctioned to merchants and princes from far shores, Yan was unimpressed.

They stopped at a pavilion of faded blue and orange sailcloth. Tattered reef-points showed it had once been a sail. Omer called out in a tongue unfamiliar to Yan. "Ay, mayun, ouzin deha? Abi Omuh, mamayun, nabi hiyatsee mafreyun Billih. Uindeh, Billih? Ugo lemiyin?" The strange, liquid sounds rolled off his tongue like syrup, and a deep baritone answered from within.

"Adonono Omuh, mayun. Yubi bahn a selun?"

"Abi waintsee yu mufan facindeha. Abi wanno wusapnin, mamayun."

Yan stared at a strange face: beneath a round red cap with gold embroidered patterns, the Burum slaver's hair was grayish seafoam, his skin old wood waxed and polished until it shone. Yellowed eyes fixed on Yan and he smiled broadly, his spatulate yellow teeth punctuated with gaping voids. "A spek dabohi deha aynsino rihul mayun weya hikum frum," the slaver murmured to Omer, who laughed and translated for Yan's benefit. "He says you stare like you've never seen a true human before, Yan. Better not let your jealousy show so."

Yan managed a feeble grin. "Tell him I mean no offense. I'm only beginning to realize what marvels the world offers." Omer repeated that, earning a satisfied nod, and the merchant motioned them inside. Hangings of sky blue, mauve, and emerald cloth divided the space into rooms. Their host had seated them on low leather stools, pushed a hanging aside, and departed. Omer motioned Yan to remain silent, and they remained so for several minutes. Yan heard only the tinkling of brassy objects beyond.

The slaver emerged with a tray, three thimble-sized brass cups, and a flat-sided green glass bottle. He made a ritual of pouring clear liquor into tiny vessels, sniffing each one with exaggerated pleasure. He and Omer swallowed their drinks in a gulp, so Yan did, too. It burned like cheap brandy and warmed his stomach; the cool tang of mint lingered in his mouth. They sipped second servings slowly, with murmurs of approval.

Following the ritual, the older men launched into discussion, and though Yan's academic nature allowed him to turn within himself for hours, he was overjoyed when a parting drink was poured. When they emerged from the tent, the orange disk of the sun rode the tent-tops at the market's edge.

Omer recounted what he had learned: the dark merchant knew several of Omer's acquaintances who called Innis home. Omer suggested their mutual aims might best be served by dividing their tasks. He would seek out his cronies while Yan made the rounds of the city's archives. Though uneasy about being away from his sole friend in this foreign place, Yan admitted that the idea had merit.

Yan's task, conspicuous as it was, might benefit from a disguise, Omer thought. Over a supper of batter-fried fowl, steamed vegetables, and a light local wine, they decided he should become a refugee noble from the Apostate Isles. Islanders were common in Innis, easily identifiable by their distinctive dress, yet not so common Yan could not avoid close contact, revealing his fraud. With the islanders' fetish for genealogy, one more haunting the record halls would not be noticed.

They retired to their upstairs room after eating, and even bright silver moonbeams penetrating their vine-colored windows failed to keep Yan awake. In the heart of his enemies' city, he slept well.

CHAPTER NINE

"Where is your God now?" the preacher cried over the crashing waves. "Where is the God of Noah, who made covenant with his people? Where is the Fire? I see only the rising sea."

"Faros!" the multitude called out. "Faros!" they pleaded. On their knees and their bellies they called out to the God, and he heeded their prayers and supplications, and sent down his Ship. By ones and by twos they ascended, strong men and young women, firm in their faith. The old and the faithless turned back, and the floods took them. "Faros!" they cried, but the great Ship ascended. "Faros!" they howled, but the ship rose away in the sky.

Walking the Water's Edge by Heim Stinson. Purportedly refers to Hekkor the Apostle, ca. 3000 C.R., but reference to Shreveport places it about 2400. [Lazko]

Awakened by streetside bustle, the travelers washed and dressed. Setting the chamber pot by the door, they descended for breakfast. Hot bread and sweet chocolate were all the breakfast their coin had paid for, but when Yan grumbled about it, Omer assured him he had expected no more. Chocolate was a long-awaited treat, produced south of the equatorial sea and seldom available in the north.

Yan's first project was his disguise. He purchased a cotton kilt from one elderly seamstress and a sleeveless blue tunic from another. A flat black hat, wide-brimmed, presented greater difficulty, but after much peering in vendors' stalls, he was directed by a drayman carrying bales of raw wool to a small manufactory where wool was beaten into felt products, hats among them. As most island nobles were dark-haired, he sought dye, from a barber. A curio-shop owner produced an enameled brass medallion on a gold-colored chain. If its intricate geometric pattern was not, as the shopkeeper swore, a true devil-bane of the cult of Inoo, then only an antiquarian would know it.

Returning to the inn, Yan laid scissors and razor on the washstand. With a sigh of regret for his carefully trimmed beard, he set to work. Later, he put on his new clothes, then tilted the washstand mirror to survey the results of his efforts. Satisfied, he swirled a threadbare travel cloak about his shoulders, leaving its hood hanging down his back.

Evening approached, and Omer would be back soon. Yan descended the stairs and took a seat outside the inn. "Bring me ale," he told the waiter. When Omer arrived, his eyes passed right over Yan, who called to him in a low voice, "Ser, a word with you, please." Omer looked at him blankly; then his eyes widened. He sat down with a barely suppressed laugh, surveying the "new" Yan in his beige kilt and sky-blue shirt, medallion glinting green and gold on his partly bared chest. His hair, cropped short beneath the hat, was dark like the mustache that drooped to the corners of his mouth and gave him a sullen air.

Yan tweaked the leather-bound queue of dark hair that remained uncut. "An islander I met in Nahbor wore his hair so, in mourning. My haircut may put off idle questions from genuine refugees. If not . . ." His eyes traveled to the great war axe, which now hung openly, unsheathed, at his belt.

"Your adopted countrymen are indeed a touchy lot," Omer agreed, "but I think you'll fool them, and the Church's informants, too. If not . . . you handled that chopper well enough in the smith's courtyard."

"Just so. But if I must use it, we've failed. I prefer to remain unnoticed. The islanders' obsession with ancestry, with the dates when their families converted to the Pharos Church, will be my excuse to delve in old records, and my mourning queue will allow me taciturnity. But what of you, Om? Any news?"

"P'raps. I'm sure our presence is unsuspected, as yet. Th' harbor is quiet an' vessels aren't being inspected more closely than usual. Brownshirts all over, like flies on shit, but tha's t' be expected in Innis." Omer's most significant discovery was an addition made to the Cathedral since last he'd seen it. Strung between two corner towers was a heavy tarred cable, visible even at a distance. Closer inspection, with a spyglass, revealed fine-drawn greenish wire suspended by glass insulating rings.

"An antenna!" Yan exclaimed. "A wire dipole. The priests

may be speaking to each other across the whole continent . . . the whole world. And you're sure it wasn't there before?"

"It wasn't there a year ago," Omer asserted. "I'm not th' first one to notice it. Others have wondered; nothing th' churchmen do is without effect, so they're watched diligently."

"That settles it, Om. We have to get in there."

Omer protested, but he knew Yan was right. "I'll see what can be done. No promises, though." He waved at the innkeeper's boy. "Let's eat." While they waited for their food, Omer gloated over Yan's disguise. "We both talked with tha' boy last night," he observed with glee, "yet today you're a stranger t' him."

The following morning, Yan shouldered his way past dun-clothed workmen, tradesmen in rainbow hues, priests and lay churchmen in brown robes appliquéd with silk of every shade. His destination was the Library of Inoo, named for the demon his medallion purportedly warded off, a lesser god of the Church. Inoo was the chief god in the Apostate Islanders' pantheon. Yan suspected that if he were to find records of alien ships that had once landed in those islands, he would discover that the beings that crewed them had called themselves Inoo, Inoue, Inoy . . .

He passed the slave market again and walked for an hour along the riverside esplanade, fondly remembering the open streets of Nahbor and the broad avenues of Pittsburg, where traffic flowed freely on wheel and foot. In Innis, he had yet to see a street wide enough for two drays to pass. But for all its compactness, Innis' air held no traces of the garbage and sewage that assaulted urban noses elsewhere. He caught only whiffs of cooking, pungent sweat, leather and perfume, and scents of flowering trees. Even flies were scarce, except about haunches of meat in butchers' doorways. The flies' droning was replaced by the deeper tones of the oddly striped, gentle bees that hummed among weeds and flower trays and in trees overhead.

Beyond the market loomed the Cathedral compound wall. The esplanade narrowed at the bulge of a watchtower, where a stone bridge led directly to a gate. Red-tunicked mercenaries watched over those entering the Cathedral compound. The Library of Inoo was a short walk beyond. Yan hesitated, intimidated. Tight against the wall was a foodseller's booth and four small tables, where six acolytes with green-striped sleeves and hems sat head-deep in conversation. A leather-aproned artisan occupied another table. A single stool was unclaimed. Yan gratefully sat, temporizing. He ordered kaf and a sweet sausage baked in pastry, all the while eyeing the watchful mercenaries he must pass.

As he finished his sausage, one of the young churchmen spoke. "Ser Islander, did you recently arrive in Innis?" Yan's legs tensed as if to propel him running, but he forced a conversational tone. "I've been here a fortnight," he lied. Then, remembering his role and the abrupt arrogance of the islanders, he spoke more sharply. "Have you reason to disturb my breakfast, or have you no study to occupy your thoughts?"

Taken aback, the acolyte inclined his head, mumbling. "I meant no offense, ser. I was born in Tenzie, within sight of your South Island, and I merely wondered how the war to recover your soil progresses."

"I know no more than the news sellers tell. War continues, and I wait for its conclusion to press my rightful claims." He stood abruptly, letting simulated annoyance propel him past the guards and on to the Library. A stone portico engraved with patterns like those of his medallion marked its entrance. A central court within, lit by a glazed skylight, was surrounded by tiered balconies, with shelves of books receding into dimness beyond. Patrons wandered at will. Clear labeling of each section's subject matter, in conjunction with posted floor plans, made attendants unnecessary. Yan explored, and noted those sections that seemed promising.

He returned to the inn after dark, stumbling often, once getting lost. The city at night was forbidding, confusing, without visible landmarks. He had had no midday meal, so he was grateful for the cold meat and potato cakes Omer had saved him. They agreed that their inn's location was no longer suitable; Omer's business was nearer the harbor, and Yan begrudged his own long walk. Tomorrow Yan could find a room near the Library. Omer would sleep on the fishing boat of a former crewman, and they would meet in three days at the head of the wharves.

Yan found a room a hundred yards from the Library. In his element, the world of books, time passed rapidly. Each morning when ale-yellow rays probed his bubbly glass windows, he rose and waited at the Library door. When sunset faded and written words grew indistinct, he departed. After a frugal supper, he burned a slow candle while he organized and condensed his notes.

On the third evening he carried a single sheaf of papers with his few belongings as he walked to meet Omer. His initial notes were ash, stirred until the last scrap of coarse yellow paper was consumed. Omer awaited him at the head of the wharf, and led him to a fine stone house facing a wide intersection. "This place belongs to Ailf Lunnon, a shipmate who's done well in local trade," Omer explained. "We'll stay here."

A night guard opened an iron gate entwined with ornamental snakes, vines, and leaves. Yan followed Omer into a fairyland courtyard, a colonnaded cloister no more than twenty yards across, which moonlight and dark contrast expanded into a vast, mysterious place. A fountain trickled. Statues of heroic scale seemed to wink and smile, a trick of the moon and the clouds that drifted over it now and again. Yan bumped into a low table surrounded with cushioned chairs. Omer led him beneath the balustrade and motioned him through a doorway with wood shutters. A light flared, and Omer touched match to lamp-wick. "Toss your sack over there," he said. "You'll meet our host tomorrow."

Yan was accustomed to sleeping in new places, with new sounds and scents, but that night he lay long awake, hearing the fountain and the blood rushing in his head. He fell asleep trying to identify the heady scent of the flowering vines twining up the columns outside the door.

Droning bees and the clatter of crockery awakened him. Warm, scented water and towels waited on a commode. Omer was already up; Yan found him at the fountainside table, serving himself eggs, fresh bread, and spicy meat patties. A servant pressed juice from a green and orange fruit. It was tart, acidic, and refreshing. "Oranges," Omer told him. "An import from the Taiksa interior. I s'pect these new bees came with them, or with another import."

Yan was eager to hear what Omer had been up to. Was this "shipmate," now wealthy and influential, going to assist them? Did he have a way into the Cathedral's archives?

"Lunnon's a smuggler," Omer told him. In Innis, he explained when he saw Yan's frown, Church law was civil law, and taxes were tithes, and tithes upon tithes. "Smugglers are th' nearest thing t' a resistance movement there is. They're men of *your* sort, Yan, and my own," he concluded. "Ailf Lunnon's an honest merchant who believes in a free market, an' only th' Church could claim he's cheated them. An' besides, with his dislike a' th' brownshirts, he'll help us, if we show promise a' thwarting and confusing *his* enemies.

"Now," Omer said, "What I've found can wait. Those pages will start smoking if you squeeze them harder. What's on them?"

"History," Yan said. "Even with the twisted truths the Pharos Church promotes, *facts* remain unchanged. The lies are omissions and interpretations. *My* interpretations are different from theirs. As will yours be—so I'll give you what I found just as I found it, and see what conclusions you draw."

The servant interrupted them, bringing kaf in a large jar with a wool wrapper. Omer thanked him and told him to go about his usual business. Yan began his narrative when the door to the kitchen closed. "The founding of the Brotherhood of Pharos was around three thousand, Current Reckoning. Priests claim greater antiquity, of course. Early references allude to the 'Compact of Pharos,' a legendary document of which no copies seem to exist. It was an agreement between a former Christian clergyman and the 'god' Pharos. The man's name was Hector William Anderson. Does that ring any bells, Om?"

"Hekkor the Apostle! The founder a' th' Church."

"Exactly. And the Compact, as best I can tell, was a bargain with 'Pharos' to establish a 'church' *to serve him*. 'Pharos,' in return, agreed to protect Doctor Anderson—Hekkor—and his followers from the wrath of four other 'gods,' who would otherwise destroy Earth, Hekkor and all.

"Some later sources give ominous accounts of *active* intervention by 'Pharos' in Earthly affairs. Listen to this." Yan pulled a neatly copied sheet from his folder and began to read.

" 'Following the death of Hekkor the Third, the lords of Roke and Innis each claimed sovereignty over the Holy Domains and invoked Pharos' name in support of their claims, but the God was about His realm, and His holy fires did not shine in Earth's skies. It was a time of troubles. Christers grew in power. Oma was lost, and Senloo. Witches walked the streets of Nahks, Chatoo, even Nobi in Burum. Warlocks and heretics reigned in Bama, and witches were their whores. They raised towers in the form of Ships, and claimed the God's right as theirs.' "

Yan glanced up at Omer. "Aya," the older man said, "there y' have everything in one pompous mouthful. Witches, Pharos, an' spaceships—though not th' real thing, I suppose."

Yan continued to read. " 'At last, in the seventh year of Athel's reign in Roke, Pharos appeared and bade Athel gather a great army. He armed them with His fires. From Heaven the God guided Athel's armies. Athel met the hosts of the faithless and burned them with holy fire. Where ashes lay, the land remained dead for generations. Who ventured there died, burned with the unseen fires of the God. Women gave birth to monsters. Plagues came and not even the beasts of the forests escaped them.

" 'When the faithless were punished and the false Ships torn down, Athel begged the God never to venture so far from His Church, and a second Compact was made in Roke: in the form of black beasts, Pharos' Sons would rule Earth in his name. Pharos caused Athel to build temples in Innis and Roke, and in cities far across the Earth. Athel caused images of Pharos' Sons to be placed in every shrine, and bade the faithful to keep fires burning before them in remembrance of the God's vengeance.' " Yan took a deep breath. "That's not the only account, either. There are four others. What do you think, Om?"

Omer held up a hand for patience while he pondered. He sipped kaf. He shook his head as if in disbelief at his thoughts. Yan, expecting a more enthusiastic reaction, felt miffed. Finally the older man spoke. "One," he said, "the ferosin were complacent. Th' Earth was their cattleyard, an' they ignored it, thinking their breeding stock safe. But we humans surprised them. P'raps we've more pluck than others they've encountered out there—and others there must be, as different from us as from ferosin. When they returned after long absence, we humans had recovered from devastations past. Their 'compact' was voided, and th' Bamians were building starships a' their own—or so th' towers must ha' seemed, from up there.

"Two," Omer continued, "they found a willing pawn, Athel, hierarch of a dying Church. They supported him wi' ship-borne fire, tossed down like pots a' burning oil. But they were pots a' *unholy* fire, I'd say. Fire akin t' the Great Bolide.

"But tha's na' all, Yan. You've just told me what the ferosin are: great black, ugly crabs."

Yan's raised eyebrow telegraphed his skepticism. "What makes you think that? Crabs? Even if 'black beasts' describes the ferosins' true color, I've seen no descriptions of them."

Omer snorted derisively. "Crabs, lobsters, or enormous black bugs. Don't look at me like I'm mad, Yan. I've *seen* them. I didn't know it at the time, is all." He reached for kaf and poured some, black and steaming, into each cup. He made a lengthy production of stuffing his pipe with black tobacco, scratched a sulfurous match under the table, and drew flame into the bowl, quietly savoring Yan's indignant curiosity. Good for the boy, Omer mused contentedly. He needs to learn patience.

"When I was a boy," he began when the air was thick with

pipe smoke and Yan's annoyance, "my father took my brothers and me to Thaka, on business. Not knowing th' town, an' being young, we had t' stay in th' rented house an' courtyard. But being boys, an' restless, we explored every inch a' th' place, which shared a common wall wi' a monastery. Hearing stories a' monks' bones an' gold buried under such places, wasn't long 'fore we were scratching mortar loose in th' cellar an' pulling bricks free. We made a hole large enough t' crawl through.

"On th' other side were dusty crocks, not bones or treasure. Soon we'd infested th' whole building like rats. The dozen-odd monks never knew we were about." Omer paused to sip kaf and relight his recalcitrant pipe. "It was a large place, an' half th' summer went by before we found treasure, a' sorts."

"Well? Are you going to relive your whole childhood, or tell me what this has to do with—"

"Impatient, aren't you? As I was saying, we found it, behind an iron-bound door. Th' monks were in an' out all day so we couldn't even peek. We watched from an airwell in th' hallway. They had a regular routine: one monk in th' room a' all times, and every two hours another'd come, get down on his belly like a worm, as if tha' big door was a bitty hole. Shiniest floor I'd seen anywhere. Being boys, th' challenge a' tha' room was like offal t' a gull, and 't wasn't long 'fore we found a way t' peek in. See, th' occupied rooms and hallways had ceilings a' about eight feet, but th' storerooms had higher ones. They'd lowered th' ceilings once, and the spaces between were like highways t' us—there was a transom above th' big door, so we wiped th' glass clean t' peer in." He fell silent again. This time Yan waited only seconds before pressing him to continue.

"So what did you see? What was up in there?"

"Th' room was plain, and almost empty 'cept for a firepot t' one side and a statue in th' middle." Omer smiled prankishly at Yan when he paused, and continued rapidly even as Yan drew breath to urge him on.

"It was solid gold, near's we could tell, a treasure as big as a man, ugly as anything ever crawled from a crack in th' wall. Like a ten-legged bug raised up on its hindmost legs."

"So you saw monks worship a statue of a giant bug? Perhaps of a ferosin? I have this feeling you're holding something back."

Omer grinned. "That 'statue' didn't just sit quietly on its pedestal. Every once in a while, it moved."

"What? It was alive?"

"I didn't say that. It sat still for hours, wi' a monk watching it quill in hand, before its legs and claws started t' move. Then th' monk got busy, scribbling as fast as he could. Oh, aya—there was an ornament on th' wall. At least, I thought it so, then. A dark-bronze panel wi' inset gems of all colors. When th' bug-thing moved, th' jewels lit up like tiny lamps, a few here, a few there, an' never a pattern I could fix on." Again, he stopped to relight his pipe, which made moist, clacking sounds as he drew on it. "Wha' d' you make a' that?"

Yan frowned and shrugged. "It wasn't alive? You're sure?" He shook his head almost angrily at Omer's nod. "I don't know what to think. Could it be an elaborate device 'speaking' in the ferosin manner, using gestures for words? Perhaps the 'Sons of Pharos' are machines, like radios—though the ones in the university archives seemed simpler. But ferosin devices are bound to be *alien*, especially if they were designed for ferosin themselves."

"Aya, perhaps," Omer agreed, nodding. "But they're not signaling in th' bugs' own tongue. You've seen semaphores?"

"Signal flags? Yes. In Pittsburg port. But for monks to go to such lengths when simpler means would suffice . . ."

"But tha's my point, Yan. P'raps no such simple signals would convey *ferosin* thoughts. How different might they be? I marvel that things so unlike us could communicate with men at all, or that men could frame thoughts suitable to send back to them. I suppose the churchmen, not knowing how t' reproduce th' machines, are stuck using them to communicate amongst themselves, clumsy as they are, though the ferosin are long gone."

"Did the monks reply to the 'messages'?"

"They moved the bug's legs into different poses, as if they knew what such might signify, an' lit the colored gems in patterns a' their own by touching them." He shrugged. "Tha's all I recall them doing. I was young, remember."

"What did you do next? Surely you didn't just leave and not come back."

"We watched, but saw nothing new, only monks 'worshiping,' as we thought then, not knowing a' radios and such. It wasn't very exciting, an' as there was no chance for us t' break off a gold leg, or steal glowing jewels, we tired a' it. When we asked our father about it, he whipped us wi' his belt, made us swear not t' speak a' it, and bricked up our hole. We spent th' rest a' th' summer chasing over th' roofs wi' th' Thakan boys."

"So Athel's edict still held then," Yan said, nodding thoughtfully, "and it does now, too. The ferosin were like insects, black—surely the gold of their 'statues' is merely decoration—

and there are surely such statues in Roke, and right here in Innis . . . in the Cathedral.'' The look he gave Omer was utterly clear. Omer knew his thoughts before he framed them: ''I *must* get in there, Om. I have to *see* it.''

Omer had known he would say that from the moment he began his story. ''P'raps,'' he murmured, ''but not tonight, aya?''

Yan grinned. ''Will your friends help us?''

''Again, p'raps. But I'll not bother Ailf right now, at his affairs, t' ask him. Nor would you hint at it, if you'd met th' man.''

''He must be formidable,'' Yan replied, then couldn't resist changing the subject. ''You said they had ten legs. Can you remember other details?''

''Like yesterday. Give me your pen and inkpot. I've a fair talent for map sketches—let's see if I can draw a crab-thing.'' Yan withdrew his pen case and removed its tightly fitted wood plug, then shook out brass quills. He unwrapped a worn sharpening stone and gave Omer coarse paper and a flat ink flask. Omer arranged tools and media to his satisfaction and began to draw. After several minutes' dipping and scratching, he swore and turned the sheet over. Yan leaned back, careful not to press him. The sun rose several fingerwidths above the roof while Omer hunched over the table. Finally he leaned back in his chair and pushed the finished sheet to Yan, who looked upon the God Pharos for the first time.

He saw a five-segmented body connected at wasplike waists, each rounded body part covered by overlapping armor plates. From beneath the plates sprang hairs that seemed to vary from jagged quills to fine down. Rippled edges on the central body plates allowed a single grasshopperlike leg to project from each side.

Yan's skin drew tight on his neck and arms. He became acutely aware of his coarse undergarments as his body hair, responding to ancestral commands, attempted to stand fully away from his skin. No finely detailed drawing of deadly spiders or scorpions had had the disturbing effect of Omer's crude sketch. Next to this creature, Earthly nasties were little cousins; poor bedfellows, but kin. The drawing drew his eyes against their will. Horror was to be avoided, but the sight of it still compelled him with a force greater than mere curiosity.

The thing's segments, Yan noticed, were unequal. The topmost segment—for ''Pharos'' stood almost upright—had small, feathery-fringed appendages resembling antennae. Omer concurred that the black spots that he had placed at intervals around and atop the segment represented beadlike bosses that might be eyes. The next segment's limbs had serrated medial edges, like crab claws. They looked like mandibles but there was no sign of a mouth. More "eyes" studded its surface. The third and fourth segments were larger—two feet or more in diameter, according to Omer's estimate, though he conceded that the statue might have been more than life size. The two largest segments each had a pair of the grasshopperlike legs, pairs opposing each other as if their owner could have leaped forward or backward with equal ease. The fourth segment's legs were the "forward" ones, while the "backward" ones were tucked up against segment three. The last and lowest segment was virtually identical with the first. "A bug with heads at both ends," Yan said, shaking his head, "and eyes everywhere. How must such a creature perceive the world? It's hard to believe that it's an intelligent being, isn't it, Om?"

"Not as hard as imagining what kind of world would produce it," Omer replied, shaking his head at the thought. "It must be an awful place."

"Oh? and why is that?"

"What Earthly creature needs eyes t' watch its back, th' ground b'neath its feet, and th' sky above all a'once? And wha' kind a' grasshopper needs legs to jump forward or back wi' equal ease? An' those lobster claws . . . I wonder what it *eats*? Even its prey must be formidable. Can you imagine a creature that could prey on *it*?" His shudder was not entirely feigned.

"Myself, I wonder how it shits," Yan said, trying to lighten the dark mood that had descended on his friend.

Omer smiled. "My curiosity has bounds. I ha' no desire t' know about that. Dan was bad enough." He made a fruitless attempt to relight his pipe, then set it down. "Would such a creature fit the disconnected 'pilot's seat' of your spacecraft, Yan? If it were indeed a pirated ferosin vessel . . ."

"Yes, I think it might," Yan replied, holding Omer's drawing up, squinting and visualizing the mechanism he'd excavated. "If so, its whole body would have been enclosed, and its eyes, too . . . That's it, Om! The human pilots. The 'witches'!"

"Slow down, scholar. You've lost me."

"Your idea, Om. The ferosin evolved in a hostile place where it needed legs to jump in any direction, with eyes and sensory feelers all over its body, just to survive, right? It must be able to respond to complex stimuli without being overwhelmed. It may even have *multiple* brains . . . those segments all seem similar enough." He barely waited for Omer's slow nod before continuing. "If the 'environment' experienced in the faster-than-light universe is enough to drive humans mad, it may be akin to the conditions ferosin evolved in. They may be *preadapted* to starflight in a way that humans are not."

"Aya, I see the course you're laying, I think. Go on."

"If our 'witches' were indeed 'mind readers' able to communicate among themselves *at the speed of thought itself*, together they may have done what ordinary humans could not. That's your 'magic.' We *must* find them, Om."

"I s'pose you're right," Omer agreed reluctantly, "but if the witch-folk can do that kind of thing, why haven't they? Or, if they've lost th' ability somehow, then why should we bother?"

"I have to *know*, Om. If there's the slightest hope . . ."

Omer grinned broadly, his face crinkling like a walnut shell. "Then you'll be happy to know what *else* I discovered while you pored over old books." Seeing the fiery look in Yan's eyes, he didn't stall or tease, but continued immediately. "The Church still takes 'witches' quite seriously. The Brotherhood's slave buyers place standing orders with all the traders for them."

"And do they get any? Real ones, I mean."

"My sources couldn't say. Once such slaves are within Cathedral walls . . ." He shrugged elaborately. "As they're all women or girls, p'raps th' less twisted priests find other uses for them."

"Whatever their fates, this corroborates what I've found in the Inoo library—that the Church is convinced of a relationship between witches and spaceships! But is that everything? Did you hear anything else?"

"I have more t' tell, but it concerns other matters. Let's put t'gether what we know so far, eh? A list. You write it—I'd waste too much paper."

Yan took pen in hand, talking as he wrote. "We know," he said, "that the Church once was aided by ferosin, that it has access to alien technology, and that ferosin supposedly protect Earth against an unnamed threat from four other alien races. What that threat is, or was—if it was even real—we don't know.

"Further, we know that the Church seeks true witches—people with unusual abilities—as much for study and interrogation as for 'religious' ends. We know that such people once had widespread political power in the southern kingdoms, and we know that the ferosin were *actively* involved in the destruction of their power base, four hundred years ago.

"We know that until the time of Athel, ferosin came here

only occasionally. Their tame Church handled things on Earth, but after having to intervene to save their 'factors' here, they could no longer afford to ignore Earth for generations at a time. They left signaling devices, the so-called Sons of Pharos, in Innis and Roke and perhaps elsewhere."

Yan slapped his palm down. "The connections between Church, ferosin, and witches are no longer speculation. The question, still, is 'Why?' " Omer was silent, but he raised a questioning eyebrow, so Yan went on.

"This is what I think happened: When Earth first experimented with starships, extrasolar groups found out about it, perhaps by emanations from the experimental ships themselves. Those alien races seemed to encourage human efforts at star travel, but once they found out that human pilots couldn't adapt to the stresses involved, their treatment of us changed radically. They began treating us as herdsmen treat their stock—selecting breeding cattle for their own use and leaving the wild herd for future picking. But why such a change? What does it suggest, Om?"

Omer sat with his eyes closed. When he spoke it was quietly, with hardly a trace of accent. "The ferosin are traders on a great dark sea with many islands. I traveled wi' traders on our own Southern Sea, giving clever tools in exchange for island resources, at great profit. Sometimes we took willing folk from overpopulated, disease-ridden islands an' settled 'em in places they couldn't reach in their own frail canoes, creating new captive markets for us. As long as th' islanders were incapable of building their own ships or navigating th' open sea, we exploited them.

"Some Earthly islands I've seen were settled generations ago. Their people grow kaf bushes and spices, an' trade whole shiploads of rare cargoes for cheap iron tools. Th' islanders stay poor an' in debt while th' traders grow rich indefinitely. I think the ferosin are just such traders, Yan. Th' humans who went out with them have been settled on far, bright islands, forever slaves, wi'out ships a' their own to sail the dark seas above." Omer poured himself water; the kaf was gone.

"It all makes sense, Om, and the analogy may explain other things as well. Out there on some colony 'island,' humans learned to pilot alien ships without going mad—using a mental trick or discipline rather than technology. They stole ships, modified them for human use, and then returned to Earth in them, expecting that the planet would be recovered from the turmoils of earlier years, believing that they and their discovery would be welcomed. Perhaps they went elsewhere as well, to other human-colonized worlds. I don't think they expected the ferosin to have left human spies and quislings behind to deal with them.

"Some were killed on arrival, as were those in the ship we excavated, but there were others—like the Great Bolide of 2884, which landed or crashed in the polar ocean. At least one ship's crew and passengers survived to become the witches of Burum, and perhaps the ancestors of the present-day witches as well—people with magical-seeming mental abilities that must have some rational explanation.

"At one time, when it seemed that ferosin had forgotten Earth entirely, those 'witches' came out of the mountains and became involved in political affairs. Perhaps they hoped to gather the tools and technology to build starships again, to flee beyond the limits of alien reprisal or even to make war upon them. Who knows? We only know they were taken by surprise when ferosin actually returned.

"They must have been upset that Earth's 'islanders' were seemingly making instruments of navigation and ships of their own. And they found their 'trading post' ashes and embers. They threw the weight of their weaponry behind the human traitor, Athel of Roke. With alien weapons at his call and ferosin spying for him from space, Athel reconquered the Church's lost territories and killed witches and rebels. Only a few escaped to the mountains, where ferosin weapons and surveillance were of no use because of the rough terrain."

"Makes sense," Omer agreed, "but there are still loose ends. Why would ferosin have to 'protect' Earth from destruction by other kinds of aliens? For that matter, why, if th' witches were still a threat, would ferosin leave anything at all alive here? I suspect that after so many hundreds of years their other 'islands' would be able to provide breeding stock, if that had been their reason for not having destroyed us in th' past."

A clatter of pans interrupted him. The house servant had returned, but the door into the kitchen remained shut. Omer continued, "Let me answer my own questions. P'raps ferosin protection a' Earth is a ruse. Th' other alien races—Piroon, Inoo, or whatever—ha' no further use for us. On th' other hand, they may be competitors of ferosin, who could offer us better terms than slavery. Perhaps they are a threat to the ferosin, not to us. All I am sure of is that whatever the Church says is a lie.

"As for ferosin not destroying Earth entirely, perhaps tha's another bluff. Our south sea traders might threaten destruction, but they'd never be able to destroy a whole island. A world is no small thing t' be crushed like a nutshell."

"So you think that there's no real threat, as long as we of Earth make no overt move to develop beyond our present primitive level?"

"I didn't say that. Actually, I'm inclined to think that not only could the ferosin destroy us, but that the other races may have good reason to, as well."

"Damn it, Om. You're leading up to something. Give it to me in one bite—the explanations can wait."

"Aya, I s'pose I've teased you enough." He chuckled. "Those other races—Proon, Inoo, whatever—are ferosin's competitors in trade war between th' stars—war over such distances, I'd think, tha' small advantages ha' great effects on profit. They'd be seeking ways t' shorten travel times and minimize costs, just as Earthly merchantmen do wi' more an' bigger sails, efficient rigging tha' eliminates th' need for large crews, and slick, fast hulls. An' it's just such an improvement I believe our 'witches' represent."

"A *better* way to pilot starships, you mean? But how could that be? The human-piloted ship we found was crudely modified, but I strongly doubt it was *improved*."

"Aya, an' tha's my point, Yan. The 'improvement' wasn't a technological wrinkle ferosin could copy. It's something only humans can do." Omer thudded his gnarled fist on the table for emphasis. "Only humans. And tha's why ferosin agents—the Brotherhood a' Pharos—still hunt witches: because they *haven't been able to duplicate what th' witches can do*."

"I see," Yan said, nodding. "But if this trick or talent is specifically human, and ferosin can't use it, why don't they destroy us—as I must assume they can—and remove the threat of *us* becoming competitors?"

"Because they want witches t' work for *them*. They won't destroy Earth as long as there's a chance they can control witch talent; but they don't dare give humans a chance t' build ships a' our own again, because some might escape in tha' vast universe out there, an' come back t' haunt them later. So they keep Earth under th' thumb a' their Church, ignorant and primitive, an' they keep hunting for witches. I s'pose they may even check on things every few centuries—just so things don't get out a' hand."

"But they let us live," Yan concluded, "as long as there's a chance they can use us. If those other races *know* what humans are capable of, then the ferosin might indeed be protecting us against them." He shook his head and sighed mightily. "Damn, this is complicated. We're threatened by alien species that want us dead, so that the ferosin can't take advantage of us to those others' detriment. The Church seeks witches for their God's use, but ferosin will kill us if they lose hope of using us—and if we show signs of using our 'talent' ourselves, they'll kill us to prevent it. The stakes pile higher and higher. What can we do?"

Morning. It was time. She removed her last two small companions from their box. They were limp from the drug-saturated cloth. She was careful—they were delicate, and while unmoving they could not breathe. Only the drug's suspension of their metabolisms kept them alive at all. She wrapped each one in fine gauze and tucked it in place within a seam of her embroidered shirt. A few quick stitches and they were invisible.

She slipped on her dirty coat and left her possessions in the dingy room. She would need nothing. Her last silver coins were sewn into her high-topped shoes. They would suffice for her homeward journey, if and when she began it.

She had paid the portal guard twice—once in coin, and again with her maidenhood. It was a small price. Lingering among the memories of her passage rite were a dozen deflowerings, some pleasant or poignant, others far more coarse and degrading than hers.

She suspected the guard would arrest her for "trying" to bribe passage into the Cathedral grounds. It would be safer than honoring his bargain, in case she was caught later, inside, and questioned by Pharos hounds. But if she was arrested, she would still be taken inside. If they suspected she was indeed a witch, they might even take her into the Sanctum, the upper levels of the great ugly stone pile, where the Senior was said to reside.

It didn't matter what happened. Of course she preferred to go about her last task undiscovered, and to win free of the place; neither the rite of the False Flower nor her training had reduced her to an unfeeling doll. She wanted to live. But either way, unfound or caught, she *would* win free. She would go home with her tale, to tell to her grandmother and the Others, or she would go more silently, her mortal covering abandoned. Either way, she only needed a minute or two, unobserved, to free the last of her tiny saboteurs in the heart of Pharos' shrine.

CHAPTER TEN

Houston—(IPS)—The Almec consortium has been awarded the contract to develop a means of communicating directly with the alien visitors now orbiting Earth.

It is widely believed that the aliens communicate among themselves using pheromones, volatile airborne chemicals, augmented with biologically generated radio signals. "When we determine how the Ferrosians interface with the physical universe," an Almec spokesman stated this morning, "we will be able to use the same stimuli to communicate with them in real-time."

Market Reporter, August 15, 2172.

Yan was relaxed after his hot bath in a huge copper tub where he had rested for almost an hour, immersed to his chin. He donned the soft wool house robe laid out for him by a servant.

Emerging from their room, he and Omer were met by their host. Ailf Lunnon was a boarish man, Yan's height and twice his girth. Curly brown hair fringed his temples, but his forehead rose interminably to the top of his bald pointed head. He walked with difficulty, puffing and wheezing through his great red nose like a corpulent gelding. His jowls bobbed with each mincing step, and his voice was shrill for a man of his stature. Yan suspected that he might be a gelding in truth, but he kept that thought to himself.

The dining room had no windows. As Yan's eyes adjusted to the clustered glow of oil lamps over a trestle table, he saw that six places were set, with three chairs already occupied. Lunnon introduced them to their tablemates. One small fellow's birdlike manner matched his staccato speech. He wore spectacles like those of an elderly scholar, and his bare robe might once have been churchly brown. "Brother Hant is a 'retired' priest," Lunnon said. His cautious tone and crooked smile intimated that whatever Hant might be, he was neither priest nor retired. When Yan stretched a hand across the table to him, the small man looked at it, then at Yan's face, and laughed.

"No business in Ailf's house for poor Hant," he trilled. "No rings on hand that reaches. Riches up your sleeve, young scholar?"

Yan didn't understand. He looked at Omer for clarification. "Brother Hant jokes, Yan. He is a skillful thief, a true master of the art." He turned to the birdlike man. "We've no need a' th' cutpurse's art tonight, Hant. Th' thievery we contemplate is on a grander scale. Ha' you brought those things I require?"

"Ah! Long-gone sailor on a bloody sea. Maps and charts—tools to rob the God—are in Hant's sack. Hee, man of many names, you were as dead these years."

"Dead to my enemies as well, I hope. Was there talk a' me?"

"New times, new talk. Old men die, ships founder. Women weep and laugh again." Omer seemed to understand the strange little man, to be satisfied, but Yan thought he detected a pensive air about Omer after that. He hoped he'd someday break through his friend's secretiveness, but that was for another time.

Across from Omer was a thin muscular man with close-trimmed hair and beard. Lunnon introduced him as Esmin Rubinsser, his "first officer," a seaman who commanded Lunnon's smuggling fleet. At present, they were told, Rubinsser was also in command of Lunnon's shoreside enterprises, an even more exacting task.

The third man at the table was Hekwit Smid, who had the posture of a landbound soldier. The neat trim of his waxed and curled mustache hinted he might be more than a common man-at-arms, as did Lunnon's introductory comment. "Hekwit is my childhood friend. He's burrowed in a strange hole and has come up only for strong reasons, which friend Omer will provide in good measure. He holds the key to our endeavor—he is the captain of our fates, in a sense."

A mercenary, Yan thought, and obviously connected with Cathedral security. When Yan addressed him as *Captain* Smid, the man's lack of protest confirmed the guess.

Dinner was an excellent roast smothered with assorted roots and vegetables, served with a fine light wine. Lunnon provided table talk almost singlehandedly, mostly anecdotes of his and Rubinsser's exploits. Hant uttered cryptic phrases that sounded snide to Yan, even though their meaning invariably passed him by.

When the table was cleared and the servants dismissed, Brother Hant brought forth several rolled charts, spreading them out and weighting their corners with kaf mugs and candlesticks from the sideboard. The charts showed the Cathedral compound's streets and buildings in good detail. The Cathedral plans were presumably accurate, too, though those had many blank areas with only stairwells and corridors lightly inked in.

Yan and Omer had to memorize the charts. They would cross the compound wall where the soldiers on duty were of Smid's choosing. Three escape routes had been laid out, each allowing for different contingencies. They would be watched by Rubinsser's men, who would provide diversion if required, and would spirit the escapees away. It was imperative that Yan and Omer know their exact location at all times in relation to those routes.

By the time arrangements had been made, several oil lamps had flickered out. Yan yawned inconspicuously into his hand. The men departed, Yan and Omer in one direction, Lunnon and Rubinsser another way, and Smid to the outside door. Hant was there one moment and gone the next. "*Hant,*" Omer explained "means 'ghost' or 'spirit.' His talent is for getting in and out of places unseen. I'm sure he knows other ways into th' Cathedral, too, ways he's keeping to himself."

The next day they studied Hant's charts and their notes while lunching in the courtyard, where they squinted in sunlight and focused their eyes on objects thankfully more distant than arm's length. They saw no one but servants. After a dinner of cold roast, green onions and salt, with pale bread and red wine, Yan pored over maps again. Omer, less inured to studious activity, visited a tavern. When he returned, late, Yan was asleep.

Yan pulled the coarse brown cowl over his head for Brother Hant's inspection and walked back and forth. Hant peered first through his spectacle lenses, then over them, his head bobbing like a flicker pecking ants. Hant finally gave his approval—or so Yan interpreted it: "You'll pass for schoolteacher, pass for priest," Hant chittered.

Then, frowning, he pondered Omer, and shook his head. "Old no-name's sailor gait gives robe and sandals the lie." He dipped to the ground and picking up two pebbles, then gestured for Omer to approach him. Yan, too, observed his friend's rolling walk. Some clever priest might indeed notice it.

Hant rummaged in a wooden case, removing a cube of ocherous yellow stuff from a tray. He popped it into his mouth and chewed noisily; Yan recognized the sharp scent of spruce gum. Hant squatted by Omer and separated the softened gum into two parts. Rolling them into balls between his palms, he fixed each glob to the inside sole of Omer's sandals beneath his heels. He then pressed a pebble into each wad.

"Walk now," he commanded. Omer complied—or attempted to: the stones bruised his heels with each step. He swore under his breath as he walked about the room, but he rapidly developed a new gait to avoid the pain in his heels. "Old fairy priest, now." Hant giggled. "Old tiptoe pervert. Ah! No sailor now."

Yan failed to suppress a snicker, earning him a glare from his companion. "Watch your behind tonight, sweet thing," Omer growled. "A fine pair we'll be, mincing like girls," Yan laughed aloud and Omer's face darkened further. He was not intolerant. In some places, even outside the Church, homosexual relationships were accepted; the sailors of Senloo had had a warrior cult that encouraged such bonding. The practice was not unknown even in rural Michan, but the stylized posturing and simpering affected by priests and thespians was almost universally considered ludicrous, and fair cause for ridicule.

"Om, it's perfect! You don't walk like a seaman anymore," Yan reassured him. "Besides, I've seen dozens of old fairies in Church clothing here in Innis. It's the best disguise you could ask for." Omer grumbled that it was indeed a clever device in spite of his discomfort, but he removed the sandals immediately and hung them over the back of a chair.

They went out and Rubinsser walked with them, showing them their route into the compound. As they passed beneath the walls he pointed out alternate exits. They went over it all one final time on Brother Hant's charts, reassuring Rubinsser that both men knew the exact times and places his men would be able to aid them.

With that done, the two "priests" left the house at a moment when no one was on the street and headed directly for the Cathedral. Their immediate destination was a stable built in a niche of the compound wall directly below a watchtower.

Originally laid out to give defending archers a clear aim at any point on the rampart, the zigzag walls had long since been encroached upon by buildings. The stable was one such structure: its roof was only six feet below the parapet's edge at the highest part of its wood-shingled slope, which attached directly to the rampart. A door had been left ajar for them. Omer and Yan climbed to the loft to await the onset of darkness. Both attempted to doze as they waited, but for Yan the effort went unrewarded. At regular intervals the clink and squeak of arms and stiff leather reminded him that mercenary sentries paced only a few feet above. According to Smid, the guard on the wall took two minutes to walk each way, but in the hot darkness of the loft it seemed longer. That guard was one of Smid's troops, but a recent recruit, whom Smid suspected was more directly in the Church's employ than through the company paymaster. Still, there had been no way to remove him from the roster without arousing suspicion. The only help Smid had finally been able to offer was to arrange for the guard to be delayed momentarily at the southern end of his route while Yan and Omer climbed over the parapet and ran along the wall to the north tower.

The last splinters of daylight made vermilion streaks on the stable wall. Omer checked their exit, a patch of roof where workmen had conspicuously removed a crumbling chimney only the day before. The new shingles over the hole were fixed to a wide board which had not been nailed down. If all went well, they would be able to push it up silently, make their exit, and return it to proper position again in the little time available to them.

"Time, Yan. The moon's not up yet." With the hatch raised an inch, the two men tucked up their robes and poised to scramble onto the roof. Yan rechecked the lashing that held his axe against his belly and snugged his sandals under his belt. The sentry's footsteps grew distinct. He could see nothing in the dark loft. Omer's face was pressed against the meager opening.

"Now!" Omer whispered harshly, lifting the board and slithering out onto the shingles. He pulled Yan up beside him and they fitted their door back into place. Climbing up to the edge of the roof abutting the compound wall, they looked toward the guard, still walking away from them about thirty feet distant. Yan felt Omer's hands on his robe, pulling him over the parapet and onto the wall. They ran. There was no time to look back at the guard, no time to breathe. Bare feet fell in silence on the smooth-worn stone. Yan's heartbeats seemed minutes apart. The tower grew no closer—surely the sentry must be turning around by now. Yan had no memory of passing Omer or hurtling through the tower doorway, clutching the jamb, and swinging around into welcome darkness. He didn't see Omer arrive a full four steps behind him, but when he peered through the arched opening he realized that the sentry's back was still to them and only seconds had elapsed. To his adrenaline-altered senses the guard's every step seemed to take forever.

The next stage in their penetration happened just as slowly. He knew it was he who was racing, that the world around him continued at its accustomed pace. Madness, he thought. My fear calls to the demon inside me. Angry at his lapse into Gran'ma's superstition, he forced the thought away.

The other door looked over a stretch of wall at right angles to the one they'd just run, ending at another tower. Two guards walked that wall. Yan knew their routes crossed in the middle of the wall, and that one guard was Smid's trusted man. Another loyal trooper would be on the wall if possible, but they were not to count on it; there had been too little time to set things up. Smid had pressed them to wait another week until the roster was changed, but Yan and Omer felt that they could not afford to wait.

One guard walked toward them, still distant. Yan looked above, where the conical wood-shake roof lay on withe and light poles. The poles rested on a ledge about two feet wide. He caught the ledge with his fingertips and swung up a knee. Omer did likewise. They settled in the darkness as the guard drew near. "Om?" Yan whispered. "Wait to see what he does. He could be the wrong man." Omer's nod was the barest flutter of violet shadow on blackness. The guard approached, turned sharply, and began his walk back.

"Either Smid didn't have time to switch men or we're not expected yet," Omer hissed. "We'll wait for the next one." Long minutes later they heard footsteps again. This time the guard didn't stop at the door, but entered the tower.

"If you're here, wait till the other fellow comes and leaves again," they heard him whisper. "When he's halfway back, get to the third building, with the yellow tile roof." Yan drew breath to reply, but the sentry continued. "Don't speak. I know nothing, and don't want to. Climb down and hide in the wall's shadow until my partner's passed you going *each* way, got that? Then jump to the lower roof. Both buildings should be empty, but watch out for loose tiles." He departed, wiping his mouth on his sleeve as if he'd taken a drink from the water jar by the door.

The hidden men waited. Would the other guard never arrive? When they finally heard his footsteps they waited for him to turn and depart, tense and ready to jump down. Yan trembled uncontrollably as the guard walked to the water jar. He tipped it to his mouth, and several gushes slipped by his lips and down the front of his uniform. When he walked back outside Omer dropped to the floor. Yan followed. They paused, measuring the growing distance to the guard's departing back.

"You first," Omer murmured. "Save me a patch of shadow."

Yan slipped by him and began to run. The yellow tile roof neared, but Yan was also closing the distance to the guard ahead of him. If he should turn, Yan would be caught in the open. He forced his legs to slow and tried not to stare at that leather-clad back, willing the man to keep looking forward. Ahead of the sentry, a voice echoed. He saw the guard who had spoken to them approaching from the far tower.

He heard murmured conversation. The two guards stopped for a moment's chat, one stalling the other to give him and Omer time to get down. The roof was just ahead and Yan walked stealthily, feeling Omer's breath on the back of his neck. Both men sprang up on the parapet at once and dropped down the other side, their bare feet making no sound on the cold tiles. The roof sloped gently, and they crawled down into shadow. Moonrise tinted the gray-shingled tower with silver. Again, footsteps sounded along the wall above.

"Close," Smid's man said quietly, never breaking his step as he passed. "You started too soon. Get down as fast as you can now." His footsteps faded.

"Yan, move it!"

Omer's sibilant command jolted Yan, and he let himself slide a few feet down the slope. "Careful—that one's loose." He could sense Omer next to him as he backed down, feeling the tiles with his toes. There! The edge! How far down? A quick look revealed moon-shot darkness. His eyes strained. Indistinctly, something resolved itself just below the eave, so he let himself slide until he was bent at the waist, his legs dangling. Stretching his toes, he felt the welcome texture of rough wood. The second roof! "Om! Drop! It's only a few feet." When he heard the soft thud of Omer's feet, he moved. "Over here! We can drop to the street."

In a narrow alley between buildings, Yan rubbed his bruised and splinter-ridden feet. Both men pulled their sandals from their belts and strapped them on. They brushed out brown robes, and Yan adjusted his axe. Omer had knives strapped to his wrists and calves, and carried his short sword on his thigh.

By the time his feet touched ground, Yan's world had resumed its normal pace. His arms and legs were like jelly; he had to force his hands not to tremble. He refused to admit that his greatest relief was that he'd not soiled himself. I wonder if Om noticed anything, or if it's all subjective?

Forcing himself to think about the present, shutting his eyes, he concentrated on Brother Hant's charts until he could "see" them as red and yellow phosphenes swirling against his eyelids. He concentrated until he saw even the loops and flourishes of Hant's ornate lettering. Then, peering around the corner into the street, he fitted each building visible in the low-angled moonlight into place on those mental maps, like tiles on the chalked cartoon of a mosaic. Two doors east was a shuttered brick building for storing bookbinders' cloth and paper. It would not be locked. Little of value was kept outside the institutional buildings of the compound.

They walked into the street together, a tall young priest and his effeminate elderly companion, apparently having completed a brief assignation in the darkness of the alley. Had they been seen from some upper window no alarm would have been given, for the Church encouraged behavior that isolated its members from the heterosexual world around them. Only small-town and rural clergy set a different standard, more in keeping with chaste and celibate behavior, especially in the Old Christer areas.

The storehouse door opened to their first effort. The interior was cool and smelled of old leather, paper, and fish-oil inks. Dawn was hours off. To be seen walking about in darkness might arouse the curiosity of early-rising busybodies, so they arranged themselves on bales of paper and attempted to sleep.

CHAPTER ELEVEN

True madness proceeds from voluntary choice and failure of imagination, or it is not mad, but mere sickness. Humans set physical and mental limitations early on, and adhere to them henceforth. Those limits are not carved in immutable stone, nor are they the same from one being to the next. A pain that drives one person mad only angers another; a nagging spouse can unhinge the mind of a saint, while a soul less fine may endure vituperation with saintly resignation.

Wherein lie the differences? In the rules each defines for herself. "Thus far, and no further." But how far is far? "To endure the unendurable," advises a sage, "extend your limits a bit at a time. Do not succumb this day, this hour, this breath. *Choose* the moment of madness by choosing the limit of your endurance. Live one second beyond your preconceived limit, and thus pass beyond it by minutes, hours, days, a lifetime."

The Book of Choices, Nahbor University copy dated 2973 C.R.

Daybreak announced itself with a growing murmur of activity. Rising to brush off his robe, Yan's first coherent thought concerned the lack of a convenient chamber pot in their hideaway. Hant's maps had shown no public conveniences, and his aching bladder could not wait upon further explorations, so he thinned the ink in a half-full crock. They ate bread and cheese from their meager supply, then secreted the remaining oiledcloth packets in a high cabinet, out of the way of rodents.

The building housing the archives, their first goal, was across the street from their warehouse hideout, but it was large, and its public entrance was a hundred yards away. They stepped out into bright sunlight. To their left, the Cathedral loomed impossibly high. Its unadorned stone wall was broken only by limestone columns at the north portico. The Cathedral was so vast it could not be seen in its entirety from any one vantage point except by the pigeons that flocked around it. So many buildings crowded the narrow compound streets, and such a profusion of tall elms thrust up from between them, that even a bird might not be able to capture it in one visual sweep.

Yan's mind filled in the unseen: the Cathedral was square, two hundred yards on a side, with round towers at each corner and a three-story portico at the center of each wall. Those walls rose six stories, unbroken except at the highest level, which was festooned with a ribbon of arches wrapping the entire edifice. The corner towers were two stories higher than the walls, their steep conical roofs adorned with red and gold tiles. The central roof ascended pyramidally to a point level with the towers, and the large tower that penetrated the center of the pyramid arose from ground level to a total height of twelve stories. Fifty yards in diameter, that tower was topped by a steep shingled cone that raised the total height of the entire structure by another sixty yards.

Of the four porticoes, two opened into the streets of Innis; the others were within the compound. Inside, four immense hallways, wider than streets, ran directly to the central tower's base. The bulk of the Cathedral was thus divided into four quarters, each one a maze of rooms, levels, and corridors open only to the select of the Church.

The two porticoes in the compound were guarded. Hant had provided no papers or passwords; to enter by the doors, they would have to provide their own. As they planned to examine the separate building that housed the archives, Hant had suggested they seek another entrance to the Cathedral proper, perhaps within the building. He was not certain that such an entrance existed, but he thought it unlikely the high clergy would *not* have easy access to their records. The Outbound School, a training center for missionaries, was another possibility, perhaps built above a connecting tunnel.

There was enough foot traffic, mostly brown-robed, for them to stroll by the archival entrance a time or two safely unremarked. On their first transit a green-trimmed acolyte greeted a pair of elderly priests by name as they entered. Omer caught a glimpse of maroon and glitter within—a mercenary guard.

They continued walking, turning left beyond the archival building to circumnavigate the missionary school. Unadorned stone three stories high, the school stood surrounded by sheds and dormitories which leaned against it but seemingly gave no access. Only one gate opened onto the forecourt, where they glimpsed a pebbled path and banks of mauve and yellow blooms. The quietness within didn't tempt them to enter. It was too late in the year for missionary students and priests not to know each other, and strangers would be subject to curious inquiry. The archives were their best bet.

Returning by a different route, they passed the northwest gate, beyond which lay the stone bridge and the inn where they had stayed their first night in Innis. Yan felt an urge to turn there, to regain the freedom of the city beyond; the walls towered so high around him that he stopped as an abrupt rush of claustrophobia took away his breath. Omer's elbow in his ribs knocked loose his psychic obstruction and he resumed his pace, but the brief glimpse of the world beyond had lowered the high adventurous spirit with which he'd begun the day. The pressure of piled brick and stone all around bore down upon him.

As they passed the archives, three priests in silver-gray embroidered robes went within. The acolyte at the door merely nodded, and they in turn ignored the young man entirely, never stopping their conversation. Omer flashed Yan a toothy grin, but waited until they were well beyond the doorway to explain.

"Th' gray trim's of a western order na' common on this side a' th' Inland Sea," he muttered breathily. "Their beliefs differ and it's only years since they've been accepted here. If they can walk in wi' out question, I s'pect any fool in a brown skirt can. Let's try it." Yan agreed there seemed no other way, but he wished that they had an explanation at hand in case they were questioned. Nothing suggested itself, so he shrugged and walked directly to the door.

Their entrance was anticlimactic. Acolyte and guard hardly looked up as they passed into a hall with open stone stairways and heavy oak doors. Beyond, an immense room's red-tiled floor bore heavy trestle tables and backless stools. Several tables were strewn with books; nearsighted priests hovered over them. Yan responded to Omer's questioning gaze by walking right in. No one paid attention. As their eyes adjusted to dim light, they saw that the room was actually a roofed courtyard, with skylights far overhead. On the upper floors, balconies went completely around, and they glimpsed stack after stack of bookshelves receding into dark recesses beyond. Neither man knew where to begin, but to stand unoccupied might have brought unwelcome attention. They walked to the side of the court where padded benches let them sit inconspicuously while they decided what to do. The answer to their dilemma arrived shortly.

An acolyte entered with twenty young monks. In the middle of the court he addressed them in a clear, ringing voice. "On these floors are copies of Church records for the past five hundred years." His singsong chant demonstrated that it was a prepared speech given often. "Copies of almost all texts in existence are stored here as well. The archivist instructs that you spend an hour familiarizing yourselves with the archives before pursuing interests of your own. The bell cords at the head of each stairway will summon assistance in finding specific work, but make sparing use of those. Do not go beyond the open shelves, or open closed doors.

"Shelves with glass doors contain sensitive works or fragile volumes of great age. Permission to view them must be obtained from the archivist. Refrain from unnecessary speech and other noise. Latrines are on the lowest level, and facilities for light meals as well. May your studies be fruitful for the greater glory of Pharos." Finished, he turned and departed rapidly without acknowledging raised hands among his former charges.

"Tha's all we need t' know, Yan. Let's just wander wi' th' crowd. Keep an eye on our bench and we'll meet when we're ready."

"Agreed. You take the next floor and I'll take the topmost."

They followed the monks into the hallway and up the stairs. Shelves covered the entire floor area to the outside walls on Yan's level. Each aisle terminated in a narrow window. He realized with a sinking heart that it would take most of a day to walk all the aisles and glance at titles. His despair intensified when he realized that though the cloth- and leather-bound documents were probably arranged in rational order, there were no placards, no visible means of locating works. He doubted he would find anything of value without luck or a lifetime to spare. Asking for assistance was out of the question. After covering half the floor in a brisk fashion, he was reminded by his rumbling stomach that the sun was halfway down the nearest window. He had missed the midday meal, and it was only hours to sundown. He spotted Omer on the bench far below, so with a relieved shrug he headed for the stairs. Descending the hard stone steps, the jogging made him aware of another biological demand.

"Let's find the latrine before we decide what to do next," he said softly. "This is a waste of time. Did you see anything?"

"Books. Dust and books."

They found the latrine. Though the odor was neither as powerful nor as complex as that of Dan's harbor, it was an adequate guide. Once relieved, they set out exploring on the pretext of finding the refectory. The lower-level doors were all closed, and it was unlikely that a hidden entrance to the Cathedral would be marked with a sign and arrow. Counting turns, they worked their way south to the wall where a connecting passage would have to be. Each door looked like every other. None showed excessive wear on the tiles at its base or greater sheen on handles. Discouraged, they sought the dining facility in earnest. Again, smell guided them, and an open door gave access to a low-ceilinged room lit by candles and light wells. An acolyte stood over a pot of stew and several loaves of bread. A keg of ale stood on a rack beside the table.

"Bread and soup are free to all, Brothers," they were told. "If you wish other than water to drink, a donation placed in the bowl yonder would be in order—a copper or two, if you please."

"Aya. A mug a' ale tuh wash th' God-damned dust from your throats." The voice addressing them was shrill. "Will you join me, Brothers?" The speaker was an obese monk whose robed buttocks flowed over his three-legged stool. His profanity indicated either a relaxed attitude toward his vocation or else a bit too much ale in his distended belly.

"Can't hurt t' chat," Omer murmured. "Ask a question or two." With bread, soup, and ale in hand they joined the fat man.

"New faces, eh. You must be a' th' group tha' came in today."

"Aya, just so," Omer agreed. "And t' whom do we speak?"

"I be Asmot Darro, assistant archivist's assistant still."

"Still?" Yan queried.

"Still. Forty years in this pile a' bricksh an' bookworms. Passed over for assistant archivist again. I wush—wish—y' better luck wi' your own stay here."

Yan realized Darro's slurred speech was indeed the result of drunkenness, and his hopes rose. A drunk and dissatisfied man was an opportunity.

Omer was equally aware of their tablemate's state and its potential. "Passed over, you say? After forty years here? Sounds like a waste a' good experience t' me."

"Aya! All a' forty an' mos' a' another.'S a damn dirty thing, I say. Ready t' retire me, an' not a promof—promorsh—not a kick upstairs t' salve an old man's pride 'fore he's put out t' graze. Mildew an' worms take their God-damned books." He raised an eyebrow at Omer. "You're a bit old f'r a 'prentice, Brother. Your pretty frien' here's more th' age for't." He leered muzzily at Yan.

"Aya. I'm here with him," Omer replied, gaining his revenge for Yan's laughter at his pebble-induced mincing. "T' see he's settled in and"—he spoke with a raised eyebrow and a leer of his own—"t' find out where he'll be sleeping nights."

"Hee! Hee! No chance a' that, y' poor fool. Unlesh y' have a pash—pass for th' Cathedral." He laughed wheezily. "Y'r pretty friend'll see no light a' day 'cept through th' windows, neither. Not till he retires, too."

"Oh? And why is that? I've a nice room down th' street. What's t' stop us seeing each other?"

"Because he'll be living on th' other side a' tha' door ri' there." Darro pointed to the hallway. "An tha' goes down under th' Cathedral wall t' th' dormitory. Better ha' your fun t'night, old man. Come t'morrow he'll be snuggled up t' me, eh, boy?"

Yan's robe moved. He felt plump, soft toes crawling between his calves. He could not shrink further without moving his stool, so he covered his consternation by lifting his tankard to his mouth, preparing to jump up choking and spitting if the foot probed any closer to his crotch—and his hidden axe. Much to his relief Omer chose that moment to rise.

"I'm in need a' th' latrine again," he pronounced. "Be a good boy and lead me. I'm lost once more." Yan got up willingly, and together they went into the hall.

"By all the gods, Om, don't leave me with that old pervert," he whispered hotly. "He'll crawl up my leg as soon as you're around the corner."

"I got you away from him, didn't I? But think, Yan. Th' dormitory's under th' Cathedral wall. There *is* a passage through here. But he's not going to take *both* of us through it."

"And you expect me to find it with him sniffing along behind me like a dog in heat—or worse? Think again!"

"Just pretend you're interested in his . . . proposal. I'll follow as close as I can, and once we're inside we take care a' th' old . . ." Omer grinned mischievously. "Your turn in th' barrel, Yan," he said. "Do it." He turned as if to leave, but actually went no further than to hide in the shadowed hallway. From there he motioned Yan back into the refectory.

Taking a deep breath, Yan entered and sat down again, next

to the fat monk instead of across from him, but with an empty stool between them to deflect probing feet and other extremities.

"Shall I show you your quarters, boy?" The shrill voice was perhaps more sober than it had been minutes before, but the round, oily face was redder, twisted into a disgusting leer. "Perhaps you can move in early, eh?" Another leer. The monk was sweating profusely and his breath was short. "I'll show you my room, too. I have it all t' myself—for now, that is."

"But should we leave without my friend?" Yan faked a conspiratorial grin. "He'll be concerned when he can't find me."

"Ach, he'll recover—and he can't follow us, in case it worries you." He produced a large iron key. "You can find him later—if you still want to." The man's gurgling laugh was like retching, or perhaps Yan's own thoughts colored his perceptions. Darro continued to giggle and wheeze as he rose laboriously to his feet. Yan hung back, but felt a guiding arm around his waist.

"Don't be shy, boy. I'll be nice to you. Oh, yes, I'll be *so* nice. You'll need a friend, you know, someone knowledgeable, influential. I'll be a good friend, you'll see. Oh, yes . . ." He rambled on, squeezing Yan to his jouncing hip as they passed into the passage below the walls through one of the doors Yan and Omer had examined earlier. Yan glanced desperately around to see if Omer caught the door before it latched, but saw it close and heard the spring-driven bolt snick home.

He tried to memorize the turnings and the doors they passed through, and tried equally hard to ignore the hand stroking and fondling his buttocks as they walked. "Where are we now?" he asked, masking his revulsion. "Are we in the Cathedral?" Was that a proper tone of schoolboy awe?

"Oh yes. The steps over there lead directly to the Senior's own offices. We bring all his requirements from the archives right through here. I myself climb those five flights of stairs almost every day, and speak with him often."

The old gasbag would die of a burst heart climbing those, Yan thought. He was happy to know there was a way to the upper floors. Without Darro, he and Omer could have spent weeks hunting through the torchlit depths. But where was Omer? Could Yan get back to him? What could he do about this horny fool?

"Here we are, boy," Darro warbled. "Here's the dormitory. The new boys sleep here." He gestured around a room lit by an oil torch. Four-tiered wooden bunks crowded it and gray deal tables lined the walls. The stone vaults were smoke-blackened, the walls brown with ancient soot and patched with white and yellow efflorescences from groundwater leaching—indicating that the room was along the outside wall of the Cathedral, north of the archives. Yan's mental map flashed before his eyes. He knew exactly where he was.

Darro was still talking. "And here is my room—forty years does bring some comforts, some little privileges, eh? But you won't have to wait so long for a soft featherbed, will you, my pretty? Here, see how you like it while I—"

The monologue ended with Darro's fat body sprawled across the bed. Yan set the hefty candlestick back on the shelf where he'd found it and checked the inert monk. Still breathing. I've never killed in cold blood—never wanted to, until now. He whipped Darro's waistcord from his robe and bound his wrists and ankles. Then he wrapped the featherbed around the monk's head and face several times to muffle any moans or cries for help.

Now to find Omer! Yan retrieved the iron key with a minimum of fumbling. He ran past the stairs, through one door and another. He saw that the third doorway was hung in a deeper recess—the thick bearing wall of the Cathedral. Then came the maze of corridors under the archives. Did he remember correctly? It was difficult to be sure with his direction of travel reversed . . . Yes! He remembered the tiled doorjambs ahead. Omer would be waiting on the other side, he hoped. Yan fumbled with the spring-loaded bolt.

"It's about time, 'boy.' I'd begun t' wonder if you were enjoying your new friend's attentions. Where is th' fool?"

"Friend, indeed! I've burnt our bridge back there—I had to club him. He's tied up in his love nest in case he regains his senses. There's a way into the Cathedral—right up to the Senior's own quarters on the fifth floor. I got that much out of him before I knocked him out."

"Will we need keys or passwords? I can't believe we'll get in easily."

"I don't know. Perhaps we can squeeze him for more information. He's the only one in the whole place until the new 'boys' arrive tomorrow."

They retraced passageways, closing Asmot Darro's door behind them when they arrived. The priest was conscious. He had wriggled to the floor and the featherbed was half-unwound from his head and shoulders, but his bonds still held. His hands had swollen, burying the thong deep in his soft flesh. Omer cautiously pressed the comforter over his face and uncovered an ear.

"If you want to live to bugger pretty boys, keep silent," he said. "I'd as soon slit your throat, but p'raps you can buy your life. Agreed?" Darro wriggled and moaned, and Omer could feel him vigorously attempting to nod his head. "I'm releasing you now. Remember, one squeak and my knife will give you a new smile, a few inches down from your present one."

The pale, red-blotched face that emerged was no longer drunk, but was none the prettier for it. Darro's eyes faithfully tracked the small knife that Omer skillfully flipped over and over in his palm. Meanwhile Yan, pawing through their unhappy host's possessions, found paper and quickly transferred his mental map of the Cathedral to it, placing a small X on the spot where he believed them to be. They hefted the obese priest onto his stool and Yan placed the map on the table before him.

"We are here, am I right?" He spoke sharply, angrily, still reacting to the shame of the old fellow's unwelcome attentions. He felt as he imagined a first-time whore must feel, and he hated the monk for it. "The Senior is five flights up?" Darro nodded gingerly, in pain. "The Son of Pharos—the God's statue—is kept nearby," Yan snapped. "Where?"

The priest's triple chins all trembled at once, and a string of drool bobbed down to his robe. "What do you know about . . . what do you mean?" he stammered.

"I think you know what he means," Omer said, flinging the knife to the table, where it stuck, waving side to side. "Refresh your memory. Where is the great bug stored?"

"There are . . . that is . . . I know only rumors. The corridors west of the Senior's offices are blocked off. The only access must be through the tower, or through his offices."

"And those stairs lead directly to the offices? Are they locked or guarded?" Omer watched his sweating face intently, attempting to read the truth of his reply.

"The top-floor door is barred. There's a guard beyond it."

"Then there's a password?"

"I don't know it. I haven't been up there in months. I'm too . . . rotund to ascend all those stairs."

"You're lying," Yan interjected. "What happened to your daily trips to the Senior? You know the codes." He was more inclined to believe Darro's new claim over the previous one, but disagreeing would keep pressure on the monk. "Here, Om. If he's through helping us, I'll cut out his tongue." He reached for the knife, still the focus of Darro's attention.

"No! No. Please! It changes every day. Yesterday it was 'Pharos rules the heavens,' so today . . . no, wait . . . today is . . . is . . . 'By Pharos' grace Earth lives.' Yes, I'm sure it is."

"He's still lying, Yan. Cut him." Yan grabbed Darro's greasy nose between two fingers and pulled his round face back. He brought the knife up and slid its point between the man's drooling, quivering lips.

"No! I'm not lying. I didn't lie. Oh, God, I'm telling the truth. It's 'By Pharos' grace Earth lives.' "

"Let's tie him up better, Om, and give it a try." Yan thought for a moment. "Where are the others, Asmot? Your coworkers?"

"Gone now. I thought you were one of the new . . . you're not a brother at all, you're . . ." Yan waved the knife. "No, wait. The assistant archivist is in the infirmary. No one else is here. You can't leave me here!" he wailed. "I'll die of thirst. My hands are numb. They'll fall off, tied like this."

"If we're successful, we'll free you on our return. Otherwise we'll probably be dead soon, and you may indeed die before anyone finds you. Have you lied again?"

The priest shook his head. Omer re-bound him, with bedding to pad the thongs. Darro's hands would survive the constriction, yet Omer's skillful ropework would not easily be undone. A wad of leftover strips was stuffed into his mouth and bound in place. They left him sitting uncomfortably on his small, hard stool.

"Shall we go, monk-killer?" Omer jested. "I'd hardly know th' p'fesser anymore."

Yan smiled sheepishly. "I don't know if I could have killed him, but I've never felt as dirty as I did playing his simpleton whore. When I hit him, I thought for sure he'd be dead."

"Heads are surprisingly hard to break," Omer observed knowledgeably.

They began climbing stairs. Each level had four flights separated by landings. At the top of every fourth landing were brass-bound oak doors, barred from within. They met no one on the stairs and reached the fifth level within minutes, breathing heavily. Yan was grateful for an open portal on their right, not only for the cool breeze that stroked his face but because he felt less trapped. The tiled roof and tall archive windows were directly beyond. Omer pounded on the door, and the speaking slot shot open.

"By Pharos' grace Earth lives," Yan said loudly. He heard the rasp and rumble of a heavy timber bolt sliding free. The man who opened the door was dressed in the maroon and brown of the Church Militant, not the less-decorative mercenary uniform.

"Where's Fatty?" he demanded. "Too tired to do his own work?"

"Brother Asmot tends to the preparation of the dormitory for the new brothers who are arriving soon," Yan stated with a pompous sniff. "I am Brother Jossig and this is Brother Brosk." He refrained from saying more, afraid of making a verbal misstep.

"What, have the new trainees arrived a day early?"

"Only some. Others will be here tomorrow."

"Well, then, report to the archivist, through that door." The guard gestured behind himself with a large, flattened thumb. "Go two doors down the hall. Don't be straying, now. There's delicate business goes on here. Just keep to yours, hear?"

"As you say, Sergeant," Omer agreed, stepping to the door with Yan on his heels. The hall beyond was empty. "We're still lucky, Yan," Omer whispered when the door behind them had swung shut. "It must be th' dinner hour. And p'raps no one'll be working late. Can you place our whereabouts?"

"Aya. The door at the end of the hall—there where it turns to the left—that must open on the Senior's suite. The temple—or radio room—must be beyond. We'll have to go through there, I think."

"The statue, you mean? Would such be kept nearby?"

"I suspect everything really secret is kept on this level. The radio whose wire you spotted is surely kept in the tower, so the wires can be kept short. But let's get out of this hallway. Our luck may not hold forever."

They approached the Senior's door. Omer put his ear against it while Yan watched the hall and listened for footsteps. The hallway around the corner had once gone further to the south, but it now ended a few feet past them in a wall whose stone and mortar, though as dark with lantern soot as the others, was laid in unornamented ashlar fashion.

"The 'Pharos Son's temple' has been blocked off for a long time," Yan commented. "Perhaps Athel of Roke himself oversaw that wall's construction."

"No sounds within, Yan." Omer pushed on the latch. There was no keyhole or lock. The mechanism gave an audible snap and the door swung inward. Omer stopped it before it opened far, and raised a finger to Yan while he listened. Yan heard nothing; nor did Omer, for he pushed the door wide and motioned Yan to follow.

The hall's oil lamp failed to pierce the darkness. Their footsteps were deadened by a floor like tough, springy moss. After waiting for their eyes to adjust, they were finally rewarded by a faint glow on their left. They crept around obstacles, weaving like wild grapevines through broken foundation stones—and, Yan thought, not much faster. The light became a thin bar of sunset-colored light at the base of a door. He heard the click of a latch, and a vertical line of brilliance blinded him for a moment. Then Omer's silhouette was framed in the doorway.

"No one here, Yan. It's an office. There are windows onto the balcony." Yan turned back to the room they'd crept through. With increased light, he saw opulently padded couches and chairs. Small tables, carved and inlaid, held lamps and cendriers. Chandeliers of glass or jewels hung low over the clustered settings. The resilient floor was layer upon layer of expensive rugs, in the Oman style.

Omer reported that a large meeting room lay on the other side, its main entry even with the landing and the stairway they had ascended; as another possible escape route it was welcome. Further exploration revealed a service kitchen and a dining room hung with embroidered tapestries in the 'Eye of Pharos' pattern, black threads on a ground of gold and ocher—a pattern commonly seen on Church artifacts. With his new knowledge of ferosin anatomy, Yan recognized the stylized circles within circles as a representation of the "head" and "eyes" of one of the creatures. Small sharp triangles in the circles' interstices surely represented spines or hairs. He made a mental note to add that to Lazko's compendium.

Finally, they discovered the Senior's bedroom and office, accessible through the sleeping chamber. Both opened onto the loggia that appeared as a continuous arcade from below. The office held only a table and hard wooden chairs. On the far wall were massive wooden doors, battened and riveted with soft iron.

"They're barred on this side," Omer observed. "That's strange. You'd think they'd want to keep people out, not in. Let's find out what's in there." He carefully lifted the bar from its brackets, pulled the door open an inch, then another, and then pushed it shut. "Pfaah! Something dead in there. Smells high as last week's stew.'' The sweetish odor of rotten meat filled Yan's nostrils, too.

There was another scent as well, a vaguely familiar one. What was it? Yan pulled back the curtain of years, remembering the highest attic over his childhood home, the lone window. The wide sill had been covered deeply in attic dust and the husks of dead flies and moths. A dead, abandoned smell. Dust and flies . . . insects, and the musky reek of long-dead mice.

Omer cracked the door again. Flickering light from a poorly trimmed wick illuminated a corridor ending abruptly at a wall of fresh bricks. Lamplight came around a corner, casting long, wavering shadows on the wall ahead, as if a barred gate were between lamp and observers. Yan peered over Omer's shoulder, inadvertently nudging the door open. Over their heads a small bell tinkled. Both men froze, not even breathing.

''Just a moment, Holy One.'' It was a gruff, soldierly voice, and came from some distance down the hall. ''I'll unlock the gate as soon as I awaken the God for you . . . but he seems no more cooperative than this afternoon.'' Heavy-shod footsteps receded, perhaps to activate the golden ''semaphore'' device.

''Om, let me by. I've got to see it,'' Yan hissed. He pushed past and peered around the corner through a grillework of heavy bars, liberally strapped and riveted, secured with chain, padlock, and massive hinges. Yan noticed that the pintles were set in fresh white mortar. The guard was about twenty paces away, standing before an identical grille, his back to Yan. He lifted a black flutelike tube to his mouth, and a single tone, shrill almost to inaudibility, filled the air. A short silence was followed by different sounds: a sibilant hissing and scratching, a crackle like crumpling paper but with a rhythmic repetitiveness, an atonal whooshing like air from a faulty bellows.

Beyond the second gate a shadow rose up: a shade with an aureate glitter, a complex, oily shine that shifted and coruscated in the flickering light. It rose above the guard, who drew back from the bars. The dark thing struck with a dry, chitinous clatter. Bouncing and reverberating from the stone walls was the shrill chittering of crickets, magnified a thousandfold. Vibrating undertones made the insides of Yan's ears itch fiercely.

He heard the guard call out over the din. ''It's no use, Holy One! He's no less mad than before.'' Omer and Yan pulled their heads back as he turned toward them. ''Perhaps tomorrow he'll—Holy one? Senior, are you still there?'' He approached the gate. Yan was on his hands and knees at the door to the office and Omer stood on his back, grasping the tethered bell in his hand and pulling on it. The cord holding the tattler snapped. Over the insect sounds they heard the clatter of the chain being pulled through the closer gate's bars. They slipped back into the office and pulled the door partway closed, then Omer reached around and carefully laid the bell on the tiles. He pulled the door shut and replaced its bar. Perhaps if the guard believed that the bell had fallen of its own accord, with a broken string . . . If he believed that the heavy door had not been opened, or that the Senior had departed, disheartened . . .

"Well? what now, P'fesser?" The door cut off all sound from the other side. "We were wrong. That's no *statue* in there. Shall we get out of here, or . . ." Omer gestured at the other barred door with a lopsided grin on his wrinkled face.

"Give me a moment to swallow my heart. I can't see yet, anyway. Are your eyes burning, too? How can that guard stand it in there?" Yan leaned to the door. "Can you hear anything?"

"Nothing. Let's wait and see. I don't see how he can give an alarm. There were no bell cords, no other doors. He surely can't go past that *thing* in there. Did you recognize it?"

"Did I! God, how wrong we were. The 'Sons of Pharos' have been *real* ferosin all along. It really is like an insect. Can it actually be an intelligent creature? The guard said it was still mad. I wonder if he meant angry or insane?"

"Or both, from th' sound a' it."

They waited. Yan counted a hundred heartbeats, then two hundred. Probably not a long time, the way his heart still pounded. There was no knock, no sound. "Let's try the other one now, Om." He reached for the bar on the second door, but stopped with his hand poised halfway there as a rich baritone voice issued from the bedroom behind him, loud in the close silence of the small room.

"That's right, Yan Bando. Open the door to my little prison. You'll be going in there soon enough." Yan and Omer whirled, reaching for weapons, only to find Church Militant guards in rattling chain-mail shirts holding swords at their throats. A man in a plain cassock stepped into the doorway and leaned on the frame.

"Clever of you to find your way here," he said. His intonation was effete. "We'd have had you brought here anyway if you hadn't slipped by us in Pittsburg. You were on the *Pride of Cansi*, weren't you? I told them so—the Juniors, I mean. You *will* tell me how you did it, won't you? Oh, yes, you will."

In spite of the malicious twist of the churchman's face he was extraordinarily handsome, with the noble features seen on busts of ancient rulers, forgiven in memory the flaws they carried in life. This man's flaws were in his behavior, which was distinctly odd. He didn't look at Yan or Omer when he spoke. Instead, his deep, dark eyes darted about, from side to side and in little circles, as if he followed the flight of a fly buzzing about his head, yet all the while maintaining his pose of studied languor. He's crazy, Yan thought in amazement.

"Oh, yes. You think I'm mad, don't you? Don't be fooled. I sometimes wish my penance were so light. No, I'm no madder than you, coming all this way to see me, to answer my questions. Now sit down over there. Yes, those stools. Plain, but such elegant butts have warmed them—kings, councillors, and Seniors. Sergeant, bring another stool in here, a plain one. I think best on a hard seat, you know, and I must think well on what you're going to tell me." Shortly, he sat down facing them.

"And who th' hell are you?" Omer rasped.

"Fisherman, fisherman, whose chair am I warming? Whose office is this? We've never met, have we, fisherman? But you know me, don't you? I am the interpreter of the God's will for Earth, the highest priest of Pharos, the keeper of our black friend in there." He gestured lazily at the door to the ferosin's chambers.

"And what is it in there?" Omer wanted to keep the Senior talking. Could they get past the guards to the loggia? Perhaps take the wordy Senior hostage? No, hopeless, he realized as he stared at the gleaming sword inches from his throat. Even when the guard had fetched the extra stool, there had not been time to get to their weapons.

The sun had only just set, Yan realized. The Senior was still speaking, but Yan's mind wandered. How strange that a madman—for Yan was all the more convinced that he was mad—could have such a mellifluous voice. A shrill cackle like Asmot Darro's would have been more fitting. Yan was aware that his thoughts wandered, that their edge was gone. Had he been drugged? Was the foul air of the ferosin's chamber having some belated effect? He forced himself to listen.

"You won't talk either, fisherman? You will, you know. Sooner or later . . . lock you up for the night . . . chat with the witch-girl, then. She won't talk either, just hums an awful little tune. Captain Ortis, lock them up. Get them out of here."

Yan was falling asleep on his stool, and offered no resistance to the guard who guided him through the door. Beyond was another corridor, lined with cells. He hardly heard the guards' admiring words when they discovered his axe. Their weapons were piled on the room's single cot, then carried away.

Bereft of hope, Yan slumped onto the cot. Vaguely, he felt someone tug at the thong around his neck and pull the tiny caged wooden ball out for examination, then drop it again. Someone—Omer?—pushed him down on the straw tick. *Depression,* Yan silently quoted from some almost-forgotten text: *lassitude, lack of interest in surroundings and situation, excessive and inappropriate fatigue* . . . He was too sleepy to continue.

CHAPTER TWELVE

Hemp grows lush in Burum's gardens.
Taken in the ancient rite,
Mothers shared their tale with girls, and
Reaffirmed the Oath of Innis.
Excerpted from "The Women's Song," from *Folktales of the Bamian Highlands*, Chapter VII, "Cryptic Tales & Nonsense-songs."

Minutes later, or so it seemed, voices penetrated Yan's dreamless sleep. His mother and father were in the front room of the old stone house, and he listened from the top of the stairs.

"He's a bright boy, May," his father said, "but not strong, if you take my meaning. Aya, he's well-built, I know. Good with tools and weapons, but he's too . . . gentle . . . to run the estates with a firm hand. There's no fire in him."

"The men like him, Carl." His mother used her most inoffensive tone. "Even the soldiers."

"They like him, true. But respect him? Will they follow him, take his orders? For that matter, can he *give* orders? He's indecisive. When old San was jumped by that tree cat, I saw Yan freeze up. He stood with his mind miles away. What would he do if he had to lead men into combat? Freeze?"

Oh, Father, Yan wept silently, if only I could have told you. I saw the cat in the tree. I saw old San. I even saw you there in the brush with your crossbow. I could have killed the cat with my knife before you could put a quarrel in the slot—I was mad even then. But afterwards? Could I have come to you and told you, even if you hadn't guessed? You couldn't even talk to me about girls; how could you have understood *that*? Should I have been brave and faced you? Which shame would you have despised most—cowardice or madness?

Momentarily, Yan became aware that he was not on his parents' staircase, but in some other place, lying down, but the other place faded, and again he heard his mother's voice. "Times are better now, dear. There's no war, and he does so well with the accounts and such; he's organized everything since he's been running the farms. I'd hate for him to be hurt, and Enri is still too young to do a man's job."

"I know my sons, May. Yan is good at what he does, but he's no fighter, no leader. He'll have to swallow his pride. I'll buy him a position in the Church."

"Carl, you can't do that." His mother's voice had turned sharper than Yan had ever heard it before. "I understand your reasons—perhaps I can even agree about Enri, but Yan deserves better than life with those . . . those horrid old men. Why not let him go to Nahbor for a year or so? Give him time to accept things? He loves books and learning so."

"I'll think on it, dear one." His father spoke more softly now. "I love him, too, you know."

Bitterness and anger welled up in Yan like raw bile. He stifled a sob as he ran to his room and flung himself on the bed. He wept aloud, muffling the body-shaking sobs in his pillow, letting them carry him along like a twig in swift, rushing water until his hurt and grief had been blunted and his loss mourned. He slept.

He awoke to a hand on his shoulder. "Yan, you can wake up now," his mother's voice murmured. He opened his eyes and was surprised to see that the face looking down at him was not his mother's pale one. Instead, a haze of fuzzy red-brown curls framed a face whose not-quite-black eyes met his blue ones. He saw a pert nose, generous lips, and a high forehead with skin the color of milky kaf—a lovely, exotic face. The girl looked no more than sixteen.

"D'you think he's better now?" Omer's voice came from behind Yan's head. "Morning, Yan. At least I think it's morning."

"I think he'll be better than ever." The girl's tones were high and smooth, with a trace of some accent Yan had not heard before. He raised himself on one elbow and looked silently at her. She was slender and small-breasted beneath an elaborately embroidered muslin shirt that was still brilliant, though smudged and frayed. Its entwined leaf clusters and tropical-looking blooms drew his eyes: they were executed with a scientific precision that rivaled botanical drawing, and he recognized some common species. But most of all, he noticed how pretty she was.

"Would you like water?" she asked him. "The guards should be bringing breakfast soon, but until then it's all we have. Are you feeling better?"

Yan tried to remember what had happened. "What did I do, faint?" He felt drained, but clean, as if his dream had purged him of an ancient hatred, not just his recent sense of failure.

"You fell asleep. It's nothing to be ashamed of, just a reaction to stress and fatigue."

"Where are we? Who are you?"

She pointed to the barred door in answer to his first question. "I'm Illyssa. From the mountains north of Nahks—a witch, or so your Senior is convinced." Her moue belied the churchman's belief.

"A witch? How strange," Yan said, his eyes mischievous. "I'd have thought witches were old women, not pretty girls."

She frowned. "I said *he* thinks I'm one. But his mind is unbalanced. Grandmothers use witch tales to frighten children."

"A pity you're not one," Yan murmured, ignoring her circumlocution. "We're looking for witches."

She glanced sharply at him. "You *were* looking, perhaps, but no longer." She gestured at the grilled iron door, with its chain and huge, ancient padlock. Then she leaned close to him and whispered, "We've been put here together for a reason. They will listen to everything we say."

"Can they hear these whispers?" Yan asked.

She shrugged. "There are strange devices in this warren—machines that make speech over many miles. Perhaps there are others that 'hear' whispers through stone walls."

Despite this possibility, Omer put his head together with theirs. In close intimacy they shared their stories. Illyssa had been bound into marriage to a man she'd never met, she said, a wealthy trader—or so it had been claimed. After weeks of travel—over which she skipped with a lightness that seemed far too facile—she ended in Innis, where she discovered that her husband-to-be was a mere shopkeeper. She spurned him, and took up with a mercenary, a Cathedral guard. When he had tired of her, she claimed, he tricked her into entering the Cathedral precincts, then had her arrested as a witch.

In spite of his recent awakening, Yan felt sharp enough to suspect she told less than her full story, whether from suspicion of him or fear of the priests' listening devices. She seemed more than the rebellious tart her words portrayed. Her eyes, Yan thought, were far too old for such antics. Yan began to press her with questions.

She had been in the Senior's private lockup for several days, or so she guessed—there were no windows in the cell—and had been questioned several times, without success. Most of the Senior's questions were incomprehensible to her, she said, and as witches were widely believed to have the ability to will themselves dead if tortured, she had been caused no pain. That anyone could "make themselves die" was a new concept for Yan, but it explained why the Church had had little success interrogating witches, and why so many captives were never seen again. Illyssa claimed no knowledge of the black beast kept nearby, and professed ignorance of spaceships and alien beings alike, but she admitted that the Senior's questions had been similar to Yan's.

Later, while Illyssa dozed, Yan and Omer discussed their cellmate. "A pity she's *not* a witch." Yan sighed. "We need 'supernatural' talents right now."

"And you believe her denials?" Omer asked, the light of mischief in his eyes. "Why should she tell us the truth? We could be that madman's accomplices, for all she knows."

"Then you think she may really be of the witch-folk? That's too much of a coincidence, I think."

"Incredible," Omer said with a mocking smile. "You, who spin tales of wonder from no more than old wrecks, books, and bones, cavil at the *coincidence* of our finding a witch after coming all these hundreds of miles looking for one? It isn't coincidence that *we're* here, or the Senior, or the ferosin, is it? This is *Innis*, after all. If it were Wain, or New Roster, or some unnamed prairie village, *that* would be coincidence—but not here. We are here after considerable effort. The Senior is here because this is the seat of the Church's power. The black bug is here for similar reasons. I see no coincidence at all. The girl claims to be from the mountains north a' Nahks, doesn't she? The very place we've been aiming for all along?"

Yan surrendered to logic. His reluctance to believe in her, he admitted, stemmed from his unwillingness to accept that she didn't trust them, if in fact she was a witch. There was another factor he didn't recognize, let alone admit. Being a scholar with little time for dalliance, and because the "demon" in his genes had steered him from intimate relationships, he didn't recognize the source of his dissatisfaction: until now, "infatuation" had been only a word to him. Omer, wiser, was not about to explain it to him.

When Illyssa awoke, Yan asked her how, if she was really a witch, he could gain her trust. "If I were one, I wouldn't need to *trust* you," she said with an air of condescension. "Don't you know anything about witches? It's common knowledge that witches—if they really exist at all—have the truth sense."

That was new to Yan. His sources had never mentioned ability to read truth in unnoticeable cues of voice, posture, or gesture, as Illyssa described it. Yan thought it more likely that ancient starfarers, if indeed they had spoken mind-to-mind, had passed some trace of talent to their descendants. No wonder the Senior seemed a bit crazy—he couldn't torture a witch, nor even fool her. His frustration must be driving him mad.

When Yan heard heavy footsteps approaching in the hall, his first thought was for his empty stomach, but Illyssa's speculation proved false. The guard carried no food. Instead, the prisoners were to appear before the Senior immediately. They were led through the Senior's office and bedroom; either the bed had been freshly made or their host had not slept that night. They passed through the other office, now occupied by a wizened monk of indeterminate age. Their guard opened the door to the hearing room and escorted them to a raised platform where the Senior sat behind a long table. Though rows of benches were laid out behind them, they were not allowed to sit.

"How fare my three pets this morning?" The Senior's rich voice filled the large room. "Fitch and wisherman and . . . no, that's not right, is it? My witch and fisherman and my clever antiquarian." Bags under his unnaturally mobile eyes confirmed that the Senior had spent a wakeful night. Yan maliciously hoped that it had been on their account.

"Will my little songbirds sing today? I've opened your cage, so give me a happy song." Suddenly the handsome face transformed into a mask of erubescent rage. The Senior held his breath like an angry child, then let it out with a bellow. "If you don't sing for me, I'll feed your squirming bodies to that cursed Pharos-Son this very day!"

His outburst was followed by a fit of uncontrollable coughing. When he spoke again, he was calmer. He almost wheedled, then sentence by sentence built up to another bellow: "He *is* mad, you know. He won't talk to me! What's the use of the translation machine if he won't sit in it? I had my guards force him, plug the wires into his head—if indeed it is a head—but they failed. He *ate* them! The guards, not the wires. Six he ate, before I commanded them to stop wasting themselves.

"He'll eat you too, fisherman—and your friend, and you, little witch. Shall I tell you how he eats?" A sick gleam in his watery eyes confirmed he would indeed tell them. "Oh, yes," he chortled. "He'll jump on you and he'll sit on you, and the little pointy feelers on his bottom will pierce you. Like a spider, he'll suck your juices until bones rattle in the dry sack of your skin." He paused, panting.

His eyes flashed around the room, never lighting in one place, following that buzzing invisible insect. He smiled crookedly. "And when he's done, he'll shit out your black blood from the same end he ate you with. Did it smell nice in there last night? I know you were in there. The bell didn't fool me, not one bit. What you smelled was my dear, dear friend, the Senior of Roke—and my foolish guards, too. My colleague came here because *his* Pharos-Son went mad, too, and then fell apart. At least that's what he said it did. It didn't die, it just came apart and all the parts ran around on horrid little legs.

"Poor Hernock! I knew him since we were boys, right here in Innis. He wanted my Pharos-Son to tell him what to do, but it ate him instead, just like it's going to eat you, you, you." He pointed at each of his prisoners in turn with a trembling forefinger, then fell silent, still panting.

"Holy One, may I speak?" Omer's tone was oily and servile. The Senior nodded jerkily. "With the Sons of Pharos acting so strangely, and with the Senior of Roke dead, only you stand between the Earth and sure destruction. If the Compact is broken, what will become of us all?"

"Why do you care, fisherman? You're going to die long before the rest of us, you and your friend and the witch."

"I only wished to offer our help, Holy One." Omer was so humble that he was hanging his head. If their situation had not been so dire, Yan would have laughed. Surely the Senior was not so detached from reality that he couldn't see through Omer's ludicrous performance? Even their guard, Yan saw with a sidelong glance, looked disgusted—but with Omer or the Senior himself? Shortly, Yan was forced to admit that Omer had indeed judged the mad cleric well. He was used to being surrounded by sycophantic priests, and Omer's behavior must seem commonplace to him.

"How could you help me, fisherman?" The Senior's mellow baritone had returned, slow now, tinged with fatigue and sadness. "There have always been Sons of Pharos to advise us, and now there are none. Always, the ships of the God brought new Sons when ours grew old or sickened, but now it's all happened too soon. It's been only twenty years. The last one didn't sicken or go mad at all.

"Oh, yes, I remember. I was no older than Yan Bando there. There were two Sons of the God right here—yes, this very room. The old one was brown with age, and the one in there now was all black and shiny-new. I was appointed his servant, you know. The old Son was going home, retiring just like the old Senior, him and his pretty little boys."

The present Senior whined, a pitiful, sickening noise. "I don't have any of those, you know. I work too hard for that. There's no time for me to enjoy my life, my rank. It's fine for other priests to have . . . friendships, you understand, but I am the Senior. You do understand, don't you?"

"We understand, Holy One," Yan said sympathetically, joining the charade. From the corner of his eye he could see the guard's face, and peering around the corner was the Senior's secretary, the wizened man. Guard and secretary alike displayed expressions compounded of pity, disgust, and anger at the two who were gulling the crazy Senior. This ridiculous game isn't going to get us anywhere, Yan thought. Those two know he's mad and they'll talk him out of whatever Omer has in mind.

Nonetheless, Yan talked on. "Your responsibilities are too great for such frivolity. Why, the burdens you bear would truly drive a lesser man to madness. We only wish, in some way, to shoulder some small part of your heavy task." He looked at Omer, not sure of the other man's plan. Omer took the cue.

"We must send for a new Son of Pharos, Holy One. You can't be expected to go on like this, without counsel. How long will it take for one to arrive?"

"How should I know. One year? Five? Perhaps never, if my poor luck holds." The Senior seemed about to cry. "No ship is expected for five years. Once ships came and went, but not now. And how can I ask him to send for another? He refuses to get in the talking machine."

"Then we must go to them—up there," Omer stated flatly.

"Oh, no. Don't you know, fisherman? Our kind go mad in the darkness above. Besides, we have no way to do it."

"Can a message be sent? With a radio, perhaps? Are there not still other Pharos-Sons on Earth, in distant cities?"

"Ahhh! Clever fisherman. You know about radios, do you?" Like a wisp of sanity, a taint of suspicion rose in the Senior's wild eyes. Then it faded. "No," he said with resignation, "there are no others. For generations, there have been only two, in Innis and Roke. If my Son would enter his machine, if I could speak with him . . . but as it is, the problem and the solution are one."

"Perhaps we can devise a solution of a different sort. If we were free men, we could help. But here . . ." Omer shrugged expansively.

"A trick! You seek to trick me." Mock-sanity and suspicion returned. "What would you do if I freed you? Run. Besides, what could you do? How could you find Pharos? The God doesn't hang in orbit around our puny globe, waiting to hear from us. His domain is wide—you'd need a ship. And how would you fly it? Do you know how from your researches, young Bando? Have your old hulks and bones taught you to fly? At any rate, you'd go mad as men always do, even if there was a ship."

He paused and peered up at them. For once, his eyes held still long enough to fix on each of their faces for long seconds. They lingered longest on Illyssa. Then he leaned back in his chair and laughed. He laughed for a long time, scarcely pausing to suck in a whooping breath between each spasm. Eventually he quieted and spoke again to Omer. His eyes steadied and he seemed once more in excellent spirits.

"Clever scholar, clever fisherman. You thought you could fool me, didn't you? You know even more than I thought. You know where there's a ship. The witches' ship. You hoped I'd let you go, to steal it from me. It's mine, you know. I've spent a lifetime trying to get it from these stubborn witches. Pharos wants it. And I'll bet she's told you where it is. But you were too clever for your own good. Now I know it still exists, and I will find it. I won't have to torture her and have her *die*." He said the last word as if it were something dirty, investing it with black disgust. Yan wondered how many witches had already died in his little prison, to so shape his bitter thoughts.

The madman continued in a breezy manner at odds with the subject. "I have to torture only *you*. You won't die for a long, long time. I can take you apart piece by piece, and you won't die until you tell me what I want to know, and more. I'll write your life's story before you die. And then I'll start on the scholar. He and the witch can watch you die first, to put them in an anticipatory mood.

"Watching *others* die will have no fatal effect on the witch, you see? Perhaps she'll beg for your release from life and pay with her cooperation. A new experiment, indeed. Perhaps I've indeed found a way around this death wish that has thwarted my predecessors for centuries. Isn't it strange, scholar? The answer is love. Ah, don't fool with me. I can see it in your eyes. You must be a fool, to fall for a dark little witch. But there's more. The fisherman loves you like a son, and the slut seems attracted to you. Perhaps my predecessors would have succeeded if they'd taken *groups* of witches. Torment any one of you, and I'll hurt the others worse, won't I?"

He leaned back and stared at the ceiling, a smile playing about the corners of his mouth. His eyes resumed their flickering. "Yes, I'll have the witches' ship, and their secrets. Pharos will reward me. Do you know how He rewards faithful servants? He gives them a world. Not a dingy, worn-out world like this one, either—a new, green world filled with palaces and lovely people—women, boys, or whomever I might desire."

Yan was disgusted with the idiot face the Senior assumed as his mind retreated into fantasies of Pharos' rewards. Saliva glistened in the corners of his mouth and, behind the table, his robe rose up with the pressure of his erection. Yan had no desire at all to know the fantasy that stimulated him.

He was equally disgusted with the way Omer's plan had backfired. Nothing they could say now would convince the Senior that they had not discovered any ship except the wreck he and Lazko had excavated. The Senior would believe what he wanted to hear, not their speculations that human pilots of such ancient vessels depended less on special technology than on a mental twist. Such witchery would not please him, for it would put him back in the situation he'd been in before, torturing witches and watching them die. But if they could have avoided torture before, there was no way they could do so now.

"Guard! Lock them up. Don't feed them—it's too messy when they puke and shit. I'll start on the fisherman tonight. Gnist! Come with me. We must try again to talk with Pharos' Son. Surely he'll listen now. I know it. They're going to give me the witches' ship, and Pharos will give me a world. I'll *make* him talk with me." He hesitated, eyeing the prisoners speculatively.

"On second thought," he added, wild eyes gleaming maliciously, "bring them along—they can see the Son, too. Perhaps their presence will inspire him to speak with me."

The guard prodded them into motion. Gnist, the secretary, followed behind with the Senior, attempting to caution him, but the Senior was determined to communicate with the beast and the secretary had no luck dissuading him. They all arrived together in the Senior's office, and the Senior lifted the bar from the leftmost door. As it swung open, a thick gust of carrion, rotted blood, and dead insects filled the air.

Gnist and the Senior led them into a high-ceilinged room. Far above, amid arching roof timbers, were light globes of blinding red intensity. They cast unnatural shadows, ultramarine and deep green where they blocked the crimson glare that mimicked the natural light of another star, of ferosin sunshine. Where was the black creature? Yan's eyes darted as madly as the Senior's. He expected to be pounced upon and devoured.

When his eyes adjusted to the odd light, he gasped, nudged Omer, and nodded at the dark mass ahead. "A pilot station," he murmured from the corner of his mouth. "A ferosin pilot couch like the one on the wreck. This ferosin must use the device's sensors to communicate with humans through those panels on the wall. Are those like the ones you drew, Om?" Omer glanced at the glowing jewels arrayed in dark, metallic frames and nodded.

The Senior motioned them to sit. Four chairs were arranged at a semicircular table, all black metal made by no Earthly smith. "Here, my guests," he said ceremoniously, with no rage, fear, or animosity. "I will fetch the Son." Far from reassuring Yan, the man's nonchalance only highlighted his madness, and his "guests' " danger. The guard prodded them again, and they sat.

Yan recognized the objects arrayed before them as computer keyboards, human-styled, no different from the worn, ancient ones at Nahbor, except these were made of black, chitinous stuff whose oily gleam reminded him of ferosin.

Sitting, the Senior was behind them, unseen. Yan shuddered, listening to him. "Come, my black friend, my pretty, great bug," he crooned. "Come see what I've brought you."

Yan felt Illyssa wiggling beside him. In spite of their predicament, his thigh felt hot where it touched hers. He hardly knew her, but he suspected he was already half in love. Even the mad

Senior had seen it. Scholars, he reflected, are fools where women are concerned.

Thinking her wiggling signified terror, he grasped her hand, but drew it back when he realized she was fumbling in her clothing and had torn loose the hem of her shirt. She palmed something small and yellow-brown, tossed it away with a flick of her wrist, then smiled reassuringly at him and squeezed his hand.

Behind them, a rising chatter of locust wings answered the Senior's continuing exhortations, growing louder and nearer. "He's entirely mad, you know," a voice said from behind. Yan recognized Gnist in those dry tones. "It won't speak with him. It may be as mad as he, and if he angers it, none of us will leave here alive."

"I've brought you a witch, Son of Pharos," the Senior cooed, his returning footfalls almost unheard beneath the rattle and scrape of chitinous appendages on the stone flags. The stink of dead flies and carrion was stronger than ever, and Yan resisted the urge to gag. He heard both Gnist and the guard gulp, either suppressing compulsions like his own or from fear of what they could see that Yan could not.

"Your couch awaits you. Come speak with me. I have good news!" Only the guard's sword at his back kept Yan seated with his face straight ahead. Somewhere a bee droned melodiously, a warm, earthy sound out of place between stone walls, beneath red glare, among alien machines. The Senior, too, heard it. "Oh, no," he rasped desperately. "A bee. Kill it. He hates bees. Quickly now, before he—" The Senior's voice cut off suddenly in a rattle of chitin, a rising trill like a thousand crickets, and resumed as a shriek of inarticulate human terror and pain.

"Gods!" the guard swore. "It's got him."

"The gate!" Gnist spat. "Use your key while it's occupied with *him*." Yan and Omer turned simultaneously. Only Illyssa remained still, as if she could see what was happening without turning to face it.

Yan and Omer saw their enemy clearly for the first time. The ferosin must have stood eight feet tall upright, but now it was not standing. It was hunched over the sprawled figure of the Senior, its segments rippling, expanding and contracting. Bristly grasping limbs held the struggling figure to the floor while spiky tendrils penetrated it. Animal sounds gushed from the hierarch's throat. "Out," the guard whispered. "Now, while it's busy eating." Gnist, Yan saw, half hugged, half climbed the barred gate. "Your key, fool!" he hissed. The guard obeyed, fumbling badly.

Once outside the ferosin's chamber with the gate relocked, Gnist recovered shreds of his aplomb. "Lock the prisoners up," he said imperiously. "I'll decide later what to do with them." He shook his head, and turned toward his office. "What now?" Yan heard him murmur to the guard. "The lesser hierarchs will demand explanation. What can we say? It was his own fault. You saw, didn't you? He angered it. He should never have gone in there."

"What about that bee, Brother?" the guard asked, looking directly at Illyssa.

"Bah! That was his madness. The bee meant nothing, caused nothing. The creature was angered by him, or by the witch's presence. Say nothing of bees." The guard nodded cautiously. Obviously, if there was fault to be found, heads would roll. Better that things go as Gnist wished. Better Gnist's head, if anyone's. No need to mention a mere bee overlooked when he had searched the girl days before. Besides, it *could* have come in on the Senior's own clothing, or . . .

The prisoners heard the huge old padlock's tumblers clack home with an ominously final sound. "They'll be busy for a while getting their stories straight," Omer reflected. "Best we talk now. Later they might remember to listen in on us."

"What's the use?" Yan asked. "We can't get out of here."

"P'raps not," Omer replied, "but assuming we got out a' this cell, where could we go?"

"We might make it back through the archives," Yan said with no great enthusiasm. "If we got to the balcony, we might sneak in on the landing, and take the stairs through Darro's dormitory. But the office door is surely barred again, and first we'd have to get rid of *that*." He pointed to the boxlike padlock that secured their cell gate.

Illyssa broke her silence. "The other door, where the guard went, leads into the tower. The guardroom there has a window. And *that* door hasn't been locked since I've been here. He just kicks it open."

"We still have to get out of this cell. Too bad you're not really a witch. We could use your help."

Illyssa raised her head with a jerk, as if to snap at him, then changed her mind. Omer paced the cell, examining mortar joints and gate hinges. Reaching through the bars, he hefted the padlock, all the while whistling breathily through his teeth.

Yan stared at the hexagonal floor tiles, allowing them to go in and out of focus. Illyssa poked at her shirt, loosening a thread. It seemed a nervous habit, like a monkey fiddling with leaves or a predator pacing, but Yan remembered the bee and watched her from the corner of his eye. Pulling the thread and unfolding the hem, she shook out a tiny oiled-silk packet no larger than her small fingernail and held it a handbreadth before Yan's face. "Perhaps we witches do have a trick or two."

Omer looked at the tiny object in her hand. "What is it?"

"A drug. It's made from this plant," she said, pointing to a delicate cluster of leaves picked out in shades of light yellow-green on her embroidered shirt. Yan didn't recognize the toothy, palmate leaves, but Omer did.

"Hemp," he said. "Ships' rigging is hempen rope. In Burum the flowers are smoked or eaten for a pleasant, happy sensation, something like drinking wine or ale. It's no good if one has t' think quickly, though. Wha' d'you plan t' do with it? Bribe th' guard?" Omer's speech, for a while delivered in the best Inland Sea manner, had shifted back to his habitual soft patter.

"The stories about witches aren't all lies," she replied with a trace of nervousness, "even though they've been twisted by ignorance and superstition. Some . . . people do have odd . . . talents. No one talks about them with outsiders—I would be chastised for even admitting what I just told you. I may yet be. But I *must* escape. I was willing to die if I had no other choice, but it's important that my folk know what I've seen and heard here. Our elders hoped that the Masters would . . . I mean . . ."

Yan pounced on her slip. " 'Masters?' Is that what their former slaves, or descendants of slaves, call them? You knew all along that there was a ferosin in there!"

"It was suspected," she admitted, confessing, with her lack of denial of Yan's supposition, that she was indeed a witch, and that the witches had once been slaves of the aliens. "The elders know about the ships that touch down in the ocean and rendezvous with the Church's boats. They have not known whether . . . ferosin . . . were *always* here, or only periodically. But they do know there's no hope of human redemption while the Masters can frequent our world at will. They learned *that* lesson all too well."

"The lesson of Bama?" Yan queried. "And the witch hunts

in ancient Tenzie? Then your elders must know of Athel of Roke as well."

"*Know of* him?" she retorted sharply. "Just as you *know of* your mother. Do you *know of* your father's belt on your backside? We are not ignorant savages who have forgotten what we were."

Yan felt crushed. It was ridiculous to play at romance at a time like this, but he had wanted to impress Illyssa with his erudition, not have her think of him as an ignorant savage. "I begin to understand what you are." Yan reached in memory to Captain Haige's books, on the *Pride of Cansi*. "Hemp grows lush in Burum's gardens," he quoted. "Taken in the ancient rite—"

"Mothers, sharing thought with daughters/Reaffirmed the Oath of Innis," Illyssa finished the verse, gazing thoughtfully, intensely, at him. "You know the Women's Song, Yan Bando? I think I have underestimated you. Perhaps your scholarship isn't all useless pottering with dead things."

Yan was again quite taken aback. He had been prepared to be admired for his erudition, to be plied with questions about his findings—if there was ever time and freedom for that. He had definitely not expected to be dismissed as a . . . a potterer. In his momentary dismay, he failed even to notice the vast difference a change of a few words made in the sense of the lines she had cited: "Mothers sharing *thought* . . ."

"What else do you—or is it only your elders—remember?" he asked, mainly to cover his chagrin.

"Pain and degradation, helplessness and servitude, a thousand years of frustrated hopes. Is that enough? Would you prefer specifications for a star drive, or an ephemeris of the dark worlds in the Oort cloud? *Some* knowledge is easy to find . . ." She shook her head and turned bitterly away from him.

He knew her cryptic outburst was at an end, but questions welled up inside him. He suspected that she, not just her elders, "remembered" such things. Was it mere rote learning, or something more? Could she, or her kind, really *remember* how to build a star drive? And what "dark worlds" were there? There might be many things these witches remembered! Whole histories never recorded, sciences forgotten or never known on Earth . . .

Thinking of sciences, one question, one group of questions, momentarily overwhelmed all the others that he wanted to ask her. "You let that bee loose in there. Did you *know* what would happen? Did you plan it that way? Is that why you were here?"

She answered in a murmur no louder than a breath. "I knew."

Then Yan understood. Those two small words were the key to everything he suspected, everything he hoped for. The witches had not forgotten Athel's destruction of their renaissance in ancient Bama and Tenzie; they had not forgotten their ancestral sojourn as slaves on some far world. For with caustic hatred they still called the ferosin "Masters"—and they had not given up hope. Mankind's ancient quest for the stars could be reborn—but only if the aliens could be kept away . . . *Could* they be kept away? What secret plans and abilities did Ilyssa's people have?

Yan considered the disparate facts at his command. In Roke, a ferosin went mad, and subsequently broke up into smaller, unintelligent creatures. Like a tapeworm whose segments each form the nucleus of a new worm . . . was that how they reproduced? Would the mad ferosin here do the same? Two things Yan knew: mad or fragmented, it was not by *their* design, nor was it a desirable state for them, not here, not now. And the bees were the key. Superficially, the ferosin resembled concatenated gene-twisted crickets; did they have other similarities to insects—internal, chemical ones? Could a ferosin be affected by an earthly insect's chemical signal? Was their "madness" an involuntary physical response to some effusion given off by bees?

He reflected upon the new bees that had swarmed over his jam and the old ones they had supplanted. Had Illyssa's elders *known*? Had they known that chink in ferosin armor from their captivity and bred such bees to drive ferosin from the Earth, or had they discovered them accidentally? The distinction was unimportant, he decided. What *was* important was that if ferosin were barred from direct intervention on Earth, if their contact with their Church minions were limited to radio messages from orbit, then humanity would gain one small advantage. He envisioned starships built in caves beneath the forested southern mountains he had never seen. He imagined them leaping suddenly skyward past dark, alien vessels into trackless, timeless eternal night . . .

"We'll help you get back to your people," he promised, "but when we do, I must speak with your elders."

"That may not be possible," Illyssa murmured. "They have no contact with outsiders."

"We'll help anyway. Perhaps they'll change their minds."

That, Illyssa knew, was unlikely. Yan didn't know them, or

what they could do to curious interlopers. But that could wait. If they could help her get free . . . "I'll need your help with what I'm going to try," she said decisively. "I'm not an adept, though, so I can't promise this will work at all."

"What do you want us to do?" Yan asked.

"If I open that lock, can you overpower the guard? I need your help with the lock, too."

"Tell us what you require. We'll help any way we can." But Yan was dubious; it sounded as though she was going to try some paranormal feat. Neither he nor Omer would be of much use to her.

"Then listen carefully. I may be able to make the tumblers move without a key, without touching them. But I'll have to eat this first." She pointed to the dull greenish powder in her palm, the contents of the tiny packet. "I may become confused, even silly. You must hold my hands and do my thinking for me." Seeing Yan's puzzled look, she elaborated. "It enhances the ability—or my belief in it. Once my ancestors had a kind from another world, a variety that didn't promote confusion, but its seeds were lost long ago. Now we make do with ordinary hemp. My thoughts may—will—open the lock. You must act as guides for me. Just think very hard of the lock. Picture it falling open. Can you do that?"

"I can try," Omer replied slowly, "but—and I mean no offense—it all seems prepost'rous t' me. Mightn't my doubts do more harm than good?"

"You don't have to *believe* it will work, Omer. Maintain a mental picture of the lock opening, and I'll do the believing."

Yan had long accepted the concept of paranormal abilities like the one Illyssa proposed to demonstrate, at least in theory. But, like Omer, he doubted his ability to close the gap between acceptance and participation. Nevertheless, he too agreed to try.

Illyssa dipped her fingers in their water jar. Sprinkling a few drops over the powdered herb, she kneaded the mixture and formed it into two balls the size and color of unripe huckleberries. She tossed them to the back of her mouth and swallowed with visible effort, making a wry face. "I try not to taste it. Well, now we wait. I'll tell you when it's time."

They settled down as comfortably as they could on the narrow bed. They heard no sounds but their own breathing. Yan became unusually conscious of it, first attempting to synchronize his breaths with Illyssa's, which were slower, then with Omer's, more rapid and far more noisy—the air whistled slightly in its passage through the hairs in his large nose. It's like waking up in the night with someone you've never slept beside, he mused. Your lungs aren't used to their pace and you end up either out of breath or hyperventilated and wide awake.

He concentrated on relaxing his hands and feet and then the rest of his body, a technique he'd learned to quell excitement before important meetings or lectures. Picturing tension as a nebulous blue gas diffused through him, he mentally compressed it and pushed it inward to the center of his body. When he had gathered it all into a small bright cloud, he exhaled it with a long, slow breath. He did this several times, until he felt loose and heavy-limbed.

Again, he listened to the breathing, this time not attempting to match it. Three rhythms entwined, merged, and strengthened, then came together again moments later, repeating with minor variations like complex music. The cycle went on and on.

"It's time." Illyssa's voice came from far away, curiously muffled, as if Yan's ears were wrapped in a woolen scarf. She took his hand. Every motion felt exaggerated, immense and sweeping. He knew exactly when Omer grasped her other hand, feeling the tiny shiftings in her posture transmitted through the straw tick. The sensation was uncomfortably, frighteningly familiar to him. The demon. His madness. But now? Why now, when there was no immediate threat? He had to struggle to maintain his detached calm, to let the padlock become the focus of his existence.

He stared at it, then closed his eyes and "saw" it hanging before him. He pictured it in meticulous detail, pendant on its dull gray-brown chain. He tried to imagine its massive body dropping away from the shackle to hang open and askew, to visualize the black, finger-sized hole no longer filled by the end of the notched, U-shaped bar. His picture wavered, formed, then faded. He was tired, frustrated. Angrily he willed himself to concentrate on the lock, to sketch it in hot red against his tightly squeezed eyelids.

Glowing dully at first, it intensified, passing through crimson and cerise to straw yellow and then bright white. Through his closed lids he "watched" the shackle stretch and flow, at first like thick honey, then faster, glowing raindrops falling to the floor as misshapen gray pebbles. He heard a dull clatter, then a harsh whisper from Omer. "We did it. By all the mad gods, we did it!"

* * *

In a faraway place, old, tired minds awakened from dreams of fire and heat. *Did you feel it?* The question touched other minds whose thoughts were a silent babble, a wordless hubbub of anxious, puzzled mentation.

Who was that? one asked. *Whose dream was I dreaming?*

Not mine, another replied, and yet another, until eleven minds denied producing the hot, metallic dream. Eleven minds grew fearful as one, fearful of the faint, powerful emanations that had awakened them, afraid that the smoldering hopes it had ignited in their odd old hearts might once again fade into embers.

Could it be, the youngest asked with relative innocence, *that we might not have to wait another long thousand years?*

Yan opened his eyes, blinking. The lock lay on the floor, just as he'd "seen" it, and part of the shackle still hung from the chain like a distorted horseshoe. Illyssa's eyes were likewise open, but they were staring far away. He helped her to her feet. "Om, get that chain off. And the lock, too."

"Ow! Damn thing's hot as a griddle," Omer spat. He looked for something to hold it with. Finding nothing, he folded the skirt of his robe over the lock body and carried it across the cell. Smoke and the odor of burning wool followed him. He dropped the hot metal into the water jar, which bubbled, spattered, and gouted steam. Removing the cooled lock, he carried the jar to the gate and knocked the dangling shackle into the water, where it cooled with a brief hiss. "Let's get out of here," he muttered.

He eased the chain from between the bars and let it hang loose. Then he tossed the lock body in the air, and Yan winced at the thought of it hitting the floor again, even though the noise they'd made so far had gone unnoticed. Omer caught it.

"Not as good as a club, but better than a rock," he whispered. "Yan, get through the gate and take Illyssa with you. Drop her if I need help with the guard. Let's go." When they were in position, he crouched by the door, slowly rotated the lever, and pushed inward. He turned with a wide grin and raised a finger—*wait*—and then disappeared into the guardroom. Yan heard a dull thump and Omer's whisper: "He's sleeping like a child. Bring her in."

Illyssa was regaining her senses, though Yan still guided her by the elbow. Omer's robe lay crumpled on the floor and he was busy undressing the unconscious guard, who was only slightly larger than he. Yan looked at the unlocked window and saw their weapons laid neatly on a table beneath the sill. He strapped on his axe while he peered outside. He was relieved that the balcony was clear as far as he could see, ending on the left at the corner tower, diminishing into distance and dusky shadow on his right.

Sunset gilded the irregular glazing on the west-facing buildings in the compound below. The view from their height was impressive. He could even see the roof of the stable where they had first entered this insane place.

Omer approached, his arm around Illyssa. Yan pushed open the sash and stepped over the sill, then helped her through. He moved off in a half crouch, keeping the north wall of the compound below his line of sight over the stone balustrade. Compound guards on the wall might see movement of shadows, but no more. Pausing at the Senior's office window, he peered within, saw no one, and motioned for the others to follow. The bedroom, too, was empty, the bed undisturbed.

In the rose and yellow glow of sunset, the light in the next window could have been a reflection thrown from another window in the compound. Yan peered cautiously through dirty glass. A lamp flickered within. Gnist, the secretary, sat furiously scratching with a steel pen. Motioning Omer and Illyssa to stop while he hitched his robe up about his hips, Yan crawled past the low sill, gritting his teeth at even the slight sound of coarse cloth on the paving.

Without rising, he continued to the next window, where he heard voices and risked a quick peek. The Senior's audience hall was full. He saw blurred faces and brown shapes that were surely robed figures. There were scattered brighter colors among the browns—laymen. He didn't dare raise his face too high and silhouette it against the glass. The next window was open, and he could hear a dry, papery voice addressing the gathering.

"—as our late Senior is now in the house of Pharos. The Juniors will meet to pray for the God's guidance in selection of his successor. Customarily, this decision has been announced on the eve of a Holy Day so all people might take time to meditate and pray for the God's acceptance of the new Senior. This time, due to rare and unusual circumstances under study by the High Council, the choosing of two new Seniors will be postponed until the members from Roke can be sent for. No public announcement of these matters will be made for at least a fortnight. It is urged that all of you exercise the utmost discretion. A spate of disruptive rumors would not serve—"

Yan crawled past two more open windows. The next should give access to the hall at the top of the stairs. What had happened in the hours they'd been locked in the cell? It sounded as if the Church was in a state of disruption. Who besides the guard and Gnist knew of their presence? Would he, Omer, and the girl be forgotten in the present confusion?

The hallway window was closed. He squinted through the dirty glass, then wiped a patch clean with his sleeve and was startled to see broad buttocks in maroon trousers surmounted by a chain-mail shirt. Their escape route was blocked. His intestines knotted and spasmed with frustration until he realized that the room beyond the guard's legs was not the final landing of the staircase, but some kind of anteroom. No fewer than six or seven Church Militant soldiers stood formally at ease around its perimeter. The *next* window was the one he wanted, and it was open. A hundred heartbeats later he looked happily at the empty landing and the staircase a few steps away.

He almost motioned for Illyssa and Omer to join him, but a better idea struck him. Crawling rapidly back the way he'd come, he squatted beside them, rubbing raw knees and elbows, and explained his plan. He then crawled forward again, just past the window with the flickering lamp, where Gnist now squinted at the pages of a large book.

Omer flattened himself against the wall, holding his recovered knife left-handed. Yan, standing at the other side of the window, withdrew his axe and spoke in a low aside: "You realize something must be done about Brother Gnist, don't you? He has seen altogether too much of this." Then he changed his voice slightly and muffled it in his cowl. "Yes, I suspect he must go. But how? We can't just have him transferred. He must never be allowed to speak of what has transpired."

Yan and Omer watched tensely as the window was slowly, silently pulled open from the inside. When Brother Gnist's scrawny neck had extended almost far enough for him to see Yan, Omer's right arm encircled it and his knife-edge pressed hard against the monk's throat.

"Not a word out of you, Brother. Not if you want to live." Omer held him absolutely still while Yan brought the gleaming axe up under his nose, forcing him to look cross-eyed at its razor edge. Illyssa, now almost fully recovered from the effects of the drug and her extraordinary efforts, began to undress Gnist. She slipped into his cassock and pulled the cowl over her head.

"Take me with you," the shivering monk whispered, his small eyes alight with more than ordinary fear.

"You?" Yan snorted softly. "You're as mad as the Senior if you think—"

"They'll torture me. They won't believe I didn't release you." He glared at Illyssa. "They'll think *she* witched me, and they'll take me apart to find out how. Besides, if I go with you, who will tell them how she killed the Senior?"

Yan looked confused. "What? She didn't—"

"The bee, you fool," Gnist hissed. "The bee drove the black bug mad, so he killed the Senior. I know about the bees, but no one else does—now. I know the Son feared them. I know that masons bricked up all the windows in there to keep them out, to no avail. Now it's done as the other Son did. There are *eight* of them in there now. Eight horrid bugs scurrying around stupidly, the size of washbaskets. I hope they don't *grow.*"

"They'll blame you for the bee's presence, won't they? Unless you can hold back that detail when they question you. A pity. I don't envy you, Gnist. But *we* can't save you, nor would we. You'll have to make your own good fortune, if you can."

Omer slipped his knife back in his belt and placed both hands on the goose-pimpled monk's scrawny throat, thumbs inward. "Be silent, Brother, and I'll stop short a' killing you." His grip tightened. "When you awaken, give no alarm. There are men beyond the compound wall this very moment, with weapons trained on you." A convenient lie. Omer had no idea where Rubinsser's men might be, nor what weapons they might have, but Gnist obligingly kept silent and was soon unconscious. Omer pushed him back through the window and under the desk.

The three of them crawled past the other windows. As Yan passed by the open ones he heard the same dry voice: "—nor speak of these matters. When the situation is resolved, you will be called here again. Now you may go."

Yan crawled faster, motioning to the others for haste. Their plan depended on all three of them being inside and on the stairs before the meeting broke up. He jumped in through the landing window, floated across the tile floor feeling as light as milkweed fluff on a dying breeze, and dashed down the stairs. On the first landing he waited for the others to catch up.

"When the doors open," he gasped, out of breath, "walk down the stairs slowly. Let some of them pass, then mingle with them. Follow the ones in secular clothes—they'll be going directly outside the compound. Illyssa, stay with me—the monks go in pairs oftener than not. Om, if we get separated try for the old bindery. We can try to go over the wall tonight."

They heard voices above as the anteroom doors swung open. Omer hugged Yan quickly, then moved down the stairs ahead of the two robed "priests." Two well-dressed laymen clattered past in hard-leather shoes and tasseled jackets of mauve and purple silks, followed by a high-ranking priest with shimmering cyan appliqués on his cassock. Below the fourth level, two more men in ordinary dress passed them, then another priest. All seemed in a hurry to leave the oppressive stone hive, and none spoke.

Yan felt sure they were eager to get out and get their own irons into the fire of circumstance before it burned low once again. Idle chatter wasted time, and they had all been admonished not to discuss the information they had been given. Who were they? Why would the Church give information to laypersons? Were they spies, or relatives of influential monks? But no matter. Disorder within the Church would enhance the fortunes of some and destroy others. All were eager to save what they could while they held an advantage—the three fugitives not least among them.

By the time the second level was in sight, all were strung out in a rough line on the stairs, by ones and twos. Most of the churchmen left the stairway at the fourth and third levels. Those who continued departed through the wide first-floor doors now held open by Church Militant soldiers. Omer passed by them without eliciting a glance. Yan experienced a moment's panic when the push of others behind him and Illyssa forced them past the door to the lowest level. If the soldiers didn't let the two of them by, he knew the way to Asmot Darro's territory below, but they would have to get back to that door. He allowed himself a deep breath when the guards let them pass unremarked.

Once off the stairs, the crowd broke into smaller groups according to their different destinations. Omer was ahead of them. They passed through more guarded doors, into a wide arcade with a vaulted ceiling almost lost in darkness above. Yan recognized the curving wall of the central tower from Hant's charts.

Some departees went right, but Omer took the left passage, leading to the east exit of the Cathedral, a public one opening onto the streets of Innis. As an Apostate Islander, Yan had eaten sausages and conversed with acolytes before that very gate.

If all went well, Rubinsser's men would be expecting them. But he didn't know if they were within a planned time bracket, as the sun had set and he had heard no bells in the Cathedral.

He followed Omer's lead. Illyssa came up behind him and took his hand. Here's one monk I wouldn't mind cuddling with, he mused irrelevantly, his good spirits bubbling over. He no longer felt trapped or deadened by the enormous weight of brick, tile, and stone which had been squeezing him like a huge gloved hand. And he was thinking of Illyssa: now, perhaps, there would be time to find out if his attraction to her was reciprocal. The prospect of getting to know her better was as exciting as the sight of stars ahead of them as they passed through the two-story doors into the free, fresh air of the city.

Yan had one more tense moment when two dark-clad men appeared from the shadows and matched their pace to Omer's. When Omer put an arm over one's shoulder and inclined his head to talk with him as they walked, Yan knew they were Rubinsser's men. He was impressed. The closed and shuttered shops told him that they had missed the meeting time by an hour, but still Omer had been picked up right outside the Cathedral. Thank whatever gods there are, he thought, that the Church's minions aren't so efficient. Lunnon is a lucky man to be so well served.

When a small cowled figure in brown homespun pushed between him and Illyssa, he saw light reflect from a pair of spectacles.

"Ha! Quick in, quick out. Good. New friend, eh? Pretty friend, Hant thinks. A real girl, Hant sees. No tiptoe fairy."

"Hant! I never thought I'd be happy to hear your mockery. Illyssa, meet Brother Hant, priest, pickpocket, and master spy." The three of them walked arm in arm for several blocks until Hant steered them into a side street where a cloth-covered wagon waited. They found Omer already inside. After a word with the driver, Hant faded into the shadows. The driver clucked to his horse, and they were off.

Yan recognized the tents and bare dirt of the slave market as the wagon passed next to the creek. He thought he saw the watchtower where they had hidden. It seemed that weeks had passed since then; his time sense had been distorted by the fast, tense pace, by dark depression and disturbed sleep. Peering out, he had determined that they were almost around the north side of the Cathedral compound when Omer drew his attention. He held up the sack with the notebooks in it and Yan made a quick inventory of its contents. Everything was there, complete and unharmed.

Yan and Omer changed into ordinary clothes in the wagon and Illyssa turned her embroidered shirt inside out, exposing its plain green lining. Out of the corner of his eye Yan watched her, catching more than a glimpse of slender shoulders and pert breasts. An electric jolt, like static in a boat's rigging before a storm, surged through his groin, making him shudder.

When she stuck her tongue out at him, he blushed, but was relieved. Aware of his interest, she was neither angry nor frightened. Had she perhaps taken longer than necessary to arrange the garment and put it back on? The only light in the wagon was behind him. He realized that she must have night vision far superior to his own, to have seen his eyes on her. Or had she only guessed he was looking—or hoped he was?

Their driver pulled his horse to a halt across from the stone inn where they had stayed that first night, and the three of them walked across the bridge arm in arm, feeling as if all danger were past. They agreed that morning was soon enough to rehash their adventures, promising themselves a whole day to do so, and to plan their course from there on. Rubinsser had rented them a room. "I'm surprised that he didn't rent one with three beds," Yan said, laughing. "He seems to know everything else—I'm almost surprised he didn't know we'd be bringing a friend."

By the time the two men found the window with its balcony, and had pissed over its edge into the creek below, Illyssa was sprawled across one of the two beds, sound asleep. Omer shrugged his shoulders and smiled at her diminutive form. "Friends always, eh, Yan? Fight together, sleep together. Just don't crowd me too much. I'm an old man, you know."

Sometime in the morning, before the sun was fully risen, Yan awoke with Omer's elbow in his face. Illyssa's bed was empty and one of the towels shelved by the door was missing, so he took over the empty bed and slept until noon.

Asmot Darro surveyed his new accommodations through tear-blurred eyes. The gloom was relieved only by flickering candles and the glowing brazier beyond his iron cage. Clothed only in his fat, goose pimples, and blood, he was thoroughly chilled. He both craved and feared the brazier's heat.

Stretched over the stone table beyond, the skinny priest, Darro's companion in misery, was again being entertained by the inquestor. His howls of agony had long since diminished to grunts and moans. Even the bouts with whip and hot irons no longer drew screams. Surely, Darro thought, the poor fellow has told all he knows. No man could withstand such harsh treatment without yielding.

Darro watched the writhing shadows on the far wall, screening their images through a chaotic mind in which black, bubbling terror vied with sick desire. When the Indic tired of using that unresponsive meat, it would be Darro's turn on the block. But to his own horror, and in spite of his fear, Asmot Darro maintained a continual and impressive erection.

CHAPTER THIRTEEN

Fourteen years the slave of Samel,
Ilse, in honor, raised Martina,
Teaching her the names and stories
Pledged that final night in Innis.

Child no longer, Ilse's daughter
Went to Samel's bed and there
Conceived a son of blood redoubled,
Carrying the Gift of Seeing.

Excerpted from "The Women's Song," from *Folktales of the Bamian Highlands*, Chapter VII, "Cryptic Tales & Nonsense-songs."

"I think we've gained time t' breathe," Omer said over a candle-warmed pot of kaf, "but when th' ruckus dies down it mayn't be easy t'leave Innis. I say we leave now, and talk when we're on th' open sea. The Apostate Isles're two days' sail at most, even with th' wind against us."

"Sail in what? Our noble rowboat?" Yan was skeptical.

"Half our journeying's passed t' th' music a' your snores, P'fesser. Are you sure you're na' still home dreaming all this?" Wearing a great grin, Omer paused to let Yan stew before he explained. "Illyssa and I went shopping while you slept half th' day. We made a side trip t' th' harbor, where a sloop caught my eye—a fast, pretty craft tha' belonged t'a merchant lost a' sea two years gone by. She hasn't sold, being a pleasure boat, but she's seaworthy and looks as fast as a gull."

"Ha! You left me sleeping so you could sneak around looking at boats," Yan exclaimed, "and now you've fallen in love with some leaky apple crate." Seeing that his jibe had dug deeper than he'd intended, he squeezed Omer's shoulder. "You're the sailor, Om. When do we leave?"

"Morning." Omer was appeased. "Illyssa's going with us as far as th' Apostates, at least. Maybe you can sweet-talk her into sticking with us further on."

Yan was taken aback. Remembering what she had said before they had escaped from the cell, he had assumed that it was settled: they would all travel together. He looked at her with hurt in his gaze. "Why? I thought you'd agreed to stay with us."

"I was upset and frightened. Now, when I think about the danger to both of you if I brought you to my people, I'm more afraid than ever." Her eyes would not meet his.

"I don't understand. What would happen to us?"

Omer, reading hurt and anger in Yan's stiff shoulders, interrupted him. "Lay off for a while, Yan. We'll ha' time later t' tell her more a' our own plans, give her time t' decide on her own."

Yan realized that Illyssa's knowledge must be woefully incomplete, pieced together from brief, clandestine conversations in the cell, and from her questioning by the Senior. Besides, the "trick" with the padlock—however unreal it now seemed in the clear afternoon sunlight—had left her quite vulnerable. Considering her people's xenophobia and her own experiences with foreigners so far, even her agreement to sail with them as far as the Apostates could be interpreted as a measure of desperation, not trust.

Yan's unease had no single cause. He wanted Illyssa to stay because he was attracted to her. That was straightforward. But she was his key to the witches, too, and that reeked of callousness. He ordinarily scorned "pragmatic" men for whom others were only means, but now . . . the stakes had been upped. He was no longer an itinerant scholar, sniffing posies in passing, with no real objective or plan. Nor was he a mere fugitive, seeking knowledge only to save his pale, northern skin. Yan was surprised to discover that Innis had made a driven man of him. He wanted more than mere knowledge: he wanted to change the world.

Ferosin could not be allowed to continue their millennial hoax. Men *could* fly between the stars. What stopped them now was malevolent alien greed and a corrupt Church that had sold humanity's birthright for temporal gain. The Church had to be brought down. Ferosin were bound to have exploitable weaknesses. The witches, with their bees, had found one; were there others? He would not allow the reticence of a frightened girl, or the xenophobia of her people, to stop him. If the witches had other tricks, he had to know. And if they in truth had a starship, or knowledge of such ships, he had to know.

I'm thinking like a general, he realized, or like Omer must have once. I need knowledge now for practical reasons, and I *will* have it. Knowledge? No, what I need is "military intelligence." I have to know everything about my enemy. I need to know what weapons exist to set against him, what terrain I must fight him on—and how to get there. "Aya," he finally agreed. "We do have a great deal of talking ahead of us. I hope it's an easy sail."

They used up the remaining daylight recovering the gold from its watery hiding place and selling the small boat to a fisherman. Purchase arrangements for the sloop were concluded by lamplight. Yan did not get to see it until afterward.

Sea Serpent, as gold-leaf letters on her transom proclaimed her, was a decked sloop with a small cockpit aft. High coamings sweeping back from her low deckhouse hinted that she was intended to sail with her deck awash, and that she would probably point well into the wind. Her mast was tall for a boat of her size, and her running rigging was simple. Omer explained that she would carry a triangular mainsail with no gaff, with a choice of three foresails, one large enough to overlap the mast when sheeted in. He claimed it was an ancient configuration whose virtues were speed and good performance in light air. She would be swift because of her oversized foresail, the seaman explained, in spite of the tall, narrow main her stubby boom would carry. Also, she was shaped more like a fish than a bathtub.

The seller's agent allowed them to sleep aboard. As a precaution against their unannounced departure, she was rafted between two other boats. The agent had a token payment, but Yan was unwilling to release any of the telltale gold until the last moment. Perhaps churchmen would trace it back to this mooring eventually, but once out on the Inland Sea, the chances of pursuit would diminish as the last hills sank below their wake.

That night Yan dreamed again, a mélange of things remembered and events that never were. His dreams were ordinarily forgotten when he awakened; this one remained clear from its beginning to its conclusive end:

The stone house was deep in evening shadow of aged elms, and portico lanterns painted wavering ovals of orange light on the clean-dressed stone. His bag was heavy across his shoulder. Strange, a part of him thought. Why am I leaving home at dusk? It's too dark to ride. There's Father. He looks so old.

"You're all ready, eh?" the elder Bando asked gruffly, at a loss for further words. Yan's horse stamped its readiness to be off.

"Aya, Pa. Ready as I'll ever be." What can I say? It would have been easier to slip away without this farewell, with a note and a promise to write later. I even have the note in my pack. He tossed his bag up behind the saddle and strapped it down, sweeping a stray tear away while his back was turned.

"We'll miss you, Yan." Not *I'll* miss you. He can't say that. He's as trapped by his own fears as I am by mine. What is he really afraid of?

"I know you will, Pa. Let Ma know that, will you? She already knows, I suppose. But if you tell her, she won't feel so alone." See how he resists even that small token of weakness? I wonder if he'll say anything? Why? What makes him so tight?

"I'll try, Son. Will you come home after harvest time? She'd like that."

"No, Pa. I won't be back. You and I both know it." He'll slip into cheap pleasantries if I let him. For all his cards-on-the-table bluntness, he'd still take the easy way out.

"I don't understand you, Yan. But I suppose you know what you must do."

Yan felt a rush of anger. Damn him! He's pushed me out, couldn't wait to be rid of me, and now he wants me to absolve him, to make it *my* burden. Why can't he admit how relieved he'll be when I'm gone? But anger gave way to understanding. He's afraid of me. He knows what I am, and he's terrified. Why? He's living a lie. They all were: all the uncles and grandfathers who were never mad were not free of the trait. They were only lucky. Lucky, and good liars. What a battle it must be to live with such a lie, to wake up every morning and tell himself he's still sane. At least I know what I am. Perhaps I live a lie, too, hiding my madness from the world, but I don't have to lie to *myself*.

The revelation swept his anger aside like a futile crab in heavy surf, and the emptiness it left behind was soon filled with new emotion: astonishment mixed with . . . pity? How controlled he is. He's pushing me aside as if he'd never sired me. I don't have that control. I might break loose, and if I did, it would force him to acknowledge the source of my madness in his own loins, his blood. He's not strong enough for that. It would kill him.

That was the final truth of the dream. Yan soared for long moments on rising currents of elation and understanding. It's not me who's weak. It's not me who's afraid. I am strong. I know what I am and I can live with it. I have lived with it. "Aya, Father. I know what I must do," he said gently. "I don't fit in here. My life lies elsewhere." Yan laid a hand on his father's thinning shoulder, feeling the age-shrunken muscles there fill with new strength. Like a priest, he thought, I've absolved him of his sin. Now his life can go on.

Yan swung up in the saddle. He'd get no parting hug from the frightened old man. But he understood why, now, and his pain eased. His father looked small from Yan's perspective in the saddle. The tall stone portal dwarfed him even more when Yan reined in by the road for a final parting wave.

The three escapees arose before dawn to take on fresh food and water. Rubinsser paid them a visit. Omer counted out five tablets of yellow gold and wrapped them in soft leather. Lunnon would be well paid. Omer smiled, raised an eyebrow at Yan, who nodded back, and then handed a sixth chip to Rubinsser for his own part in things.

They did not eat breakfast until they were under way, with the low morning sun angling beneath the boom. *Sea Serpent* cut crisply through long swells. They sailed on a broad reach with a light easterly breeze, and Omer said that they were making good time and were sailing almost directly toward the Apostate Isles. They might sight land before the next morning.

Both men talked enthusiastically of their discoveries. Innis had indeed been a fruitful stopover, and though still without a radio, they felt their goals had been realized. They were able to make sense of much that had puzzled them before. Illyssa listened thoughtfully. She seemed bemused, whether by the extent of their knowledge or its gaps. Yan brought out the notebooks and read anecdotes to her. The ensuing discussion lasted until sunset, then died with the wind. Their pace slowed to a glide across glassy water, trailing a wake that smoothed out behind them. No other sails had been seen all day.

"So you believe that my people, with their uncommon talents, are direct descendants of star travelers," Illyssa summed up. "But the *genes* originated here on Earth, I think." She shrugged. The sweet motion of her shoulders and the way her breasts rose slightly tantalized Yan, taunting him with the knowledge that she might soon be gone. "I wish I could tell you more, but I've already said—and done—more than can be forgiven. I'm afraid of what will happen when I return. If the old women who keep our history *would* talk with you, it's possible you might learn more, but outsiders have never brought us anything but harm, so you wouldn't be trusted."

"I'll still have to try," Yan replied. "The Church has destroyed so much of the past already. The knowledge left needs to be built upon. I owe it to Lazko to further his dream—and witches' were an important part of it. Besides, we're free of the ferosin for almost five years, if the Senior can be believed. There's no telling what may happen when they return. They may destroy all of us this time, and we're helpless as babes. Five years is hardly time to find out how to save a world."

"I'll do what I can, Yan, when we get there. Now I'm going to bed."

But Yan was satisfied. Her words implied that she would continue to travel with them.

Even with almost no wind, they made headway during the night, and before the sun cleared the horizon Illyssa saw a gray line of coast to the east. "North Island," Omer identified it. "We made good time." He thumped the deck with all the affection a landsman might show a favorite horse. "She'd be no good for fishing or hauling, but how sweetly she sails!" They coasted southwest for an hour before Omer pointed toward shore. "We go in there. It's no harbor t' brag about, but if you want t' stretch your legs a mite . . ."

Yan and Illyssa thought that was a good idea. Yan had decided to start another notebook describing the peoples and places he visited, and the Apostates would provide him with his first opportunity for scholarly observation. Perhaps he would write of Pittsburg and Innis later.

Until the day before, most of Illyssa's travels had been in closed wagons or ship cabins without windows, or hooded like a monk, seeing only the trail ahead. Though eager to get back to her familiar mountains, she dreaded the thought of having done so without seeing everything of interest along the way. Free and with friends, her spirits bubbled like winter cider, infecting her companions with partylike gaiety as they prepared to go ashore. She made a special attempt to tease Yan out of his scholarly reserve. He was attractive in a pale, gangly way, and she'd already had one very private fantasy about him. Though he was stuffy, she'd caught glimmers of his other self on occasion, and his boyish discomfiture when she had caught him peeping in the wagon had been enchantingly innocent. She was sure her own folk were much less inhibited than his. No longer a boy by a decade, his behavior was as retiring as that of a mountain youth just entering puberty. She sighed, vowing to change *that* if she stayed aboard past the Apostates.

Their outing ashore was pleasant, though the Apostate harbor was a less-than-enjoyable place. The islanders' hard-won freedom had its costs; decades of war with Church and Church followers, including former aristocrats such as Yan had impersonated, had created a fortress mentality among the survivors. The town *was* a fortress: tall stone walls surrounding a hundred acres of closely packed two- and three-story houses and shops. The townsmen's mouths were as tightly guarded as their walls, and Yan was reduced to describing the town itself for his journal.

The buildings were fireproof brick and stone—sometimes both—with little thought of architectural continuity. Windows were small and few, confined to the upper stories, and streetside doors were uniformly plain and heavily built. Though no exile troops had trod Apostate soil for years, the islanders were prepared for the eventuality: should the enceinte be breached, each house was defensible against troops who attained the narrow streets. Both islands were so defended, and every harbor had such a town. Granaries and warehouses were within walls, and even farmers lived with stockpiles of oils and poisons at hand to pollute wells, denying the enemy even the least resource.

After a shorter visit than Yan had anticipated, they decided it was still a fine day for sailing, and they were soon back aboard *Serpent* with letters to deliver on South Island. Once beyond the harbor Omer began singing a sailors' chant. Yan and Illyssa soon learned the simple melody and repetitive lyrics, and then improvised harmonies; the disastrous clashes that occurred were cause for much laughter. They matched their phrases to the plunge of the sprightly vessel on steepening swells:

Pull 'er up and tie 'er down,
We'll drop 'er off in our home town
And sell 'er for a piece of gold
T' buy our ale when we're too old
T' sail upon the Inland Sea,
Or drop a hook in Burum's lee.
So heave 'er up and stow 'er tight,

We're leaving with the morning's light.
So heave 'er up and stow 'er tight,
We're leaving 'fore the sun is bright.

Omer claimed that "she" was a wine tun from Cansi, or perhaps a bale of rare silk. Illyssa insisted—suggestively, she hoped—that the subject of the song was an obese slavewoman on her way to market in Bama, where copious flesh and minimal intelligence were allegedly of more value than other charms. She even got Yan to abandon his north-country prudery and laugh at the imaginary sight of enormous buttocks popping through the squares of a cargo net. Still, Yan did not follow up. Too bad, Illyssa thought. Even Omer seemed to catch my message.

The wind held steady until after dark. Stars moved back and forth over the masthead as *Serpent* bobbed and plunged. Omer went to his bunk, but Yan had no desire to be belowdeck while the craft leapt and cavorted in the following breeze, and one trip down the companionway ladder was enough for Illyssa. She popped back out the forward hatch and thereafter kept her eyes fixed on the horizon, the only stable thing in sight. Yan had experienced such swells and winds aboard the *West Wind*, so he had not even considered trading his still-settled stomach for the dubious comfort of a swaying bunk, however soft.

They sat silently as the wind died and the swells diminished. Omer found them asleep, huddled close against the nighttime chill. He shook out a blanket and tossed it over them, then untied the tiller. Changing wind patterns, and the smells of wood smoke and barnyards, told him that South Island was only a few miles off, but he would not be able to find port by moonlight. He continued to sail offshore until dawn, rounding the southern cape and heading east toward Shebbol, the capital of the island nation.

When Yan awoke, Omer was surprised to see him get up quietly, without awakening Illyssa. He could not imagine himself being so restrained at that age. When he raised an eyebrow, Yan blushed hotly. "I don't want her to feel pressured—after all, she's alone on a boat with two men," he whispered.

"I think she's helpless t' make sense out a' a great northern lout who treats her like furniture," Omer muttered more softly than Yan could hear.

They did not linger in Shebbol. Yan delivered the mail to the harbormaster, then scouted the diminutive waterfront—fragile docks and oil-soaked catwalks which would burn quickly, leaving no foothold for aggressors. Just another fortified town, he mused. People trading off the privilege of walking free and without fear for the freedom of worshiping their own Earth-born God. Even knowing the sham that was the Star Church, he wondered if it was a good bargain for the islanders, and he returned to the sloop with deepening resolve to see his world free of the puppet religion and its chitinous black abominations.

The wind was out of the southwest all day, so they sailed on close reaches, or sheeted in with the deck almost continually awash. There was no time for conversation. Omer was in his element and, in spite of initial anxiety when a gust heeled them over until water rushed by the coamings, Yan and Illyssa were exhilarated as they slashed through the rolling water at great apparent speed.

Shebbol was on the east coast, so the first hours' sailing retraced the course Omer had followed the night before. They continued west, and a thick overcast enveloped them. They were out of sight of land until dusk, and no sails were sighted off the south Tenzie coast. They sailed through the night.

Tenzie, the land Athel of Roke had retaken with alien aid. Following his devastating conquest, the common folk of the land had turned their rage upon surviving witches and Christians, blaming them for the death and destruction. Like hostages and torture victims, they adopted the values and faith of their conqueror with great fervor; even now, with Athel's name almost forgotten, they were still the backbone of the Church. Of all the lands the Church controlled, Tenzie provided the greatest single portion of revenue through tithes, bequests, and taxes. Tenzian priests and scholars filled the ranks of the Brotherhood. Omer steered well away from the Tenzian shore.

At some undefined time they passed beyond Tenzie and entered waters claimed by Gram, a narrow peninsula free of Tenzian domination only because inhabitants were few and had little of value. The peninsula jutted westward into the Inland Sea, a skinny finger pointing at Senloo below the horizon. The shore was a line of gray-green hills unbroken by harbors.

The wind held until after sundown and no one rested. Small refuge was had by huddling tightly against the companionway hatch, the only spot free of spray. They rounded Gram and ran before diminished wind through the night. Yan thought "running" was an absurd term for their rocking, wallowing progress, with the mainsail so far out from the hull that the short boom seemed ready to dip into each swell. Omer replaced the jib with a larger one that swelled fatly opposite the main, held with a light pole. Though it was off their course southward, they prudently decided to put in for water and supplies at Gram, the city that gave its name to the duchy. The next leg of the journey would take three days—a week if the winds were foul. The entire distance paralleled the Tenzie coast again, so they planned to stay several hours' sail offshore, out of sight of land.

Illyssa was happy to avoid the country where she had spent weeks in closed wagons or sweltering under a hood. And neither Omer nor Yan had forgotten the lesson of Pittsburg, nor excluded the possibility that even a village temple might possess a radio. Yan wondered if the churchmen had radios that transmitted words, not semaphore code. It was too much to hope that with the ferosin incapacitated, all communications would be cut.

The city was at the head of a deep-cut bay, a bright accent on the otherwise gloomy coast. It sparkled in the clear morning light like ivory dice on a cloth of dark pines, oaks, and contorted gray rock. Boats filled the harbor or were drawn up on sandy beaches, and large schooners lined the wide stone wharves. Yan saw that the streets winding up steep rocky slopes, though narrow and roughly paved, were scrubbed clean. As they walked through the town—or climbed, for Gram was built entirely on the steep slopes that formed its harbor—his first impression was strengthened. No grass tufts pushed between the paving stones, and no dung or offal lay about. Flowers made splashes of gold, crimson, blue, and violet both in stone and wood troughs below wide, shuttered windows and cascading from espaliered vines on walls. Even the tints of the lime-washed houses varied only within a narrow range of tones, though every hue was represented. The result was a play of light like a watercolor with washes of fine pigment.

They dined in an open-air restaurant a quarter hour's climb up cobbled alleys. From their vantage at the edge of the uppermost terrace, the flat roofs of Gram stepped irregularly down to the sea. Parapets no longer concealed Gram's bustling activity: weaving, baking, sailmaking, cordwinding, and the countless tasks that make up the commerce of a healthy seaside town were spread out on the flat roofs. The sounds of voice and tool were attenuated in clear dry air, reaching them only as a tinkling whisper.

They ate fresh fish and bread hot from the oven, which they

smothered in pale sweet butter and washed down with water-clear wine, sweet without heaviness. Talk was inconsequential, a vehicle for holiday spirits, but when Illyssa asked their serving girl about a particular large dark building, the conversation darkened. The edifice departed from the pattern in Gram, having no wash of color over its gray stone walls. Its steep, slated roof was more appropriate to a rainy northern clime.

"That's the Church of the Sailors," the girl said. "No one goes there but foreigners. My father says it's a silly faith. Who wants their soul to be taken from Earth when they die? I'd prefer to be reborn when the Wheel turns, not carried off to a far place." Her gesture encompassed city, lush fields, vineyards, and azure ocean darkening to emerald with distance and depth.

"The Star Church," Yan stated flatly. "If only foreigners use it, why is it still here?"

"There are visitors. The brown priests hardly ever come out in the sun, even for festival. Buggering each other in the dark, my father says." She giggled. "He says they're spies for Innis and Roke—big cities out there." Her gesture took in most of the southern ocean, opposite the direction of either city. "Our duke has to let them stay, Father says."

"So they've a foothold here," Omer reflected as the girl walked off. "Gram's never been conquered—na' by Athel or since. I hope we're na' seeing th' beginning of its fall."

"Can't we warn them? If we told their duke about Innis and the Sons of Pharos . . ." Illyssa sounded plaintive.

Omer shook his head. "Who'd believe a tale a' unearthly things who've manipulated us for two thousand years? Giant black bugs? Look around. They've made heaven here. They've na' even th' experience a' conquest t' make them fearful."

"It is hard to believe. Everything is so pretty, so calm and sane. The rest seems like a bad dream—crazy priests, slavers, all of it." She shuddered expressively.

"Yes. And disease, flies, and shit," Yan added. "Torture and war. I don't think these people would listen. My fear is that no one will, that five years will be up before we can convince anyone of the danger. Your people may be our only hope."

Illyssa regarded him sadly and shrugged.

"There may be other hopes. Gram isn't typical," Omer said. "It's been too isolated too long. It'll go along like this until some king or Senior sees something he wants, and then . . . *psst*! Gone. But other lands, other princes, have no love a' th' Brotherhood. They don't control the whole world—yet."

They ate a confection of lemons, honey, and cream frozen into soft ice. The delicious stuff was made in a machine that made its own cold, and Yan got the owner of the establishment to show it to him. Though the man used it, he could not explain its workings—which, Yan reflected, was typical of the intellectual state of the world. The innkeeper's grandfather had bought such a machine, and that one had been repaired and parts duplicated for almost a century, but no one knew what "magic" made it work. Yan deduced that a small spirit engine drove an iron pump, which caused fluid to flow through copper coils and a sawdust-insulated box. An ammonia odor permeated the shed. Yan sketched the machine carefully, labeling materials and components. He thought he understood the principle of the device—or devices: motor, pump, and condenser—but not knowing what might prove critical to its function, he omitted no detail.

"There's so much to rediscover," he moaned on his return to their table. "Think of the knowledge that must still exist in such out-of-the-way places. The Church suppresses scientific thought and method to gain power, the universities for profit, and the world sinks deeper in squalor and ignorance with every morsel that's lost. Consider this machine. People sicken and die from spoiled food. Fishermen's catches rot before they're sold. Is the Church's plan, and the ferosins', to keep us so busy grubbing and laboring that we can never challenge their mastery, or afford the time to learn how?"

Omer and Illyssa agreed. Together they fantasized the creation of a great compendium of knowledge, a body of scholars and scouts roaming the world in search of lost devices and books, adding them to an immense storehouse of knowledge open to all. Together they cursed the Brotherhood and its alien masters as the instruments of Earth's decline.

As pleasant as Gram was, they were still reluctant to linger long. Weeks from their destination, they knew that the passing hours could not be regained; they put to sea in midafternoon.

By their second day out, Yan became aware of a change in his relationship with Illyssa. On previous legs of the journey she had kept close to him. They'd spent nights huddled beneath the stars like small children, and shared turns at watch. Yan had been careful not to press his growing desire. She had nowhere to run on the open sea, and he did not want her to leave at the next port of call, so he had decided to wait. But the way things were turning out, his chance would never come. For three nights Illyssa had kept her own watches and then had gone below.

At first Yan attributed her behavior to the calm, oily waters. *Serpent*'s motion was gentle. Disorientation and seasickness were no longer a problem as the long, easy swells imparted a relaxing motion to the sloop. But he soon realized she was not avoiding him on watch alone. Her jokes and bubbling laughter were now reserved for Omer, and she changed her idle waking hours to match the old sailor's watches.

Yan chided himself for churlishness when he grew jealous of his friend. On the rare occasions when she and Yan were both about at the same time, she sat far forward with her feet on the bow rail, staring at approaching seas for hours at a stretch. At other times she would not converse with either man, defeating all their attempts at small talk with brief, flat replies.

The two men found plenty of time to plan and speculate. They had no maps or charts of the seas they now sailed, but Omer's decades of experience on the Inland Sea and beyond enabled him to sketch their proposed route in adequate detail for Yan, who filed the rough charts in the back of his journal. In spite of Yan's interest in the discussions, Omer frequently had to wave a hand in front of his eyes to break him from a spell of cloud-gazing.

At noon on the fourth day out, Illyssa saw land and popped her head down the hatch to alert Omer. "If there's land ahead, we've sailed in th' wrong direction," he grumbled, rubbing sleep from his eyes. "I'll be up for a look." In a moment he was squinting into the glare. "Tha's no land, honeybee. It's a storm. We're in for rough weather. If it's na' too bad we'll make up time even running wi' bare poles. May end up in Tenzie in spite a' ourselves, though. Yan! Head up a bit. Storm's coming an' we'll need sea room."

Yan pushed the tiller over. The winch pawl clacked vociferously as Omer and Illyssa sheeted in sail, and the sloop seemed to jump ahead, pointing just south of the main mass of storm clouds. Estimating that the courses of storm and sailboat would intersect in two hours, Omer had Yan stretch canvas over the forward hatch grating and the deckhouse portholes. Illyssa went below to secure gear and supplies, then took the helm while Omer assembled ropes and spare sails into a drogue, a sea anchor that would keep the boat's bow safely pointed into the oncoming seas. "It's a good chance we'll need this," he commented. "If following seas 're too high we may have t' heave to. We'll want it ready." He measured rope and made quick splices, attaching the loose ends to deadeyes at bow and stern.

The remaining rope was coiled in the cockpit, and the lashed-up sail laid on top of it. After last-minute checks on their readiness, they relaxed as best they could.

The storm continued to build on their right and ahead. Tall white cumulus piled higher and higher, soon covering half the sky. Below it, darker masses advanced successively from the sea's edge and the visible horizon drew nearer minute by minute.

"May as well drop sails now," Omer ordered. "No sense reefing. This's going t' be th' grandfather a' all storms. Bring 'er into th' wind, honeybee. We'll be running with th' storm jib." Tension crackled in his voice like the sound of the raindrops now slapping the deck. Daylight was smothered in the dense cloud, a featureless expanse of gray that matched the leaden sea. The wind died as they lowered the mainsail, and when the tiny storm jib was raised, it flapped idly without filling.

"If we can keep 'er headed a few degrees south a' east we'll run out th' storm; otherwise, there's danger a' running aground in Tenzie. Good luck'll have us in th' sound north a' Burum in no time 't'all."

The raindrops became larger, angling from the west. Forceful drops stung their exposed skin. Air quickened in gusts, and *Serpent* swung off the wind. Omer took the tiller and motioned the others to go below, but Yan shook his head and sat facing aft to watch the storm as best he could through the beating rain. Illyssa also stayed above, but sat on the opposite side of the companionway, pointedly avoiding Yan's squinting glances.

At Omer's insistence, Yan finally went below to rest and dry off. He'd have to relieve the old sailor at the helm in an hour or so. The rain had turned cold, and even a hardened seaman would not be able to tolerate it for long without oilskins and warmer clothing than they possessed. Later, Omer would shake his head and wonder aloud if he was becoming too old and soft in the head to command even a cockleshell like *Serpent*, having overlooked such an important thing—but as it turned out, it didn't matter. Yan had not been below for more than half an hour, fighting uneasy feelings in his gut brought on by *Serpent*'s motion, when Illyssa stuck her head in the hatch.

"Omer's going to put out the sea anchor," she yelled over the wind. "He wants you to drop the jib when he's ready. Go forward belowdecks and use the small hatch to reach the fife rail. It's too rough to get forward up here."

Yan went forward. When he attempted to open the hatch, the canvas cover he'd put over it held it down—he'd tied it wrong.

He pushed up hard. The wet lacing stretched and pulled tight, and a shower of water, half salt and half rain, drenched his arm and shoulder. The hatch opened only a few inches. He staggered aft, trying without success to anticipate the boat's rolls and twists, and cracked his forearm painfully against a bunk. *Serpent* plunged and rolled in nauseating double motion. Something was beating on the small vessel like a drum, with a rapid bang, thud, bang.

Swallowing bile and tightening his gut muscles, he fumbled in the cook box for a knife. Holding it well away from himself, he crawled toward the hatch. *Serpent* rose beneath him and kept rising. At the giant wave's crest a sideways gust heeled her violently and Yan was thrown hard against the boat's ribs. His back and shoulder were numb. Nothing was broken, but he feared neither he nor *Serpent* could take much more knocking about. He struggled forward.

Finally, the hatch was overhead. He pushed head and uninjured shoulder against the hatch until it opened a crack, then sawed at the lashing. It snapped, but the hatch was still not free. He cut the cords on the opposite side. It flew open and he was inundated. Blinking cold salt water from his eyes, he groped for the sheet. He felt a rapping on his sore back and heard Illyssa's voice, muffled and faint, from below.

"Just cut the sheet, then the halyard. Omer says let the jib blow away." Yan squinted. Which one was the sheet? He could see the tiny sail pushed out ahead, and he tried to follow the ropes back to the fife rail behind him. Three lines were belayed there. What would happen if he cut the wrong one? He shrugged. May as well find out—I can't see to tell. He sawed at the closest cord, and when it was halfway cut through, it parted. The little cloth triangle straightened with a loud clap, then droned and clattered in the wind. That had been the sheet. When he cut the second line, the sail flopped down over the bow. That was the halyard.

Serpent lost headway and Yan felt her swing sideways. Rain came first from his right, then, as the boat swung around, beat directly into his face. He felt a jerk through the hull and, through a gray curtain of rain and spray, saw a line spring from the water ahead. Omer had gotten the drogue over the side, and it was dragging ahead of them—no, not ahead, because they were making sternway—it was downwind of them, and the calculated lengths of line at bow and stern held *Serpent*'s bow to wind and the enormous cresting waves. The drumming noise had stopped.

The water at port and astern was still rain-beaten, but no longer torn and contorted by wind. *Serpent* created a patch of shelter alee, and slithered backward into it over each wave. Her sleek bow parted the white-edged crests to windward. It looked as if each glassy-faced mountain of water would crush the boat. Each time she sped down a rain-chopped following slope, Yan was sure she would keep on plunging until she was buried at the bottom of the trough, but somehow she kept bow and stern out of the water.

When he felt a tug on his pants leg, he was no longer too anxious about their survival to drop down into the cabin. He pulled the hatch cover over against the strong wind that tried to twist it off its hinges, and Omer reached up and tied it tight. It was almost quiet in the cabin, and Omer spoke without raising his voice. "Nothing t' do but wait 'er out, now. We're about sixty miles offshore, I think. No worry for a while—if th' wind lets up in six, seven hours we'll sail south a' Tenzie."

"And if it keeps up?" Illyssa asked. "Then what will happen?"

Omer chuckled—feebly, Yan thought. "Then we'll all walk ashore." Or die on the rocks, in the surf, Yan suspected.

They settled down in darkness to wait out the storm. *Serpent*'s motion was regular now, but she still rose with each wave, tilting at the crests and sliding sickeningly into the troughs. The air in the cabin grew thick and steamy, and water rushed back and forth beneath the sole. A cider jug rolled first one way and then the other, rumbling and clunking. They watched it, but no one made any effort to pick it up. Its cork was gone and the smell of cider added a sickly tang to the thick atmosphere. They dozed fitfully. Once Yan crawled to the soil bucket and hunched over it, vomiting dryly, then sat limply against the damp hull with his empty gut pointlessly spasming. He thought Omer went past him, and he felt a change in the light, as of the companionway opening, but he had no energy to open his eyes. Later, he stumbled to a bunk. Had *Serpent*'s motion changed? It had not seemed as hard to move about. He slept again.

A wisp of cool salt air tickled his face and nostrils, breaking through the acid reek of sweat, cider, and vomit. The hatches were open, and gray light streamed in. He pulled himself upright. Illyssa was still asleep, and Omer was not to be seen. Yan stumbled to the companionway, climbed to the cockpit, and knelt with his chin on the coaming, gazing at the verdigris expanse of rolling hills only a few miles away.

"Tenzie," Omer said from the deck above. "We won't have t' walk after all." He was lacing wet wrinkled canvas to the boom. It draped over the deck and almost into the water. The sea-anchor lines were coiled at Yan's feet.

"Storm's over, uh?" Yan mumbled dully. His mouth felt full of sponge and his tongue tasted like something unspeakable. "Wha' d'we do now?"

"Rest a bit. I'll get th' main up, get us moving offshore. Then we clean up. Shit bucket's kicked over and th' bilge's full a' puke. Pump's clogged with it, too. Your puke, you dip it out—tha's a sure cure for seasickness *next* time, anyway."

Yan moaned, but when he got moving he was surprised how fit he felt. He was lightheaded, but no trace remained of the nausea he had thought would never go away. After washing his sour mouth with salt water and then fresh, he steeled himself to the stink and went below to carry Illyssa up into the fresh air. She was only half-awake. Tenderly he wrapped her in a damp, clean blanket, then trailed his shirt in the water to slosh it off. Gently, he washed her forehead and eyelids with the shirt-tail, and she opened her eyes momentarily to meet his own.

She was so small and delicate. Her deep brown eyes glistened, and a peculiar expression flitted across her face. He kissed her forehead lightly and then stood up to go below, but she raised herself on his arm and pulled his head down to her. With her eyes wide open, she kissed him. Her lips were full and soft against his, and her tongue darted between them briefly. He held her tight against himself and felt the twin pressures of her small breasts; her nipples were like two hot coals against his chest. His swelling manhood pressed against his coarse trousers. He ignored the scratching and the rough, ill-sewn seam to press closer. She pushed a small hand between herself and Yan and slid it beneath his waistband. Grasping him firmly with a warm grip, she spoke for the first time: "Finally! I love you, too, silly. Now let's get this mess cleaned up."

Avoiding his clumsy grasp, she twisted away from him, as light as thistledown and as full of energy as ever, and ducked back into the cabin. "Pheeeooo! Here, Yan, start rinsing this out," he heard from below. A great lump of bedding and clothes mushroomed through the hatch. He held it over his persistent erection as he carried it to the rail. A quick, embarrassed glance let him know that Omer had not seen. He grinned stupidly at the floating blankets as he swished them about.

Within an hour, *Sea Serpent* was washed down inside and

out, and bailed almost dry. The sole boards were back in place, and they were sailing away from Tenzie on a broad reach, heeling more than usual and making leeway because of the blankets and clothes flapping from every stay and line. The sky was a uniform silver-gray and the ocean was slaty, with glassy swells. Yan still grinned like a schoolboy, and Illyssa favored both him and Omer with bright, white-toothed smiles, and hummed incessantly.

Asmot Darro was a free man. Broken in body, spirit, and rank within the Brotherhood, true—but free. No longer would he rule his small domain, or take his pick of choice new acolytes, but that was a small matter. He had seen Hell firsthand, and he was happy to be posted to a small rural parish as a subannu, an assistant clerk. He was alive, clothed, and not permanently damaged by his ordeal. That, he reflected with great satisfaction, was more than could be said for his companion in adversity, who even now held his jaw clenched to hold back his agony. "Where will you go?" Darro asked him. "Have you been given a posting?"

"I am now an aide to the Junior of a border town by the Mountain Freeholds," the gaunt, grim-faced man replied. "Though the hierarchs' torturers were free with me, my superiors in the Brotherhood have promoted me. As a Hand in the Order of Pharos, I will outrank the one I serve. That will be interesting. I myself will hunt witches, and teach them to die slowly. I will experiment upon them with drugs and instruments, and take my poor pleasure of them." His grimace revealed bloody gaps in his teeth.

Darro shuddered. Poor pleasures, indeed, considering what the fellow had lost of late. Had not the man had enough of torture and degradation? Had his mind snapped in the red-lit subbasement of the Cathedral, or was his evil mania a hallucination resulting from the pain-killing pills he ingested one after another?

Darro was relieved, when their paths parted at wharfside, that their brief relationship was at an end.

CHAPTER FOURTEEN

> In fifteen hundred years' wandering, one thread of continuity stretches across chasms, around mountains along our unplanned trail. We are the distaff side of our race. From us the thread unwinds. The Book of our God provides wool for our spinning. There are other fibers, too—history and biology. We rage at the slow progress of experiments, the length of generations, the intractability of genes; we demand answers to unanswerable questions.
>
> "Hope is the evidence of faith," the Book states, "the substance of things unseeable." We advise impatient ones to examine coincidence, to study the political and genetic accidents that have made us, to ponder the improbabilities of our continued existence, the unnatural strength of that single thread.
>
> *Essays on Education*, (20) Ludmilla (132), ca. 3420 C.R.

Following their accustomed watch schedule, Illyssa took the hours between supper and midnight. Omer was next, then Yan until breakfast. Shortly after sunset, having moped about the boat while Illyssa had the helm, Yan went below; *Serpent*'s motion was easy, and he would not get seasick. He sat on his bunk, not trying to doze, and made several trips to the companionway, always stopping himself before climbing up. Finally, feeling frustrated and ridiculous, he undressed and lay down, but no sleep came.

Above, Omer watched stars and glanced occasionally at Illyssa, who sat rigidly at the tiller instead of sprawling across the seat in her usual manner. "Nice night for sailing, eh? Na' enough wind t' have t' work a' it."

"Yes."

"Nice night t' watch th' stars and think a bit. Mull over th' high points a' life, eh?"

"I suppose so."

"Young woman might ha something else in mind?"

Illyssa looked up sharply. Omer was grinning, a gentle grin that crinkled the papery skin by his eyes. "Aya, I'm na' sleepy, little witch. I'll take your watch. Go see th' young fool, if he won't drag you below. I'll call you if th' wind rises." He sat down on the opposite side of the tiller and lifted her hand from the bar. Illyssa stood, rounded the tiller, plopped down on his lap, hugged him, and planted a wet kiss on his bald head. "Thank you, Papa Omer!" she said, darting for the companionway.

Her silhouette darkened the hatchway. Yan heard the swish of her coarse sailor's pants. "Illyssa, I—" One small hand covered his mouth while the other unbuttoned her shirt. He heard it fall, then sensed her movement as she knelt beside the bunk. The air seemed charged with Saint Elmo's fire, a tingle that made every hair stand on end. She replaced the hand over his mouth with her lips. A small nude breast brushed his arm, and he pulled her up beside him.

In the cockpit, Omer crossed one leg over the other, shook his head, and grinned again. Then he scowled at the bright, sharp stars. "*Papa* Omer, shit!"

"Could you get—I mean, what if you . . ." Yan stammered.

Illyssa smiled mischievously in the semidarkness. "Do you want to be a father?"

"No! I mean, I do someday, but—"

"I would bear your child, Yan. But that won't happen. I'm a 'witch.' I won't get pregnant until I choose, and I can't make that choice alone."

"I understand—I want to wait, too. I'm glad we won't have to worry, because I—" He reached for her again, and she pushed him down and swung her leg over him, kneeling. "—Want you again and again and . . ." She covered his mouth for the second time and moved on him slowly, smoothly timing her thrusting to the low, soft waves. Much later, they both slept.

Omer's hot black kaf, white glare, mauve shadings of the rising sun, and a freshening breeze greeted them on deck. The seaman blew out the fish-oil burner and stowed it, pouring the used grounds over the side. "I think I'll have a nap," he said, smiling. "Been up here all night. You know our course?"

Yan nodded wordlessly. He was almost becoming used to being tongue-tied. The color and intensity of his blush compared favorably with the luminous clouds on the eastern horizon. Omer patted Illyssa's cheek as he passed. "Papa Omer, shit!" he repeated.

"What was that about?" Yan asked when Omer had gone below.

"What was what about?" Her pure, innocent air mocked him. She giggled and would say no more.

Yan pondered what she had told him during the night. At the time, he had accepted the simplest meaning of her words, but now, thinking back on one comment, he had begun to doubt that he had understood her correctly. "Illyssa?"

"Hmmhh?"

"What did you mean about not making the choice yourself? Babies, I mean."

"I didn't want you to worry," she said, smiling mischievously. "Are you going to worry now?"

"I don't believe you. I love you, Illyssa—can't we trust each other?"

The plaintive note, and the openness in his clear blue eyes, melted her resolve. She looked first sad, then angry, but not at him. "God knows I don't *want* secrets between us, but I showed you more than I should have in Innis. I wasn't ready to go out in the world; I'm not an old woman with a lifetime of discipline. I was impetuous. I betrayed my people by what I—we—did with the lock, and I didn't even do that right; it wasn't supposed to burn. If I had been better trained, it would have just come open." She began to cry silently, keeping her hands over her face as she spoke. "My people have been hunted and killed for hundreds of years because of what we do. We have to keep secrets to stay alive. Don't you see how I've betrayed them?"

"Illyssa, I love you. I don't know your people at all, but I could never, never betray you. Don't you see *that*?"

"I . . . I understand that you wouldn't want to, but I can't tell you any more. Please don't ask."

"You've already said you have to go back to them, to tell them of changes in the Church, and of the ferosin. You did what you had to do." He moved closer, pulling her under his arm. "So you're not an old woman. How can they hold that against you? Why did they allow you to go? Whose fault was that?"

"Mine." Her voice was muffled by his shirt as she buried her face in his sleeve. "The choice was mine. Let's not talk about it anymore. I want to be happy now, while we can."

So they talked of trivial childhood things, of friends and pranks, parties, houses, and chores, bridging with words the chasm their bodies had already crossed.

That night, while a refreshed Omer kept the helm, they made love again. Afterward Illyssa changed her mind. "I want to tell you about us, Yan. I don't care what happens later."

In those dark hours, drawing memories from Others who haunted the recesses of her mind, she told him of her ancestors' trek from their downed starship, seeking a rumored "enlightened city" in the south, where their knowledge and talent might be used. She told him of capture by the sea earl Prahhl, weeping as if she truly remembered that black-hearted villain's division of his spoils—the star crew's menfolk sold west as laborers on Cansi's walls, and the women south into the harems of Burum. She told of the Oath made that last night in Innis' slave pens: like would seek like, though a thousand miles and years might separate them. She told of the women's vow to . . . remember.

Her people were gentle, she said, loving mankind, as their Book commanded, by healing wounds and diseases. Ailments of the mind and spirit were especially vulnerable to their ministrations. They lived high in hills and deep in mountain valleys. Few outsiders saw their farms or villages, but their reputation was known and, as happens when understanding is lacking, they were feared. Only the terminally ill and incurably insane were brought to them by relatives desperate enough to try a last resort. Patients were left at the border of the witches' land, a border everywhere known, seldom violated. Some returned to their families, healed, but with no memory of time's passing. Others never returned. Their empty clothes were returned in neat bundles, but no explanations were made.

"White witches," people called them. Why white? Illyssa did not know. In the north, white was good, black evil. Perhaps outsiders so named them because they practiced no evil. But in Burum, black was holy, white a funeral wrap, and "white witches" had been hated by Burum's kings for centuries. Illyssa was darker than Yan or Omer, and there had been black-skinned "white" witches once, so skin color had nothing to do with the name.

The witches believed they were different. Their healing talents supported that belief. They believed they possessed a unique combination of genetic structures of unspecified value to humankind. Only the elders knew the nature of those genes. Their witchcraft, they insisted, was comprised of traits intensified through breeding; it was not supernatural.

They were a tolerant folk, adhering to no fixed rules: "Live with whom you choose, worship as you please, do as you will, harming no others." They were hard, too: "Live as you choose," they said, "but bear no children; the elders decide whose children you will bear. Should you resist them, a day will pass without remembrance, and soon your body rhythms will change; you will be with child. Never ask who the father might be, for the elders answer in riddles. A man centuries dead? No man? What answers are those?" Mysterious genes took precedence over womanly love, over desire to look at a son and see a husband's features.

Perhaps the "white witches' " skin, darker than surrounding folks', hinted at a relationship with the peoples of Burum and Bama whence they had fled. If so, the heritage had been watered down. Their hair was finer, less kinky, and their skins varied from gold to light brown. Only rarely was a child born with ebony skin and tight-curled hair.

Once, seeking a key to their genetic puzzle, witch-folk left their mountain hideaways and became powerful in other nations, sitting on councils, teaching in universities. They ranged widely, seeking what they had lost, until they were driven back to the hills by evil men allied with devils not of Earth. Trapped, landbound, and isolated, only women whose breeding years were over sought the mysterious key in the outside world. None returned with answers. Few returned at all. There was another secret, too, a sacred place far to the north: the site of their origin, where the cycle of years would be completed, a gift given, an ancient oath fulfilled.

Long after Illyssa finished, Yan sat silently. She had answered some questions, but had raised others. The cabin was stuffy and hot. When they climbed on deck, Omer watched them go to the bow without speaking. He said nothing, willing to wait until they had something to say.

"You know I *must* talk with your elders. You know what the sacred site in the north is?"

"Yes," she replied softly, hesitantly. "A ship of space."

"They *must* talk with me. There has to be a way for an outsider to get in and see them, and still keep his mind and memory intact. Will you help me?"

"I'll try. You know that. But I love you, Yan. I want to go

somewhere like Gram to live and make babies and forget Pharos and starships. I don't have to go back. Perhaps we can send a message and not have to go ourselves."

"Perhaps, someday. But I'm driven, Illyssa. I can't stop now, can't promise you anything at all."

"I know." Tears glistened on her cheeks. "I'll help all I can. I'll beg them to see you. But I'm afraid. If you anger them, if what you know frightens them, I don't know what they'll do. What I did to that lock is nothing; healing is work, but destroying takes no effort at all."

He held her close. They were both shivering more than the cool air warranted. "Let's see if Omer will make kaf," he suggested. "We'll have to tell him what we plan to do."

They went aft, but kaf and talk were postponed. Omer estimated they were far enough south so that if they changed course now they would make good speed for the North Burum coast. Only when they settled on a new tack was there opportunity to outline their tentative plan. When they had finished, the older man pondered their idea.

"Nothing changes till we're north a' Chatoo. Then we go up th' Tenzie River past Nahks and th' big swamp. I'll be able t' keep a deck under me. But then it's mules and shanks. I should keep an eye on *Serpent* and let you go on ahead." That was a jest, but it had merit. Yan said as much, then explained what he meant to Omer, who was stung by Yan's willingness to leave him.

"If Illyssa's worst fears come true," Yan said, "then you'd have the notebooks. You could see that they got into good hands—the university, perhaps. Besides, if Illyssa's elders turn out to be hostile, at least *you'll* know what *we* know, so there'd be no point in silencing us."

"They'll be more likely t' talk than act, eh? Makes sense enough. But no, I've come this far, I'm na' going t' warm a bunk anchored in some upriver mud puddle. I may ha' a better way t' cover ourselves. Depends on what we find in Nobi."

"Nobi?" Illyssa asked. "Isn't that off our route?"

"Only a morning's hike. By water it's a week, but it lies a' th' narrowest part a' Burum." Illyssa pleaded with Omer to tell her his "better way," but he was proof against importuning, batted eyelashes, and pouts. Yan knew Omer's stubborn taciturnity, and let him have his secret.

Yan was first to see land. When they were close enough to spot details, Omer recognized a familiar headland and became jolly. "After th' storm, we could a' been on the Bight a' Burum, two day's sail south, but tha's Bagad ahead, North Burum Island. We're where we want t' be. I wasn't sure until now."

"The old sea wolf thought he'd lost his touch," Yan said in a vocal aside. "All those years fish-dragging on the Reach, y'know."

Omer tossed a hank of line at him. "Fix that. Eye splices a' both ends. Use a new thimble on th' one tha's worn half through. Lost my touch. Hmmph."

Ahead, a harbor was enclosed by massive riprap moles. The northerly one supported a round stone tower. "Th' Refuge Light," Omer commented. "Built by th' first Mayan a' Burum t' rule here. It warns ships off th' shoals." Yan contrasted the impressiveness of the light and moles with the dowdy town beyond. Omer elucidated: "Burum's th' most civilized country on th' Inland Sea. Libraries, lighthouses, schools are all free. There's a marine guard corps, and no pirates in their waters. We'll need papers t' travel here."

Docking north of the commercial harbor, they walked for ten minutes before finding the guard post. Registration was simple: names, vessel's name, route, cargo, and destination. Yan was fascinated by the dark and light brown faces everywhere and wanted to linger; after all, was not this where pipe dreams and legends met? Burum, whose rulers traced their descent unbroken across two and a half millennia, whose palaces towered above the very hills, antedating even the ancient dynasty? Burum, whose capital had been built when rivers flowed in the bed of the Inland Sea? Omer, knowing that given free rein Yan would question and scribble notes, assured him that more interesting visits were in store. Yan reluctantly returned to the pier.

That night they anchored in Harut, a short sail east. They slept aboard, as it was too late to find an inn. Illyssa awakened Yan at sunrise. He remembered that he had dreamed: he remembered elated victory following upon hard-earned success, but unlike his last dream, which was still oddly clear, this one yielded only a faded fragment which evaporated in the hot morning sun.

Omer agreed to spend a day in Harut, though he would have nothing to do but scrub *Serpent*'s deck, drink wine, and lie in the sun—better, he hastily appended, than following Yan around, poking ancient monuments and translating Burumese for him.

No palaces towered over Harut, but a short distance from town was a double road. They hired a carriage whose driver promised an extensive tour. Such was the fame of Burum's ancient works that guides spoke several languages, and the rates for tours were fixed by royal decree, posted for the benefit of polyglot gapers and gogglers. Such remnants of ancient prowess snaked like twin ribbons through many countries, ignoring natural and man-made borders, defying fens and valleys, and cutting through bedrock as if it had once been soft butter. Where such remnants cut across otherwise impassable terrain they were still used, but more often they terminated abruptly at unbridgeable chasms, or marched inflexibly into the sea. Nowhere was more than one roadway in use, the other usually choked with scrub forest or eroded beyond repair.

Their driver's patter was well-practiced. He informed them that carriages had once been so wide that a road was required for each enormous wheel; steel axles spanned the forty meters between wheels. Yan knew otherwise, for elsewhere he had seen remnants of such roads divide around obstacles, or enter twin tunnels.

This particular roadway was paved with hard-fired brick of recent manufacture, bedded in sand atop an older surface. Dips in the terrain indicated places where other thoroughfares had once passed beneath their path, but present bridges were narrow arches, only wide enough for passage of a wagon. The ancient spans had been steel, their guide proclaimed, but those had become unsound and had been replaced centuries ago. Impressed by the ancient wonder, Yan was more awed by the wealth of the Burum lords who maintained such an extravagance. The road cut across all North Burum, and was used almost solely by carriages like theirs. Serious travelers followed the sea route.

The tour consumed most of the day, and they returned to Harut during the dinner hour. They dined on icy gelled consommé with tiny suspended slivers of crisp vegetables; Yan suspected the restaurant had a freezing machine like the one in Gram. After a course of tough noodles and meat chunks in peppery sauce, and another of crushed ice with sweet fruit syrup, he was no longer able to restrain his curiosity. He asked the table boy and was disappointed to learn that the ice was carried overland in sawdust-filled boxes from a mountain source. The servant assured him that it was a laborious and expensive journey that few inns could afford, but one that a superior house could not omit.

It was again too late to search for rooms in town. That was just as well, for they planned an early departure.

* * *

Pain and pleasure, as always, entwined like lovers. The Tenzian countryside flashed by Gnist's carriage windows like magic-lantern pictures, and the jolting ride sent shafts of agony through the ghost-pale man. His fellow passengers saw only the skeletal rictus that passed for a gap-toothed grin. What pleasures he contemplated, they had no wish to know.

The prosperous merchant sharing his cushioned bench surely did not. It was enough to endure the foul effusion of old blood, a bowel ailment, and slow-healing wounds. Though the mountain air was chill, he met with no objections when he pulled the coach window open yet another inch.

The fat middle-aged widow and the one-armed mine owner who faced the emaciated priest—by his satin sleeve facings, a Hand in the Order of Pharos, not to be snubbed lightly—found ample excuse in each other's charms to ignore him without being patently rude. Under other circumstances neither would have given the other a glance, but having cuddled and fondled for hours and miles, they found each other attractive enough to disembark together in search of an inn and a capacious bed.

Solemnizing their coupling a week later in a village chapel, neither offered prayers to the cadaverous Hand who had provided impetus for their liaison. Better such men be forgotten.

CHAPTER FIFTEEN

In the seventy-eighth of Gold-eye's years, the witch Martina fled from his house with his seed. Sam-el's wrath was bright in the land and, though his eyes were thousands and his ears countless, she was never found in Burum. With her she took a daughter, and her slaves, and in each was the seed that was Sam-el's hope for eternal rule.

Chronicles of the House of Burum, Volume XLVII.22.

They sailed at dawn and made good time, entering the Bagad Channel at noon and arriving in Nobi Harbor a few hours later. A carriage took them across the isthmus to the town. Illyssa wanted to tour the cloth market, a center for weavers, dyers, and sundry other trades. Omer set about business of his own, refusing to say anything about it. Yan insisted on going with Illyssa, and Omer agreed; women's status in Burum was improved over past centuries and they were no longer slaves, but it was unwise for them to venture into public places unaccompanied. In spite of her disgust, Illyssa was not about to risk abduction, so she accepted Yan's presence with little grumbling.

When Yan assured her money was no problem, she ordered yards of exceptional fabrics—silks imported "from the other side of the world," locally woven in intricate patterns resembling embroidery. Others were hand-decorated in motifs like the botanicals on Illyssa's faded shirt. She ordered wools softer than Yan had ever imagined, wool from a creature neither sheep nor goat, a denizen of mountains far south of the equatorial seas.

By the time she finished, Yan had made a mental note to ask Omer about exchanging gold for local coin; Illyssa's buying spree had put a dent in their reserves. Sensing his annoyance, she explained that the cloth was not for herself. "Where would I wear fancy clothes, even if I had time to make them? The elders are women, with grandchildren to dress for festivals.'' Opulent gifts might not soften the elders' hardness, but they could not hurt their cause. Illyssa's feelings were bruised by Yan's implied criticism, and they remained so in spite of his apology. For an hour she kept as much distance between them as good sense permitted.

But the minor storm abated quickly. Illyssa stood in front of a woodcarver's stall, and called Yan to join her in admiring the tiny toys and figurines. She seemed to be waiting for him to say something. ''Well? Do you see it?'' she asked impatiently. ''Behind the whistles.'' His eyes swept the display twice before he saw what she had discovered. He motioned the carver to bring it forth.

''It's like yours, isn't it?'' she exclaimed. ''A ball in a cage. I think I'll buy it.'' She looked sideways at him beneath lowered lashes. ''If it isn't too expensive.'' He assured her that it would not be, if she were prepared to haggle. His smile was teasing, but she did not accept the seller's first price, or his second. She laid a copper coin on his stand and raised an eyebrow. He made as if to put the carving back. When she laid another copper beside the first, he shrugged and handed her the purchase.

''Isn't it strange that this ball is blue, too, like yours used to be?''

''I don't know. It's only the second one I've seen. My father made mine, I think. I may have chosen the color myself, but it's been so long, I can't remember.''

''Now I have one, too. Let's find something to hang it on. A necklace chain, not an old bootlace like yours.''

When Omer later commented that they'd have to sleep on the deck to keep all Illyssa's purchases dry below, involuntary tears sprang to her eyes. Angry at herself, she started to stalk away alone, but saw the slight smile beneath his mustache just in time. She resolved that she would have to do something about both smug, superior men. Whether their joking was condescending or not, she was easily hurt by it.

For the time being, she shrugged off her unease. Omer had news. ''I remembered something Yan told me,'' he said. ''Remember the name Azzar ab'd Onskill, Yan?''

''I think so. Perhaps I've read it somewhere.''

''He's prob'ly the greatest living historian. You told me about him.''

''I did?''

"Not by name, but you did. When you were a cub in Michan, one a' his informants took note of th' wreck you'd discovered."

"Of course! He put me in contact with Lazko, and . . . ab'd Onskill is here?"

"I used Lazko's name t' set up a meeting. I didn't tell him Lazko's dead. We'll see him in th' morning."

Yan wanted details of the man's studies, and Illyssa needed reassurance that neither Yan nor Omer would compromise her by revealing what they knew about her folk.

"My thoughts, little witch, are t' use *him* in the same way Yan wanted t' use me, t' protect your man and me from certain murderous old hens we've discussed. Think on't. If *they* think Onskill'll spread word a' them from here t' Oma unless we get an agreement, they may be willing t' bargain. Na' that we have t' tell him everything, mind. Just enough t' get a letter, some evidence or other tha' he knows everything we do."

"No wonder you were an admiral, Papa Omer." Her tone was syrupy. "You think of everything."

"Yan tell you that? 'T's a drunken tale. I'm a fisherman like my father and grandfather."

"Were they admirals, too? What fleets did they command? Yan didn't mention them."

"Let's find something t' eat," Omer grumbled.

Later he told them more about Azzar ab'd Onskill—or Onsill, depending on dialect. Brother to the Mayan of all Burum, Azzar had once been governor of the city of Onskill and the chief patron of the university there. When the overthrow of Onskill by fanatics and priests had removed the last unbelievers from Tenzian soil, Azzar had organized a flotilla, evacuating city and university across the bay to Nobi. He had arranged for last-minute transportation of centuries' accumulation of documents and artifacts to Burum; most were now in the Royal Archives and Library in Burum City. Azzar lived modestly in Nobi, spending his stipend from the royal house on his immense personal library and financing itinerant students and scholars who recorded their findings much as Yan had set out to do.

Morning came none too soon for Yan, who was eager to meet with a scholar of such dedication. Omer instructed them in proper behavior and address. Scholar or not, Azzar was a prince of the royal family of Burum and should be treated with care. His house was near the port, atop a hill commanding a view of southern ocean on one side, the isthmus and sound on the other.

On a clear day, Omer speculated, it might be possible to see the Tenzian shore beyond.

They were ushered into the house by the largest man Yan had ever met. He exceeded Yan's height by a full span and his girth by a factor of five. Contrasting with his walnut skin, he wore a white cotton loincloth mostly concealed by his paunch in front and his massive buttocks behind. From his thick neck hung a heavy gold chain with a bronze medallion. He was hairless—even his eyebrows had been plucked.

Communicating with gestures, the fat man led them to a courtyard garden. Omer followed, as befitted his age, then Yan. Illyssa would remain outside until their host himself summoned her; though women in Burum were less oppressed than before, the forms were punctiliously observed. At the end of the garden was a conversational setting of three wood-and-canvas chairs and a heavy wooden one with a pillowed seat. When they were seated in the light chairs, the huge man bowed and departed. "Now what?" Yan whispered. "Is he going to get Azzar?"

"I s'pose so. Stand up and bow when the prince comes in." Both men were puzzled when the fat man came back with Illyssa at his heels. She was offered the remaining canvas chair and, to Yan's consternation, their guide settled himself in the pillowed one. Once comfortably arranged—a time-consuming process—he spoke for the first time, his voice a smooth tenor which contrasted with his bulk. "Scholars and lady, Azzar, son of Avdool, welcomes you." Yan and Omer were chagrined and confused. Where was Azzar himself?

The huge man held out both hands, palms down. "I am he. Stay seated. We have satisfied custom, and it is my eccentricity to play the servant. It offers a rare chance to observe without being truly seen." His bulging eyes fixed on Omer. "I greet you, Knight-Admiral Omar Valon, erst-Senloo. I have read your treatise on gunship tactics, and your history of the Senloo merchant navy." He noted Omer's—Omar's—discomfiture, and his gaze went first to Yan, then to Illyssa. His meaty, hairless brows rose in mock surprise. "He hasn't told you? Either of you? Ah, then I am indeed flattered to have been so honored—and so should you be—that your companion has sacrificed his anonymity for your cause."

He turned to Illyssa. "I greet you, too, many-times-great-granddaughter of Martina Schorr, who so thwarted my ancestor, Samool of the Golden Eye." He raised an admonishing finger to silence her pending outburst. "How do I know your pedigree?

I didn't, until now. I merely assumed that, after many generations, every one of your people is directly descended from the original few. Your expression confirmed my guess." He shook his massive head, making his jowls and earlobes bob. "Don't fear. Samool's hopes and hostilities alike have long evaporated. You are safe here, and your secrets, too. Welcome to my home."

Finally, his gaze fell on Yan. "Master Yan of Michan—Yan Bando. Surely *you* know you are welcome in my house. Kemal ab'd Selm invited you when you were a youth. Don't you remember?" He grinned broadly, enjoying Yan's surprise. "Of course Kemal reported to me. Do your friends know the tale?"

"In brief, Prince Azzar."

"There's too much reticence in this company. Lives and stories are to be shared." He laughed softly. "That, at least, is my opinion, as a collector of lives and tales. May I share yours with your companions, Master Yan?"

He took Yan's silence for assent. "Years ago," he began, "I received an intriguing letter from remote Michan, requesting entry into my service. The writer was a brilliant, articulate child but, as my man Kemal averred, too young for the rigors of the long road. Kemal described the boy's partial excavation of an ancient spaceship, and sent me notes and drawings the boy had executed. Such talent and dedication, I felt, should not be wasted." He sighed. "And wasted it was to be. The Pharos Church, long covetous of the Michan dukedoms, unable to take them by force of arms, had prepared a subtler plan: they held younger sons of ducal families as 'student' hostages, 'educating' them and corrupting them with perversion and priestly nonsense. Once their charges reached their majorities, they would assassinate the *elder* brothers, the heirs."

He cleared his throat. "This boy, Yan Bando, determined that the only way to save his younger brother from brownshirt perversity was for him, the heir, to 'die.' The young hostage would be returned to his family because he would be the new heir, and no longer superfluous. Thus he would be freed from the Star Church's deviates." Ab'd Onskill paused as he noticed the look of mingled surprise and apprehension on Yan's face.

"You didn't know about the Pharos Church's scheme, Master Yan? Then your subsequent act is more noble for your ignorance. No, say nothing. Allow me to tie up the tale.

"Young Yan hid at his excavation site all one summer, having laid a false trail leading to his 'death' in the swamps. I received his letter, but not soon enough. The brownshirts found him, and he was to be publicly executed . . ." Ab'd Onskill paused.

Yan had stood and was stiff as a mast, his face white as a sun-bleached sail. "I beg you say no more, Prince Azzar. To you, this is but a tale. To me, it is a life I've long put behind me. These friends know nothing of that life, only the one I've lived since then." The demon. He knows why I left Michan, and he's going to speak of my madness aloud. Yan was sick at the thought of Omer knowing, of Illyssa looking upon him as a monster. Gran'ma's conditioning ran deep.

Ab'd Onskill smiled—sadly, it seemed. "I have overstepped courtesy. My lust for a good tale has overridden what good sense I possess, and I apologize. But one word of caution, Ser Yan: the past can *never* be abandoned. It must be faced as surely as must the future. It must be taken in hand and turned to advantage, or it will destroy you.

"At any rate," the prince continued lamely, "my letter to Lazko got through at long last, and you prospered with him. I know this, for I have watched you from afar, with great interest. Welcome, Yan Bando."

Grateful that his shame was not revealed, Yan was nonetheless aware that he had put himself and his companions in a difficult position. The apologies of princes were not light burdens, and he feared he might have destroyed their chance for aid. "I wasn't aware that it was you who brought me to Lazko's attention, Prince Azzar. I thought Kemal had merely given the notes and drawings to him, not to you. I have you to thank for whatever has been made of my life."

It was the right thing to say; Ab'd Onskill's piercing eyes warmed noticeably. "Knowledge is my trade and my obsession, young scholar. I further it where I can. No thanks are necessary. But what gift do you bring me? What news?"

"Only a bitter tale, Prince. The wrecked ship was stripped and reburied by Pharos' hounds. Lazko is dead, and his worst fears confirmed."

For a brief moment, the fat man seemed taken aback. "I am a lover of tales, as you know," he finally said. "Have you objection to my scribe's presence while you recount yours?"

"I have none, but the events, and the conclusions drawn from them, are of more than academic interest. Our lives are at risk for what we know, and there may be danger even to you. Does the scribe enjoy your utmost confidence?"

"He does. But, being cautious, I have other protection. He is mute, knows no hand signs, and writes only in a mnemonic of my own devising. Would you kindly pull the cord over there? It will summon him."

Yan's ringing summoned the scribe, who also brought cool, mint-flavored wine, water, and maize cakes sweetened with syrup. Yan told their tale, omitting only some details of their escape and Illyssa's demonstration of witchly talent. Though he admitted his and Omer's desire to meet the witches in order to find out if they had kept any of their spacefaring ancestors' lore, he avoided sounding as if he implicitly believed the extraordinary tales about them.

"You understate, scholar. You illuminate areas I have long puzzled over and raise new questions as well. But let us not be circumspect. You"—he pointed a fat finger at Illyssa—"are a witch. No need to answer me, girl. That was no question. You are pledged to silence, and I do not require you to be an oathbreaker. I will give you facts without asking confirmation. First, you are a witch. Your people are witches. That is to say, they have concentrated in their blood abilities which occur only rarely in the ordinary population.

"Second, they are descended in part from my ancestor, Samool Gold-eye." Seeing surprise neither Yan nor Illyssa could conceal, he said, "Oh, yes! We are truly distant cousins, small witch. The theft of Samool's seed is a touching story and I honor the dedication of your ancestresses, especially now, with the information the young scholar has given regarding their true calling."

"I'm not sure that I understand," Yan interrupted. He felt that Azzar was speaking to Illyssa alone, and that much was assumed and left unsaid.

"Fact three, then: Samool, my ancestor, bought slaves—blond, light-skinned exotics captured in the far north—who convinced him they were travelers from another world. This I have seen, written in Samool's own hand a thousand years ago. To convince him they were no ordinary slaves, and to enlist his aid, they demonstrated minor abilities of an unusual nature—mental control of small objects and of fire, 'seeing' the contents of closed rooms and boxes . . .

"Had they been owned by another man, their ploy might have succeeded, but Samool was himself a witch, able to sense emotions, to ascertain motives behind words. His successful reign in Burum was a product of that talent. Samool was a prince, a selfish man, and the owner of their bodies and talents. He saw in them a chance to found a dynasty that, combining their talents with his, would reign forever. He believed their account of their origins, but for Samool, Burum was world enough."

He looked directly at Illyssa. "I see no contradiction in your face, so I will continue. Your ancestresses' talents were man's hope for the stars, it seems. For some reason, no others have returned to Earth or, if they have, they have suffered similar or harsher fates. To preserve their hope, your ancestresses swore an oath not to let their talents vanish from Earthly blood; thus they bore children in captivity. Perhaps others of their kind, sold apart from them, did the same. Be that as it may, in 2948, two of Samool's women escaped from Burum with his seed quickened in their wombs. Samool lived thirteen years longer, to ninety-three, and in those years he recorded rumors of witch-women in the highlands of Tenzie—the beginnings of your people.

"You can see, witch-girl, that I am no Pharos priest, no hunter of your kind, nor will I publish what I know. We must make common cause." He took a sip of wine and awaited comment.

"Earlier, Prince Azzar, you said Yan's account answered some questions, but raised others." Omer's Eastern Reach accent was replaced by the same broad vowels and precise diction that marked the Burumian's speech. Yan smiled inwardly.

Taking a draft of his wine, their host replied. "Aaach! My throat's dry. Yes, the question answered: How did Athel of Roke succeed in breaking the superior armies of a dozen states with his rabble? Until now, I had suspected that he had dug up some arsenal from ancient times.

"More current questions answered are: Why have so few of my adventurers returned from Pharos-dominated lands? Also, what has been the Pharos Church's reason for suppressing purely historical research? I see now that the stakes were not dogmatic consistency; they feared close examination of their millennial hoax.

"The questions raised concern the nature of these . . . ferosin." He nodded to Omer. "There is merit in your suggestion that they are merchants on a grand scale, merchants who ply the dark seas between those bright islands we perceive as specks in the sky. Still, your hypothesis fails to explain why, for many hundreds of years, they have not exploited us, though they continue to rule our world secretly. It does not tell us why they fear us. Could a few puny humans in jury-rigged spaceships frighten them enough for them to threaten us all with extinction?

"That raises another question: If they are capable of destroying us entirely, and if we indeed pose a threat, why have we *not* been destroyed? Your speculation concerning the utility of the witch talent may be one reason, but might there be others? Four other races are mentioned. Do those other star travelers hold the ferosin in check?"

"That's a good question," Yan said. "During the first years of contact with the aliens, all five races were involved. But only the ferosin continued to visit us and strip us of whole populations. I ask myself why."

"Perhaps the witches will have answers for us—if they will speak with you," ab'd Onskill replied. "To that end I will draft a letter for my brother's signature. The overlord of Burum, descendant of Samool, will beg forgiveness for his ancestor's treatment of theirs, and will offer their envoys an honored place in his court, that we might discuss how we of Burum can aid them in reaching their long-sought goal. You three will deliver it." For a moment, the prince's eyes grew distant, his thoughts far away. His gaze then lit with pleasure. "I have just thought of another gift for you, one my seekers find useful."

Yan wanted to know more, but Omer, with a better grasp of the ways of royalty, cut him off. "We are grateful for your help, Prince Azzar. Grateful, and astounded as well."

"Astounded? How so? Did you not want me to do just this?"

"Aya, but consider: we came with a tale unsupported by evidence except these poor notebooks, and we end with your support and that of the Mayan, your brother. You need na' have listened at all, nor believed us."

"Ahhh!" Azzar's eyes glittered; his grin was sly. "Did I ever claim that Samool's own talent did *not* breed true?"

More wine was sipped and lighter conversation made. The prince arranged for Lazko's notebooks and Yan's to be copied for his records. He explained that it would take three or four days for him to travel to the court at Burum and to return. They were to wait, and to enjoy the city at his expense. Final arrangements would be made when he returned.

The priest was no surgeon, only a medi in the Order of Pharos specializing in male complaints that priestly inclination made common, but the execrable fellow who commanded his services had no ordinary malady. "You have been . . . much abused, Brother," he told his patient. "Caution dictates that you refrain from carriage rides until your injuries heal."

"My posting commences one week from tomorrow," the Hand grated through clenched teeth. "Patch me up and give me drugs for pain. I am sure my—condition—was taken into account by those who send me thither. If I die, the better for them. You do our mutual superiors no favor, advising me to caution that might lengthen my span. One day of rest, no more. Now, the drugs, man. I must have sufficient to last the month."

The medi scurried to gather compounds, tinctures, and binders, to mix them and press them into pills. The Hand of Pharos, meanwhile, pulled blood-soaked rags from his underdrawers and selected fresh, boiled bandages to pad his injuries.

Later, looking upon the sleeping Hand, the medi was glad his patient would move on quickly, to die or recover elsewhere than in his clinic's bed. The man's rigid, crenellated grin never relaxed, even in the depth of sleep.

CHAPTER SIXTEEN

Theory? What theory? Plate tectonics? Look, the whole Appalachian region is sinking—sixteen centimeters this year alone. The lab boys are going nuts. It's *unnatural*. No earthquakes, no sensible readings. It's like the lower crust has turned to goo, and something's sucking it out like a coon sucks eggs. Before long, we'll be needing those TVA dams to keep the *ocean* out.

Unnamed source in newly established Tennessee Valley Authority geological unit. Undated.

They sailed from Burum with mixed feelings. They were eager to press onward and their hopes for success were high. Ilyssa was glad to be rid of the repressive burden of Burumian tradition, able to be her ebullient self once more. On the other hand, they had been relatively free from worry during their stay. The death of the Seniors of Innis and Roke, and the destruction of the Sons of Pharos, had thrown the Church into confusion, though it might still function on inertia alone. Burum had been safe; Yan was unhappy to return to lands dominated by the Church.

Yan had spent his last days in Nobi among the books and papers of ab'd Onskill's library, filling out his knowledge of Burum and Bama—particularly the period from the Great Bolide in 2884 to around 3150, after the purge of the Bamian witches. The latter event stood out from all others in his mind:

In 3125 a grandson of Samool conquered a collection of independent small kingdoms on the Bamian Peninsula. This grandson, Semal Blackfellow, fought not against opposing armies, but against an entrenched corps of viziers, advisers, and regents who directed the affairs of his conquered kingdoms as if all were a single state. Blackfellow believed those powers behind his throne were a single extended family of witches. After eighteen years' fruitless attempt to direct their influence toward his own desires, he grew impatient and took direct action against them.

With their properties confiscated, their movement restricted, and their political power shattered, the "Witches of Bama" fled into the forests of Cloon. Blackfellow's troops harassed them as far as Chatoo but pursued them no further. After Chatoo, the "Witches of Bama" evaporated. Tales of wonder sprang up like mushrooms on their path through Bama and Cloon, becoming more wondrous with each passing year, until beasts and devils were said to have sprung from the soil to hold Blackfellow's troops while the witches escaped through burning forests.

Yan wondered if the incipient Pharos cult had been behind Blackfellow's actions. Though the Church had existed for over a hundred years by then, Innis was still only a slave market and Roke a Lannick fishing town. If the Second Compact, the elusive document that heralded the Pharos-Sons' appearance, were fact, then there had been no permanent ferosin presence on Earth until 3550.

The witches, safe in Tenzie, were free to pursue their goals for four hundred years. Tenzie, the last land to recover from geological cataclysm, became prosperous. Schools rose on old foundations, hospitals ministered to rich and poor alike, and fine roads sent tendrils into the furthest valleys. It was obvious to Yan that the "Witches of Bama" were behind that remarkable efflorescence. The Tenzian renaissance stood out like a beacon in the foggy aftermath of worldwide devastation, a light not ignited by chance. It was not a slowly evolved culture, but one guided and created by folk with a vision of what should be.

There were no tales of star-flying witches in Tenzie, or of aircraft crossing Tenzian skies, but if the descendants of the Bolide were responsible for the Tenzian buildup, they would have been cautious, remembering that ferosin Masters might still be watching from afar.

Did they build starships? Did they, in Semal's genes, find the lost key they sought? Yan doubted it; repercussions of their success would have been evident. And if ferosin had felt threatened, he suspected no humans would be alive to wonder. Only negative evidence hinted that the ancient Tenzians had been on the right track. Athel of Roke had destroyed Tenzie with atomic fire, dropped with pinpoint accuracy, guided by ferosin from orbiting ships. Those were draconian measures, direct intervention that would have been unthinkable to the subtle ferosin of earlier ages.

Athel's conquest, and the Second Compact, legitimizing ferosin overseers on Earth, hinted at pressures on the ferosin themselves—driving forces Yan could not imagine. Had they, failing to obtain results from their Earthly experiment, simply used Athel to wipe clean their laboratory retorts?

Had others, the tsrath and inouwa for want of better names, hounded ferosin as Church tales implied? Yan did not know. Was there some intrinsic flaw in the ferosin system that forced dependence on humanity, saving it from annihilation, but pressing it ever further into ignorance and servitude? There were no answers in ab'd Onskill's archives.

Unable to find answers to his burning questions, Yan sought information from a source near at hand, a brass-bound wooden box bolted to the chart table: ab'd Onskill's surprise gift. A thick copper wire snaked down the table leg, through the cabin sole, and out through the hull to a copper plate tacked to the keel. Another wire led forward, then up the mast to a rotating spar, an antenna. Ferosin and churchmen, it seemed, were not the only ones to have had radios for some time.

Azzar's radios were old technology, built from plans and ancient prototypes. Their builders were, the prince complained, skilled craftsmen, but without a scintilla of theoretical knowledge of their craft. He and Yan commiserated about the state of men's thinking—how could ferosin be confronted by those who considered their own craft an application of complex magic?

The actual antenna was a length of copper wire strung from the ends of stiff twelve-foot poles lashed together at their midpoints. The butt of one pole rested in an iron socket atop the mast. The diamond-shaped plane of the wires could be rotated, by hand or by changing *Serpent*'s heading, to maximize a signal. Yan had received instruction from Azzar's chief technician, but he was not convinced he knew how to make good use of it.

He spent hours each day twisting verniers and gazing at glowing dials, but heard no intelligible sounds. One particular adjustment yielded clicks, another a rhythmic peeping that might have been code, but that was all. Yan kept at it. He had a copy of the click code Azzar's seekers used, but neither signal matched it. A human code he could decipher, but if the churchmen used some ferosin code, he suspected he could spend a lifetime at it without success. Still, he kept trying.

The letter from ab'd Onskill's brother was everything he had promised. The overlord proposed full alliance with the witch people, including the freedom to live and travel unmolested in his wide lands. His only condition concerned their spaceship, should it exist. If it were ever brought to working order, he wished his dynasty to be represented among its officers by his youngest brother Mamood's two sons. His request for ambassadors from the witches to attend him in Burum was accompanied by gold: coins minted in Tenzie, Chatoo, and Burum to pay expenses and passages, should they accept his hospitality. And it was signed, "Your cousin in blood and spirit, Gamaal ab'd Burum, Overlord of Bama, King of Cloon and Bagad."

They sailed northeast along the Burumian coast, with many changes in tack, progressing slowly. Contrary winds swept from the Cloon highlands, creating gusts one moment and calm the next. They put in at Chongan, a border town noted for sulfurous waters bubbling up from the earth. The springs, trapped in tiled pools, were patronized by the affluent and arthritic of Burum and beyond.

Sleek, brightly canopied pleasure boats lined Chongan's wharves, and yachts lay at anchor. A quick sortie in the town convinced them that prices were inflated beyond reason. The shops and marketplaces offered nothing they had not seen in Nobi.

Azzar ab'd Onskill had furnished charts of the South Tenzie Sound, and of the waterways that led north and east to Choke Marsh, north of Nahks. "This is th' most dangerous stretch," Omer said as they studied the charts, indicating length of twisting waterways with his callused forefinger. "If we arrive a' Chatoo at midmorning, we'll go unnoticed in th' heavy traffic between islands, but past th' head a' th' sound, th' river's never a mile wide, an' *Serpent* looks less like a river craft than I'd like. We'll have t' have our stories down pat. Even if we're not stopped by Tenzian patrols, we'll still have t' pass three locks an' th' wagon portage a' Nahks. Got our papers handy?"

Papers had been prepared by an acquaintance of Azzar, who had performed similar tasks for the prince's itinerant scholars. He prided himself on the verisimilitude of his forgeries. Yan and Omer were less positive—after all, had not Azzar lamented the agents he'd lost in Tenzie? But the travelers kept their doubts to themselves, and resolved not to test their documents except as a last resort. There were letters of credit, receipts and customs checks from South Tenzian towns, and a bill of sale for *Serpent*, therein called *Lady Sefonee*, with stamps indicating she had been purchased in Onskill weeks earlier. Her gold-leafed name had been painted out and the new one lettered on.

Yan was to assume a familiar identity, now given a name: Vridz Hundrik Smidson, Apostate Islander, exiled and seeking his fortune in trade. They had no reason to suspect that browncoats had uncovered his earlier masquerade, and now he had documentation for that identity. Illyssa, her hair and skin darkened to Burumian swarthiness, had no papers of her own, but Yan carried a receipt for a slave's purchase in Lonce, near Onskill. Omer was Hiolmar Sarganoon, retired from the merchant fleet of Demoyne, now trading for his own profit. After spending the evening lamplight reviewing their roles, they retired early.

Ashore in Chongan, the populace was hardly stirring when they cast off. Stoves were being lit and oven flues belched smoke, which dissipated rapidly, leaving only heat-shimmer over the roofs as the fires took hold. The wealthy tourists would have fresh, hot bread when they rose at midmorning. As they pulled away, a dray clattered along the waterfront esplanade, loaded with melons and wine.

The domelike heights of Chatoo loomed as *Serpent* struggled north before a fitful breeze. The Vald coast of Tenzie lay ahead between two islands. By midmorning they sailed into the narrows between Chatoo and Tenzie's Red Island. Numerous small craft paralleled their course, and a four-masted schooner was being warped into the stream ahead. Sails hauled up its towering masts filled immediately with winds not apparent to lesser craft. A flock of oared harbor boats cast off and pointed back at Chatoo, among them the harbormaster's galley, flying Chatoo's ultramarine and ocher. From the Tenzian shore the hoot of a steam whistle echoed across the water, its rhythmic blasts softened by distance, evoking in Yan some faint, familiar memory, perhaps the call of a marsh bird he'd heard in Michan as a child.

When the sun had ascended to midsky, Yan pointed out the buildings gleaming whitely on the city's highest ridge. "That must be the fortress Athel built for his conquest of Vald. He headquartered there for several years." Illyssa and Omer gave him sour looks; neither needed reminders that they were in enemy territory. But once beyond the narrows, the sound became Chatoo Bay, ten miles wide and thirty long, and they felt less cramped. Their relief was unfounded, though; there were rocky shores in every direction, and no freedom to sail away from danger.

After anchoring that night in a cove on the east shore, at dawn they entered the estuary of the Tenzie River, still so deep that no current was evident. At the first locks they paid the toll and were passed through without a glance, their papers untouched. The locks elevated *Serpent* over fifty feet. The waterfall they bypassed was an immense dam, repaired and refaced many times, so overgrown with ancient trees that Yan could not guess its age. He knew such dams had once generated electricity, and he could imagine no other use for them besides keeping lockmen employed. The river would have been more navigable without it.

The day passed as had the one before, below rolling forest-covered mountains. A second series of locks raised them higher, and the terrain remained monotonous in a wild, pretty way. At dusk on their third day on the river, they tied up at the base of a wagon portage. A road across the dam-top—all the river's obstructions were dams—led into Nahks, but though no Tenzian brownshirts were evident, they decided to forgo the luxuries of a hotel and sightseeing in town.

In the morning, they unstepped *Serpent*'s tall mast, stowed her rigging, and guided her along the wharf with ropes and poles. A small lock's upstream gate opened not on a waterway, but on a long ramp with log rollers. A hemp cable thick as a man's calf snaked down from a summit lost in overhanging trees and branches. When *Serpent* floated inside the lock, naked men slipped into the water and disappeared; bubbles hinted at their whereabouts. Yan and Illyssa were curious, but Omer just raised a finger and said, "Watch." The men surfaced, drew air, and dove again, then flopped alongside the lock and lay gasping. Hearing the crack of a teamster's whip, Yan saw six mules pulling into harnesses, and a great capstan turning, tensioning a cable that ran uphill out of sight. *Serpent* jerked and moved forward, pulled by the cable's trailing end. As she progressed up the ramp, Yan saw she was supported on timbers cleverly hinged to adjust to any hull shape. As the hull emerged from the final inches of water, he saw the heavy wooden platform that supported the boat. Rusted steel beams that ran its length met beneath *Serpent*'s bow at a huge clevis mated to the cable. One diver struck a metal triangle, sending bell tones across the water. The cable groaned, and boat and platform moved more steeply upward. A diver rode the platform, placing wooden blocks between the after rollers. Just as one set of blocks was placed, another man removed the lowest set and ran them forward to his coworker. Slowly the boat rose up the long grade.

An hour later they poled *Serpent* onto open water. They did not restep the mast; no sails were needed. Instead, they warped and poled her to the last position in a line of flat-bottomed barges and made her fast. In the morning they would be towed into the channel, a bright bauble on the end of a crude wooden chain. Omer was morose. No longer captain of a vessel, he was now a passenger, with no control over *Serpent*'s course or destination.

Yan worked on the radio. He bolted the iron antenna socket to the tabernacle and restrung wires from point to point on the crossed spars. The clicks and chirps came in clearly. He had just settled down to listen in the hope that something recognizable would be transmitted when something clattered on deck. He heard Illyssa's wordless exclamation, and then, "What's *that* doing there? I might have cut myself on it."

"That's the antenna," he heard Omer say. "Here, I'll turn it so you don't—" His words were drowned in the shriek of the radio as the peep code swelled to an intolerable level. Yan twisted the volume knob, muffling the noise. He stuck his head out the companionway. "Om? Illyssa?" They turned. "Will one of you turn the antenna again, slowly?"

Illyssa turned it while he stood in front of the radio, scribbling on the back of a chart. "That's it!" he exclaimed. "The signals are directional."

"Well, of course," Omer commented, peering down at Yan. "They have to come from somewhere."

"No, don't you see? If we figure out where the signals come from, then there'll be clues to what they *mean*."

"Well," Omer said again, "where *do* they come from?"

"I don't know."

"I thought you just said . . ."

"I did, but I'll have to listen several times, from different places. I don't know if the signal is strongest when the antenna's parallel to the source, perpendicular to it, or . . ."

They agreed they would have to experiment at several places along their route—"Establishing a baseline," Omer called it. But right then, as Illyssa pointed out, dinner was ready. They dined on bread, smoked fish, and cheese, then shared their last bottle of strong Burumian spirits in silence. Yan and Illyssa had caught the lure of the free, open sea, and felt as confined as did Omer in the close waters. They prepared for bed without a thought of making love, and were asleep before the sun was properly abed. Omer spread a mat on the foredeck and waited out the sunset, mingling thick pipe smoke with the gathering mist.

Yan awoke in the small hours, covered with sweat. He'd been dreaming again. He was thirteen. Thaddy, old San's son, no older than himself, had taken a breeding pig of Yan's to be slaughtered. Thaddy was bitter and angry, resenting his father's servitude and the family he served. He'd long ago discovered Yan would neither fight him nor tattle, and the mean prank was only the latest in a string of cruelties Yan had endured for years.

An adult might have believed it an honest error, but Yan read gloating satisfaction in Thaddy's eyes. Rage built like a fire in a closed barn, ready to burst into conflagration. He struggled between rage and tears, afraid to show either. "Tears are shame and rage is . . . madness." He repeated that phrase under his breath like a mantra, over and over.

Another internal voice, quieter but no less clear, demanded recognition. *He shan't get away with this. I must fight him and win, or I'll have to live with his torments. I am in control of myself. I can conquer my demon, and Thaddy, too.*

No! Stop! the louder voice cried. *Rage is madness. Fighting is rage.* A silent dialogue went on. *He can't get away with this. I can't let him.* And: *I can't fight him. I can't fight the madness. Everyone will know my demon.*

The cooler voice carried across his mental battleground, passionless, reasonable: *I can fight him without anger. I can thrash him like a mischievous dog, without malice. Without rage, the demon will not come forth.*

The danger! the voice of fear persisted. *Madness! They'll all know. I might foul myself.*

I'll not fight, then, the cool voice soothed. *I'll just cut him down like I would a tree. Purpose without rage, without madness.* The internal discussion lasted only seconds; Thaddy's grin remained unchanged. Fear surrendered to the calm coolness of decision. Yan recognized harbingers of madness: the attenuation of ordinary sounds, their bell-like clarity, the ponderous beat of his own heart thundering like the engine of a harbor tug. But where had he seen a tug? An engine? Without rage, with cold dedication to his task, he advanced on Thaddy.

The other boy crouched unreadily, suddenly aware that the figure now closing the distance between them was no longer the same boy who'd so meekly endured his persecutions. "No more!" Yan's words were like solid objects striking. His fists, pummeling Thaddy's face and chest, were more solid still. Yan's blows broke past Thaddy's upraised fists and spun him about. Yan's lesser weight, backed by the impetus of his charge, bowled Thaddy over with Yan on top. Yan's left hand, at his throat, pinned him down even as his right one drew back for a crushing blow. Yan saw blood over Thaddy's eye, and watched a droplet fall in slow motion to the dusty ground. *Enough,* the cool voice told him. *Purpose is served. True madness lies just beyond your fist. Stop now, and your demon is thwarted.*

"No more, Thaddy. Do you understand?" Yan's internal struggle to halt his poised fist was evident to Thaddy, who turned his head away and eyed Yan askance. That look was the essence of human submission, spoken in a language that predated words, so elemental that words had never replaced it. Yan needed no other reply. He released the other boy, drew his feet under himself, and arose to walk away without looking back. The sounds of the farmyard regained the fuzzy density of normality, and his heartbeat slowed and quieted, becoming an unnoticed body rhythm once again.

In spite of sweat and coarse, clinging bedding, Yan felt as cool as the voice in the dream. Stars clustered thickly overhead as he climbed from *Serpent*'s cabin. I wish it had really happened that way, he thought. We might have become friends later. Stranger things have happened. Yan made no attempt to sleep after that, though he returned to his berth after his sweat dried. Illyssa slept on. He pondered the strange, coherent dream, seeking symbols, archetypes, dual meanings—but it was only a dream, parallel to reality, to a point. If I hadn't let my fear of madness stop me, it *could* really have happened like that. The more he thought, the more real the dream seemed, until the events his mind called "true" were less substantial than the dream.

From Nahks to Choke Marsh was a three-day trip. *Serpent* rode smoothly, only occasionally lurching at her tether. Far ahead, a woodburning tug spat smoke and embers skyward; they fell again as fine ash, thick on *Serpent*'s deck. It was a monotonous voyage. When they first entered the river the forested slopes on either side had been a relief from open sea, but it soon seemed that they traveled on a circular stream: the mountains repeated themselves over and over, and only the locks were different.

Yan fiddled obsessively with the radio. He checked each signal's strength at regular intervals, reasoning that since the steam tug's speed was constant, each interval would represent an equal distance traveled. Omer whittled a wooden disk from soft driftwood and carefully carved a compass rose on one surface. He blackened the incisions with soot from *Serpent*'s filthy deck, then fixed the disk on the antenna pole. When it came time to check the signals, Omer or Illyssa rotated the antenna until the signal strength was greatest, then called the bearing on the disk and the heading from *Serpent*'s binnacle to Yan, who noted them on his chart.

On their third day, as the barge train emerged into the vast openness of the marsh, Yan yelled, "I've got it!" He spread his charts for Illyssa and Omer and pointed to a line of dots. "That's our course," he said. "When I assumed that the strongest signal came in with the antenna in line with the source, I came up with that." He showed them lines crossing their course at acute, changing angles. "That didn't make sense, so I tried this." The second chart's lines crossed the course baseline at more moderate angles, converging on a single point Yan had labeled "Roke."

"The strongest signal is always perpendicular to the plane of the wires," he told them. "The bearings converge on the signal source."

"Then does the clicking signal come from Innis?" Omer asked.

"I wish it were that far away. It's from Jossity—days ahead, but on our route. We can't avoid Jossity. It's the only place we can cross into the Mountain Freeholds."

That was not welcome news—the signal was surely sent by churchmen—but still, there was no reason to believe it pertained to them. Yan was as frustrated as ever; he still had no clue to their code. Sometimes a burst of peeps sounded almost familiar, but that, he thought, was because he'd listened so long he'd heard it before, or because he wanted to recognize it.

When Omer fiddled with the frequency knob, they heard first the clicking code, then the chirps, and near the end of the knob's travel a high, continuous tone devoid of rhythm or meaning. The sailor shrugged. "We know who they are, but we still can't understand what they're saying." He shook his head and went above.

Choke Marsh was the soul of monotony. It stretched for twenty miles, a sea of reeds and tortuously entwined channels where no breeze twitched the thinnest cattail spear. Stinging flies circled and burrowed into their hair and clothing; Illyssa's face and wrists swelled and she became nauseated and dizzy. Tying their beechwood washbucket to a boathook, Yan scooped up a noxious mass of gray swamp muck. Methane bubbled in their wake from the disturbance. Yan worked mud into his hair and spread it thickly on his neck and hands.

"A mudman!" Illyssa laughed at him. "I wish I had a mirror." She picked fine-leaved weeds and stuck them in his caked hair. "This is how a well-dressed mudman should look."

"You're right, you know," he replied with a grim smile too slight to crack his mask. "Hunters do just this. Bugs can't bite through the mud, and the switches keep them circling. Now let's make *you* a mudwoman."

He approached with the half-full bucket. "Oh, no! I'll die of flybites before . . . Yan, let go of me!"

His playful grab evolved into a wrestling match, and most of the mud was soon strewn in *Serpent*'s cockpit. Yan was surprised to find himself aroused by the struggle. Their lovemaking usually began quietly, building slowly to its height. This time, still half wrestling, he fumbled loose the cord holding Illyssa's coarse canvas pants and roughly pulled them below her knees. She helped, lifting her trim buttocks from the cockpit floor, but continued to wrestle and resist. She writhed beneath him, fighting with all her lithe strength, pushing his face and chest away as he climbed between her pale brown thighs.

She was ready even as he thrust into her without foreplay or hesitation, but she still struggled wildly, thrashing to free herself. He held her shoulders against the deck. His legs bore against her crumpled pants, holding her legs and ankles down. A small part of his mind drew back in appalled denial of his mindless rut, but it was a small voice, quickly drowned by the rush of blood in his ears, the triphammer pounding of his body against hers. She was crying. Her sounds beat against his eardrums without resolving into words. His thrusts pushed her head up against a seat, twisting her neck sideways. His own forehead drummed the light wood panel as he bore down on her toward his release. She stiffened and arched as he emptied himself into her, then with a convulsive shudder he sank down on her small body, the rigid strength ebbing from his arms. He felt the wetness of her tears on his neck as he sank into semiconsciousness.

They lay like that for several minutes. Her voice awakened him; her hand caressed his cheek. "I love you, too, great beast.

You can poke me anytime—even with Omer and the whole barge train watching—but there's a horde of flies poking my legs right now, and if I don't brush them off I'm going to scream." Yan, still engorged, slowly lifted himself again. He slid gently back and forth, then withdrew with a groan. He sat up unsteadily while she flicked flies from her legs. One left a smear of blood behind.

Again? Was it the same mind? Did you feel it?

The ancient minds that answered the silent question all held the same tinge of sated heat.

The same, I think. Closer now. Untrained, unclear.

Danger. Fear. Hope. The thoughts of the oldest among them swept through their own minds like the hot and cold spasms that had so recently embroiled them. *Who? Where?*

Nearer than before. Strong, so strong. I sensed lesser minds as well.

Traces? Traces? Patterns? Some old minds were less articulate, but no less strong.

None. Gone now. There were no more questions. The thought-images divided like clumps of fog before a breeze and dissipated as if they had never been.

Yan heard several voices talking at once and looked up at the barge ahead. Several men, and two women with small children clinging to their skirts, waved their arms and gave bawdy cheers.

"Oh, no! Illyssa, get your pants on."

"Get *your* pants on before these vicious flies consume my favorite toy! Of *course* they were watching. I tried to tell you that. One of them started it."

"Started what? I don't understand."

Seeing that the brief respite from the boredom of the barge train was over, their watchers began to depart. Illyssa nodded in their direction. "See that little fellow up there? The boy in the blue shirt? I think he's a sensitive, one of those outsiders with a snatch of . . . witch talent. He'd been peeping at me for some time, thinking very sexy thoughts. I felt them as clearly as I feel yours." She smiled, a frank, lascivious expression that discomfited him. "It's not uncommon among my people. If someone's got a very strong need—not just lust; it could be loneliness, boredom, grief—someone else feels it and responds." Illyssa must have felt Yan's own uneasiness at her words, for she hunched her shoulders and turned away from him, but she kept talking. "Once, when my father and my uncle Jasso returned from a hunt–when they were both young and horny–my mother felt them so strongly she met them outside the village and had them both, there at the side of the trail."

Yan desperately tried to assimilate what she was saying without letting fear, betrayal, and prudishness sweep him away. There was much he still had to learn about living with a witch; it was not all clever fireside tricks and handy talents. Part of his mind attempted to analyze, to sort out the differences between Illyssa's world and his own, differences resulting from the subtle and not-so-subtle meshing of thought and emotion that colored every aspect of her society and behavior.

Another part of him danced between disgust at his own rutting—especially his willingness to accept that the responsibility for the near-rape had not been entirely his–and the fear that nothing, not even lust, was under his own control. "It wasn't me, then?"

"Of course it was." She smiled at him. "You can't get off the hook so easily. But his need was strong. Can't you remember being thirteen? I just let it into my head. You and I reacted the way we wanted to anyway, so you're still a rapist–my favorite rapist."

Relieved, he could not help responding to her infectious grin. A surreptitious glance showed him that the last observers had gone back to their own affairs–perhaps literally, considering the stimulus–and the two of them were alone again. "I think your randy friend up there must be feeling better now. I saw a wet spot on his trousers."

Illyssa giggled. "He didn't have as much fun as we did. For some things, you really have to *be* there." Her words trailed into laughter, which started Yan chuckling, too. Once started, neither could stop. Each whooping spasm instigated the next and they did not fall quiet until their breath came in ragged gasps. Mud-covered, flybitten, and satisfied, they leaned against the coaming, all tensions forgotten for a time. Ahead, the tug's steam whistle hooted its noonday signal, twelve short blasts followed by a flurry of long and short ones, always the same. It was a mournful, empty sound, and it dissipated over the vastness without returning echoes.

Omer came aft from the foredeck where he'd been napping. "Wha's so funny?" Though he had not witnessed their lovemaking, some intense sensation had touched him. "I dreamed a' getting drunk and chasing women. Must be th' heat, eh?"

Illyssa looked long and intently at him, then at Yan. She was considering, Yan could tell, debating whether or not to ask him something. He thought he knew what it was, but he was unwilling to think about it. Their relationship was still new, strange—and perhaps getting stranger. Her casual mention of her mother having sex with two men, one her husband, had appalled, disgusted, and titillated him. He'd had as much sharing of her as he could handle, as much shock as his ill-defined moral code and tenuous self-esteem could tolerate. Perhaps, when love had deepened and matured, he would be able to share her with someone he loved as he'd come to love the old man—but not for a long time. Illyssa raised her shoulders in an almost-imperceptible shrug. But her eyes seemed to say, *You haven't heard the last of this.*

They reached the end of Choke Marsh before nightfall the following day. Yan and Illyssa kept a bit of distance between themselves most of the time, as much from Yan's lingering self-consciousness as from their sated desires. They both felt as drained and sexless as young children. Yan imagined he felt an occasional flicker of thought from her, and once, attempting to picture what their last coupling had been like for her, experienced a transient impression of being small, of pebble-sized nipples being scratched by his/her shirt, and of a slick emptiness at the base of his/her belly. Imagination? He shook his head, unwilling to speculate just how far such strange witch talents might extend.

Ansel Kornvetz paced the tessellated floor of his empty study. His walnut desk, matching chairs, and side table had been taken upstairs to his new, larger office already, and only the heavy woolen drapes remained. Those he would leave for his successor, the estimable Effredi Gnist. "I wonder what trouble he was in in Innis," Kornvetz said aloud, then: "Pharos take me, I'm stuttering!" Talking aloud was a long-standing habit, one that possibly contributed to his having been passed over for promotion in his order; the Brotherhood frowned on such eccentricities in its middle ranks.

"I wonder if he's good-looking? No, that would be too much to hope. There's not a priest under forty in Jossitytown, I swear. And no more local boys for me. Not seemly for the new Junior of Jossity to be tavern-cruising, is it now?" Kornvetz smiled smugly. He was fifty, but he'd finally made it. Now he could relax. East Tenzie was a quiet district, far enough from Roke to deter superiors in the Church from visiting. True, his rank in the Brotherhood remained low, a mere medi unlikely ever to gain even sub-Hand status, but even an Arm of Pharos who held lesser churchly rank would be unlikely to gainsay him—or so he thought.

He flung open the seven-foot balcony door. "Brother Dennik, has he come? The new man?"

A fat priest in the courtyard replied. "No, Junior. He wasn't on the boat this morning. Perhaps he stayed in Soin or Kort." Kornvetz resumed his pacing.

In truth, his new aide was not yet at Soin. Brother Gnist was not the same man whose robe Illyssa had borrowed a month before. Recent experiences had left him with a black nut of bitterness where he had once had a heart. His wrists still itched as scabs came loose, leaving bright pink scar tissue. His back and belly were matrices of slowly healing burns, and he did not expect his fingernails to grow back at all. The loss of his manhood to the surgeon's knife had been the final stroke, unhinging Gnist's mind, now fueling his anger and his obsession.

Considering his wounds, his hemorrhoids, and his involuntary surgery, he had not been about to sit a mule for an hour, let alone days. The sea voyage from Innis to Tenzie had been tolerable because he had been drugged, and he had hired a well-sprung carriage across the Cumber Neck. But his drug supply dwindled, and he was terrified that some new pain or injury might yet surface.

So he waited in Nahks for a barge train to be formed, confident that he would still get to Jossity in good time. His new duties would be a far cry from the privileges he had enjoyed as secretary to the Senior, but there were worse places, and he would be near the borders of the highland tribes—the Pharos-cursed witches. Once acquitted, he had been given his choice of posting by way of reparation. The witches had been his sole reason for choosing Jossity.

The council of regents that substituted for the dead Seniors would retain power for some time, he had reasoned, at least until the Pharos ship arrived with new Sons some five years hence. Until then, they would bumble and piddle to little effect, and would likely be purged soon after. Gnist had no desire to be purged with them. He knew the landing coordinates for Pharos' visitations, and he planned to meet the ship. His plans had not developed beyond that moment, but he anticipated that high positions would be obtainable, and, with them, revenge.

In the meantime he would apply himself to the God's goal on Earth: the capture and interrogation of witches. Jossitytown was a convenient place to begin. It sat square across the main route out of the highlands, it was near enough to Nahks for him to use its mercenary garrison, and the soldiers at Jossity Keep were competent as well. The keep would serve as a prison. When the time arrived, he would have something to show the Pharos-Sons. And the witches would curse the name of Effredi Gnist.

One witch in particular would feel the effects of his rancor, and soon. What incredible luck! What good fortune attended his wise choice of mission. Gnist made no effort to pray or to thank his black lobster-god for any of it. He was far too sophisticated to believe that Pharos had any power over events that superior gimmickry did not provide. Instead, he congratulated himself again. He had picked up the trail of the fugitives who had caused his agony.

Two days earlier, there had been a commotion at the rear of the barge train. He had walked painfully aft over barges and across flexing gangplanks, arriving too late to witness what had transpired; those who had seen were reticent. But he had seen a small sloop with graceful lines, and caught a glimpse of the same three whose trail he had lost at water's edge in Innis. They had evidently lingered in Burum or South Tenzie, for though his overland journey had been shorter than the sea route, he would not otherwise have overtaken them.

Now there was no further choice of transport. No carriages left for Jossity soon enough, and it was too far for a man in his deplorable shape to walk. But even the pain caused by the accursed mule he now whipped unmercifully was dulled by his anxious desire to get to Jossity ahead of them to prepare his trap.

CHAPTER SEVENTEEN

Don't count miles; measuring your journey in steps, miles, or days, you will accumulate a head full of heavy numbers. Instead, keep note of bridges and byways, fords and detours, and measure yourself against where you have traveled, what you have done.

(11) Adrianna (8), *Meditations*

The objects of Brother Gnist's evil thoughts were at the moment packing their possessions on four mules of their own. *Serpent*, or *Lady Sefonee*, had been sold to a merchant who planned to keep her there on the narrows. Omer was downcast by her loss, swearing she was the sweetest, most responsive craft afloat. Yan and Illyssa felt sad, too. Yan equated it to leaving home knowing that even should he return, nothing would greet him but ashes and overgrown ruins. The sale had been firm and final.

Beyond Jossity, they would still have six days' travel to the witches' domains. They purchased equipment from southbound travelers with no further need of it. Owners of mules and trail gear had been glad to get rid of them, for they would have been left behind in any case. One of their mules carried Illyssa's purchases from the Nobi cloth merchants and most of their other supplies. The other three were saddled. Tarpaulins rolled behind the saddles concealed bedding and clothing, and could function as impromptu shelters.

Yan packed the bulky radio in a canvas sack and rolled the wire carefully, trying not to flex it too much. He planned to unpack it nightly to listen to the elusive codes. Illyssa suspected he would sleep in his saddle during the day and listen all night, and her bed would be solitary and cold.

They decided to take the trail on the east and north banks of the river. It was infrequently used, and there would be less chance of meeting curious travelers or churchmen. The other route was smoother, without steep inclines or dangerous crossings, and was several miles shorter than theirs. Their mules, Yan reasoned, were mountain-bred, used to rough trails and narrow paths, and were trained to follow one after the other. With no other beasts to distract them, no one would have to work hard to guide them. Of course, he pointed out for Omer's benefit, none had a tiller or a wheel, so whoever rode in front would have to guide his mount with those silly leather straps. Illyssa guessed he was challenging the old seaman to take the lead so he could sleep while he rode and play with the radio at night.

Game was plentiful, and Yan brought down four stupid birds with flung stones. The creatures had fled directly down the trail when he flushed them and had made no attempt to evade his missiles. They fluttered clumsily, not leaving the ground for more than a yard at a time. Yan speculated that their behavior was intended to decoy the humans from their nests; a quarter hour of thrashing in the brush proved him right, and they dined on meat, eggs, and wild salad, a welcome change from the fish and grain that had lately sustained them.

They met no one else. The only sign that the trail saw use at all was a single set of hoofprints. Drawing on childhood woodsman's lore, Yan noted that the prints were from a light riding horse or mule with no great burden—a woman or a boy. At first the tracks were fresh, an hour or so ahead. As the day wore on, it became evident that their fellow traveler was widening the gap between them.

They camped early. Yan would have pushed on, but Omer started swearing, cursing flies, mules, face-slapping branches, and the unnavigable river that glistened tauntingly through the trees. Illyssa's attempts to cheer him by singing sea chants only intensified his own vocal efforts, which, though not set to music, were original, resoundingly euphonious, and eloquent.

Yan supervised the erection of their shelter, a three-sided tent with a gauzy insect curtain that they pulled aside to have a cheery fire and to brew kaf. The netting was welcome when the fire died. But soon the local mosquitoes, their wingspans wide as Omer's broad thumbnail, found their way in, in spite of the curtain, and kept them awake and slapping until fatigue overcame them.

Before sleeping, Yan cut poles and set up the radio. He listened to chirps on one setting, clicks on the other, then the odd, monotonous signal on the third one Omer had found. Oddly, the latter was strong in every antenna position. Yan was intrigued enough not to budge even for dinner. He ate with one hand and fiddled with dials with the other, stopping periodically to make notes. Could the mule's jostling have broken something? That was preferable to the alternative, that there was a mysterious signal he could not fathom. He endured the bugs. The signal faded briefly near midnight and then gained strength again shortly after. He had noticed that once before. Was it significant?

Though he had less sleep than Omer or Illyssa and more insect bites, Yan alone was cheery the next morning. He had dreamed again of home. All he could remember was a sense of childlike contentment, and his mother's face, smiling. The birds wakened him, and he sat outside the tent feeling as if he *were* at home, for with few exceptions the birdcalls he heard were familiar ones. He noticed large canine footprints around their camp—wolves had visited while they slept. The tracks meandered between tent, gear, and firesite; an inspection tour, he decided, as the mules had not been disturbed. He knew that northern wolves were intelligent creatures with great senses of humor, and he saw no reason why their southern brethren would be different.

"My father's great hounds," he told his companions later, "were outbred to wolves every few generations, which accounted for their superior intelligence and vigor. I myself raised a she-wolf from a cub and can attest to her superiority over dogs."

Omer suggested, not without sarcasm, that Yan stay up the entire next night to make friends with such splendid neighbors. Yan countered by recommending that Omer drink large quantities of water and kaf throughout the day and pee in a circle around their entire camp the next night instead. The older man thought that a poor rejoinder, lacking wit, until Illyssa spoke on Yan's behalf. "Fences won't keep them out, but wolves are law-abiding where *wolf* law is concerned." Yan added that wolves always respected such determined efforts to delineate boundaries. Nonetheless, Omer drank no more kaf than the others, at breakfast or later.

They did not get going until midmorning, and Yan stretched his three-day estimate of the trip to Jossity to four. He suggested they travel until dark and sleep later in the morning to give their gear and clothing a chance to dry; heavy dew beaded everything exposed to night air.

Most of their route that morning was along silty riverbank, and they followed directly in the tracks of the traveler who still preceded them. "He's making good time," Yan pointed out. "He started before down—those deer tracks are over his, and deer drink at daybreak." He looked at Illyssa for confirmation that the mountain deer did indeed follow the pattern of the woodland variety. At her nod, he continued. "If he keeps up all day he'll have a useless mule by nightfall. Even on this ground it's likely to stumble and injure itself. I wonder why he's in such a hurry?" They made good time themselves, eating in the saddle and not stopping until dark, within sight of Soin, a nondescript town too small to have an inn. "I wonder where our 'trail-breaker' is staying," Illyssa said. "Should we find out?"

"Let's wait until morning," Yan cautioned. "He's in a hurry, and that disturbs me. I'm curious, but I'd as soon not meet anyone until we're out of Tenzie, especially people on urgent business." Omer agreed.

At midmorning, after kaf and a porridge of boiled roots sweetened with Burum honey, they rode down the only street in Soin. Yan estimated that a hundred people occupied the town—a double row of unpainted sheds, widely spaced and linked by split-rail fences. The spaces between held pigs and gaunt cows standing in mud churned to a consistency not unlike the street itself. Since the travelers had no desire to dismount in the slippery muck, they refrained from conversing with townsmen. On the far side of Soin, on higher, less-soggy ground, Yan spotted the tracks of the one they followed. An old man leaning on his fence at road's edge took note of their interest. "Friend of yours?" he asked reedily.

"In a manner of speaking," Yan said.

"Won't catch up before Kort, you don't hurry."

"He may not be who we're looking for, anyway. What did he look like?"

"Looked dead, or on the way."

"Dead? That doesn't sound like our friend."

"White as a mushroom. Whipped his mule. Damn shame, that. Mule won't last. Coulda used a good mule, hear?"

"A pity. Did he stay in Soin last night?" Yan asked.

"Na. He'uz through in a split.'Fore dark."

"Ah, no matter. We must go, too. A pleasure talking with you."

"Ummh. Maybe."

Omer nodded as they filed past, eliciting not a grunt. "Sa much f' our myster'ous rider," he said when they were out of earshot. "Don't sound like plezzunt cump'ny." He had duplicated the oldster's tone and accent exactly, and Yan laughed aloud.

"Om, can you imitate every accent? How about other languages? I know you speak Burumian."

"Zhe connay zunpudda too. Cumprahn suhsi?"

"That sounds like Bekwah. Have you been that far north? Somehow I imagined your travels were to the south."

"I've been as far as Nuffin Cape. Bought sails from th' Norvik once, when we broke a mast off Nuffin Island an' lost our rigging. We'd planned t' sail 'round Hudsin, but snow fell for three months. We hardly saw th' sun. We gave up, sold our cargo a' dried fruits, an' sailed home."

"Are there other languages?"

"Spannol. Tha's spoken 'long th' west side a' th' Inland Sea and t' th' South. Then there's hill-tongues further west. Mostly there's Inglis, Spannol, and Bekwah, enough dialects a' each t' make it hard t' talk from one village t' th' next. Like Burumian. Tha's Inglis, you know."

"Are you joking? It sounds nothing like it."

"Th' sound's different, but it's put t'gether th' same. When they write it, it's Inglis."

"Try me. Say something in Burumian."

"Aya. Something Azzar might say to you: 'Aiman, obbi dabrutha damayan.' See?"

"No. *Mayan*, I think that's 'overlord.' "

"In a sense. If I wrote it, you'd read 'Aya, man, I be the brother of the Man.' "

Yan mulled that over a while, his lips moving as they rode along. He shook his head and laughed. "I never would have suspected. I wish I'd known in Burum, or at the market in Innis."

"There's another place where they speak almost th' same. Baltum, on th' Lannick Coast. They claim no common ancestors, but both 're dark and curly-haired."

"Then at some time past they must have been related. If I ever have the time, I'd like to—"

Omer cut him off. "Read th' whole Chronicles a' Burum, I s'pose, an' then go t' Baltum t' dig and scribble?"

"Will you take me home first?" Illyssa interjected. "While

you do that, I think I'll stay in the mountains and find some nice, uneducated farmer to marry."

Yan grinned superficially and made his mule crab toward hers as if to push her into the brush. Her words, though in jest, had struck a tender chord. She's battered by the world as much as Omer, or me, he realized. But for her there's always an option, a woman's choice: to follow a path only so far, and if it leads in an off direction, to find some farmhouse beside the road, some dumb farmer who'll be there this year and the next and . . .

He flexed his throat muscles to push down the lump that had formed. Illyssa was nearing home, and at every mile his fear grew. She could joke about leaving him, but he could not joke back.

I find my friends fortuitously, he thought. I just hitch myself like a mule to their wagon, and there I am, stuck in the traces until they let me loose. I don't pick my associations; they just happen. Like Lazko. I just drifted into his world without a plan, but then I was committed. I didn't specify Omer, either, but he's as much part of my life as Illyssa. Gods pity me if I ever have to choose between either of them and my quest.

If Illyssa really wanted to settle down, even with him, or if Omer set a new course, Yan did not know how he would handle it. He supposed if she found the farmhouse, he'd stay, but he would never stop staring down the road, watching the sky for un-Earthly fire. He would hate himself, and if Omer rode up with two saddled mules . . . Yan shrugged. If he was to remain a drifter on a sea of circumstance, so be it. His method, or lack of one, had served him well enough. He had companions he loved dearly; he had confirmed and expanded upon his mentor's speculations; he had enlisted the aid of a powerful prince; and he was less than a fortnight from the goal he had originally set.

The day wore on. The trail narrowed severely at a looping river bend where a ledge had been cut into a clifflike bank. They led their mules carefully several man-heights above the foaming, crashing water. Then the trail faded completely. Picking their way among jumbles of fallen rock slick with river spray, they found no place to stop until after sunset.

Again Yan stayed up, listening. Again the clicks and chirps sounded familiar, but meaning eluded him. The third signal again faded near midnight, then resumed. When he finally turned the set off, Yan stood outside their makeshift tent and stared at the sky. Deneb, Altair, and Vega, the summer triangle, glittered like jewels, but clouds encroached on them and finally snuffed them out. He was missing something obvious, he knew, but what?

By morning light, they could see they had reached the end of a narrow gorge. Their camp was on the verge of wide, hilly country. Omer climbed a crumbling knob of contorted bedrock and called down that he could see a town—Kort—at the opposite end of a stone bridge they had passed by unaware in their last hours of travel, after dusk had fallen. When Omer came down from his vantage, they agreed there was no point backtracking through rocks and water to cross there. There would be another bridge in Jossity, which was a fair-sized town.

After a half-mile ride the trail took up again, only to leave the valley entirely. It headed in a southerly direction at right angles to the oak-covered ridges. They climbed steadily, by afternoon reaching the crest of a ridge. The river was in sight below, winding tortuously through eroded hills, and they plotted a course toward Jossity. Columns of woodsmoke marked its location: a few hours' ride, mostly downhill. Finding a frigid spring and a level patch of sod, they halted early; the mules were fatigued from the long climb. They took icy baths and made as good a meal as they could from their dwindling supplies.

Descending to Jossity, Yan commented on the trail they followed. "Have you seen that the clefts we've gone through aren't natural? They're smooth, and have tool marks in places."

"More ancient highways? In my country there's a place where . . ." Illyssa hesitated, wishing she had not spoken.

"Where what?" Omer prompted her.

"I suppose you know enough already," she said, shrugging. "There's a tunnel with such marks leading to it. It's not a cave. In legend, it's where my people stayed when they came to this land. Now only elders go in there. It's said to be miles long."

"Big enough to hold a spacecraft, I wonder?" Yan was musing, not questioning her. "Wouldn't that make things easy?"

"How big would a spaceship be?" she asked.

"In Chongan, there was a pleasure barge with a red canopy, remember? A spaceship might be that size, but cylindrical."

"And smooth? No masts or such?"

"Exactly."

"Something that size might fit in the mouth of the tunnel, but it's rough country, and the mouth is halfway up a steep slope. There was a stone bridge there once, I think."

"It's a possibility, at any rate. I only hope that we can reach an understanding with your old women."

"As I do. Then we can settle down—unless I trade you for a blacksmith with no interest in spaceships."

Jossity was a stone city. A walled keep occupied a tight bend in the river, connected to the town proper by a bridge to the west and a tall gate on the north. To gain the northbound trails to the highlands, travelers had to pass through town and travel along the river's edge for several miles. Jossity was on a water gap where the river had cut through a northeasterly ridge. That ridge was burnt bald of timber, and stone watchtowers stood along its crest, grim reminders that they were not yet free of Tenzie. The far side of the ridge was a land of ungoverned hill tribes. Illyssa's folk were beyond those, to the north.

Yan had never seen a fortified border before. "Is there no way around those towers? Surely they can't encircle all Tenzie like that."

"They don't go twenty miles south," Illyssa replied, "but they follow the ridges north for over seventy. Sometimes our menfolk slip between them to trade, but mostly, people go around. The towers supposedly protect against raids by the hill tribes."

"Supposedly?"

"They were built not to fend off the tribes but to trap them; above all, to trap witches. The tribes have never been warlike. Like my own people, most of them are Old Christians."

"Your people follow the old god? I didn't know that."

"Well, Professor Bando! Who would witches worship? Pharos and his demon-dogs? Why do you think they call us witches?"

"Books about witches say they worship natural objects, spirits, wild animals—that sort of thing." Yan was flustered by his faux pas, and Illyssa was just as obviously having a good time rubbing his nose in it. Omer kept his eyes on the trail and said nothing, though he missed none of the exchange.

"But those were *witches* you read of," she said. "Everyone knows *witches* worship such things—trees, mountains, the moon. Oh, yes, and demons, too. One mustn't forget them."

"Well, that's what I read, and—"

Illyssa interrupted his confused exclamation. "Silly professor! Those were *real* witches—I mean people who really believe they *are* witches. My people are just people. Only outsiders call us witches. We've always been Christians, I think. Not good ones, though."

"Why not?" Omer asked.

"We're too permissive. The Mennites claim that we're loose and sinful. Their Book is like ours, and it supports their words, so my parents say. But Mennites all wear the same clothing and never sing except in church. My uncle Jasso says they're upright and drive hard bargains in trade, but I wouldn't like to be a Mennite. They believe lovemaking is wrong, most of the time."

"I think if I had t' belong t' a church, I'd pick a Christian one," Omer reflected. "At least your god is an *Earth* man, honeybee." Illyssa did not correct him. Perhaps the elders understood the Trinity, but Illyssa's beliefs were simple: she suspected she might be more like those self-professed witches Yan read of than like a Christian Mennite. The moon, at least, smiled on lovers.

"Is there no route except through Jossity? That keep reminds me of Innis Cathedral." Yan eyed the great structure's thick walls and tall, star-shaped tower. Perched on the cliff opposite them, it seemed ready to spew soldiers or demons. Sunlight did not lighten its stark, threatening aspect. "I'd hate to be trapped, now that the border is so near." He caressed his axe nervously. He had donned his Apostate trappings and Pittsburg chain shirt shortly after Jossity had come into view.

"We can ask in th' town. I 'spect th' Tenzians 're more careful who comes in than who goes out." Omer scanned the bridge. "I wonder if there's a toll? Do we have Tenzian coin?"

"Enough. A half ounce of gold and five quarters of silver."

The near side of the river held half the town. The mules' hooves rang on cobbles as they searched for an inn. Pairs of armed men walked the streets in a manner Yan considered arrogantly inferior—the look of police everywhere. Their spectacular uniforms were the color of hard-tempered steel, with violet braid. Gleaming buttons, buckles, eyelets, and rings served no purpose but intimidating display. They wore no mail or armor, but carried metal-ferruled clubs.

There were no signs to indicate what businesses buildings might hold. Shop windows with roll-up shutters were denoted by their visible wares: fabrics from Burum, wines of Cansi and Tawnyo, gold figures of saints, and squat cylindrical spaceships of base metal and bright paint. An inn was proclaimed by an ornate weather-checked headboard, once part of a commodious bed, that hung over the street from black, frayed ropes. Feeling conspicuous, they decided to ride no further. They ducked beneath the precarious sign to order two rooms, then stabled their mules in a shed across the street.

At dusk, as they ate a fine meal of roast pork and cabbage at the inn, several bells chimed, marking the end of the workday for laborers. A deep-toned horn bellowed seven times, then closed with a series of slow and fast notes. "That's the same pattern I heard from the tugboat on the marsh," Yan remarked. Suddenly he grew pale and dropped his fork with a clatter.

"Yan?" Illyssa asked. "Are you choking?"

"That signal! I've heard that on the radio, too!"

"Whistle code?" Omer asked. "That's just ordinary whistle code. Every seaman knows it."

"Om, that's the Church's code!"

"Shut up, Yan," Illyssa hissed. "People are staring."

"I have to get to the radio and—"

"You can't. It's packed with our things, at the stable, and you can't use it here, under the priests' noses."

"She's right, Yan," Omer agreed. "Tomorrow, on the trail, we'll stop so you can listen."

Yan gave in grudgingly. "I want you to write that code down tonight," he muttered. "All this time, and you've known—"

"Oh, shut up," Illyssa said affectionately, squeezing his leg. "How could Omer have known? You've been the only one listening."

"I know. I'm just frustrated that I've wasted all this time. We could already know what the brownskirts are up to."

Before they settled in, Yan handed Omer pen, inkpot, and paper. "I suppose you want it right now?" Omer asked dryly.

"Morning will do. I'll study it on the trail before we stop to listen again."

That night, alone for the first time in days, Yan and Illyssa made love slowly and tenderly, forgetting the vast differences between them, differences that became more apparent each day. Later, they talked.

"You know about so many things, Yan. I know you love me, but you treat me like a clever child instead of a woman. I'm not sure I can live with that for the rest of my life."

"I know. Your jokes about dumb farmers and blacksmiths aren't just idle teasing, are they?"

"I don't know. I mean, I tease you, but it's *serious* teasing. I want you to accept me. I deserve your respect—I'm as intelligent as you, and I'm surely less obtuse." A smile lightened her words. "Neither am I thirty, like you."

"Twenty-eight."

"Yes. Sometimes you're distant, as if I don't even exist, and then you surprise me by being all warm and loving for a while. You turn me up and down like a lamp wick. Which man are you?"

"That's easy enough. I'm both. I'm confused, too. I feel like the man who loves you, but I suppose it doesn't show. The other me, the scholar, is real, too. I get involved in my books and ideas and ancient things, and sometimes I hide there."

"You hide from me?"

"From what you are. From the differences. It's easy to say that people are all alike: men, women, scholars, sailors, even 'witches,' but they're not. We're not, and it scares me."

"Because I'm a witch? Or because I would have made love to Omer back on Choke Marsh?" Her words bored into him like hot needles. So it was true, he thought. She would have.

"What if it's so?" he asked her. "For you it's a natural thought. He's lonely and randy, so make him feel good. But me? I wasn't brought up like that. I felt betrayed. In my grandmother's day, adulteresses were killed in horrible ways. How do you think I feel, that you wanted to bed my best friend?"

She rolled out of the narrow bed suddenly. Had he said too much? Was she leaving him? Frustration and anger gave way to a cold, empty premonition of loneliness—but Illyssa didn't leave. She stood with her hand stretched out to him. "Sit up and look at me." She took his hand and pulled him up. His eyes were level with the dark fluff at the base of her belly. He raised them, past her navel and her small, pointed breasts, to her face, at once a small boy looking at his angry mother and a man swept up in a rush of desire.

"Yan," she said, holding his eyes with her intense gaze. "I love you even though you're a stupid, narrow-minded, smug, selfish, and ungrateful savage who doesn't know what 'friend' is *capable* of meaning." She sucked in a gulp of air; Yan drew breath to reply. "Shut up!" she hissed. "Don't say a word until I'm done. Then, if you still want me to, I'll listen—or you can write it in your damned book.

"Do you think I've got an *itch* for Omer? Do you think I can't wait to get him between my legs? Are you afraid I'm going to spend my life on my back, under every lonely fool who's got a hard-on and nowhere to put it? You *savage*!" she said again. The word bothered him more than all the other epithets put together. Wisely, he listened, saying nothing. "He's *your* friend," Illyssa continued. "*You* should care what he's feeling, what he's going through. But you refuse to notice your so-called friend. You're so smart—how could you miss it?''

''Illyssa, I'm sorry . . . I still don't understand. What did I miss? What's wrong with Omer?''

''Sorry! You're *sorry*? You're a sorry excuse for a friend and a sorry scholar, too!'' She sat on the edge of the bed and turned toward him, then spoke more softly. ''If those people on the barge train, that boy and the others who showed up to watch, could feel something of what we were feeling, then what about Omer? And not just that time, either. Every time we made love, from the very first, Omer was there, too, only *he* didn't have anyone to hold him or love him. Are you going to go on pretending you don't know how he suffered in silence, how he's cried out loud for his own dead woman? How could anyone be *more* alone, with only stupid, selfish *you* for a friend?''

Yan reached up to brush tears from her cheek, but she deftly, angrily twisted her head aside without taking her eyes from his. ''You and I have tormented him and turned all his old scars back into raw sores, and he keeps right on hurting and staying with us because he loves you like a son.''

She had finished. Her eyes met his, but he couldn't see them through the blur of his tears. ''It's true, isn't it? Omer, you, me, all caught up in each other, all hurting.'' She had opened his eyes not only to Omer's pain but to her own. Like a child who clung to its parent, demanding time and love and caring without understanding that spouses and other children had needs separate from its own, he had demanded all that was Illyssa without understanding, without compassion or even love. When he put his head in his hands and wept, she knelt before him and held him against great wracking sobs that coursed through him, surging waves breaking roughly on a black granite shore.

''There's no blame,'' she whispered later, when the sobs subsided, when the storm was past. ''No remorse. Only understanding.''

''How could you stay with me? Why? And Omer . . . what kind of a 'son' have I been?''

''You've been like a little boy. You looked up to him, deferred to him.''

''A boy who doesn't know that his father's a man, not a god.''

''That, too. But little boys grow up.''

''Aya, they do. And none too soon.'' He leaned back until he could see her eyes, until her nipples just brushed his chest.

''Tell me about your father, Yan. And your mother—you were

dreaming about her the first time I saw you. Do you remember?"

He recounted that dream, and the telling led down a long path threading through his childhood. He told her about Enri, the bear, madness, and his flight from it. At times his voice was a young man's tenor; at others it fell to a mature baritone. When he finished he felt weak and hollow, but clean, as if he'd emerged from a bathhouse purified by steam and heat, then rubbed himself with cold snow. Just before he slept he asked her a question. "Would you still go to Omer some night?"

"If you asked," she replied sleepily.

The Junior of East Tenzie faced a thin, haggard priest. He had known the man a single day, enough time to form indelible impressions and a dislike that bordered on hatred. Effredi Gnist was thin, ugly, and too old for the job he was to fill. What was Innis thinking? Kornvetz was too new to his own position to take Gnist's autocratic manner lightly. "A fanatic," he muttered. "By the God and His Sons; they sent me a fanatic. I will not, absolutely not, began my Juniorcy knuckling under to my own so-called aide—past secretary to a Senior or no." Kornvetz's fantasies of a young brother, wise in the perversions of the Holy City, had been cruelly crushed by the arrival of this scarred viper of a man.

"It's quite simple," Gnist told him. "They are in Jossity this very moment. They will depart within a day, and if you refuse to cooperate in their capture, you will hold your new post for but the briefest moment. Their escape would be a blow to the Brotherhood, to the entire Church, and consequences would redound on you alone. Think upon it, but not long." Gnist arose to leave, thinking, How strange it is. A month ago I would have sniveled and begged of this man, my superior-in-name. The torturers took much from me, including my fear. I am pared of all but hatred.

"Wait, Brother!" said Kornvetz. "You've come to Jossity under a geas—whose or what, I don't know. I don't want to know. Since you're prepared to upset and go on upsetting the order of things, I must know your view of our future relationship. Much hinges upon it."

"I will have my captives; you will have East Tenzie. I will hunt witches; you will rule all else. It's that simple."

"That's it, then? Your interference will be in matters of witchery alone, and you will otherwise be my loyal aide?"

"Exactly so. A bargain?"

"Agreed," Kornvetz said flatly.

"Then I must see the captain of guards. Excuse my haste." The emaciated man was already out the door. Ansel Kornvetz reflected that a man obsessed with witches would be less difficult to deal with than one whose goals were rank and power. Sighing mightily, he placed his feet upon the polished wood of his desk.

CHAPTER EIGHTEEN

> "Don't think about it now," Gran'ma used to say. "It will all come back to you by and by."
>
> *Yan Bando, Journal 7*

After breakfast—corn cakes with honey and slabs of fried pork from last night's roast—Yan and Omer looked after the mules, gear, and goods stored under lock and key at the stable. Omer handed Yan his ink, pen, and a sheet of paper, now filled. "I took care wi' my hen-scratchings," he said apologetically, "but you may still find them hard t' read."

"Not as hard as 'reading' the code without them," Yan replied, folding the paper and slipping it in his jacket.

While the men loaded the mules, Illyssa returned to their rooms to pack personal articles and to bring them down.

The men heard a commotion in the street, but thought nothing of it until they heard Illyssa scream. They rushed to the stable door, colliding with each other and with two bright-suited constables. Yan stumbled, and even as he fell he saw men holding Illyssa's small, thrashing form. Another man stood at one side, passive, dark-clad, and thin. "It's Gnist! From Innis!" Illyssa managed four words before a hand was clapped over her mouth.

Gnist. For a moment the name meant nothing to Yan. Only the terror in Illyssa's voice meant anything at all. He desperately wished that now, of all times, his madness would come to his aid. Gnist! His recognition of the name was the necessary prod. His head swirled with memories of the Cathedral compound, of a black crab-beast in its dark cell, a glowing, melting padlock. Pictures dissipated, leaving only dew-clad cobbles and polished boots before his nose as he lay on the paving. He saw Illyssa, held fast by guards. The scene was like a painting. Nothing moved. His hand crawled to his axe. He raised his head slowly, as though his body were immersed in syrup—the very air was palpable, resisting his effort to rise. He recognized what was happening: I've been given time to plan. I must use this gift while I have it. For Illyssa.

He drew his knees under himself. The guard he had collided with was still off-balance. Yan's axe came free of his thong like a living thing. His wrist twisted it, accelerating it toward the man's throat, and he planned the follow-through even as the axe swept a swarm of round red droplets after it. Yan did not watch the ball-shod butt collapse the face of the second guard, for he was already running toward Illyssa. More men emerged from shops and houses. The two holding Illyssa backed into the inn, leaving their arriving comrades to face Yan with drawn clubs.

This is almost easy, he thought. They're so slow. He barreled into their ranks, clipping heads with both ends of his axe; one head was crushed, another fell open from a slash. Good. His satisfaction was unemotional, technical, as though with a neat test-pit or a well-turned phrase. He whirled, pulling the flying weapon into a circular path. Momentum drove it through thighs and shins as it dropped. Yan saw everything as a series of still images. He continued to whirl and slash. Five were down, then six. Screams and moans were drowned by a louder voice, an undulating, throaty bellow that went on and on. More unfortunates fell like broken dolls before Yan recognized the eerie howl as his own. A blue-jacketed foe stared dumbfoundedly at a slash across his chest, not yet aware that the gaping slit went deep, that his heart no longer beat in lively rhythm, that he was dead. Another stared wildly at the sky as his head slipped sideways, held to his slumping body only by a stretching flap of skin. Blood fountained from his severed neck, covering his hair and his still-bright eyes before his knees had time to buckle. The axe sang and Yan bellowed. Men arrived, fell, and died. He was a mindless machine, hewing human timber into piles of red-sapped cordwood.

He felt Omer at his side even as he swung the jaw-crushing ball at yet another foe. "There's too many, Yan! We can't hold them." The voice came from a far distance, it seemed. "I'll hold them," his friend called. "You get away. Knowledge, Yan! What you know mustn't be lost. You *must* go!" More pretty uniforms rose before Yan, and for a long moment Omer said no more as the slaughter resumed. They backed from bloody refuse and slick red cobbles, to fight again on dry stone. Yan knew he was being struck, heard the thud of clubs across his back and shoulders, experienced brief annoyance as he turned to destroy the club wielders. Everything occurred with ponderous slowness; his every move was planned in advance, and he forced himself to wait for every swing and thrust to arrive at its intended target. Each impact went unseen, for he knew the blows were true, and turned to focus on his next goal: a face to be crushed, an arm or thigh to be slashed, a head to be freed from its neck.

"You've *got* to get away, Yan!" Omer's yell broke through his shell of concentration. "I'm tiring. Illyssa's captured. Get the mules and go before it's too late."

Between methodical, careful swings, each drawing its calculated draft of blood, Yan forced out words. "I'll be back for you." He fended off a slowly approaching club. "Stay alive." He spun, taking out another guard with his blade, and made for the mules. Drop-reined, they had wandered only to the stable door. Two panicked as the blood-sodden apparition appeared in the doorway, but he caught the third. Yan threw himself chest-first over the saddle, and the mule crab-stepped into the street. He pulled himself up and over as his mount's clattering hooves drowned out receding battle sounds. The high tinkle of metal on metal told him Omar still fought on.

At the edge of Jossity, streets climbed the ridge a short way and petered out at the forest edge. Yan dug in his heels and his durable mount pushed on—still slowly, it seemed. Behind him, he heard the clatter of hooves, so he spurred his mount to greater effort. Shadows swept over him as he entered the tree zone. Ahead lay the burnt ridge where nothing grew but stone towers. I'll cut west under the trees, he thought, with the machinelike precision of his altered mental state. I'll come out on the burn beyond the third tower. I won't be expected that far down the line, and if the beast holds up, I can make it. He slowed his lathered mount to a walk. The trees were large, spaced with parklike precision twelve yards apart. Though there were no landmarks, he knew that his direction was correct, that he would emerge where he planned. The forest floor was hidden beneath bright ferns, which brushed his mount's legs and belly, then swung back up, undisturbed. Looking over his shoulder, he saw no pursuers and no sign of his own passage. Keeping ridge-top sunlight on his left, he traversed the slope.

Somewhere inside him a small boy sobbed. *It's over!* The mule's slow pace seemed to quicken. No, not yet! I'm not free yet! The slowed time of madness was fading. He knew that when it was gone, pain would come, and he would no longer be able to fight. For the first time in his life he made a conscious effort to hold on to what he'd hated most. He forced himself to remember his battle with the bear, picturing details of terrain, recalling bog scents and the rank, hairy stink of his foe. Still, the world about him, the pace of his mule, and the oak leaves twitching in the breeze sped up. He felt dull aches now, sensory messages that would soon be agony.

The fire! Think of Lazko, of thugs dying beneath my bare hands! The images flashed, obscuring reality. Sunlight glittering between heavy-shrouded limbs became sparks cascading from Lazko's attic. Still, his pain grew, and he swayed in the saddle, knowing he was failing. He could not hold the strength of madness. "So be it," he murmured. "This is the end. It no longer matters. I did what I could, and now I'll die." He felt no bitterness, no grief for Omer or Illyssa—only vague regret that he had not reached his ill-defined goal.

Only then, with his mind empty, did the lingering sparks of Lazko's pyre change course, ascending upward in a column of impenetrable black smoke. A new picture rose before him: a ponderous machine of great power and weight, chuffing and straining inside him. He reached a mental hand out and grasped a lever, pulling it slowly. Steam surged through clanking tubes. Hot flames rose up a tall, constricting flue, emerging in showers of bright vermilion sparks and gouts of black coal-smoke. In the depth of his being, a massive flywheel rotated faster, shaking its timber-seated bearings, and again Yan felt the slowing, the bright, emotionless clarity of madness. But this time, in a hidden place deep within, a small boy laughed and hooted exultantly. "I did it! I did it all by myself!"

Sunlight streaming between oak boles was blocked by the third tower, just a few yards on. Yan slipped from the mule's sweat-soaked back and drop-reined it among some ferns. He walked, then crawled belly-down, to the forest edge. Blackberry canes choked out ferns at the juncture of grass and forest, but his bramble pricks and thorn scratches went unnoticed. There was the tower. Anyone pursuing him would concentrate between the first two towers, nearer the town. He listened with adrenaline-augmented ears for the least sound or hint of motion near the tall building. Nothing. The tower was ten yards high, and not much less in diameter. On its crenellated parapet, poles interwoven with wattle shaded the interior. At least one sentry would be there; more were probably below. He caught a whiff of horse scent downwind, not from his own sweat-soaked clothing or from his mule. Glancing back, he saw that his pursuer was his own well-trained pack mule, who had followed doggedly the whole way. There was no sign of the other riding mules. Yan felt momentary regret; his own mule, exhausted, could not survive much more of this.

He crawled back through the brush, remounted, and turned toward the sunlight. The exhausted mule staggered. "Don't die now, half-ass. Give five more minutes of your best and I'll feed you oats and apples forever." He kicked his heels with no result. Further kicks, hard ones, did no more; the mule's strength was gone. Good mule, he thought. A horse would have died already. Yan still gripped the slippery handle of his axe; even during his crawl through the brush he had been unaware of it. His knuckles were white and bloodless. Truly, Father, your lessons were well taken. *Make it a part of your arm*, you said. Now see what's happened. Will I live to break loose this death grip? He reached behind himself and poised the spiked peen over the mule's broad hindquarters, then let it fall. With an agonizing half snort, half bray the mule broke through clinging blackberries into the bright, morning sunshine. So much for surprise, Yan said to himself as the mule continued upslope at a fair pace.

The grass was tall and sere. Birdsong faded as he rode out beneath the sky. Nothing moved. Ahead was the ridge-top. Was more forest beyond? Had he been seen? The mule strained onward. The stone cylinder was the largest thing in view, the only thing besides grass and the slowly nearing line where ground met cloud-strewn cerulean sky. He heard only the rustle of dry grass parting, the coarse rale of his mount. And inside, a faint chuffing as if some distant engine beating in time with his heart.

Concentrated sunlight danced at the corner of his eye as a sentry flashed his mirror. From the angle, he knew a message was being sent not to the tower nearer town, but to another to the south. Still, no troops emerged from the tower nearest him. Had they been called to reinforce the line near Jossity? Whatever the message, Yan knew no tower but one was close enough for its occupants to reach him before he was over the border. His mule plowed ahead ever more swiftly, or so it seemed. The madness ebbed.

A youth's sobbing rose in him; his chest drew air in response, making the ghostly crying real. He wiped real tears from his face with the back of a bloody hand. "Not yet, son. It's not over yet. Time for tears on the far slope, later." Had he spoken aloud? The voice had been Omer's, or his father's.

Movement! A shadow detached itself from the watchtower and resolved into a mounted man. Steel and purple contrasted against the grass; buckles flashed oblique sunlight into the air. Yan concentrated on the image of the great, pounding engine, but his mind refused to recall it. He shrugged listlessly. He was finished. Well enough. Exhausted, he could do no worse than die, and he was so very tired that it no longer mattered.

The horseman's course intersected his where the slope leveled. Years of wintry winds had swept soil from the hilltop, and metal-shod hooves crunched on the brittle frost-cracked chert. Between Yan and freedom, the rider raised a long, curved sword. They were close, a few horse-lengths part. Yan saw stubborn fear in his opponent's eyes, in the tight set of his smooth, beardless jaw. What have I become? The boy's terrified. A bloody apparition, I must be, but tired—as tired as this poor mule who's already dead. I haven't told him, is all. He forced a grin and raised his axe level with his chest. His eyes never left the young soldier's. His vice came deep like his father's, like some distant, mad ancestor hoarse from shouting as his enemies fell before him. "I've already gone by, boy. I'm down the hill and gone, and you never caught up with me. Only *you* need know what happened here." And you'll wake up nights wondering if you should have done otherwise, Yan added silently. But that's your burden, not mine. You can live with it.

Yan's mule had not altered its dogged pace, but the horse stood still. Not a hair moved on its rider's head as Yan drew near, then passed by. Like an eroded statue of a dead general, the youth remained still until Yan was almost to the far treeline. Then he slumped like a sack of sand. Saber dangling on his slack arm, he returned to his tower. Yan never looked back.

The guard captain's face glowed where the imprint of Brother Gnist's bony hand marked it. A vein bulged and throbbed beneath Gnist's tight-drawn skin. Shedded hair matted the shoulders of his coarse woolen cassock, as if a cat had slept on it.

"Accelerated, premature aging," Junior Kornvetz gloated under his breath. "Will he die from delayed results of the torture which lost him his fingernails, or will he be consumed by the internal fires which drive him first?" Either way, the result would be the same, and Kornvetz would hardly mourn his passing.

"A scholar!" Gnist shrieked. "You let a bookish antiquarian

and an old fisherman slaughter seven constables and maim a dozen more? You *permitted* him to ride unhindered through a mile of city streets, right past your watchtowers, without even a *shout*?"

Stiffly at attention, the guardsman spat explanation. "A berserker, Brother! A northern madman! We were never warned."

"Two against twenty? Do you expect to keep your posting still? Have you performed satisfactorily, then?"

"I expect nothing, Brother. Another score of men might have made a difference, but I could not know. You yourself were there—for a while." He paused to let those last words sink in. He dared not accuse the new priest of cowardice, but he could remind him of his hasty departure. "You saw, before you left. No normal man could stand against him. He had no false move, no wasted effort. Blows that would have felled any man in my company, he brushed aside or ignored."

Brother Gnist had indeed seen enough to send him fleeing to safety with Illyssa. He relented. "Go, then. See to the two we have taken. The witch must talk to no one. Gag her. Isolate her where her charms can affect no one. Inform me when the man regains consciousness—if he does—but she is the important one. The fisherman is a lever, if I need one, but without *her*, the scholar can't cross the witches' borders. They kill outsiders. No permanent harm is done. He'll come back for her."

CHAPTER NINETEEN

Faith. Religion. Consider this: through millennia of cultural evolution on Earth, new faiths emerged regularly. Ancestors first, then gods and goddesses. Prophets elaborated, formulated, and one God emerged. Teachers like Buddha, Jesus, Zarathustra, Baha'Ullah refined rough creeds. Reformers redefined and purified them, theologians elaborated them beyond recognition.

Consider now *our* Earth. No creeds emerge, no prophets foresee, no reformers cut or shape. Pharos' fraud predominates, and the old faiths endure stoically and statically, in their native locales. Is there a lesson in this?

Preface to *The Fossil Creeds* by Harich Swedoon, last Chancellor of the University at Onskill, written during his exile in Burum.

Yan awakened in darkness. Was it night? He blinked crusted eyes to see if there were stars, a moon. Something weighted his hands. Coarse cloth scratched his body. He remembered: a cowherder had seen his mule collapse at the mountain's foot, and had helped him to the hut. Yan remembered callused hands removing his blood-stiffened clothing and his chain shirt. He was naked beneath the scratchy blanket; his mattress was a heap of swale grass, dry and sweet-scented. He tried rolling over and getting an elbow under himself, but that was too much effort. He drifted back into sleep.

Later he felt his head being raised by a strong hand. "Drink this," a smooth voice said. "It's a broth of vegetables. You've lost blood, and must have liquids."

"Am I . . . what's wrong with me? I can hardly move."

"You've bruises enough to have *rolled* down that mountain.

Be glad you can't move much. It will hurt enough later. I found nothing broken, though. Will you tell me what happened? These club marks are from Jossity's constables, unless I'm mistaken."

Yan hesitated, but the herder reassured him. "You're safe here, out of their reach. There was a to-do up on the ridge, but Pharos-folk don't come down here. This is free land."

"I fought with them," Yan told him. "They were waiting for us in Jossity, and only I escaped. My friends are still there, if they're alive."

"What will you do now? You can't go back after them."

"I must go north. There are people who may help me."

"You can't go yet. You barely managed to get this far. Give your body a day or so to recover—dead yourself, you can't help your friends. May I ask how it happened? Idle curiosity, I confess." The man smiled deprecatingly. "I hear little of interest from my cattle, as you can imagine."

"I don't mind," Yan said hesitantly, "but it's a long, crazy story. We got on the wrong side of the Brotherhood of Pharos. The Star Church. My . . . one of my friends was a captive before, in Innis. We were traced or followed to Jossity."

"You've come a long way. Perhaps you'll feel like talking later. Rest now." He left Yan to sleep. The broth had gone down smoothly. Perhaps one of its herbs was a soporific, Yan thought as he drowsed off.

As he pulled on his freshly washed and mended clothes, Yan asked, "How long has it been?"

"Since you stumbled in here? Only a day. You weren't unconscious, only exhausted. Your saddle mule fared less well. I might have saved him, but it was kinder to let him die."

"You acted rightly. He suffered enough."

Seeing him in daylight for the first time, Yan was surprised that for all his strength in moving Yan, the herder was not large. He was a brown man: brown hair and skin, brown eyes like his cattle's in color and expression. Brown clothing and boots and a brown felt hat completed the monochromatic picture.

Yan's meager baggage was set out beside the hut. He had weeded out everything not necessary—the mule he had taken had been Illyssa's. Her personal articles were of no use to him, nothing she had treasured, nothing he could use to prove to himself or her elders that she was his Illyssa or theirs. It had been a painful task to sort through her saddlebags, not knowing if she lived. With a strong rein on his grief he pushed those thoughts aside and concentrated on his immediate goals.

Illyssa had been carrying the letter from the Mayan of Burum and some of their coins, so Yan still had an introduction and some means. The pack mule, carrying the radio and the goods he had kept, would be lightly laden.

Perhaps there was still a chance the witches might talk with him. He had no idea what to do about Illyssa and Omer, but there was nothing to do but go to her people. Of her effects, he kept a brass comb she had bought in Nobi and gave the rest to the herder. Then he headed for a village where he could buy a horse.

Later, Yan would not remember that walk, the town, or the days that followed. He retained only impressions of grand vistas of corrugated rock and forested land with small streams. His trail took him along the crests of north-trending ridges, bare of soil, and his passage was easy. He found no horse in that first village, so he rode on a produce cart, and then on a dray filled with metal scraps, the pack mule trailing behind. He went slowly, impatient with the winding lowland roads, but he had time to heal.

He had time, too, to set up the radio, to string wire and orient the antenna. Using Omer's code table, he deciphered fragments of messages from Jossity: the click code, he discovered, was the same as the whistle code; a quick *ti-tic* was "short" and a slightly extended *tick-tick* was "long." Not surprisingly, among the Jossity signals he frequently recognized his own name. He determined that there was to be no pursuit—the churchmen believed he would come back to ransom or rescue his friends. Good, he thought. They're still alive.

The Roke messages puzzled him. Some were strong whistle code, routine communications of no import to him; others, faint ones, contained fragments of different code he could not decipher. Context suggested the fragments were numerical information, but not numbers he could make sense of.

The odd, nondirectional third signal continued unchanged, even after he opened the radio's case to assure himself that its metal-, glass-, and wax-covered components were secure in their mounting. The shrill sounds seemed to have slipped down the scale a quarter octave, but Yan's sense of pitch was not absolute, so he was not sure. He *was* sure that the signal had migrated down the radio-frequency spectrum, gradually edging closer to the other signals on the tuner dial. The brief midnight lull in the signal, he discovered, was mirrored by an equivalent fading just after noon. It was the only variation, and it told him nothing.

When he bathed at a public house in the third village on his route, he was surprised to see how colorful he had become. Scarcely a palmsbreadth of his skin was without green, yellow, and reddish-purple bruises. He marveled that he had felt nothing at all while collecting them, which led his mind back to the subject of his madness. Others, writing of similar afflictions—or gifts, depending on viewpoint—had called it "rage." Perhaps it seemed so from outside, but Yan remembered no emotion at all. The image of the pounding steam engine described how he had felt: inexorable strength, machinelike precision, fiery heat controlled and harnessed to purpose. He was no longer afraid of madness. And the loss of fear, he realized, was only partly due to events in Jossity, to his recognition of the madness's utility. It had begun with his dreams; his mind had secretly worked on it, and on all the other torments he'd carried like heavy stones in his pockets. He remembered the flight from Jossity, and calling up his demon to bolster his waning strength. Could he do that again? Could madness be brought under control by his rational, conscious mind? Could it be *stopped* at will, too? That, he knew, was the key to his personal acceptance—the final step that could turn curse into talent.

He experimented as he rode his newly acquired horse, creating images of hypothetical dangers at first. He was pleased to discover no such stimulus was needed: the steam-engine image was enough. How lucky I was to see that magnificent creation, he told himself, for I can think of no other image so powerful. He played with "flywheel" and "piston," altering his breathing and heartbeat. Subjective time flowed as fast and slow as he willed. Is this how witches cause themselves to die? he wondered, but stopped short of dangerous experimentation with his body rhythms. By the time he neared the end of his journey, he felt that he controlled the process of his talent, though he was no closer to understanding it than he had been as a child. Nonetheless, it was more his tool, less his master.

The valley town below was called Blue. Did the name originate with the dark vegetation of surrounding hills or the foggy mountains whose silhouettes formed the horizon? It looked no different from any mountain town he'd ridden through: two trails came together in a wobbly cross, unpainted clapboard buildings stretching a half mile along each one. A discerning eye might have noticed that Blue was a tiny bit neater than some towns, that its porches were more recently scrubbed than in others, and that its fretwork and carved vergeboards were perhaps more carefully executed than was the rule. The cobbles Yan rode across were well-set and evenly sized.

Previously, Yan had not needed to look further than the next hill, the next valley—immediate goals—but Blue was the end of the line. Across the valley, where fields gave way to forest, was the unmarked border of the witch tribe's land. Now he was faced with choices. He could wait at the end of the trail where witch-folk might come for invalids or madmen left for their ministrations—but he was no longer injured, and did not consider himself mad. That irony was not lost on him, and he wished his friends could appreciate it. It marked the change in his attitude toward madness that he would not have hesitated to tell them everything.

Alternatively, he could ride into the woods and fervently hope he was not shot from the saddle or disposed of by paranormal means, or he could get acquainted in the town. Illyssa had said her menfolk came here on occasion.

A carved pine slab over a door attracted Yan's attention. It portrayed a beer mug and another object too weathered to identify: a loaf of bread, or a potato. He scented roasting mutton as he rode by. He had eaten indifferently since fleeing Jossity; the smell was overwhelmingly delicious. Cautiously slinging his saddlebags over a shoulder, he stood in the doorway while his eyes adjusted to the lessened light. A long wooden bar extended the length of one wall, and tables were set on identical angles in the open space before it. An open-planked batten door led to a kitchen, where the wonderful smell originated. Four men sat at a corner table playing cards, and the owner or innkeeper stood idly by with his hands tucked in his apron.

"No food for another hour, traveler," the aproned man greeted him. "Something to wash down the dust while you wait?"

"Aya. Beer or ale would do nicely." A cedar-stave tankard was brought, and Yan drank greedily of an excellent light beer. He wiped foam from his beard with a dusty sleeve.

"You've been long on the road, I'd guess. From the southlands?"

"Aya. Jossity."

"Any news of note? We don't get many Tenzians here."

"I'm not Tenzian, nor a friend of Tenzians." Yan spoke quietly, but the innkeeper saw anger in his eyes.

"Just as well. You're among friends here, eh, Jasso?"

A tall man looked up from his cards. He was dark-skinned and clean-shaven except for a full black mustache hiding his upper lip and the corners of his mouth. If he was smiling, his mustache hid it. "It may be so. Tenzians aren't popular here, nor are their false gods. Are you a Christian, stranger?"

"I am no follower of Pharos. What I *am*, I'm not certain."

"Fair enough," the swarthy one said, shrugging. "News, then. What of events in Jossity?"

"There was a disturbance there, and constables were killed." Yan's thoughts raced. What should he say? What did he dare reveal? He took a deep gulp from his tankard to give himself time to organize his thoughts. "Some people report that a witch was captured in the fray. One man escaped."

"A witch you say? 'Witch' country is north of here. A spurious rumor, perhaps?" Jasso's smiled as if he considered witches to be the stuff of fairy tales, not a legitimate topic for grown men's conversations.

"My source," Yan said after another lengthy swig, "was only a merchant, but he claimed that a 'witch,' long-lost, was returning home." He shrugged pointedly, as if vastly uninterested in such things. "Whatever her nature," he said, "she's in Brotherhood hands, in Jossity Keep—if she lives."

"Curious indeed," Jasso said, tracing a strange spiral figure in the wetness on the table. Yan wondered if it was more than an idle gesture, but he carefully refrained from showing his curiosity. Jasso did not meet his eyes as he asked another question. "Did your informant mention a name?"

"Perhaps," Yan said, pretending sudden suspicion, hoping to put the man on the defensive. "It strikes me your questions aren't idle."

"I am a trader," Jasso replied, shrugging again. "I know many names. I've traded with witches—or men who might claim to be so. But no matter. Is there other news?"

Yan was disappointed. For a moment, he had hoped to get more from the close-mouthed fellow. "There is, should I find the ones to tell it to," he replied stubbornly. "I have news from Burum for a man called John, and for his mother, Martina."

"Old names, common hereabouts. How will you find the ones you seek?"

"I have no plans. I might wait here awhile, and noise it about that I seek words with them. If I hear nothing, I'll ride past the trees at the north end of town, come week's end."

Jasso shook his head. "A dangerous plan. Some have died in witch land. Others never return, alive or dead. Is your own life worth so little?"

"My messages are worth more," Yan snapped, tired of circumlocution. If he could not get through to Illyssa's people, if there was no way to rescue her, what did it matter what happened to him? "Can word be gotten to them?"

Jasso sipped from his mug. "It's said that witches come and go. Some here may know them, but won't talk of it. Others know nothing at all."

"Then I'll follow my plan and hope not to have to ride into their midst unannounced." Yan was done with talk. He looked around for a table not too near the card players.

"Good luck to you, then." Jasso looked down at his cards in dismissal, and the game took up again. Yan took a seat where he could see the others from the corner of his eye but did not have to look at them.

Without an order from Yan, the tavernmaster brought him a beechwood platter heaped with crisp parings from a crusty leg of mutton, nestled among sliced tubers soaked with dark juices. Wide, flat pod beans drenched with melted butter shared the plate, and more beer accompanied the feast. When he had eaten and drunk, Yan was overcome with lassitude. There were no rooms for travelers, but Jasso offered to guide him to a proper inn. Yan accepted assistance and was soon comfortable in a well-scrubbed room overlooking the street. He was too tired to bathe; at any rate, hot water would not be available until morning. Out of consideration for the innkeeper's wife—and the bright quilted featherbeds themselves—Yan threw his own blanket over the top of them and slept clothed.

He slept late. He rose in time to bathe in hot water, though he was not the first to use it. The procedure for bathing, carefully explained by the innkeeper's aging mother, guaranteed that each user of the bath would have a soak in reasonably clean water. Undressing, Yan washed with soapy rags from one oak bucket and rinsed from another. After a second wash and rinse, he was ready for a long soak in a wooden tub large enough for two men. Being late, he was alone, and was able to stretch out. A second scrubbing—outside the tub, of course—rid him of the last dust of the road and of several loosened scabs.

He made contact with several people that day in the manner of a traveler buying supplies, but none claimed to know about witches except tales such as he had heard and read before. The town was small enough to walk through in an hour, and Yan had no idea of what to do next. Possible death awaited him beyond the valley unless he obtained permission to travel there, but if Omer and Illyssa were alive, he should proceed as rapidly as he could. He passed by his best opportunity for contacting witches several times without realizing it: a nondescript, single-story building with nothing to identify it but two sticks hanging from the gable. If anyone had bothered to straighten them, they would have formed a cross.

When he finally did venture in, the door swung quietly on wooden gudgeons, revealing the inside of the Christian temple—Christians called them "churches," but Yan associated that too strongly with the Brotherhood, and preferred the other name. Candles lit an altar where the dying Christ hung on a cross of black wood. The carved figure's pink-painted flesh looked orange by candlelight, while the crimson splashes on brow, ribs, and extremities seemed black. Smaller figures occupied pedestals along the side walls.

Yan was moved by the scene, feeling as he had when he'd climbed into the pit with the ancient spaceship. The wooden temple felt not seventy years old, but as if it had been there in its exact form for millennia. The ancient religion had endured so much, and still endured as if years had not touched it. How different it was from the cold, alien magnificence of Innis Cathedral! This temple is as much of Earth as if its walls were cut from sod, he thought. It belongs here, a building among other buildings—part of Blue, of Earth.

"Can I be of service, son?" The voice startled him. Its owner came through a door beside the altar, from a tiny cubicle. He was short and round, with streaky gray hair and a ruddy complexion, and his voice boomed like a healthy bullfrog's.

"I'm not sure you can, sir. Forgive me—I am a stranger. Is there a proper form of address?" Yan knew that the tight, round collar and black shirt were not ordinary dress, though the man's checked woolen shirt, worn as an overgarment, was a common piece of clothing. He had to be a priest, of sorts.

"There's no rule. I'm Rossup Andever. People call me Father Ros."

"It's a notch above Brother, then," Yan commented dryly. "I'm Yan Bando, once of Nahbor on the Eastern Reach."

"Welcome, Yan. May God be with you. Are there Christians, still, in the north?"

"I'm not a Christian, Father Ros. But yes, there are, though they're not outward about it. The Brotherhood of Pharos allows no other churches."

"You're no Pharos worshiper, are you?"

"Most assuredly not. I've dedicated my life—what may remain of it—to the downfall of that fraud."

"What may remain of it, you say? You are obviously a bitter man. Are you also a pessimist?"

"A realist. Perhaps you can help me feel optimistic."

"Again I ask: how can I be of service? You wish more than an inspirational sermon, I presume?"

"I've been told that the so-called 'witches,' whose boundary lies beyond, are Christians, though perhaps of a different ilk from yours. No one in Blue admits to contact with them, but I desperately need to cross that border, to talk with their elders. It is no idle whim. Events of worldwide importance hinge upon our meeting." Hearing his own portentous words, he grinned sheepishly, then continued. "I may sound inflated and self-important, but if I do not contact them, I will cross that border anyway. That is the weight of my mission. I prefer to die of old age, not by suicide at the second hand, as such intrusion is said to be."

"I can't attest to the truth of old tales. I've met witches, and they seemed much like other folk. One is a priest like myself. But I can't promise anything. If you can wait a few days in Blue . . . ?"

"I'm prepared to wait until week's end—four more days—unless I have word from *them* to wait further."

"Good enough, Yan Bando. If they can be contacted—and I promise nothing—what message do you wish them to hear?"

Yan took a steadying breath. "There are two people: a woman named Martina, and her son John. And two messages. First: their lost one may still live, in great danger. Second: an ancient enemy in Burum wishes to make his peace with them."

"Cryptic. You're *too* careful. If the message is misunderstood, you waste time—to your own risk, for if you become impatient . . ." He shook his head. "Whatever dangers you've seen, you're safe here in Blue. The Brotherhood has no power here, nor spies. But if you don't talk, no one will listen."

Piles of cushions lay in precise rows on the floor. Ros kicked one to Yan and sat on another. It looked uncomfortable for a portly man, but the priest seemed relaxed enough. Yan sat down also, and with only occasional prods or questions gave the priest the briefest account he could—so brief that each significant event stood baldly without detail to mellow its unlikeliness. Yan was aware of how preposterous it must sound to a stranger, in this sheltered mountain town. He was prepared for the priest to brush him off as a madman, and his statements as delusions.

"It's an interesting tale, to be sure," Ros said, an hour later. "I'm not sure that it's all true—or accurate, I should say—especially those events long in the past. But enough jibes with things I know that I'm inclined to believe it all.

"What you must do, Yan, is return to the inn and settle down. Talk as much or as little as you wish, but don't ride north until you've spoken with me once more. Will you promise that? Good! Not that you must wait until you're ready to leave to talk with me, you understand. I'm here most of the time, or in the house behind. You're welcome to join us in worship, too."

"I've told you that I'm not a Christian, Father Ros. Does that matter to you?"

"To the contrary, it only strengthens my desire to expose you to my faith. You aren't a heathen in my view, only unawakened." Father Ros' eyes traced a path upward, resting on the wooden cross and its burden. "He was a man of Earth, like us."

Yan waited. He ate well, but otherwise spent little. He filled pages in a newly purchased journal with tight, minuscule lettering that made the most of each sheet. Lazko's precious notes were gone, perhaps in Gnist's hands, perhaps destroyed, and he tried to recapture some of the more important information they had contained. He played cards with the men who seemed to have permanent claim to the tavern's corner table. Jasso, the man who had spoken with him and showed him to the inn, did not return.

He visited Father Ros several times, and attended two masses in the temple. Much of what he experienced there passed him by; the sermons assumed things he did not know, because Ros did not adjust his addresses to Yan's presence among the tightly packed worshipers. On other visits, though, he questioned the priest intensely, especially about the rules by which a Christian was expected to live. It made sense that Gods should make demands on their adherents and should provide models for behavior. The Star Church had no concern for individual morality, being dedicated to secular regulation and collection of tithes, and ferosin were surely no paragons for men to imitate. He did not miss the hooting and swaying, the competitive calling out to Pharos, the money-throwing. Father Ros' temple was a placid place.

But Ros' theology eluded him completely, and he privately discounted the importance of esoteric concepts. Most religions seemed to have such elements, of interest to priests and scholars but irrelevant to the daily practices of their followers.

The importance placed on daily practice, of adherence to stringent rules, gave him his strongest reassurance that he might survive passage into the witches' land, for even such poor practitioners of Jesus' rules as Illyssa claimed her folk to be would not violate His teachings to the extent of indiscriminate murder of mere trespassers—or so he fervently hoped. By week's end he was not a declared Christian, but he felt at home with the faith's warmth and Earthliness.

On his fifth morning in Blue, Yan returned to the temple with saddlebags packed. The cobbles were slippery with dew. Riding up, he noticed a small, twisted maple that grew from the building's foundation stones. The first time he'd seen it, it had been green, but now it glowed red and yellow in the sunlight. It was an impatient plant, he thought; autumn was weeks away. Father Ros was outside when he arrived. Smiling, he peered into the rose-washed east where the sun was emerging over the ridge.

"I don't suppose I could persuade you to stay another day? No, I thought not. Then dismount for a cup of kaf before you go. It's prepared already." Some hesitancy in his manner gave Yan the impression that the invitation was more than idle courtesy. Finding no hitching post, he twisted reins around the stunted maple's stem.

The sanctuary still held a hint of nighttime damp. Their conversation was light, and skirted topics that had involved them deeply on other occasions. Both men knew that the parting was final, that should Yan return to Blue he might not be the same man. It had happened before, the tales said. Talk of weather and the coming fall covered both men's regrets that so much had been left unsaid, unlearned. Should it all come to nothing, Yan told himself, should Omer and Illyssa be dead and the witches obdurate, I will return here. In our own ways, Ros and I both pursue heaven, and perhaps I'll learn to believe in his version, given time. There was not much more they could say to each other out loud. Yan fidgeted and wiggled on his cushion as his tall new boots cut off the circulation to his feet. Father Ros got up. Opening a carved and gilded box, he fumbled inside it.

Palming what he found there, he returned to stand over Yan, who got up.

"A mile beyond the border, I'm told, is a shrine, an ancient wayside place where travelers have prayed since early times. Would you place this within for me?" Yan took the object from his outstretched hand. It was a small gold chain with links so finely made that it seemed smooth as a tiny snake. Pendant on it was a diminutive replica of the crucified god.

"A thing of beauty," Yan said. "It's ancient, isn't it?"

"So I believe. Two thousand years, perhaps. It has no history, but I feel that it belongs in that ancient holy place."

"Should I get that far, I'll deliver it," Yan agreed. Ros, he had observed, seemed to have no fear that he would be molested—at least not until after he reached the shrine and delivered the token, he clarified silently. "Now, Father Ros," he said aloud, "I must leave before my courage goes its own way." He turned and went through the door. Father Ros stayed within.

Once mounted, Yan saw that the priest watched him from the doorway, quite solemn except for the slightest crinkle at the corners of his eyes. "You must be quite confident that this precious token will arrive at the shrine," Yan pointed out. Father Ros shrugged wordlessly. Was that a smile?

Omer had been awake for several minutes, but he continued to feign sleep. How long had it been? He was so weak. Indeed, though he was not bound, he had no strength to lift his arms against the weight of the light woolen blanket tucked around him. He felt no pain except where his body pressed against the bed. How did I get here? he wondered. Am I captive or free? But the first voices he heard shattered his hope of freedom even before the speakers reached his room.

"—and the drugs we've been giving him should wear off by nightfall. He won't be of much use to you, though, until he recovers his strength."

"And how long will that be, Brother Kinnut? I've already waited twelve days. For twelve days the damned witch has defied me while this one slept. I can progress no further with her until he's strong enough to feel the iron without dying of it. *How long?*"

"You press me too hard, Brother Gnist. He still lives, which in itself is a miracle. The man's wounds were most severe. Two of the constables he fought have since died from lesser injuries than his, and they were both young men. So—a week, two weeks? Who can say? He will be conscious soon, but his life will hang from a thread. Should he even hear you talk of torture he might lose his desire to live."

"A week, then. You have one week, Brother Kinnut. Consider your snug house beyond these walls, and your pretty wife. They hang in the balance. Have him ready for me."

Omer heard one pair of slapping sandals depart. Brother Kinnut came closer. He poked and prodded Omer's limp form, then peeled back his eyelid. "You're awake. I'm not fooled. You're even hardier than I'd thought—as well you must be, soon. Gnist is insane. Heal fast, old man. I'd rather you be the focus of his madness than me."

Omer tried then to speak, but all he managed was a constricted hiss far back in his throat. The effort exhausted him. Brother Kinnut departed.

CHAPTER TWENTY

Ilse, the third to bear the name,
Bore a daughter called Martina
To the Overlord of Burum,
Samel of the Golden Eye.

Excerpted from "The Women's Song," from *Folktales of the Bamian Highlands*, Chapter VII, "Cryptic Tales & Nonsense-songs."

The road north out of Blue narrowed to an overgrown trail. Yan's horse pushed aside the scrub oak and sumac that had grown up in it. Deep ruts told of past centuries of heavy use, but now it saw none. Yan could only guess when he entered the witches' domain. The first sign that he had arrived was a glimmer of white among the trees ahead, a building of a strange style. White stone walls held tall windows that drew to points at their tops; a heavy wooden door was similarly shaped, latched with a freshly whittled oak bolt; the steep roof was of flat reddish tiles, much weathered and patched. A miniature tower as wide as the building itself reached skyward over the front and tapered to a sharp pyramid topped with a wooden cross.

The door swung open on well-greased iron pintles and Yan stepped into a bath of color. The windows! From outside they had been black, but here, wherever sunlight penetrated, bright beams of color bathed the tiny chamber. The windows shone like jewels, and at first Yan thought that they were indeed gems, for the only colored glass he'd seen had been the dull green and brown of medicine bottles and beer jugs. Even as he stood admiring, another part of his mind analyzed; the work was ancient, he was sure. Another lost art, another magnificent human accomplishment buried, here in these woods. Someday, once again . . .

Two tiny pine benches crossed the cramped room, where four or five worshipers might sit facing an altar shelf. A cross was deeply carved in the stone wall there. Yan stepped forward hesitantly and hung the tiny gold pendant from the altar's carved corbel. He turned to leave, but thought better of it. It was a place for travelers' prayers. He had much to pray for, but no god of his own to pray to, so he compromised, sitting down for several minutes to bask in the polychrome light.

Outside again, he shut the door. Above it was a weathered inscription whose archaic characters would have been difficult to read even when new. Nonetheless, he took out his journal and sketched them as best he could:

R ADSIDE CHAP L
1998
Unit d Prot stant Chu c s
Bluef ld, Virg i

"Roadside chapel, 1998, Blue . . ." That much he thought he understood. Could the tiny place be two thousand years old? Was *Bluef ld* now Blue? Could the town have extended this far, once? The other words were meaningless to him.

As he sketched, some sixth sense or subtle change of light warned him that he was being watched. He raised his head slowly and turned. The first thing he saw was a pair of very small scuffed boots not five feet from his own, then two skinny wool-clad legs, a belt that would have fit around his thigh, and a bright plaid shirt, yellow, red, and black. Expecting some shrunken, dwarfish face, he looked up and his breath hissed in between his teeth. Fuzzy brown hair surrounded a face that he knew better than his own—a soft, brown face whose focal points were two eyes brown almost to blackness, whose lips were full and red-tinged. Illyssa's face. Hers, but not a day over seven years old.

He said nothing, only letting his sudden breath whistle back out between his teeth. What did you expect? he chided himself. You're in her country now. Did you expect her people to be blue-eyed and blond?

"Hello," the tiny girl said. It was Illyssa's accent, her own mellow tone, but an octave higher. "Can't you talk?"

"I can talk. You startled me. I thought I was all alone here. Who are you?"

"Martina. And I know you. You're Yan Bando."

"Yes, I am," he said. "Did you come here to meet me, then? I hope so, because I'm almost lost."

"I'll take you to my house. My father wants me to. Can I ride up there with you?" She pointed to his saddled horse.

"How about right in front of me? Think you'll fit?"

"Yes. My uncle Jasso has a horse, too. I ride with him sometimes."

"Jasso, eh? I think I met your uncle in Blue." Several things fell into place at once.

"Uncle Jas goes everywhere. He's a trader. Nobody can go with him, though. It's dangerous."

"Yes, I imagine it is. What's your father's name, Martina?"

"John."

"Then I'll bet your grandmother's name is Martina, too."

"How did you know that? Who told you?"

"A very dear friend of mine did. A long time ago." He had a hard time keeping the grief out of his voice. Everything felt unreal and sad, a strange waking dream. Illyssa's land, her people, even her little sister. But no Illyssa. What had little Martina's parents told her of Illyssa? What should *he* say?

"What's his name?"

"Who? Oh, my friend? She's a girl."

"What's her name?"

"That's a secret. Maybe I'll tell you sometime. Shall we mount up? Your house must not be far from here."

"I didn't have breakfast yet. I had to walk a long time, even in the dark."

"Well, let's hurry, then. Perhaps there'll be something for you when we get there."

It was not a short ride. After an hour at a walking pace they reached a clearing with a timber cabin and a fairly new slab barn. It would indeed have been a long walk for a small person, though Yan suspected that she had tried to lead him on a roundabout course to the house. They had made a great circle in getting there. His own acute directional sense had detected their curved track, and at first he had assumed it to be due to streams or other obstacles. Or was it just caution? Had Martina been so instructed? But no matter. His tension at the beginning of the day's journey had entirely dissipated. Instead of meeting him with crossbow bolts or "supernatural" influences, the witches had sent a small girl.

Who could be uneasy with a warm, chattering child squeezed in his saddle, playing a birdsong game they had made up? Yan noticed that some of the commoner birds of his homeland were less familiar to little Martina, sometimes known to her only by their songs, while others, rare or unknown to him, were ordinary. They quizzed each other about them. Martina whooped enthusiastically at each example of Yan's ignorance, and blithely shrugged off his countering victories.

The house was a common backwoods cabin, with two rooms and a loft. Its waist-thick logs were neatly hewn square and the corners were lovingly joined with half dovetails still tight after years of weathering. Six flat rocks kept the structure off the moist ground.

The woman who stood in the doorway was another Illyssa look-alike. Too much so, Yan thought. There must have been severe inbreeding at one time, or even now. No wonder the old crones exercised such firm control. They must have had to cull their population severely to produce healthy Jassos and Martinas—and Illyssas. How expert were they?

The woman stood silently as Yan dismounted and lifted Martina after him. She had ignored Yan's polite nod, but whether out of hostility or mere caution with a stranger, he could not tell.

"I'm Yan Bando," he said. "Martina brought me here to speak with her father, John."

"I know. My husband is out milking. Will you come inside? There is no kaf, but I will make tea if you wish it." She spoke in a guarded monotone. Were all her people so suspicious? Were all outsiders so feared?

"Tea would be fine, if it's no inconvenience."

"Sugar in mine!" Martina piped up. "Or honey. I'm hungry, Ma. Did you save my breakfast?"

The woman thawed ever so slightly. "Of course I did. It's in the warmer. Be careful—the stove's still hot."

Yan tied his horse to the porch post and mounted the steps. The unpainted walls inside were whitewashed, and the pine floor was worn and fuzzy-grained from much scrubbing. Finely crafted cherrywood cabinets hung on one wall. There was no clutter. It reminded Yan of a room in a clean inn: freshly straightened and devoid of personal touches. A tinned pot steamed on the black iron stove, the only artifact of daily living not stored away.

"I'll pour the tea, Ma," Martina insisted. "You sit down and talk with Yan."

"Be careful. It's full." She motioned Yan to be seated at the small trestle table, which with its four rush-seated chairs was the room's only standing furniture. Her daughter's obvious attraction to Yan seemed to be loosening her reserve. They sat together while Martina found cups and served them, sharing the air of faint conspiracy that strange adults assume when a child is playing matchmaker. "Please forgive my lack of conversation," she said as she sipped her tea. "I don't mean to make you ill at ease, but we're so isolated here. A new face is almost beyond my experience."

"No matter. I don't suppose that whatever you've heard about me has been reassuring, either."

"That may be," she said cautiously. "Did you discuss anything with Martina on the way here?"

"Nothing of note. I was shocked by her resemblance to . . . to another person I know. Not knowing what she had been told, I thought it best to say nothing of it."

At that moment he heard footsteps on the path outside. A shadow filled the doorway. "Welcome to my house, Yan Bando." Martina's father. Illyssa's father. His voice was light and dry, mellowed by the soft southern inflection. This man, John, resembled the other, Jasso. Brothers, Yan realized. "I heard you ride in, but cows care little for human guests.

"Martina, is that tea I smell? Bring it here, child, and then go tend your goats. They're no less in need of milking because we have a visitor." Yan was surprised that the girl did not protest being dismissed. She carried a third mug of steaming tea to the table. There were crumbs around her mouth from her snatched breakfast.

"Bye, Yan," she said as she darted out the door.

"Shall we get right to the subject, then?" John asked, his tension obvious. "Is Ilse still alive?"

"Ilse?"

"My daughter! I was told that you claimed she hadn't died. Is it so, man?" Exasperation bordered on anger as he leaned forward over the table. His wife put a restraining hand on his arm.

"John, wait," she said, and then to Yan, "Perhaps you know her only as Illyssa?"

"Aya! Forgive me. I never knew her otherwise. I saw her alive twelve days ago. She was with me, coming here. Now, I don't know, I only hope."

"What chance she still lives? A guess, man! I've been too long without hope."

"He who captured her knows that she can't be tortured, so there is hope, depending on his plans for her, and for my friend who was taken also. But if only revenge suffices him . . . But how much have you been told? About Illyssa and me? I don't know where to begin."

"Assume I know all that you told the priest. We'll sort through the details later." Yan felt that he could read the father's face as he had the daughter's. They, too, were much alike. They were all so much alike.

"You know what our goal was, then," Yan began, "and why we were coming here. But that can wait. If she and Omer are still alive I've got to try to get them out of Jossity Keep, and I can't do that alone. I need help. How can I get it? What sort of aid can I expect?"

"I'm inclined to accept what you've told Father Ros and us," John said, "and Cora feels you've been level with us." His glance at his wife was returned with the slightest of nods. "We'll do what we can, but you'll bear the greatest burden."

That had an ominous ring to it, but Yan decided not to question him more right away. "I'm glad that you'll help me. I'm aware that it is a preposterous tale on the face of it, and I realize the shock to you both also. I had little to introduce me here, only Illyssa's mention of your names. We hadn't planned for my coming here alone, without her, and she was reluctant to disobey the injunction against discussing you with outsiders.

"But what can we do now? Can I expect aid in freeing her and my friend Omer?"

"You've opened a box of worms, Yan. I can only prepare your way to the elders. Our secretiveness and reclusive behavior stem from their wishes, and they must decide the nature of any aid we give you. It has been this way for centuries. But you know that story, I think."

"Athel of Roke, aya, and the two Semals."

"Convincing them to change a centuries-old policy won't be easy. As Illyssa's father, my weight on your side will be discounted. I've long been considered a hothead by the elders anyway. It all hinges on you and on Jasso, my brother. He left for Jossity even as you came here. As a trader, he's known there and has friends. He will find out if they are still living, and where they may be kept. Then you must convince the elders that Ilse and your friend are worth the risk of outside involvement. You can assume that they will have all the facts at hand, and you must concentrate on the timeliness of your plans. They must be shown that never again will there be such an opportunity, with the Pharos-Sons incapacitated and the Star Church in turmoil. They must *believe* that such a chance will never happen again, that our common destruction is otherwise imminent.''

''How will that convince them? Can't they just take what I know and act upon it? Even escape in the ship, if it still exists?''

''The elders are passive regarding events outside. They exert only subtle and occasional control. It's been that way since Athel's time. If the news you bring is judged true and the significance you place on it is accepted by them, then they'll be forced to act. They'll need you and others like you to bridge the chasms they themselves have created down through the centuries. If you convince them that you'll not cooperate willingly until Illyssa and your friend are either freed or—'' He hesitated, and his smooth voice sounded suddenly harsh. ''—or until they are proven dead, they may bend their rules to aid you. And concerning the ship,'' he continued doggedly—forcing his mind to stay with practicalities, Yan realized—''I suspect that there may be more to it than just climbing in it and flying off, else why would it not have been done generations ago?''

''I've worried about that no end,'' Yan admitted, ''hoping that the know-how still exists, if nothing else. I see no devices or unusual technology in your home . . . yet you, for one, don't seem ignorant or unschooled.''

''Hah! That's easily explained. I am a farmer, but like any man in Ararat, I've cross-trained—I'm a passable engineer. Take electric lights. I could build a generator myself, from schoolbook illustrations. An ordinary steam engine, like the one at the sawmill, could light this whole valley—if we wanted to do it.''

''But why haven't you?''

''History, Yan. Tenzie. Such a network of charged wires would be a beacon. As things are, our town and farmsteads look ordinary enough. Even if a spy should slip through our borders undetected, he would see nothing unusual, just mountain folk and wood and stone buildings. You see? If we used the technology we know, the electromagnetic emanations would be detectable from afar—from Jossity, Roke, or . . . or from a ship orbiting above. No, far better we live as those around us do, alive and obscure, else this valley, so lovely, would soon be naught but a smoking, radioactive ruin. No Athel would be needed to exterminate us."

"I should have realized." Yan was chagrined. "I begin to comprehend your elders' frustrations . . . but when can I see them? Will it be long?"

"Today, perhaps. Your horse is still fresh, and I have a pony. You are expected this afternoon, so finish your tea. Have you eaten?"

"Earlier. I'd as soon get it over with. Perhaps you will tell me more as we ride?"

John, anticipating the shortness of their stay at the farm, had already saddled his pony. They rode in silence for a while, and Yan pondered the elusive way that communications seemed to flow through the witch domain and even beyond, as if the fluttering birds themselves were these folks' spies and messengers.

"John, I've known your daughter as Illyssa, but you call her something else—Ilse? Is that a nickname?"

John laughed. "No, not at all. Illyssa is the nickname. To the old women—the geneticists among them at any rate—she's known as fifty-four Ilse seventy-five."

"The numbers meaning what?"

"She's of the fifty-fourth generation since the Return, and the seventy-fifth Ilse to bear the name. It was the name of a woman from the ship, Ilse Lindgren."

"I see what she meant about the elders' power—they even name children for their own convenience in record-keeping. But how can you be so open with me? Illyssa and I were . . . were very close, but she was still terrified of telling me anything at all. Most of my limited knowledge of you people comes from other sources."

"She was right to tell you so little." John turned in his saddle and smiled broadly at Yan. "Just as you are right to protect her even now. I can speak freely because now you are here, not there, and because you have much knowledge already. I am inclined to trust you, to treat you as one of us, and as a dear friend of my daughter. As for the elders, you'll not leave our land without *their* blessing, for though I can't confirm the tales outsiders tell of chance wanderers departing with no memory of their experiences here, there are some among us who have been called by them as you have been. Most return tight-lipped from their visits, but others speak as if nothing at all had occurred, or only events of an ordinary nature. At times, though, the later behavior of those ones has been markedly different from before their calling. Who knows what powers the elders may have?''

"I can't say that you've reassured me. I'm less terrified of death or imprisonment than I am of losing my memory of events, my knowledge. For a scholar, such a threat surpasses all else.''

"I wish I *could* reassure you, but the elders are almost as much a mystery to me as to you. I don't know that I've ever met one face-to-face.''

"How could that be?'' Yan's puzzlement grew.

"None of us know who they are. We are told that there is a council of elders among those women who work often within the dark cave above the town, but which ones are they? My wife or my mother might be among them, for all I can tell.''

"How can I talk with them, then? Will they hide behind a curtain? Won't I hear their voices and perhaps remember them at some later meeting, on the streets, perhaps?''

"You will see and hear exactly what they want you to, I'm sure. And you won't tell a soul about any of it. It's happened before—I've seen it.''

"That kind of power is awesome,'' Yan said. "No wonder outsiders fear you 'witches.' But while I was in Blue I speculated that your Christian religion might act as a kind of check-rein on the use of such powers for evil ends. Was I right?''

"I suspect so. You've surely guessed by now that the tales of killing intruders—whether by conventional or supernatural means—are patently false, a propaganda barrier alone?''

"That thought was all that comforted me until I met Martina at the shrine. Now all I have to fear is the death of my memory. Would I know even now if I had been so manipulated?''

"I doubt it. Others, myself for example, or surely someone who knows you well, might notice a change in you, perhaps in your resolve—but then, I wouldn't inform you of it, would I?''

The rest of the way they rode in silence while Yan pushed down his fears and marshaled the arguments and persuasions he hoped to use. They approached the town from the southeast, traversing the westerly slope of a worn, timbered ridge. Across the valley that held the town was another, higher ridge, on which soil had been stripped and rock cut back to a vertical face that was several stories higher than the highest roof of the town. A semicircular blur of mortared ashlar marred the cliff face—the old tunnel mouth. Could there be a ship in there? Was the Moromen's tale of the northern Bolide and the star children false, or had the Bolide-ship been flown down here and hidden long after its landing? Yan's thoughts darted like the swifts that threw fleeting shadows over the roofs of the town. The meeting. So much hinged upon the meeting.

"No one's said what this place is called," Yan commented. "Does it have a name?"

"Ararat. After the world our ancestors came from."

"What does it mean?"

"I don't know. It's the name of a mountain in our Book, a place where men landed after a great flood. I suppose the planet Ararat was named after the mountain, and then the town after the planet. I've often thought it might mean 'refuge,' since it's been used in that sense three times."

Yan resolved to read the Christian Book when he could obtain a copy of it—if, after today, he still cared.

They were now among outlying buildings, and Yan guessed that Ararat might hold three thousand people or more. It was as neat as Blue, or as John's farmhouse. They reined in before a whitewashed stone house. Its shutters had been recently painted an intense blue, and spatters of color made shutter outlines on the grass.

"This is my mother's house—fifty-two Martina eighty-eight. You can wait here awhile. No one should be home, so make yourself comfortable." John glanced up at the chimney. "The stove's still fired up. There may be some kaf—Martina is quite fond of it." He left Yan to tie up his horse and go inside. "Someone will be along, I'm sure," he assured Yan before he rode off. A pot of tepid water was on the stovetop, over the coolest rear eye. He stirred the firebox coals and added a few oak splits, then moved the pot over them. There was ground kaf in a glass jar above, and a bowl of clean eggshells to mellow the brew.

Screams echoed among iron-barred stone doorways, complicating and replicating themselves down the long hallways, only the sharper notes damped by the angles and turns of the keep's star-shaped plan. Thus Illyssa heard the screamer's agony, but could not determine if man, woman, or child made the cries. Loud at first, they muted through the hours, through the day, until at nightfall she heard no more than the ghosts of whimpers. The next day was silent, but later the screams resumed, less loudly—or perhaps she merely grew inured to the sounds of human degradation.

Her food was sticky wheat-and-barley gruel, grains hardly

broken by the millstones. A bowl was slid under her planked door by a booted foot, and later retrieved. She saw no face, and no voice responded to hers. Only when the much-changed Gnist called on her did she have human contact at all—such as it was. Gnist was as skinny as ever, but his skin now stretched tightly over his skull.

Tanslucent waxed window parchment. Much of his hair had fallen out, and the wisps that remained were white. His hands seemed heavier, gnarled. His forearms, revealed by tightly controlled gesturing, showed iron-hard cords. Ancient memory, stimulated by the sight, commented on unnatural rigor, the isometric tension of a body at war with the mind controlling it.

"The old man will be healed enough to entertain you anon," Gnist said each time he visited her cell. "I cannot pleasure *you* with the irons and the rod, I know, but the fisherman will sing loudly. I will watch your face the while, and you *will* speak, soon enough." Illyssa never responded, nor gave evidence that she heard, but Gnist seemed not to notice or care. "When he dies, *then* I will pleasure you, entertain you as I was entertained when you abandoned me in Innis. You will die at once, I suspect, but know this: I will not stop when your heart ceases. With hot iron I will rape your corpse. With cold iron I will break your every bone. I will have a bag made from the soft skin of your breasts, and I will carry your teeth in it as a charm around my neck. In death, you will be with me always."

The darkness of her cell was a blessing; sometimes she could not stop the tears that blurred her eyes. But should Gnist have seen them, he would have misunderstood: the tears were not for Omer or Illyssa herself, but for him.

CHAPTER TWENTY-ONE

The *message* of love? How quaint. Haven't you considered that love itself may *be* the message?

Anon., in *Amorous Anecdotes*, collected by Ephaim of Burum.

It's their move, Yan reflected. What will it be? With fresh-brewed kaf in hand, he had just seated himself on a low padded couch when the door opened. At first he thought the newcomer was a slightly built man; she wore men's clothing suitable for travel or working outside. Her voice was gravelly and deep. "I'm Martina. Don't get up. I'll have a cup with you while you wait. It may be a while." She poured herself kaf in a huge earthenware mug, added a liberal spoonful of brownish sugar, and sat down across from him in a chair that matched the couch. Does everyone here know everything that goes on? he wondered, amazed. I wouldn't think there's been time to tell my tale, yet Jasso, John and his wife, and now this odd woman . . . "The crones don't do *anything* fast," she commented, smiling tolerantly. She draped a booted foot over a couch arm and set her mug down, looking expectantly at him with penetrating hazel eyes. Just as little Martina had Illyssa's face as it once had been, this older Martina had that face as it might someday be—as he hoped it might someday be. Her skin had lost the elasticity of youth, but showed no signs of harshness, and her smile was warm.

"Well? What are you going to tell them? You can practice on me."

Tell *her*? Why? Yan eyed her suspiciously. What's her part in all this? Is she only a curious grandmother . . . she doesn't act like a *concerned* one . . . or is there more to this? He shrugged.

This was a move in the elders' game, or it was not. It made no difference. Nothing he could say, or not say, would make any difference. The only hole card he had was the letter from ab'd Onskill. And he hadn't said anything about that to anyone . . . had he? He might surprise them yet. "Why not?" he said with a guarded smile. "It will pass the time."

Yan's practiced speech did not fit the informal setting, nor the woman, so he just started talking much as he had with Father Ros. He concentrated on the danger to Earth, the probability that the next ferosin visit might be a final one, emphasizing the potential for alliance with concerned nations unspecified as yet.

"You mean Burum, of course," she said. "Our ancestors' kin." Was she reading his thoughts? "With our inbreeding," Martina went on, "we all carry Samool's genes—I suppose there's little offplanet blood left. But we've no love for Gold-eye's kin, even fifty generations removed." She shook her head.

"Azzar ab'd Onskill struck me as a sincere man," Yan said, giving up even the pretense of holding back his cards. "I have little doubt that his motives are as he claims them to be. As for the Mayan himself, can it hurt to open communication with Burum? You'd risk little, for much potential gain. Ab'd Avdool's seekers go everywhere. If they knew what yours sought, it might help your own searching."

"It's a possibility," she replied, seemingly dismissing the subject out of hand. "But what of Illyssa and your friend Omer?"

Yan told her what he surmised of their situation. From her questions, he got the impression she knew better than he the layout of Jossity Keep, the priests and guards who inhabited it, and the likely location of the prisoners. She questioned everything—Lazko's speculations, Omer's description of the statue, Yan's impression of the black crablike beast, and even his relationship with Illyssa. He answered precisely, omitting nothing but the extent of Illyssa's revelations, and the part madness had played in the battle in Jossity. He was, in spite of his newfound acceptance and control, reluctant to discuss that. If she wanted that secret, she *would* have to read his mind.

Finally she stood. "Let's go. It's midafternoon already."

"Will they see me now? John said I was expected by noon."

She laughed, a harsh sound from so slight a source. "They'll see you when and if they wish it. I was thinking of food. There's nothing here, and I've not had lunch—nor have you, I imagine. D'you think you can eat something?"

"I know I can. But will they know where we've gone?" Yan

had picked up John's and Martina's stressed "they" and "them" when speaking of the elders.

"They'll know if they want to. There's an eating place only a few minutes away. Care to escort a hungry old woman? One of the boys will take care of your horse. They'll leave the saddlebags in the house. Bring the letter from what's-his-name." Without comment, Yan dug the heavy paper packet from the bottom of the bag and tucked it in his belt. They talked as they walked, while they waited for their food, and while they ate. Yan's speech was entirely in response to Martina's questions, which she fired like crossbow bolts, swift and hard. After the meal she ordered ale.

Yan had known few women like (52) Martina (88). She was self-assured, straightforward, and a competent questioner. The latter especially gained Yan's respect, for the essence of good scholarship was the formulation of meaningful questions. In spite of her age, mannish dress and voice, and the total absence of "feminine" deferral to his maleness, he was also well aware of her as a woman. Subtle mannerisms and earthy expressions hinted that she was not averse to a toss in the hay, and he did not doubt that—grandmother as she was—she'd be a splendid partner, though likely a demanding one. But he felt ashamed of such thoughts when he remembered her relationship to Illyssa, and his own mission.

"Your mind's wandering, scholar. Is it an interesting path?" Her eyes sparkled with mischief.

He blushed. If she can read my thoughts, she must be able to read my intent, too, he decided, resigned. I don't mean ill by them. Can't I dissemble at all with these witches? "Aya. The resemblance between you and your granddaughters is remarkable. I was wondering whether Illyssa would maintain her attractiveness as you have."

"That sounds like a compliment. You find me attractive, then?"

"I'd have to be deaf and blind not to," he replied honestly, "but I'm also growing impatient. How long will they continue to stall me?"

"It's no use questioning their actions, Yan. They make decisions for generations not yet born. A life—or two—means nothing to them, at least in their official capacities. Be grateful you've gotten this far. You're the first outsider in this town in years. May I see the letter from Burum?"

"I'm sorry. It was sealed by the Mayan and I've only seen a

copy. I'm not to open it. Azzar ab'd Onskill intended I deliver it to your council of elders."

They talked about Nobi, ab'd Onskill and his wandering scholars, and the low estate of scholarly activity in the known world. Yan described the radio messages, stressing how valuable a radio would be for anyone with an interest in the Church's business, but Martina dismissed the idea as if it had no real value. Only the third signal, the one that carried no message, seemed to pique her interest, and then only momentarily.

They walked back to her house by a circuitous route while she pointed out the square where social and commercial activity concentrated, the infirmary where Ararat inhabitants and outsiders alike were treated, and the tiers of wooden steps that led up to the entrance of the tunnel.

"Are there outsiders in the infirmary now? And are the elders up in the cave?"

"Yes to both questions, I would guess."

"Then I'm not truly the first outsider in Ararat in recent years."

"No, but you're the first one to set foot here. Those in the infirmary have traditionally been drugged and then carried here. Are you always this suspicious?"

"Not often enough, I begin to think. I'm trusting by nature." The sun was below the western ridge when they reached Martina's house again. Streamers of pink clouds stretched obliquely across the sky, gilt-edged nearest the dark slopes.

"It looks like you'll be staying the night. John's been here and gone already—I hope he left food for us."

"How can you tell he's been here?"

She smiled wickedly. "Witchcraft, of course." Then she pointed at the ground. "With help from the pony tracks over our own. He'll have gone to care for his livestock. My son is a conscientious farmer."

Inside, she opened a wall-hung cabinet and slid out a heavy salt-glazed jug. "Have you tried our local spirits yet?"

"In Nahbor I once bought a bottle of liquor said to be mountain-brewed, but I found it harsh, even diluted with water."

"Then this will be a new experience. The process is two thousand years old, and the stuff comes from our own distillery. We trade some, but save the best for ourselves." She poured clear amber fluid into two bubbly blue glass tumblers, set one on the couch arm, then sat down next to him with her own drink. "Enjoy it. I think you'll be a very busy man tomorrow."

"Why do you say that?" he said, then sipped his liquor. "Ahh! This *is* good! Warms me all the way down."

"I thought you'd like it. This is the first decanting of the 'Twenty-three product. Almost as old as you, I'd guess."

"Almost. I was 'decanted' in 'Twenty-two," he said with a grin, "but I probably won't continue to age as well as this—or as you, for that matter."

"Somehow I don't think that's *idle* flattery," she said as she shifted closer to him. "I think I'll pursue that topic further."

She was close. He felt her warmth across the intervening inches and was hardly suprised when his pants began feeling tight. Martina was not surprised either. She set her glass down and unbuttoned his shirt in a tentative, teasing manner, then ran her hands over his ribs and shoulders to push the shirt away. His breathing became irregular. He reached for her, but she twisted away, toying with him just as Illyssa might have. "You'll get your chance," she said. "Just let me play. Oh, what's this toy?" She hefted the carved ball and cage around his neck, and Yan experienced déjà vu. Martina's words and Illyssa's under similar circumstances were the same.

"A memento of my father. It's all that I have left from him. Silly sentiment, I suppose."

"I don't think so. It's an old symbol, you know." Seeing his blank look, she shrugged. "I suppose you wouldn't. My ancestresses allegedly made these for their male children during the Burum years, when boys were taken from them at puberty. It was supposed to be a way to find them again later on. But Burumians were so fond of clever trinkets that their carvers began making them by the hundreds—or so the story goes. The ball is the Earth, and the cage . . ."

"Interesting," he said as he reached for her again, not sure himself what he was referring to.

"Has Illyssa told you how lovely you are?" she said. It was not a question, not really.

"Shouldn't I be saying something like that? How lovely you are, I mean?"

"Only if you mean it."

"I do. You're the loveliest grandmother I've been undressed by."

"And the only one besides your own, I'll bet."

"I won't give you odds on it," he said, pulling her closer.

She nestled against him, turning her face to his. They kissed for a long moment. She expertly loosened his belt and buttons. When the kiss ended she rose, tugged off his boots, and tossed them aside. She took his hands and pulled him to his feet. He swayed and kicked his trousers from his ankles. Is this witchery? Is this really happening? How can I do this while Illyssa is captive or dead? Another thought intruded: Would it make any difference to her?

Naked and fully erect while Martina retained her clothing and her dignity, he still felt completely at ease. Witchery or not, it did not matter. "My turn," he said, reaching for her shirt buttons. She kicked off her boots as he undid the rest of her clothing. As he knelt to slip her trousers off, his eyes registered every detail. Her breasts were not youthfully firm; her belly sagged slightly; stretch lines told of children she'd born. Such details only increased his ardor. She was beautiful in the way of the tiny chapel, of the worn and ancient hills, in a way that no young girl—even Illyssa—could be.

"That's the bedroom," she said, leading him.

When they made love her hazel eyes were open, and though her face was Illyssa's, those eyes were hers alone.

Later, he told her that if their lovemaking had been prayer, surely some god would have heard, and would grant him the chance to look into Illyssa's eyes as he had hers, until the years made her young face like Martina's. She smiled and said, "Then let's pray once more and make sure of it." They did.

"You said I'd be busy today," Yan said as they dressed. "Does that mean the elders will see me this morning?"

"For an intelligent man you can be obtuse. Why not put your knowledge to use?" Her crinkling smile robbed the remark of its sting. She sounded like Illyssa.

"What do you mean? What did I miss?"

"You missed your meeting with the elders, for one. It's over already. They have agreed to help you—to a point—and today you'll get together with some of our men, to plan a rescue."

His fears of mental manipulation welled up again. What had happened? Missed the meeting? Had they made him forget? He remembered nothing out of the ordinary, except that the whole night had been strange. He remembered waking in darkness and making love a third time. He remembered talking, in those quiet hours before dawn, of hopes and plans—of a fleet of ships going out from Earth, so far out, and in so many directions, that no malevolent alien crabs would be able to obliterate them. He remembered Martina's head on his shoulder, his hand on her still-smooth hip as she slept. What had really happened? Were his memories of the night false, too?

Seeing the tightness of his face and budding panic in his eyes, she held his shoulders. "You've nothing to fear, Yan. I've heard the stories, too, even the ones my own people tell. Your mind has not been altered. What you remember happened just as you remember it."

"Then I understand less than I thought I did. Stop playing riddle games."

"I suppose I am playing games. I'm not sorry, though. I really wanted you to figure it out by yourself. Will you play one more round if I give you another clue?"

"I don't have a choice, do I?" he snapped, then relented. "Aya, of course I will."

"Then here's your clue: You could have let me read the letter from the Mayan without breaking your word."

For a moment his face remained blank, uncomprehending, before it took on a silly slack-jawed look and his eyes widened with comprehension. "You? You're one of *them*. That's it, isn't it? You're an elder."

"That's right, Yan—as far as you've taken it. But there's more to be gotten from my clue."

It would have been impossible for his jaw to have hung lower, for his eyes to have been wider. "The mind link! I said I'd only give the letter to the whole council of elders. But I told *you* everything that was in it. You've been in contact with them, haven't you? With all the others?" He reddened as another thought welled up, so intensely embarrassing he hardly dared voice it. "When? How long were you sharing thoughts with them?"

He had seen her expression before: pure, unadulterated glee, the look of a child who's just succeeded in pulling off the most elaborate of pranks. Illyssa's look, and little Martina's. He knew immediately that the worst of his current fears was true even before she confirmed it.

"You're thinking that you made love three times last night to the whole council, aren't you? Well, you're right. You did." But she was not mocking him anymore. If anything, her voice was sad. "I can assure you, without a shadow of doubt, that every one of them loved it—and loves you for it. There are a dozen old bags out there who'll be trying all morning to get the silly grins off their faces."

Yan swayed in her arms. He should have guessed. It was not as if he had no experience with such witchery. There had been that time in the barge train . . . "I can't begrudge it now, can I? But are they gone? Are you just Martina?"

"Just me." She stroked his back and ribs, pressing against him. He realized neither of them had dressed beyond their shirts. She caressed his stiffened member. "I think you've spunk to make love to a lonely old woman once more, don't you?"

He did, and they did. He missed his chance for breakfast. They bought spiced, frosted rolls from a baker's shop on the way to his "council of war." He and Martina shared a lingering kiss at the doorstep, which brought slightly embarrassed smiles to several bearded faces within.

Illyssa was led from her cell for the twelfth time. She believed the trips to Brother Gnist's chambers had occurred on successive days, but she had not confirmed it. Her guards were forbidden to speak at all, and she had not seen daylight since she'd been dragged from the street. It could have been ten days, or two weeks, but it did not matter much. What mattered was that she was alive and unharmed, and that Yan was still free. Gnist tried to convince her that he had been captured, but when she challenged his assertion he backed down.

Omer was there. She had seen his pale, emaciated form in drugged sleep in the keep's infirmary, surrounded by churchmen in white cassocks. When he grew strong enough, Gnist would use him to force her to talk. She hoped she'd have the courage to bear it, or to die. She hoped this trip down the hall wouldn't be the final one. But Gnist's office was this way, and they wouldn't torture Omer there; it was time for another tirade, that was all. Thank god Yan is alive, she thought. He's coming, I can feel it. If only there's time.

The door to the thin, scarred priest's office was open. Her guard shoved her into the room; she struggled to maintain her balance. Omer was there, and Gnist. The old seaman was awake, and his bright blue eyes were alert, aware of his surroundings, but she was shocked by his appearance; although she'd seen his matted hair, his frailty was more apparent, now that he was awake. His skin sagged like old rotted canvas. His beard had more white than gray, and it was thinner, as if whole patches had been pulled out or had fallen away. His hands, resting on his lap, trembled. He attempted to smile, but a muscle in his cheek spasmed repeatedly, more than a mere tic. She saw his hands whiten, his fists clench. Was the pain that bad?

"Aya, girl." His voice, never smooth, was a wet, raspy whisper. "You're pretty as ever." The short sentence started him coughing. He spat bloodly phlegm into a rag. A white-robed man stood behind him, seemingly concerned. Gnist sat at his desk and said nothing.

llyssa did not dare speak. Her resolve was so weak she might burst into tears, encouraging the priest. Though she was glad to see Omer awake, she wished that he had remained unconscious to postpone what would soon happen. Gnist seemed to read her thoughts.

"A fine specimen, our fisherman, isn't he, witch? A few days of rest, and he'll be strong as ever. You'll pray for his recovery, won't you?" Allowing for shriller tones, Gnist sounded like his mentor in madness, the late Senior. She refused to look at him or speak. Her eyes and Omer's were locked, and though he did not speak again, he winked at her. His cheek bulged as he pushed his tongue against it. What was he saying? Then she knew. Tongue in cheek. More than one meaning. One, Omer was dissembling. He was not as ill as he seemed. Two, the fists—he was exercising. Isometrics. Three, the blood he'd spat—he had bitten his cheek.

"Guard! Come in here!" Gnist squalled, then addressed Illyssa in mad, entirely conversational tones: "I wanted the two of you to see each other, to give you something to think about." He turned to the guard at attention inside the door. "Take her back to her cell."

CHAPTER TWENTY-TWO

If Pharos had intended that Man should fly, He would have made him in His own image.

Hekkor the Apostle

John would accompany Yan on his return journey to Jossity. Others were introduced by name. Two were Ernst; the one in his fifties claimed privilege, as eldest, to be addressed as Ernst. The younger fellow would have to pick a nickname; a common practice, Yan realized. They all used the same names, those of the crew of their ancestors' ship, and that crew could not have been large. Besides Ernst, John, and the young fellow, now called "Badger" in anticipation of a burrow into Jossity Keep, there were three others. One, a woodsman in fringed deerskin and moccasins, introduced himself as (56) Karl (37). He was pleased that Yan's own father was also Carl, though spelled differently. Next was (55) Arn (28), who traced his name to a crewman less notable than the original Ernst, whose name, he groused, was common as grass in cow droppings. The final member of the team was Jasso, Illyssa's uncle, whom Yan had met in Blue.

The news Jasso brought from Jossity was heartening. His source confirmed two new prisoners in the keep. One was a dark-skinned woman. The other was old, and was in the infirmary. Thank God, Yan thought. But seven against a fortress? What odds would any god give us?

The men, traders who had gotten in difficult places before, felt that forced entry to the keep was impossible. The west and southwest gates were accessible only via steep switchback roads above the swift-flowing river. The northern walls were as high as three-story buildings. The north gate opened to Jossitytown, but the gate itself was at the end of a narrowing passageway between walls, designed to compress attackers so they could be stoned and burned from above. Another barrier remained: at the center of the enceinte was a seven-story tower, in plan like a five-pointed star. Below the top story only loopholes and a single gateway broke its thick stone walls.

Ernst was familiar with the layout. He drew rough plans of the inner keep, indicating guard stations, offices, quarters, and the prison wing. He showed where Omer and Illyssa might be. "Here, in the basement, are long-term prisoners, felons. The main floor holds blasphemers, debtors, and the like. The next four house the rest, except special cases—political and Church prisoners to be interrogated. Torturer's rooms are located on the sixth level—our goal. The infirmary and prison offices are above. Only top and ground floors access the rest of the keep. Transients enter from the central courtyard, here, and the top level has gated hallways here and here." He indicated the interior angles of the star.

Six of the seven men agreed it was impossible to get in or out of the keep. Jasso was silent. He waited to speak until each had had his say, until discussion ground to a halt. "We've concluded only a fly could get in and back out again, right?" Heads nodded. "So we'll have to be flies, won't we? Or birds." Puzzlement replaced their glum stares.

John chuckled. "You think it can be done?" he asked his brother. "Can we build enough wings? What about membranes?"

"Will you tell us what you two are talking about?" Karl demanded.

"Perhaps we'd better show you instead," John suggested. "We have time—if we can't get in, we're just idling here anyway." Yan privately disagreed. Jasso's information about two prisoners might not remain correct. The torturers could change it. Yan was uncomfortable with John's coolness. He spoke as if Illyssa were a stranger, as if this were some almost-prosaic military mission and he its commander. Were his grief and fears buried so deeply? Had he burnt his emotional fuel in its entirety, or had the witches, the elders, "helped" him deal with his loss in their own fashion? Yan decided not to inquire or interfere.

John left to get horses. He arranged for a wagon and team as well. He drove. Yan, Jasso, and Ernst rode with him. On the way out of town they stopped at a barn and loaded mysterious cloth-bound packages onto the wagon. John and his brother ignored requests to explain. They headed up a steep switchback road, stopping beside a cliff.

Jasso unwrapped their cargo. First to appear were bundles of thin black tubes, resinous stuff that gleamed like the ferosin's chitin. "What is that?" Yan asked.

"The tubing? It came from the cave," John answered. "*What*, is anyone's guess; fibers embedded in resin—stronger than steel, and light." He tossed a tube to Yan. Even expecting lightness, he overreacted; it bounced from his hand. Picking it up, he waved it back and forth. There was no inertia, only air resistance—and it came from the mysterious cave. He flexed it. It grew stiffer the more he stressed it. Could its chitinous look be accident? If ferosin chitin was like this, the beasts had to be light, fast, and terribly durable; more deadly than he had suspected.

The objects taking shape on the brink were indeed wings, but not the flexible appendages of a dove or swallow. Assembled spars held loose membrane sails Jasso claimed would take shape when a man's weight and the wind's forces were applied. Even wrinkled and unstressed, the filmy stuff was reflectionless, clear as air. A wood-and-"chitin" trapeze hung beneath. Two cords would warp the wings for control, but the budding fliers were advised that weight shifts would usually suffice. The wings, John explained, weighed only a few pounds, assembled.

"Where did these come from?" Karl asked. "Whose idea are they?"

Jasso explained that the *idea* of flying had been John's, when he was ten. The two of them had built wings—heavy wood-and-cloth contraptions—and had come near to killing themselves several times before their mother had taken pity on boys pitting limited skill and knowledge against the weighty demands of flight. Or perhaps, Jasso admitted, she only wished to save them from killing themselves. At any rate, she had brought tubing, membrane, adhesives, and, most important of all, printed plans for a "hang glider." With modifications for the materials at hand, which were stronger than "carbon fiber," "nylon," and aluminum, those very wings were the result.

Yan felt a chill, a tingle as of static building up on a boat at sea with bad weather brewing. *Printed* plans. Plans based on technology known only as hoarded records in places like Nahbor and . . . in the cave? The witches' secrets, he realized, went beyond hoarding, beyond mental parlor tricks and clever genetic manipulation of bees. In the university archives, he might have found formulas for nylon and other synthetics, but he would have been hard put to actually *make* any without rebuilding a whole technological base first. Yet these witches had furnished bundles of tubing and rolls of transparent membrane with ease, and for what purpose? Toys for little boys. There was no question that the materials had been produced, not merely pulled from a warehouse of ancient artifacts. Both were organic and would have aged, stored in a cave for decades, let alone hundreds or even thousands of years. What was in that artificial grotto, that "unending cave"? Whole factories? Offworld machinery brought to Earth in ferosin holds?

His spirits rose. The witches had technological knowledge and the means to use it. They were cautious, but not afraid to apply what they knew even for the pleasure—and education—of adventurous youths. Was that the only reason for the wings, though? Might the elders themselves have had reason for John and Jasso to make and use them? Had they been John's idea alone?

When the last connections were made and tested, John and Jasso strapped themselves in place, each man to a wing sail. They half ran, half hopped to the lip of the precipice. The watchers saw them drop out of sight and heard the crack, the sound of sails filling; they ran to the crumbling edge, threw themselves to the ground, and crawled the last yard to peer out and downward. Two shadowy triangles skimmed trees far below, visible mostly as man shadows on the trees themselves. The watchers stared even after both kitelike wings disappeared beyond a distant hill.

"I'll brew tea," Karl said jauntily, failing to conceal his anxiety. Either the two fliers would crash and die, or they would return—and then everyone would have to try. Neither prospect was appealing. Tea water was already steaming over a pine-branch fire when Badger yelled. Above them, coming in opposite their departure point, were the triangular wings, shimmering webs with dark spider shadows slung below. They swept into downward spirals and descended within yards of the group. John landed running, but Jasso touched earth as gently as a bird alights on a branch. The groundlings ran to them, all asking questions at once. "Considering that I was only twelve, and weighed less the last time I flew this, they carried us well," John said, gathering raised eyebrows from all.

"I hope you're the bravest man I ever hope to know," Ernst said, "because I'd hate to think I'm being led by a crazy man." Others echoed him. Now that it had been dramatically established that the wings actually worked, they were eager to get the project under way.

There were three projects. Jasso would handle the first: making additional wing frames. "We won't have time to train Illyssa or your friend Omer to fly," he said, leaving unstated the possibility that even alive, they might be in no shape for it. "So two of the wings will need greater sail area to carry them and a flier. There are printed tables to match fliers with wings, but no flier was anticipated to be as heavy as two—even though one's a girl. We'll need to experiment to make sure they'll do." Jasso borrowed Arn's horse and headed toward Ararat, leaving John to answer questions and organize things.

The second project was set aside for the moment: making a model of the keep and planning their exact strategy. Timing, wind direction, details of which roofs and courtyards would be in sunlight—all would affect their plans, so several alternatives had to be considered.

The third task was key to their effort. All five men would have to learn to fly. John set about that task at once. While two put on wings and staggered about with them, staying away from the cliff, John ran through a list of conditions they would have to cope with: updrafts and down, turbulence and still air, alone or in combination. Condensation could be a danger, and frost. He himself had gotten frostbitten cheeks on one flight, though the temperature on the ground had been warm enough for sunbathing. Each condition, he told them, could be read by signs in the air or on the ground below: ripples moving across water; stiff-winged hawks following spiral paths on rising air. Terns and gulls hovering over sun-warmed beaches, Yan thought without mentioning it, knowing that only he had seen gulls on sandy Michan strands.

Images washed over him like waves on remembered beaches—the stone porticos of his childhood home, granite walls, the sawdust-floored armory where he had hefted child-size weapons. Strange, he thought, how images long tainted with bitterness rise clear in my mind with no pain, only wistful nostalgia.

Without flying, they disassembled the wings to make the long descent before darkness, and they rolled into Ararat to join Jasso for a planning session over cold sliced beef and bread. In the morning, Arn and Karl would solicit memories from every man and woman who had been to Jossity, for help in modeling the keep. Jasso would build wing frames while John worked cutting and heat-sealing membranes, assembling their conveyances, and gathering weapons and supplemental equipment they might need.

Yan returned to Martina's house after dark to find it empty

and cold. The bed had been made up with fresh linen. All traces of his presence had been obliterated, as if his time there had been only a realistic dream. He experienced vertigo, as if solid reality were now subject to shifts and changes without warning or awareness. He felt terribly alone and frightened. His mind resisted manipulation, real or imagined, and the rooms where he remembered joy had become threatening and cold.

Finding his saddlebags and bedroll, he went outside, closing the door to Martina's house with firm finality. At the stable, he tossed panniers over the pack mule's blanket, loaded the radio, and balanced it with saddlebags, bedroll, and antenna wire. He walked to the limit of the town, unnoticed, and spread his bedroll beneath the tall upland pines.

Though it was night, he had something he couldn't wait to check on. If he was right, the clue Martina had given him would confirm the nature of the third signal. If it was what he suspected, then everything had changed. Where he had felt hope before, there would be none. Only at night could he confirm it or put his fears to rest. He sunk two forked saplings in the ground, in a north-south line with enough distance between so the antenna mast, held horizontally, would rest in the crotches. The forked poles were tall enough so the secondary spar, rotated, would clear the ground. Then he mounted the antenna as usual.

The night was chill enough for a fire, but he made none, preferring obscurity over comfort. It was a lonely wait until midnight. Dreams of two Martinas and Illyssa merged and parted like figures seen through a drunkard's eyes until Yan's internal clock awakened him when the Summer Triangle was overhead.

He tuned the radio to the third frequency—even closer to the others, now. Its shrill tone, now definitely lower, had almost separated into discrete pulses. He made notes of settings and antenna position. He didn't crawl back into his bedroll, only wrapped it around his shoulders and waited for the signal to fade, as it always had.

When the tone was at its weakest, he dismounted the antenna and placed the mast horizontally in the crotches, with the cross-member vertical. Listening to the signal, he rotated the antenna toward the horizontal plane, and with sinking heart heard the faint sound swell, growing louder until the spar paralleled the ground, then fading as he continued to rotate it. He moved his support poles ninety degrees, and again set the mast horizontally. His results were much the same.

In case he had miscalculated, he huddled in his bedroll until dawn and then tested his theory again. With the cross-spar horizontal, the signal was weak. As he lowered the westernmost arm of the spar, the droning grew louder just when the antenna plane matched the plane of the Summer Triangle, now far in the west. The droning note had chittering overtones now, like massed crickets or an enormous black creature, blacker than the lightening sky. His fears confirmed, he turned off the radio.

At Martina's house, he jotted a note explaining his findings. "Check the signal," he wrote. "I'm sure you have means, in your secret place. You'll confirm my belief that a ferosin ship is approaching the Earth, decelerating, from a point in the sky enclosed by Vega, Deneb, and Altair. If your equipment is sophisticated, as I suspect, you should be able to determine from the tone's change in frequency—the Doppler-shifted wavelength—the rate of deceleration, and thus the ship's arrival date. I suspect we don't have five years to prepare, or even one." Yan left the note on the table, weighted with a fork from the dry sink. Then he settled his mule in the stable, planning to wash at the inn where the others had arranged to meet.

The companionship over kaf and sweet bread was warm and simple, restoring the good feelings he'd had the day before, the bond of men united for a common purpose. It was a down-to-earth feeling, he mused, considering the altitude of their plans.

Yan didn't fly that day or the next. Ground practice, assembly of wings, and memory drills continued through the day, and planning sessions well into the night. He was given a room over the restaurant when the others discovered he had slept rough. They were embarrassed that no one had thought of his sleeping arrangements, though he protested that he had endured no hardship. At least every "witch" isn't perfect, he mused. They don't all know everything before I tell them of it.

Meals and room were given without payment. "It's taken care of," he was told. Even subtle inquiry as to who was paying was met with warm, uncommunicative smiles. He would have preferred to pay. He felt like a mendicant, uncomfortable asking for anything extra, even a pitcher of water at night. He took walks between dinner and evening work, and observed that Martina's house was dark. Peering in the window, he saw that his note was still on the table. At the inn, his oblique references to Martina were brushed over as casually as his other queries.

In Jossity, those mornings were like any others. Traders departed with their wagons, purses lightened by the Church's stiff tolls for the narrow bridge and the precipitous trail. For Brother Gnist, the days were frustratingly similar to those preceding; the witch remained silent and the fisherman's keeper declared him still too weak for the rigors of questioning. Circumstances conspired against the skinny, obsessed Hand, and he began to suspect a more active conspiracy against him. His suspicions were groundless, of course, but, as he held them close, no one could reassure him. Brother Kinnut and his aides were Gnist's prime suspects: the fisherman couldn't be healing as slowly as they claimed. Gnist now paced his office, snapping at anyone who disturbed him. It didn't take long for functionaries and messengers to learn to avoid his chamber, and the resulting isolation from normal intercourse deepened his growing paranoia.

Omer was well enough to talk with his doctor. He could no longer pretend not to be healing at all. But his end of such conversations consisted of nods and monosyllables; he saved his breath for occasions when he had to prod the voluble fellow.

Such prodding was rare, because Kinnut was a talker. He lived with a woman, and held the mincing priests up to ridicule. He himself was only in the Church because *all* doctors in Tenzie were; he likened himself to a tailor who couldn't ply his trade without joining the proper guild. Before Omer's return to consciousness he had had no one but his common-law wife to talk to, he said, and though she was good-looking and a fine mother to his little ones, she was uninterested in deeper thought, and unable to discuss things more complex than infant diarrhea and the price of goat's milk.

Omer was an excellent listener, his interest keener than Kinnut could suspect, and the information he gathered would not have been given voluntarily. Within days of his awakening he had learned as much about activities within the keep as others might glean in a year; he had constructed a tentative mental map from no more than the brother's chatter and careful inference. He wasn't yet strong enough to make use of his growing knowledge, but it kept his mind active and away from less pleasant thoughts.

He continued to exercise, slowly, painfully shambling about his room at night. He wasn't going to do push-ups anytime soon, but if he could find a sharp instrument somewhere, he could take Gnist with him when his own time came.

CHAPTER TWENTY-THREE

If God had not meant Man to fly the stars, he would have made him a blind worm. Ultimately, nothing else would have sufficed.

(7) Adrianna (5), *Commentaries*, Archive Bay 32 in the Unending Cave

Jasso took the student fliers up the mountain for their maiden flights. Their point of departure was a west-facing slope, less threatening than the sheer cliff the brothers had hurled themselves from; a slide, years back, had cleared the steep hillside of trees and bushy growth, and prevailing winds created an updraft near the top. Jasso took the first flight, testing the air currents. Returning, he reported conditions he'd noted—it was a good measure of his and his brother's teaching skills that the novices had few questions.

Yan was first to don wings. The hillside, which had looked so gentle before, seemed to grow steeper as he ran at it, but, a few long steps down its side, the wind caught him and he was airborne. At first the ground raced rapidly by beneath him, but it seemed to slow as his relative altitude increased. He had not moved a muscle since leaving the ground, and his course was still along the strike of the slope. Below him the rocks and jumbled soil of the slide diminished to a minor disturbance of the thick forest cloak. A glance backward showed him he had gained real as well as apparent altitude. He could see over the ridge behind to Ararat, its buildings reduced to tiny cubes amid the trees. West and south, ridge after ridge progressed, disappearing in pale, slaty haze. Somewhere out there in the distance lay the Tenzian border, and the brooding stone watchtowers on a barren, gravelly ridge. Yan saw too much at once; his sense of distance was distorted by new perspectives and nothing gave a sense of scale.

A glance at the spidery framework and the almost-invisible membrane that held him up gave him a momentary chill, but, surprisingly, his initial fears had vanished as he rose. He leaned tentatively to his left; the ground rotated clockwise. A shift back stopped his turn. He squinted against the sun's glare. He could not spot the landslide scar. Looking behind, he tried to orient himself to landforms he'd seen going west, but saw nothing familiar. The sun was still low, at just the angle to blind him as he searched for Ararat. He had not passed over any ridge-tops, so the one ahead had to be "home."

Ahead? A glance to each side confirmed that the ridge was no longer below him. He was approaching it from below the crest. Individual treetops reached up, almost brushing his dangling toes. In moments he would be among them. He leaned hard right and the trees veered away. He had to get higher. His mind was blank, the drills forgotten. All he could think of were trees—reaching, towering, sharp-branched trees. He needed time to think, but he was rushing through the air, covering ground at an inestimable rate and getting more lost by the second.

Why had his demon not arisen? He was in terrible danger—the spur that goaded it—but this was different. Soaring away from the ridge, there was no immediate risk of a crash. He was still descending, and there was no place to land, but the threat was distant, unreal. There was nothing to fight against. Fighting was the stimulus—but what he needed was the emotionless, analytic madness, the time-slowing relief from the urgency of his situation, and its enhanced perceptions to guide him.

Could he bring it on voluntarily, as on the journey to Blue? There was time to try. Ahead were no obstructions; the ground still sloped in his direction of flight and the next ridge was hazy with distance. Eyes out of focus, he allowed an image of the great iron-shod flywheel to take form in the air ahead. He watched it turn slowly, accelerating with each roar of invisible steam from the heavy cylinder. He imagined brassy vapor and the thick, meaty stink of hot grease on ironwood pillow blocks. The tremor of air across his wings was the shudder of the ponderous machine. His image faded. Had he lost it? Had he failed?

The wind on his face told him he was gliding, not soaring. The ground had leveled out. The valley trees were about eighty feet in height, and he was no more than five tree-heights up.

Squinting, triangulating, he estimated he was dropping steadily; he had three or four minutes of flight before he hit the treetops. He needed to find rising air, but he was too low to catch the updrafts where wind compressed against western slopes. Was there a localized air column? A place where sun warmed the ground, where heat was not absorbed by dark leaves and forest shadow? On his right, he saw a wash of color, a small stream meandering in its outsized valley. A torrent in springtime, now the glimmer of water threaded between wide mud flats and expanses of dry canary grass. The dipping flutter of black and orange flashes were redwings landing on magenta loosestrife. Crows in search of grounded fish circled level with him above cracked, curling mud. Their wings fluttered only sporadically.

It would do. The crows scattered at his unnatural shape, cawing four times for danger, then in threes as they settled on branches among mates and companions. Crows speak the same language everywhere, he reflected irrelevantly. He felt radiating heat from the flat as he passed over it, perhaps imagining increased pressure against the wide-spanning membranes overhead. At the far end of the flat he leaned, and his tight-stretched wing responded, following the line of division between dark trees and bleached gray-gold grass. A full circle brought him over a great white oak, long dead, shining like polished pewter in morning sunlight. Later in the day the mud would be hotter, the air would rise faster. Had he gained altitude? Surely he had lost none on his circuit of the marsh. Another full circle, and he was sure; the oak had diminished, its trunk no longer as thick as a finger, but barely thicker than a quill. He held up a hand, measuring barren branches against his span. Yes, he was higher.

He circled several times, feeling tremors of turbulence through the struts above. The silvery tree was tiny now. How high? High enough. He became aware that his mind was operating with the precision of an abacus, the speed of a computer, correlating the shrinking scale of things below with the metronome accuracy of his heartbeat, calculating his rate of ascent. He could not have explained how he knew the number of seconds in each circle around the air column, or the circumference of his flight path, but he was sure he *knew* it, without guessing. His senses were unnaturally tuned, giving quantitative data, and he felt no anxiety when it was time to turn outward, to drift east and north where he could glance off the rising air of the ridge.

With smug pleasure, he realized his mind had recorded every moment since his feet left the ground, and he was no longer lost—he couldn't be lost. Deep inside, the boy Yan thrilled at his soaring flight, marveled at the immensity of the world moving so slowly by, so far away and down. The other Yan, machine-precise, calculated airspeed and rate of climb as he followed the ridgeline, still rising, the sun warm on the right side of his face.

He spotted the west-facing scar, and four specks on the grass at its summit. Four? Where was the fifth man, the other wing? He leaned back, feeling the thrum of pressure on membrane, and used the upper edge of the wind-rise to gain another few tens of feet. There—he squinted into the sun and caught a flash like oil on water, another wing aloft. Jasso was searching for him. Triangular ghost and dark man-shape passed below, and he turned, dipping the leading edge of his wing, reducing lift. A flutter warned him he was diving too fast, but a backward lean brought him out of it with only a slight snap of his straining sail. He pondered the membrane as it stretched and gave, wondering how much strain it would take, knowing he had not even approached the limit of its strength.

A downward spiral brought him level with Jasso, and he swept by tangentially, then brought himself up in small, speed-killing climbs, a butterfly flutter of dips and rises. Jasso's dark features were suffused with anger, and the movements of his lips were a string of curses no doubt aimed at Yan, for the scare he must have given them when he had not returned. Yan curved toward the landing site and brought himself around into the wind, coming to a virtual stop just as his feet dropped the last inches to the ground.

The delicate precision of that maneuver was not lost on Jasso. He landed beside Yan after a looping pass, matching his landing form, but hitting hard with his feet when his sail lost wind. He stumbled, then shed his wing with the speed of experience and approached at a run while Yan still fumbled with his straps.

"Is this your idea of a joke, you God-damned heathen?" His intense anger was compounded of relief and conviction that Yan had flown before, had concealed expertise from his fellows. "What the hell did you think you were doing? I told you to make one circle and come back down."

Yan forced his gleeful smile away and assumed a contrite face and posture. "I'm sorry," he said truthfully. "I panicked and I got lost."

"Cowshit! You handled that wing like you were born to it. Where did you learn to fly? Who else knows how to build them? You're toying with me!"

Yan responded contritely to the rapidly fired questions, realizing that Jasso was seriously angry. He felt compassion, then concern for negative effects of a rift in the team. It took fifteen minutes of hangdog apology to calm Jasso enough to listen to Yan's explanations. Yan described the entire flight in detail, omitting only the "demon" that had made it possible. That was his secret, and he was determined it remain so.

Mollified, Jasso helped Badger don the wing, and when the young man took to the air Jasso sailed with him, a single wingspan away. They returned after a short flight, and the others each took a turn, with Jasso close beside them. Their flights were short and predictably similar: a hop to the brink of the slope, a flutter into the air, and a soaring circle upward and right back down again, approaching the hill from behind. Watching them, Yan knew that Jasso would never completely believe he had not been made to look like a fool.

Ernst missed the ridge and had to make another pass. On a second try he landed, stumbling and swearing. Then there was time for each of them to take one more turn, and when Yan's came he flew carefully, precisely, obeying Jasso's commands to the letter.

That evening they checked progress on the new wings. One, a large one, was ready, and John was busy stretching and bonding the membrane in place. Tomorrow they would test it, and if that went well, would try a two-man flight.

At a planning session, the new fliers bent over a model of Jossity Keep. Until their flights, the star-shaped tower had represented an impenetrable obstacle, but that night their fingers swept and darted about it like miniature wings, landing with impunity within the outer walls and on the tower roof. Yan felt confident that he could land on the roof without risk. His own doubt was whether he could take off again from the hundred-foot tower and still clear the surrounding walls. He resolved to test the possibility at the soonest opportunity.

Again that night, he went by Martina's house. The note still lay on the table. Had the fork that weighted it been moved? Yan couldn't remember how he had placed it. He left a new message, more urgent, begging for confirmation that the elders were considering the imminent arrival of a ferosin vessel. He expressed hope that he would not have to go on the mission with that anxiety hanging over him.

The next day Jasso allowed the others to fly by twos, without him. Yan used the opportunity to scan the surrounding countryside for an outcrop similar in size and configuration to the apex of the keep. He found a promontory by an east-facing ridge that was not subject to the winds of compression that had so far eased them into the air. Takeoff would be aided by a slight breeze or none, which would show him if escape from the tower would be possible under ordinary conditions. Jasso thought well of the idea. He had Badger climb down a rubble slope a quarter mile away to establish a line of sight to the promontory. Badger marked the lowest points of Yan's and Jasso's dives and long glides, and from his observations they calculated the drop and distance covered by the one-man wings. After basic testing, they did the same with the two-man craft, with successively heavier loads of rocks to simulate a passenger.

Even heavily laden large wings dropped no more than fifty feet, and were able to maintain altitude, passing over a point six hundred feet away that corresponded to the lower, cliffside wall of the keep.

At night, the cool air of the keep would provide no upward aid, and it would be necessary to glide over the wall and along the deep water gap for miles before they could land, hopefully unobserved—but if the escape was in that manner, they would be on the wrong side of the watchtower-lined border, and it would be a difficult and dangerous trip back. An afternoon flight in bright, hot sunlight was preferable, they agreed. Rising hot air from the cobbled outer keep would provide a strong, constant updraft. Even if their spiraling rise above the keep was observed, they would quickly be out of arrow range, and the increased altitude would allow them to fly over the watchtowers to some safe meeting point in the north.

They made several two-man flights simulating conditions they might encounter with an injured passenger or a panicky one—it was anyone's guess what shape Illyssa and Omer would be in. Yan doubted either of them would panic, but he himself simulated a clutching, jerky cargo well enough for Jasso to have to fight hard for control. Happily the larger wing, though less responsive than its light brethren, was correspondingly more stable under such conditions, and Jasso felt they could handle almost anything without spinning out of control.

Two more days passed before they felt ready to depart. John, Arn, Karl, Badger, and Ernst would fly one-man craft; Jasso and Yan, the larger ones. Each man had a pack with light tools and food. In addition, the larger wings were equipped with ropes, grappling hooks, pitons, lengths of light tubing, and membrane for repairs. Yan strapped his axe across his back.

They departed without fanfare. Yan had hoped Martina would see them off, if not for his sake, then for her two sons who were flying into danger, but his notes were still untouched. They threw themselves into the air over Ararat, and the first ones aloft waited, circling like hunting hawks, until the heaviest had gained altitude. Then they formed a file and drifted southward.

From beds and armchairs near dormer windows in Ararat's old houses, from the iron-and-oak doorway into the Unending Cave, and from stoops and porches, eleven old women stood or sat as their aged bodies permitted. From a parapet atop the town's tallest house, eleven old women watched through the eyes of a twelfth who was not yet too old to climb steep stairs and a final ladder to see the seven graceful, translucent wings spiral upward and away until they grew tiny and then disappeared altogether.

That one has a strong mind, (51) Johanna (70) said. *He will be useful to us later, I think.*

If he survives Jossity, (49) Anna (37) replied wordlessly. *If indeed the weak signals from the south are the girl. If either of them return to us.*

He will. They will, another "voice" reassured the doubter. *Without our help, he'll not locate the ship.*

Should we help him at all? (50) Adrianne (48) wondered. *Are we overeager, perhaps? Could the ferosin threat be less pressing than he believes? We risk much. Is it premature?*

Can we know that? We've waited a thousand years. Shall we wait another? The ship won't survive another millennium of neglect.

He had the Sign, remember. Could that be coincidence? Such things are uncommon where he comes from. What does it mean? A new mind had posed that question.

I doubt it means much, another answered. *His mind is closed, but from old hurt and childhood shame, not Power.*

Aya, aya. Even his dreams are locked away.

We have no choice but to aid him, the oldest reminded them. *Have you forgotten the disturbances when young Ilse used her Power?*

Aya, even I awakened from dreams of fire and hot iron. Is Ilse so strong?

Anomaly. Her generation, her age, should not be so strong. We must have her. Her genes may have what we cannot create.

And if nothing comes of either of them? Will the ferosin slavemasters allow us another millennium to ponder and plot?

If young Yan returns with her, we'll give him *the seeker's task. Perhaps* his *steel will survive the heat of forging.*

Aya—whatever he may think, his journey's only begun.

They all felt a sensation of wind and lightness pass through their minds like a chill through old bones as the youngest sent her thoughts outward after the wings. *Wings such as those may soar far in the years I foresee,* she predicted. *You see? I was right to allow the children their toys.*

CHAPTER TWENTY-FOUR

> Out there, on one of Omer's bright islands, is there a race of blind worms? If so, to keep them planetbound, God would have to deny them the ability to *imagine* wings.
>
> (54) Ilse (75), Diary

Everything had felt wrong as Yan prepared his filmy wing for flight; the elders' priorities were distorted. Someone—Martina, most likely—had finally taken his notes from her table, including the one that listed message fragments from Roke that he had jotted down but not deciphered, messages that he was convinced dealt with preparations for the ferosin vessel's arrival. The elders knew everything he did, and more, but were they *doing* anything? Even if they were, would they tell *him*? Still uneasy, he put the worries from his mind and turned his thoughts to rescuing Illyssa and Omer—or avenging them.

The first part of their three-legged flight was parallel to the border watchtowers, over Tenzian territory. After spiraling skyward in a turbulent updraft that two hawks had cautiously vacated, they landed atop a bald, gray mountain where they conferred and checked their gear. John flew point position, where his experience finding rising air would be most useful. The other one-man wings spread out in V-formation like gigantic geese, maximizing the chance of finding critically important updrafts. Yan and Jasso flew behind, where they could see who rose and who did not. Their courses were zigzags punctuated by spirals as they took advantage of lift.

Two more hours brought them within twenty miles of Jossity; in a morning's soaring, they had traveled as far as Yan had ridden in seven days. They waited on another mountainside until the sun was only a handbreadth above the horizon. Their timing was perfect; there was still rising air. From a thousand feet above Jossity, they watched the sun set. Town and keep were deep in shadow, and before it was completely dark they descended in a strung-out line, circling the tower and landing on its flat roof one by one. They collapsed their wings and tucked them behind chimneys. Once oriented, they broke out climbing gear to descend to the seventh floor.

A brief half days' practice had not prepared Yan for the reality of dangling from a rope in semidarkness. He had taken to flying like a young hawk, and felt secure even with thousands of feet of air between himself and the ground; the pressure of air on the wing's fabric was tangible, reliable support. But the thin, braided rope seemed no more substantial than a spiderweb, and sweat ran coldly into his eyes as he lowered himself to the seventh-floor ledge.

John and Ernst preceded him. They waited long moments, listening; the room beyond the window remained dark and quiet. There were not supposed to be sleeping quarters nearby, but what if they'd made a mistake? Ernst slid a blade along the casement until it met resistance, then tapped upward with the heel of his hand; the latch slipped free. Moments later they were inside. Badger struck a match. The room was a storeroom for medical supplies. Glazed crocks with lead-wrapped stoppers crowded among baskets of dried herbs; equipment, exotic and ordinary, was stacked and piled about.

The door was only latched, not locked. They exited one at a time, staying close. John peered into a hallway lit by ensconced candles. Numbered doors lined it at ten-foot intervals. 704, 706, 708 . . . Their storeroom was 705, on the outer, odd side. To their left, beyond 710, an iron grille crossed the corridor. A patch of darkness hinted at a side passage.

Omer seldom slept at night. There was no light in his chamber, but he could tell by sounds of activity when morning came. He planned his sleep for when Brother Kinnut was about, reinforcing the priest's conviction that his patient recovered slowly. At night, when Kinnut had gone home, Omer exercised. At first he just walked, and rested frequently. As his strength returned, he practiced lifting a stool, then a wooden chair. He was still as weak as an infant, and his heart pounded irregularly, but his coordination was returning. He could have gained strength faster if he ate more, but appetite would have given him away. Kinnut watched intake and excretion with equal diligence.

This was Omer's first exploratory foray beyond his room. He knew roughly where he was, but his sense of direction gave him contradictory information from moment to moment—a result of his head injuries. He stood by the door, listening. Nothing—no cough or creak. His head twisted the door handle; it was unlocked. Good. He'd suspected it from the easy way Kinnut opened it in the morning. The hallway was empty. On his right, an iron gate separated the infirmary from the hall leading out of the wing.

The left corridor split in a Y, the right limb blocked by a gate, the other dark. He left his door ajar and shuffled toward the darkened passage. It joined another, well lit. He peered both ways. An unlocked gate blocked the right-hand side, and the left corridor was like his own, with numbered doors. He paused, not sure which to try first. He pushed on the gate, moving it slightly on well-oiled hinges. Hearing a noise behind him, he spun quickly, catching the wall corner when he lost his balance. Damn this weakness, he thought angrily. I should have waited another day.

A door down the hall had opened a few inches. He watched it open further, ever so slowly. Funny; whoever was in there was being as cautious as he. Another patient with a midnight errand? He backed up and lowered himself into a squat; men's eyes always looked on their own level first. The door swung fully open. A man in dark clothing and moccasins jumped out, peered both ways, and gave a come-along signal to someone within the dark room. He darted down the hall away from Omer, and another took his place at the door. He made the same motion and came toward Omer's corridor. Omer backed up a step, then carefully returned the way he'd come. Do I know that first man? Have I seen him before? Here? No, not here. In Burum? What's he doing here? Does he only resemble someone I know? But who? The man's identity continued to elude him. The second man peered down the dark hallway toward Omer, then pushed the unlocked gate open and went past. A third man took his place—a man whose identity was no guessing matter. Omer felt a great breath of exultation. "Yan," he gasped, just as his weakened body slumped to the tiles with a light, dry thud.

Yan spun toward the sound. He had worried that practice with his demon might exorcise it instead—a far cry from the days when he had so desperately wished it gone. Now his fears were laid to rest when awareness washed over him as suddenly and intensely as sunlight bursting from a cloud. He saw a patch of white on the floor ahead. Without thought he darted toward it, taking in the intersecting passage at a glance as he bent to the frail, crumpled body. He half lifted, half rolled the white-haired old man. "Oh, gods, Om! What have they done to you?" He clutched a bony wrist and felt a weak, fluttering pulse, then lifted his friend and ran back the way he'd come. Jasso and Badger were outside the storeroom door.

"It's Omer!" Yan said. Speech came slowly, as if his mouth had filled with cotton wool. "I'm going to take him inside. Arn, stay with him. He's weak, maybe dying."

"Not dying yet, P'fesser." Omer's harsh voice was more beautiful than all the birds or pretty girls that had ever sung.

"You'll make it, Admiral." Berserker clarity remained, but tears ran down Yan's cheeks and into his short-cropped beard. "You've *got* to make it."

"Illyssa. One floor down," Omer croaked. "Stairs way around th' corner. Gate back there, I think." He gestured flaccidly toward the grille that Ernst, the second man, had pushed through. "Gnist's office—he's probably there. Doesn't sleep—crazy."

"Don't talk. We'll find her. And Gnist." Yan ran quietly the way Ernst had gone. Light shone under a door near one point of the tower's star-shaped layout. *Gnist*, he thought. Yan mistakenly assumed that Omer's condition resulted from torture, and the rage directed at Effredi Gnist was white-hot slag burning inside him, consuming him—no clear rush of his madness, but a choked, incoherent mix of anger and helpless grief. He suppressed an urge to kick down the door. Ernst's sudden appearance startled him out of his fit, and he reeled dizzily, tasting harsh bile in his throat. "Gnist—the priest—is in there," he whispered. "I won't leave him."

Ernst nodded and held up a finger—*Wait*. Badger arrived, and they took position on both sides of the door. Ernst slowly twisted the heavy handle, then pushed. Yan stood facing the room within, his axe hanging heavily from his right hand.

Gnist paced on, hearing only his own muttered soliloquy, his back turned for the moment. Yan stepped forward, raising the axe high behind the pacing priest. The others slipped in behind him. When Gnist reached the far end of the room, where windows straddled the point of the star, he turned. Eyes dazzled by the lamplight behind Yan, he saw only the ghostly silhouette of a man, and the great gleaming axe poised to dismember him. He fainted.

He awoke on his back, choking as water coursed over his face.

He blinked, focusing on the gleaming nightmare before him. All he could see was the sparkle of lamplight off the three-pointed Pittsburg crown stamped on the axe-face. A deadly, honed edge pressed a thin, hot line of pain into his throat. Blood and sweat mingled on his neck and pooled on the floor under him.

"Where is she, Brother Gnist? Tell me, and I may kill you quickly, as I should have done in Innis." The scars on Gnist's neck, and the nailless fingers clutching Yan's wrist, were white, even in the yellow light. "Tell me where she is, Gnist," Yan droned tonelessly. "Take me there and I'll not add further to your mutilations. Take me to Illyssa." Gnist gargled, afraid to nod and unable to speak for fear of the keen blade pressing into his larynx. His eyes flashed up and down in assent. Yan lifted the weight from his throat. "We're getting up now, Brother Gnist. We're taking a walk. Don't make a sound. Just walk and point the way, and I'll stay very close to you." The two men rose simultaneously, Yan by himself, the priest with Ernst and Badger at his elbows. The axe never strayed, never varied its light even pressure. Close together, the four walked through the wide doorway and down the leftmost hall. John and Jasso fell in behind.

Even on the stairs, the axe remained constant. There were no sounds but the soft padding of moccasin-clad feet and the clipping of Gnist's sandals. A flutter of the priest's hand halted them at an iron-bound door with the number 652 in faded white paint. Jasso lifted its heavy bolt and pulled it open. The blackness inside was unbroken by glimmer or reflection. John fetched a lamp from the corridor wall, then went inside.

Yan waited with Gnist while Illyssa's father went in to her. Long moments went by before they emerged together, her eyes wide and unbelieving. Her uncle moved to her other side. Yan felt the tension ebb, and with it the worst heat of his rage. Illyssa, at least, seemed unharmed. Her face was thinner, and he imagined that her coarse prison gown hung more loosely than it might have before, but her eyes were clear, her steps sure and firm. Her eyes met his over Gnist's shoulder, but they did not speak. Instead, she addressed the quivering priest. "We've come the full circle, Brother Gnist. Another city, another stone warren, another blade at your throat. Shall I again borrow your robe?" A ghost of her mischievous grin crept over her face.

Turning to her father, she said, "Omer is above. You've found him? Good. Is he strong enough to travel?"

"He's very weak," John told his daughter. "Can you heal, girl?"

Her face tightened and paled. "I don't know, Papa. I've never been tested. I can try."

"It's all we can hope for. His heart won't stand stress. If you've bred true, you'll give him strength to live out the day. With luck, that's all we'll need." John led her toward the stairway. "What did the priest do to him?"

"Nothing, yet," Illyssa told him. "He wasn't strong enough to survive torture. It was the fight, his wounds."

The axe felt heavy in Yan's hands. Gnist, for all his evil intent, had not deliberately caused Omer's condition. He turned to Ernst. "I can't kill him, but I don't dare leave him either," he whispered. "What shall I do?"

"Get him up to the storeroom and we'll decide," Ernst said. They hurried up the steps and around through the long, angling hallways. Illyssa knelt by Omer's inert form. The others crowded into the storeroom. Ernst and Jasso conferred, then Jasso jabbed a thumb in Gnist's direction. "Take him up to the roof," he commanded. "We'll follow with the old man, and make sure our traces are cleaned up—if there's no sign of our presence here, we can wait on the roof until the sun is well up. At best, the searchers will waste time looking in other places. At worst, we'll have to hold them off until midday, when we can get lift from the compound paving. We can't chance the water-gap route with Yan's friend—without the altitude to fly over the ridges, we might have to stop, abandon the wings, and walk. He couldn't do it—he'll need all the help the healers in Ararat can give even if we get him there soon."

Ernst, Jasso, and Arn climbed up the thin rope. A sling was made for Omer, which they then used to haul up Illyssa and Gnist. Yan was the last to leave.

Well back from the parapet, Illyssa knelt again by Omer, but now her eyes were desperate. "I think he's dying. His heart."

"Then we've no choice," John replied. "We'll have to merge. Will you lead us?"

"I'm frightened, Papa. If I can't do it . . ."

"If you can't, then he's no worse off than he is now. Jasso and I will be with you."

"And Yan—him, too."

"He's not one of us. Ernst can help."

"No. Yan. He's strong, and he knows what to do."

John hesitated, then smiled and squeezed her shoulder. "Still breaking the rules, girl? I should have expected it. You've bred true in that way, anyway. Don't worry. You can do it." He motioned to his brother, and to Yan. All four joined hands in a circle around Omer, and Yan morbidly thought of mourners around a freshly dug grave. Standing, it was impossible for him to see if Omer was still alive.

"I'm not going to try to heal him," Illyssa said. "I'll be satisfied just to channel our strength to him for a time, and bring his heart under control. Can you think of an image we can use? One that he will know also? Yan?"

"Have any of you seen a steam engine?" Yan asked quietly, thinking of his own heart, the madness and the machine.

"There's a shingle mill in White Gap," John said. "A boiler and cylinder that drive a saw." He looked at his brother, who nodded.

"I've seen it, too."

Yan questioned them further. In the Cathedral, his last attempt to aid Illyssa with imagery had brought fire and heat, a melted lock and not merely an open one. He blamed himself for that, not Illyssa, because the image had been his, stimulated, he suspected, by the red false images of his tightly squeezed eyelids. He wanted no such accidental images to interfere this time.

"That will do," Illyssa stated. "Shall we each pick individual functions, or try to maintain the entire picture together?" She was brisk, now, like a nurse or a captain of men. There were no more hesitant looks toward her father or uncle.

"I use the flywheel in my own . . . meditations," Yan said hesitantly.

"Good," Illyssa said quickly, not questioning his odd revelation. "Yan, the flywheel. You will set our pace. Papa, the fire, our joint power, and Uncle Jas, the boiler and the steam, the channel. I am the piston, Omer's heart. Yan, your image is critical. You must keep us all steady. Can you hold it so?"

"I have to," he murmured, more frightened than he had ever been by cliff-hanging or battle. I did it for myself, he thought. There's no reason I can't do it now, for Omer. He envisioned the great wood-spoked wheel, and almost immediately his fears faded, leaving only resolve.

He knelt by his friend, feeling John's and Jasso's hands on his shoulders. Illyssa placed his hand on Omer's bony chest beside her own, then covered it with her other one. Cool clearness—no longer madness—enveloped him, and the great wheel turned slowly. The hands gripping his shoulders felt like vices. Through his palm he felt the weak *chuff* of Omer's irregular heart. From John, he sensed the roar of a coal fire as combustion and flue dampers opened; from Jasso, the roiling pressure of steam forced into the fat cylinder. Through Illyssa's hand he felt impetus; through the brothers', surging power. Cylinder pushed flywheel, and flywheel spun cylinder through its cycle: pressure, movement against inertia, then a great gout of released steam.

Omer's heart *chuff*ed again, more strongly than before, and Yan, the flywheel, responded with a ponderous half turn. He pushed against it, willing it to continue the turn, and the next beat of the heart came sooner, stronger still. Useless flutterings of weak muscle and misfiring nerves were no match for the gathering inertia of the iron-shod wheel. Hot, roiling steam could only pass into the cylinder at the proper time, when the wheel was at one point in its spin, and the heart could only beat at its appointed moment. It beat more regularly now, in rhythm with gouting steam and the wheel whose painted spokes were a blur of red and yellow.

Too fast! Yan realized. The well-run machine had overcome inertia and was shaking, shuddering. He smelled hot grease on the bearings and felt turbulent air between the spokes. Illyssa murmured something, and John valved steam with a shriek that could surely be heard across the almost-forgotten town beyond, below. Jasso shut the fire door with an iron *clang*, and slid the combustion damper sideways, limiting air to the fire. Delicately, he balanced the flue damper. Yan heard squealing, overheated leather brake pads chatter against the iron rim, and smelled the warm tang of burning hides. The engine gradually ceased its vibration and settled into a smooth, relaxed rhythm. The fire took air in an even stream, and the smoke from the tall black flue cleared. No more blackness billowed forth; no more hot orange sparks flew skyward. The steam flowed in smooth pulses, and cylinder pushed wheel just enough to maintain an even pace. Blood surged in perfect time through Omer's cold hands and feet, into his dulled brain. His eyes rolled sideways, unfocused.

"If you hear me, blink once," Illyssa murmured. "Don't try to talk." Omer blinked—a firm, controlled motion. "Good. Do you remember Innis? The padlock on our cell?" Another blink. "We're working as we did then—this time for you, for your heart." She squeezed Yan's hand. "You tell him. You know it better."

"The *River Ox*, Om. Remember the steam tug in Pittsburgh?

We're imaging your heart as such an engine, running smoothly now. Can you focus on it, too?'' Blink. ''Your heart is the cylinder, and a heavy flywheel regulates it. Can you feel your heartbeat?'' Blink. ''We've brought it under control. Can you concentrate on it? Feel how regular it is?'' Omer blinked twice. ''Is that 'yes'? One blink for 'yes.' ''

Again Omer blinked twice, and Yan saw that his lips moved, forming words. Yan bent close. ''You. Yan. The flywheel. Others . . . fire, steam . . .'' Breath whistled noisily in his nostrils. ''I'll take over. Aya. Let go.''

''You're sure? You can keep it steady?''

'' 'M sure. Let go.''

Yan leaned back, his hand still on Omer's chest. He let his tight-held image recede, feeling the strong, steady beat under his palm go on unfalteringly. ''You're running your own ship, Admiral,'' Yan said softly, affectionately. He lifted his hand from Omer's chest to caress the white, matted hair and beard. ''It's a good Pittsburg tugboat. Keep the boiler fired.''

''Close your eyes now, Om.'' Illyssa's voice wavered with emotion and exhaustion. ''Sleep if you can. In a while we'll be in a safe place where you can finish healing yourself.''

Omer blinked twice, then said, loudly enough for the standing men to hear, ''Staying awake. Ha' a ship to run. You go now.''

She stood unsteadily. ''He'll make it. How long before we leave? And how?'' She looked around, only now truly realizing where she was, on top of the formidable Jossity Keep.

''It's almost dawn. We leave in six or seven hours, then perhaps seven more to home, the straight way.''

''Seven *hours* home, Uncle Jas? Have you moved to Jossity? How will we get down from here?''

Yan drew her aside to show her the wings. She looked skeptically at the sheer membrane and chitinous tubes. ''I think I'll shut my eyes until it's over.''

''That's how I felt the first time I jumped off a cliff with one. You'll be angry later, though. It's beautiful, flying.''

''Yan, you fool. I won't *blink*. I wouldn't miss a thing.''

''I know you're brave, but it's frightening, at first.''

''Who will I ride with? You? I think not. *That's* terrifying. I'm getting more scared by the minute.''

''You should be so lucky. I'm flying Omer home as fast as I can. You ride with your uncle. Shall I ask him to drop you off somewhere? A nice cold river?''

She smiled demurely, then stuck out her tongue. "Did you miss me, Yan?"

"It's been the longest three weeks of my life. For all I knew, you were dead. Of course I missed you."

"Like a dog misses fleas, right? You haven't even kissed me. Who'd you sleep with?"

Her joking question caused a visible reaction. He couldn't tell what she saw in his face, or his mind, or how she interpreted it, but she peered into his eyes. "You did!" she exclaimed. "You really did sleep with somebody! How did I know that?"

Yan reddened, sure he'd gotten himself into an inextricable predicament. Though by her standards he'd done nothing wrong, his own mind warned him he was on dangerous ground. His relationship with Martina had not been exactly secret—not even its intimate aspects. She would find out whatever she wanted to know, he was sure.

She saw his discomfiture. "I keep forgetting what a prude you are. At least you weren't lonely, I hope—and someday you'll tell me about her." She said it in the tone she might have used to say "Someday you'll tell me what you had for dinner" rather than "Someday I'll find out." And the way she squeezed his arm showed none of the rage and recrimination he'd feared. Knowing witches' attitudes, he reflected, was not the same as experiencing them firsthand. Looking at Illyssa, it was hard for *him* to believe that he had made love, not once, but several times in close succession, to her *grandmother*. He was relieved that she didn't press him further, for he knew he would have been unable to put his tangled feelings into coherent words. Besides, as she slipped into his arms, he was much too busy kissing her to think about anything else at all.

Gnist, trussed and gagged, was thrust against a chimney like a sack of worn machine parts. His eyes darted from one witch to another, then to Yan, and to the odd contrivances they were assembling. He understood nothing except that he was, unaccountably, still alive. The team was too busy to pay him notice as they prepared for escape. They made a litter for Omer from spare membrane and tubing. Jasso instructed Illyssa in her role as passenger, and Yan sat with Omer, who alternately dozed and listened as Yan described the wings and the experience of flying. He feared the stress of flight might bring on another heart attack if the old man was not prepared for it.

The first two minutes after launch were critical. They would jump from the south wall of the prison wing. Paralleling the southern star-point, they would have five hundred feet of open, cobbled pavement, in full sunlight, as hot as it would get that day. The walls of the outer enceinte, toward the cliffs, were nowhere over twenty feet. If they turned before reaching them, staying over hot pavement and tiled roofs, they could establish an ascending spiral, gaining altitude that would allow them to put miles between themselves and Jossity even if no further updrafts were found.

Finally the most difficult hour was at hand. They sat in tiny patches of shade near the chimneys, waiting for the ideal moment when the sun passed the southern rampart. At the parapet's edge, Ernst kept watch. Though none knew the course of daily events below, no unusual activity was observed. If Gnist and the prisoners had been missed, any turmoil was masked by the thick walls and floors under them. The roof was the last place they would look for an escaped girl and a sick old man. Besides, as Illyssa observed, Gnist hardly seemed to be held in great affection. Others might hesitate long before bringing the escape to his attention by knocking on his now-closed door.

Minutes before the first shadow appeared on the east wall of the tower, Yan slipped over to John and Jasso. "I'm unable to decide about Gnist," he said. "I won't—can't—kill him. There's much death behind me, and I carry a heavy burden of it."

"I suppose any of us could manage it, if needs be," John replied thoughtfully, "but would that be any different? Killing is killing."

"Just so. But I believe he is the last churchman to have interest in me—and in you 'witches.' With him freed, we won't have five years of grace. He'll rally the Church."

"Then do we take him with us?" John mused. "He and Illyssa together can't weigh much more than one large man."

"Now *that's* a possibility," Jasso said with a broad, bloodthirsty grin. "Shall we give *him* his choice of fates? A quick death at our hands, or life at the hands of . . . our elders?" He chuckled. "He may be useful, if he knows anything Yan hasn't heard about." He got up. The others followed him to Gnist's resting place, where Jasso explained the limited choices. Still bound and gagged, the Hand of Pharos agreed with jerky nods to postpone his death for a time.

Omer and Illyssa were as ready as they could be. Gnist was seated opposite Illyssa on her uncle's wing. His wrists were tied, but he was able to secure a white-knuckled grip on a strut. An armed man, and the prod of something sharp in the small of his back, restrained any urge to flee. Besides, there was nowhere for him to go but down. There he sat while the others gathered around Omer's litter, affixed to the wing near Yan in his harness. They lifted the whole assembly, backed up as far as they could, then ran to the roof edge with it and thrust it beyond.

The courtyard rushed up at Yan. His wing membrane filled with air, cracking like a musket shot, then gained forward momentum. For a moment he thought he was going to hit ground, but as he traded speed for lift the sun-washed cobbles receded and he swept upward toward the southern buildings. Time maintained its usual pace. There was no need for his demon. He began his clockwise turn, but with the litter's drag, he missed the wall only by inches. He would have to circle several times before he could rise out of arrow range.

John passed several winglengths overhead, soaring lightly on rising air. The other light wings followed. Was Jasso airborne? Yan cursed his oversight. The large wings were adequate for the weight they carried; testing had proved that. But why had they not considered the drag of a bulky burden? Jasso's double load would slow him, too, more than a comparable bag of stones. But there was no time to search the sky for the others. Yan was approaching taller buildings and the high north wall. He fought for altitude, balancing speed and lift, perilously close to stalling and plunging toward the roofs and walls ahead in a flutter of loose fabric and overstressed tubing.

He missed the tallest structure by no greater margin than before—but he did miss it, and from then on he was in no danger of crashing. He was still at risk, though; his low passage had not gone unnoticed. The compound filled with people. He was low enough to distinguish upturned faces and gaping mouths; among ordinary folk he spotted a scattering of brown robes, and more ominously, steel blue uniforms.

Toward the end of his second pass over the barracks and stables by the southeast gate, a row of blue-clad constables formed: a squad of archers. Yan was acutely aware of Omer's vulnerability in the tightly stretched membrane litter, and of his own slightly less exposed position. At least he'd seen no crossbows or muskets. He braced himself for the tearing impact of a steel-tipped shaft. As his wing shadow raced across cobbles, two smaller ones overtook it, growing larger each second. Badger and Karl plunged ahead of him, drawing fire. He heard hoarse, shouted commands. Two more shadows rushed in from ahead: John and Ernst, banking steeply, further distracting the archers.

Yan continued his fight for altitude, and on his next pass he saw the star-shaped roof of the tower below him. No arrow could reach him now; he had time to look around. Three small wings were in sight, but he couldn't tell whose. Where was Jasso? Behind him? With sinking heart he scanned rooftops and cobblestones for a crumpled, broken wing. Nothing. If they'd fallen between the buildings, he wouldn't see them anyway. He forced his thoughts to his own flying and tightened his circle, centering it on the shrinking tower. When the tremble of wing membrane ceased to vibrate the struts under his hands, he knew he'd reached the limit of the updraft. He turned north. Then he saw Jasso's wing, not below, but ahead of him and higher. He could see only two figures suspended beneath the craft; the larger one, on the left, was Jasso. Then the other was Illyssa. Where was Gnist? Had he escaped? Yan wanted to catch up, but he could only trade altitude for speed, and had no idea when he would reach the next suitable updraft. He watched forlornly as the other craft slowly increased its lead.

John and Karl swept over and took position ahead. One wing joined Jasso's. Two were missing. Who? Where were they? Again, his eyes swept the sky. Had they gone down? Yan assumed the worst. They'd gained two and lost two. He hoped the others were dead, if they'd gone down within reach of the Jossity constables. If Gnist survived, he would have no reason not to torture them; they were witches only by birth, without the women's training and talent to put him off, and they knew enough to put Yan, Illyssa, and all the witch-folk in danger. The mad priest would stop at nothing.

Ahead, Jasso and his escort turned and gained altitude. There was a strong upwelling ahead. Yan decided he could afford to lose a bit of altitude to catch up, to find out who the other flier was, and who had been lost. He raced toward them and soon recognized Ernst. Badger and Arn was missing. He had not known either man well, for Arn had been taciturn, Badger reticent, quietly deferring to the older men. Yan mourned them both as he glided from one thermal to the next, following John's lead. Omer was silent and unmoving. Yan prayed hesitantly to nebulous gods, or God, that he'd have no one else to grieve for when he landed at last.

They did not stop on the way back. Prevailing winds from the south and west pushed them at a good rate, and they passed over Blue sooner than Yan expected, with Ararat just over the next ridge. He made the softest landing he could on the parklike green near the infirmary, wincing, for Omer's sake, at the jolt his knees could not absorb. Jasso and Illyssa ran toward him, and together they carried Omer's litter to the whitewashed stone building. "Healers waiting," John said. "How's he doing, girl?"

"Alive. Asleep or unconscious, but alive."

Healers met them at the door—middle-aged women like any red-faced farm wives, and young girls, students or aides. They took charge of Omer and shooed the rest outside. Yan did not want to leave, but Illyssa hushed him. "We're all going to the nearest inn for a strong drink or two, then we'll sort everything out over kaf, all right? Omer is in the best hands."

"Yes. But what about Gnist? Where is he?"

"Dead. He tried to escape after we jumped—and thank God he did. Uncle Jasso says we never could have gotten high enough with him on the wing, too."

"The drag," Yan commented.

"That's what Uncle Jas said."

"But how did he die? Are you sure?"

On the way to the tavern, Yan pressed for details. Her brief statement gave the bare bones of the struggle that had resulted in Gnist's demise. After the precipitous launch, the priest had clung to his perch like a molted pigeon, sinking his teeth into the stanchion, and had maintained that rigid pose through the first half turn around the enceinte. At some point he saw he was only feet above the rooftops, and had nursed the idea of jumping off until it had become a conviction that his chances were better dropping a few feet then instead of hundreds later. Too, he feared rightly that the keep's archers, once alerted, would not discriminate between fliers and unwilling passengers.

As a two-story building loomed up before him, he prepared to jump. Jasso, struggling to balance lift, load, and velocity without much success, was satisfied to clear the oncoming roof by even a foot. When the roof rushed beneath Gnist's heels, the priest thrust himself outward and let go. His forward momentum carried him over the roof's far edge in a ballistic arch that would have been graceful but for his thrashing limbs and flapping robe. His cartwheeling course ended at the rough stone wall of a stable. Some skulls, as Omer was fond of observing, were hard to break, but none could have survived that impact. Gnist's head crumpled like a ripe melon as it struck, driven by the body behind it.

"So he couldn't have lived through it," Yan stated flatly.

"We passed over him again," Illyssa replied, "and his head was crushed. There was blood all over the wall. He was dead. I wish he had come with us, to be healed of his hatred, but I suppose it's a small price to pay for my uncle's life, and mine."

"For me, it's downright cheap," Yan agreed. They reached the inn. The short walk had done much to loosen stiff muscles, and all of them felt better for it. They found a table and ordered spirits and kaf.

"What happened to Arn and Badger?" Yan asked once they were settled.

"Badger's dead," Ernst said. "He took an arrow in the eye. When he went down, they shot him a dozen times before they'd even come near him. I don't know what they thought they'd shot down—a demon, I suppose." Yan was relieved by Ernst's matter-of-fact delivery of the bad news. He felt guilty that Badger had died saving his and Omer's lives, and feared that his comrades would hold him responsible. Ernst must have read his face, for he reached across the table and squeezed Yan's wrist. "His choice, Yan. We all volunteered."

"And Arn? Is he dead, too?"

"I doubt it." John shook his head. "He was hit in the leg, but he stayed with us for a while. He signaled he was going to land to bind his wound, then he touched down on a ridge and waved me off. I imagine he'll be along soon enough."

The little group stayed together for a second cup of kaf, and a third, but Badger's death cast a pall over the gathering. John volunteered to bring the news to his parents, who lived a day's ride away on a mountainside farm. Badger had been unmarried and had left no one else to mourn him. Jasso left next, to supervise removal of the wings from the town common. Ernst went with him after a few more sips, taking a full cup of kaf along into the drizzling rain that had recently begun.

Yan and Illyssa ordered a light meal. Dinnertime trade began to fill the room, so they moved to a small table in a corner. They spoke little. Though they were together again, Yan felt a little depressed; the action was over, and he had no idea where he was going to go, what he was going to do, from that point. The goal he'd driven toward months before had been reached. It had been spring when he'd left Nahbor, and now the trees were turning russet, orange, and gold.

Here he was in Ararat, home of the legendary "white witches," and all he could think was that he was too tired to escort Illyssa to her parents' cabin, and that his single room and bed were too small for the two of them. She smiled and took his hand. Without a glance at the innkeeper, she took a key from the board and led him to a room hardly larger than his old one, but with a wide, soft bed.

He fell asleep as soon as his head touched his pillow. No dreams troubled him that night, and he was pleased to discover Illyssa small and warm beside him when he awakened to dawn's first questing rays.

CHAPTER TWENTY-FIVE

Like river catfish we swim blindly in a muddy flood of circumstance. Unlike poor blinded fish, a leap of imagination can lift us above the roiled waters, where branching channels can be seen and understood, and a Way chosen. Madness is not blind leaping, but the refusal to leap at all. From that refusal stems the blind, battered confusion by which we recognize the Mad.

Look at the faces of madness, the broken souls, and lend them your strength. Make their dreams your own without surrendering to them. Swim back with them to the place where they first refused to leap, and help them choose anew.

From *The Healer's Way*, Volume II, Chapter 23: "In the House of Madness."

Yan's plans for a quiet breakfast with Illyssa were disrupted by the tramp of hiking boots on the wooden stairs, and by a cheerful voice at the door. "It's my grandmother," Illyssa whispered. Yan already knew that. For a moment he seriously wished he had never returned to Ararat, or that he had carried his wing back to Stormbreak Ridge immediately and had flown off, no matter where. Steeling himself for an uncomfortable, perhaps embarrassing encounter, he went to the door, glad at least that both of them were dressed. He wished the bed were made up, too, but . . .

His fears evaporated with Martina's first words. "Now that you two are back, there's work to be done," she said breezily, with a trace of impatience. "You were right, of course, Yan. It is a ferosin ship, and it will splash down within a month."

Over hot rolls and kaf she outlined the situation, holding little back. The ship would touch down, if past experience held true, somewhere in the Lannick, a day's sail from Roke. It would have one or more ferosin aboard, and a slave crew, probably human. Soon after it landed, ferosin would know from the quislings in Roke what the witches' bees had accomplished, and would probably not risk close contact even with their Church minions. Since it was only one ship, the first one since before Hernock of Roke had seen his Son of Pharos divide into prereproductive segments, ferosin in general could not know their kind were not safe on Earth, but if there was suspicion that the bees were not a natural variation or mutation, and if the ship was allowed to leave with that information, the next visit would be a war fleet. That, Martina stated flatly, had happened on other worlds. "So you must stop it from leaving with its news."

"Me?" Yan asked. "But how?"

"That's for you and your sea knight to figure out. And it has to be done without help from us."

That was madness, he thought angrily. He said as much.

"Think about it, scholar. What happens if you use what technological aid we can give—we have no real weapons—and you fail? Then Earth's fate is sealed. They'll know the only way to suppress us is to destroy us. No, it must be done—but with trickery, with ordinary weapons that will lull them into believing their enemy is without resources. That way, even if you fail, it serves our cause."

Yan considered her words. "What help *will* you give?"

"A ship and crew in Shallah, south of Roke. Hand weapons. A radio, smaller and more versatile than your clunky box. Whatever you need that won't reveal our threat to ferosin."

"I'll have to talk with Omer—if he's well enough," Yan said. But before he left to visit his friend, he pressed Martina for more information. He was not happy with what he heard. Though the general landing area ferosin used was known, the witches couldn't pin it down closely, or find out when the landing would be—things Yan had to know precisely if his crude, budding plan was to succeed. When Martina departed, Yan leaned gloomily over his cold kaf. Illyssa was helpless to cheer him.

At the infirmary, the girls hovering over Omer allowed Yan a brief visit, long enough to explain what he planned. "Aya, it's a fine day when th' cabin boy expounds strategy t' th' admiral," Omer muttered. "But it's a good plan, Yan—once you figure when and where they'll land. I may have a trick or two, also. I'll think on it."

Illyssa took Yan's list of requirements. He did not ask where she took it, or to whom. Then he waited. He was getting used to the elders' autocratic, secretive ways, but he did not like waiting. He suffered most not knowing what they were working on and, worse, what they might have overlooked.

When? Where? The Roke broadcasts were monitored from the elders' burrow, and Illyssa brought him transcripts, written in a schoolgirlish hand. "Something's planned for the week after the Sailors' Mass in Roke," Illyssa commented. Yan watched her count off days on her fingers. "Seventeen days from now."

"Our vessel will be ready by then," Yan said, "but that's not good enough. Are the brownshirts preparing to meet the ferosin ship, or getting ready for something else afterward?" He had visions of another Athel—of Ararat and Blue and the southern mountains lit by thermonuclear fire. "I need to know the *hour* of landing. I need coordinates in degrees, minutes, and seconds. Our Shallan ship won't be able to tack back and forth in Lannick seas, waiting, with winter winds rising."

"Is it hopeless, then? What if there's no way to get the numbers you need?"

"Then the ship lands, and churchmen meet it, and if there are ferosin on board . . . it will all start over again, except the enemy will be forewarned of your 'biological warfare' with bees, and they'll stay in orbit to . . ."

"To what, Yan?"

"To scour life from the face of this poor, maltreated planet. Once churchmen tell them everything, they won't have a choice."

Yan and Illyssa moved out of the inn and into a small house near the town common, a whitewashed, shingled box with coarse plaster walls the color of old cheese, stained by decades of diffuse woodsmoke from its wide hearth. There was space enough in the single room for cooking and sleeping, and for Yan to write, once the dishes were cleared away and washed. A curtained composter-privy allowed them to stay inside as long as food and drink held out. When the low gray skies sank to the ground and streets turned to icy mud, they hid for days at a time, seldom bothering to dress. There were no soft chairs in the tiny house, only the high bed—the focus of their waking and sleeping hours, a place for reading and fire-watching, for loving and talk.

There were few demands on their time. They visited Omer daily, eagerly noting the progress of his recovery. Yan spent afternoons with Jasso, discussing improvements on the fliers, or whiled them away with townsmen who sought his university-instilled memories of ancient manufacturing processes. Occasional messengers from Shallah assured him that ship and crew were ready to sail on the day of the Sailors' Mass.

Despite the slow pace of his and Illyssa's lives, something was happening in Ararat. The life of the mountain town quickened, but townsmen avoided his curious questions. When he spoke of it with Illyssa, she merely assured him all was well, that he'd be taken into the elders' confidence in good time. She skillfully dodged his questions about what she had been doing on days he came home to find her boots stained and rain-soaked. Other men complained about "women's secrets" as if Illyssa's reticence was common, but he liked it no better for that. In his childhood, there had been "men's secrets"; those of women were held to be trivial. Here, the situation was reversed, though the role reversal did not extend to all aspects of life; men still worked the fields and at trades, and women labored mostly at home.

Illyssa had not been reprimanded for her indiscretions with Yan. He would have known. To the contrary, her air of confidence and control seemed to grow daily.

One day, desperate for answers, for a break in the fog of noninformation that pressed in on him from all sides, he found himself standing in front of Martina's door. It was unlocked, but when he stepped inside, he knew it had been unoccupied for some time. There was a musty odor of unheated disuse, and fine dust covered the furniture and stove. He did not stay.

For a while, just as his days were filled with frustration, his bed reeked with the sweat of fearsome, evil dreams in which he relived his madness and the slaughter of Jossity. In the dreams, there were always onlookers. Sometimes they were strangers who watched the swinging arc of his axe avidly, their faces twisted in fear and disgust. In other dreams they were family, old neighbors, even his father's house servants. Night after night, he awakened weak and shaking, afraid to return to sleep.

One nightmare stood out from the rest. The scene was the same: the street in front of the stable in Jossity. The players were identical, and he remembered every face, even those he'd glimpsed as he cut them down. But the spectators' faces were all his own. With the voices of his mad ancestors, they cheered him on as he hacked and swung, parried and thrust. How he hated them! "Why am I fighting these soldiers?" his dream voice asked, "when the watchers are my real enemies?" His rage turned then, and he spun to attack the howling, leering Yan-faces. Every blow struck home. With every impact, another leering visage winked out like a cloud-obscured star, until he was alone in the street with a shining, unbloodied axe in his hand.

That had been the last nightmare, the last time he had awakened in terror. At some time in those gray do-nothing days he had stopped dreaming altogether, or perhaps his dreams had become normal ones that passed unremarked. When he had awakened refreshed after several nights, he knew his nighttime wandering in a past that never was had ended. He stayed abed and watched Illyssa prepare warm, sweet tea.

"The dreams are over, aren't they?" he asked her when she returned to the bedside. "Where do we go from here, my sweet?" He knew her well enough to read sudden tension in the set of her shoulders, and he knew he had guessed correctly; his question had struck home. Whenever he questioned her about her witch talents, she reacted in the same manner—first tension, then anger, then, if he pressed further, silent tears. Let them have their secrets, he had told himself on other occasions, hating her silence, her sadness. He had no need to know what she was learning in the Unending Cave. But this time, it was different. The subject of witchery was him, his dreams. He had changed because of them, or been changed by them, and he had to know.

"You're more skilled than you pretend," he continued, ignoring her discomfiture. "The battles I've fought in my sleep—and my victories—have been yours, too, haven't they?"

"All your victories are mine, my love," she replied without meeting his eyes.

"I think the need for secrecy is gone, now. In those dreams, ever since that first night in Innis, you've been healing me, haven't you? My guilt and pain? Now I want to know how, and why. I'm not afraid anymore—not of myself, or of witchery."

He was adamant. Illyssa knew he would take no joking brush-off and no tears would deter him. Still, she tried. "You should be afraid, Yan. I'm a dangerous witch, as we all are."

"You see? You've admitted it—you're dangerous, all of you. Even to those you love?"

"Especially to them. We use and consume them." She had swung from mild jest to tears with no intervening step. He wiped salty droplets from her cheek with a finger. Understanding came from within, with sudden, chastening intensity. He remembered their painful talk in Jossity the night before her capture; he recalled his own childish selfishness, and how she had suffered for it.

"You are consumed in turn," he said. "I'm so sorry, Illyssa. Again I failed to see how the knife cuts two ways. You've been on trial, haven't you?" She said nothing, but she let him pull her close without resisting.

"I suppose you can't talk about it without their permission," he pressed, "so let me tell you what I think. When I collapsed in our cell in the Cathedral, it was not just fatigue, or stress. I was at the end of my personal rope, face-to-face with total failure. I had lost everything I cared about—my family, my profession—and I saw no escape except through madness. In that dream, that night, when my parents wrote me out of their lives, I wept. I think I wept aloud in my sleep. Did I?" Illyssa maintained tear-streaked impassivity. "Never mind," he said. "I'll ask Omer, sometime.

"The difference between my dreams and the events I remember as 'real,' " he continued stubbornly, "are small, taken by themselves. I wept or was silent, I spoke or was silent, I stood up or remained seated. Small, insignificant choices that had narrowed my path down to a single moment in Innis, when no alternatives existed." All the while he spoke, he held and watched her intently, reading small signs of face and body. He remembered the witches' truth sense; its obvious corollary was evident—witches were perceptive, but made poor liars. Even without saying a word, Illyssa could not have helped telling him how close his speculations were to truth.

"The dream in the Cathedral was a stopgap, wasn't it?" he went on. "It was an emergency measure to save someone who might be useful to you. It gave me breathing space to go on. Shedding those tears released me from the decision I'd made another time, the 'real' time, when I'd gone to my room and refused to cry.

"When we were free, you went against your 'mission' instructions by continuing to lead me through the decisions I'd made that kept me from accepting myself—and my talent. You pushed me to come to terms with the madness that the boy Yan couldn't accept or wholly deny." Looking at her, he was overcome by pity that went beyond even love. Tears filled his own eyes.

"You took it on yourself, and suffered with me until I could control the 'demon' my ancestors had let run wild—and they gave you a penance, didn't they? To finish what you had started, to go all the way with me, through fear and loathing, whining self-pity and ugliness, to live every moment of my evasion and failure. I think they hoped you'd get sick of wading in muck, and would stop loving me, but it didn't happen, did it? I know I'm right."

Yan was right on all counts, and Illyssa confirmed it by the small and simple act of snuggling closer in his arms. He needed nothing else. Perhaps some day she would tell him in words, share what it was like to steer another's dreams as they had steered *Serpent* on the Inland Sea. Would the elders allow it? Would she defy them again? Did it matter?

"Your tea's cooled, my love," she said quietly, still neither confirming nor denying his words. "Shall I make fresh?"

"Later," he replied as he bent to kiss her. "Now we have *your* victory to celebrate."

CHAPTER TWENTY-SIX

Detrun esklav, saydla sairconstans;
Detrun esklav propre, saydla natoor;
Davwaruh uhnesklav, say nee lun, nee lowtra, ay too layduh.

Being a slave is a matter of circumstance;
Being a good slave requires a certain temperament;
Having been a slave is neither—or perhaps both.
Marie-Claire Ailloud, transcription of a recorded conversation;
Ararat

Yan and Illyssa moved to Shallah to be near the outfitted ship. Yan's earlier hope of guessing when the ferosin ship would arrive, or of figuring it out from Roke's broadcasts, had almost died. The best they could do, not knowing, was to be ready to sail.

If the elders' spies in Roke signaled that a ship was leaving port, they would try to intercept it and follow it. There was a chance it would be the right one, for the sailing season was over. Otherwise, when all the ships of Roke set out for the Sailors' Mass at sea, they would merge with the fleet, keeping an eye out for a ship that strayed; if churchmen were meeting the ferosin vessel, it surely wouldn't be under the eyes of every Roke sailor. But many things could go wrong. There did not seem much chance of them going right. Still, they had to try.

Illyssa shook fat snowflakes from her hair and slammed the door.

"Is it bad out there?" Yan asked.

"The snow's not staying on the ground yet."

"How's Omer? I haven't been to see him today."

"Him? Feisty as ever. Smoking like a sausagemaker's chimney." When he'd found out about the move to Shallah, Omer had fumed, blustered, and threatened to walk across the low mountains from Ararat to the coast. They had had no choice but to bring him—and two nurses—with them. He was still hospitalized, but Shallan medics, at least, did not mind his smoking. He had a view of the harbor, and his soul seemed at rest there. Yan and Illyssa took a cozy apartment at the back of a chandlery, near both the wharves and Omer.

"Have you been listening to the signals from the ferosin ship?" Illyssa asked Yan. "I understand they've been changing."

"Of course I have. As the ship decelerates, the signals don't pile up on themselves, so the tone gets lower and slower and . . ." Yan was staring at Illyssa's hand, at her fingers. Something she'd said in Ararat was nagging at him. Fingers. Ten fingers. "That's it!" he shouted. He jumped up, spilling his cup, and dashed for the door.

"Yan? Yan! Where are you going?" Illyssa followed him outside, snatching his jacket from its peg. She saw him disappear around the corner, heading for the radio, now installed in a former carpentry shop. By the time she arrived there, he was powering it up.

"Set the antenna, will you? The position for this time of day is on the chart." Illyssa wrestled with two fat-knobbed cranks. Light chain rattled and, on the roof, unseen, the new bowl-shaped antenna jerked and crept into position. Below, peeping noises issued from the radio. "Listen! What do you hear?"

"It sounds like code, now that it's slower," she replied. "Like the parts of the Roke code you haven't figured out."

"Exactly. Roke is signaling the ship, and this is the reply that we're hearing. The problem is most of it hasn't made any sense." She watched him jot down numbers and letters: "1 2 3 4 5 6 7 8 9 a b c d e f g h i j 10 11 12 13 14 15 16 17 18 19 1A 1B 1C 1D 1E 1F 1G 1H 1I 1J 20 21 22 . . ." She made no sense of the sequence, though Yan seemed to be on to something.

"Can you get that girl—'Milla, is it? The one who does calculations in her head?" He did not stop jotting to ask.

"Now? She's home with her parents—probably in bed."

"It's important."

"I—of course. Wait." She draped his jacket over her shoulders and went out. Yan did not look up when she left. He thumbed through transcripts until he found the sheets of undeciphered codes from Roke, then began making small, careful marks beneath each group of "long" and "short" lines. Shortly, Illyssa returned with Ludmilla, eleven years old, wrapped in a blanket, with slippers on her feet. She was shivering.

Instead of chiding Yan for not having lit the fire, Illyssa did it herself. "Stand here, 'Milla. You can ask questions while you get warm."

Yan realized he was acting boorish, but he was too excited to wait, so he brought sheets of paper to the hearth and squatted next to the shivering girl. He showed her his most recent notations and explained them to her. "—so you understand that the letters A to J are really numbers, here?" he said a few minutes later. She nodded; her teeth still chattered when she tried to speak. "Good. Then try this one: What is one-aitch plus two-two?"

"T-t-three-jay."

"Good. What is one-one-cee in regular numbers?"

"Two hundred thirty-two. I'm getting warm now. Can I sit down?"

"Of course you can. I'm sorry, 'Milla. I'm so excited about this, I'm not very thoughtful."

"That's all right. This is fun. I didn't know there were other kinds of numbers."

"I didn't either, until just a little while ago . . ."

An hour later, Illyssa took Ludmilla home, apologized to her parents, and returned to find Yan by the fire, holding a single sheet of paper that showed only three strings of numbers:

GF–D5 = December 1, 3:54 PM
4= 3.6 deg. or 216 miles E
24 = 40 deg. N lat

Yan waved the sheet at her, too fast for her to really see.

"What do they mean?"

"Those are the date, the time, the latitude, and longitude of the touchdown site."

"You figured that out from the signals? But how?"

"Once I realized that ferosin, with ten segments and twenty limbs, might not count by tens, as humans do . . . I just looked for those repeated 'nonsense' sequences. It stood to reason that ferosin would be concerned that the meeting be on schedule. They have to land far off the regular trade routes, else some curious captain might investigate. They have to come down at sea because there's nowhere on land for the brownshirts to meet them unobserved. And it has to be at night, so when they meet the ship from Roke, there'll be time to offload cargo or . . ."

"Yan?" Illyssa had to raise her voice to stop his rambling. "Where will it be? When?"

"Didn't I say? Sorry. Forty degrees north latitude, and just over three and a half degrees east of Roke. Two hundred and sixteen miles offshore, give or take a mile."

It took Yan a while to explain how the numbers worked. "GF, base twenty, equates to three hundred thirty-one, and the three hundred thirty-first day of the year is December first."

"How do you know ferosin use the same system we do?"

"I guessed. Ferosin must have their own means of counting time, but they had to have a way to coordinate with humans, like Athel of Roke. I assumed they'd use something ordinary and understandable. One year, I-five and a fraction days; one day, one-zero-zero units long, or four hundred units, decimal, see?"

"Why four hundred? Why not *one* hundred?"

"We think in tens and hundreds—ten fingers, ten squared, and so on. Ferosin think in twenties—twenty legs, so twenty squared, or four hundred. Now do you see?"

"No. I'll believe you, though, as long as 'Milla did the figuring." She took the paper from him and looked at it. "I suppose the 'four' and the 'twenty-four' are ferosin numbers, too?"

"Aya. I suspected they'd use a well-known place to establish a prime meridian. Innis was nothing, back then, even though that's our prime meridian now, so I guessed Roke. Four four-hundredths of a circle around the Earth at Roke's latitude is about two hundred miles. It fit: convenient, offshore, after dusk . . . none of the alternatives worked as well." He got up and pulled on his jacket.

"Where are you going?"

"Omer. I have to show him."

"Yan, it's the middle of the night. You are *not* going to blow in like a snowstorm and wake him. Morning is soon enough."

Yan shook his head. "What day is it?"

"Tuesday."

"What *date*, I mean."

"November twenty-seventh. Oh! December first is . . . Yan, is there time? Can our ship *get* there?"

"Pole t' pole is two hundred a' their degrees, you figured? Why not four hundred, their 'standard' multiple?"

"It is, really, but if you think of azimuths radiating from the center of the Earth, starting with zero at the north pole . . ."

"We start at the equator and figure to the north and south. Why didn't you—"

"I did try that, Om. I figured it out several ways, and that's the only one that fit."

"I s'pose you're right, then," Omer conceded. "So what now? When will you leave?"

"The Roke ship has surely gone out with the fleet for the Sailors' Mass. It will lag behind when the ships go in. When the last one is hull-down toward port, they'll turn around and sail out to the meeting place. They'll have just enough time. We *might* have enough time, too, if we leave port at dawn—there's no moon."

"Aya, it makes sense." He reached for his pipe, earning a glare from the blue-clad "sister" who watched over him. He ignored her, and was soon puffing strongly.

"Yan, what did I say that gave you the first clue?" Illyssa asked. "You ran right out the door without your jacket."

"It wasn't anything you said. I've never been able to figure out how the brownshirts determine their holidays. The Sailors' Mass, for instance. Why isn't it the same day every year, at the *beginning* of the shipping season? When I remembered you counting on your fingers, saying, 'Monday, Tuesday . . .' I thought, 'Church holidays are Pharos days, which are *ferosin* days . . . and ferosin don't have ten fingers to count on.' "

Waves rattled on slaty beach cobbles, and spray darkened the rocks of the harbor mole. As the cargo yawl *Shallah Maid* cast off from the oared galley, her crew sheeted in the half-reefed mizzen. The small staysail forward flapped momentarily, then filled with a loud crack. Even with so little canvas, the lightly ballasted craft leaped ahead. Yan, standing aft with Mustaf Bakh, *Maid*'s captain, worried aloud over the rough weather and the moonless sky.

"The wind's fair going out," Bakh drawled. "Shallan ships don't balk at a breeze. Coming back, now, a sailing vessel might have a time—long tacks only a few points off the wind the whole way. One might have to winter in the south, if it came to that. But we'll get out there easy enough, never fear."

Yan reserved judgment. He had no desire to be blown to some unknown land on the far side of the Lannick. If Omer had been with him, and Illyssa, and had there been nothing pressing at hand, such a voyage might have been an adventure, but not now. For a moment his mind turned to a smaller vessel, to warmer, gentler seas . . .

Sailing on a broad reach out of Shallah, they would make better time than ships from more northerly Roke, which would be wallowing in westerly seas, running, if Bakh's guess was correct, under storm sails alone. Even hardened sailors would be leaning over the lee rails of the Roke fleet. Not a follower of Pharos, the captain was free with his scorn for sailors who let themselves be browbeaten into attending a blessing of ships in a fall Lannick blow. "There'll be less of this nonsense, you think, if the brownskirts have no 'gods' at their beck?" he asked Yan.

"It seems likely. But people change slowly, at their chosen pace. It could be a century before the Church is weakened enough so sailors of Roke feel free to defy its whims."

"Then someone will have to hasten its fall," Bakh muttered. "Too many seamen die because of such nonsense."

Yes, Yan agreed silently, someone *will* have to give the Church a final nudge over the edge, and that "someone" is me. He pointedly refused to think about the more-likely possibility—that he, along with *Shallah Maid* and her crew, would end up on the ocean floor, victims of ferosin.

"Where?" Yan asked, his face red and chapped from staring into the harsh wind aft. The first half day out and part of the rest it had rained, and even light spatters, driven by such winds, were like needles on his bare skin.

"The starboard quarter, just before the mizzenmast. It's under full sail. The damn fools. No appointment is worth sinking for."

Yan hated to admit that his scholar's eyes were dimmed from lamplit study and he couldn't see a thing. He did not see the white speck of sail for a half hour. "Will we fool them?" he asked anxiously, looking at *Shallah Maid*'s splintered mainmast and tangled rigging.

"We'd fool *me*," Bakh said, "and I'd hate to think a god-howler from Roke had a better eye. They have to stop for us. No captain would dare ignore the code of the sea—another time, it might be *him* in trouble."

"Yes," Yan agreed doubtfully, "but isn't our false emergency a flagrant breaking of that code?"

Bakh gave him a malicious grin. "Some circumstances compel a man to ignore lesser evils. There! See? They're lifting their main. They'll furl all but a trysail before they come alongside us, in this sea." Aboard *Shallah Maid* an odd lot of people clustered on deck, wrapped in blankets, wearing bright, dressy coats, broad-brimmed hats, and other garments appropriate to a pleasure excursion along the coast. Some even wore the voluminous skirts so popular in the Inland Sea cities, just gaining market on the Lannick Coast.

Aboard the Roke craft sailors in thick felt coats hooted disparagingly at *Maid*'s obviously incompetent crew, coast-huggers who let themselves be dismasted by such a feeble blow. Sailors on both ships made ready to lash the vessels together. Great bundles of roped sails were thrust over *Shallah Maid*'s side to ease the grinding contact between wave-tossed vessels. *Maid*'s "passengers" kept out of the way until the vessels were secure. At that instant the thin tone of a boatswain's whistle pierced the groans of timbers and rigging, the slap and whoosh of swells pumping between the two bound hulls, and the shouts of sailors.

"Women" threw off their hooped skirts and revealed not petticoats but sabers, and crewmen reached for sea-greened hafts. They swarmed over the shifting gunwales, leapt the greater gaps fore and aft, and infested the Roke ship like panicked rats.

Yan, still aft, gripped his war axe, his mind in turmoil. The fight seemed to be going well. Surprise was complete, and Shallans outnumbered the Roke crew, but he felt unworthy standing aside from battle. At the same time, a vision of cold, lone graves at the edge of a Michan swamp, the harsh echoes of Gran'ma's voice, held him back. His eyes raked the Roke deck and traveled past men battling by the mainmast. His gaze rose above their heads, and higher still—to the wrought metal mesh bowl atop the mast.

With a croak of dismay, Yan threw off his cloak and vaulted the poop rail. A quick dash brought him to a gunwale where a six-foot gap separated the vessels, dark water boiling upward between the hulls. Poised on the rail, he awaited *Maid*'s rise, and when the ship's movement reinforced his, he leaped. A sailor moved between him and his goal. Yan's axe swung at a low angle, catching the man's knee. He crumpled. Time slowed to a viscous crawl. Yan dodged Roke sailors and Shallans, never letting the double-doored companionway out of sight. In the shadowed opening, the maroon silk edging of a high-churchman's cowl gleamed like old blood, darker than the red haze in Yan's eyes.

He broke past a knot of fighters, who gave way as before a force beyond comprehension. None raised a blade against him. The brown-and-maroon shadow in the passageway receded, and he followed the clatter of sandaled feet into darkness below. Left, then right—his eyes caught a gleam from a door's opening, and darkness when it closed. Splinters flew and laths fell underfoot as he opened a way ahead with a single downward sweep of his massive blade. Light scattered in yellow shards as he burst into the radio room on the priest's heels.

Drying blood flaked from his thrown axe as it sunk into a brown-robed back. Plump priestly fingers groped in dying desperation for the brass code key, just out of reach. Yan's hand mated again with his weapon, and with one foot on the priest's back he wrested the axe free of splintered ribs and sucking flesh. Breath seeped and whistled from the priest's dying lungs. An oil lamp had fallen, and flames licked the bare planks underfoot. Yan kicked the lamp aside and rolled the dead priest over the flames, smothering them. The only light in the cabin came from the paired round dial faces of the radio. Above, the clatter of battle continued unabated, and before his mind could slow to a normal pace, Yan moved.

Unbuckling his belt, he let his trousers fall and kicked off his boots. He tore his red-spattered shirt away in a single motion. The dim electric glow from the dials turned his pale, cold skin golden, and reflected glittering crimson from his chromium-coated blade. With a brief backward glance, a silent promise to return, he left the radio room, and went to rejoin his shipmates, to finish the business at hand.

No crewman spoke to him when the battle was over. Even desperately involved in survival, in their individual fights, no one had remained unaware of Yan's reemergence on deck. He had been a pale typhoon sweeping men and steel before him, pure force moving with a speed and grace that busy eyes could hardly follow—a demon indeed, from the old, fearful tales of the dark, barren coasts. Sailors stared as if he were more alien than the Church's god, and they feared him more than any *human* enemy.

But Yan knew he was human, and that was enough. Soon men would realize that he stank of sweat as they did, that his scratches bled as red, that his words and victorious laughter were no less joyful than their own. For now it was good that they were in awe. It would give them strength, believing that the demon on their side was as ferocious as one they would soon face: the black ferosin demon that was not of their blood or their world, a true demon they had to confront, and conquer.

Both ships were a bustle of activity once the stillness of total victory had dissipated. Roke crewmen, bound or chained, were transferred to *Maid*'s hold. The Roke ship *Pharos' Grace*—quickly nicknamed *God's Grease*, then more rapidly shortened to *Greasy*—was scrubbed clean of gore. Dirt was rubbed into scarred wood to make gashes look old. Aboard *Shallah Maid*, a sheet-iron funnel was mounted, her boiler fired, and the false wreckage of tangled spars and rigging stacked neatly on deck.

The Shallans had intercepted *Greasy* a half day's sail from the splashdown site, interposing themselves between it and the Roke ship, and they were slightly north of their own ideal course to the meeting place. The rest of the voyage would be a run down the wind, the square-rigged Roke ship's fastest point of sail, so there was no real hurry, but Yan wanted to be in position to *see* the alien ship come down from the cold blackness of space.

The stiff wind abated, and they raised full sail. Slackening swells would make the following seas less uncomfortable than they had been for the Roke crew before them. From *Greasy*'s afterdeck Mustaf Bakh waved *Maid* off. Whistled commands brought sails into the wind. The gap between vessels widened, and *Greasy* was under way. *Shallah Maid* would follow, allowing the gap to grow to a dozen miles—there was no way to tell how ferosin might react to the presence of a second, unexpected vessel close at hand.

Brief questioning revealed that the Roke seamen knew little of their mission. Such knowledge lay with the brownshirt who, thanks to Yan's axe, now sank slowly to his muddy grave, bundled with the other dead in sailcloth weighted with broken swords, crockery, and whatever heavy things could be spared.

There was no plan. They hoped to approach the ferosin vessel, to take it as they had taken *Greasy*, before the starship's crew knew they were under attack. The witches of Ararat had provided basic information: ferosin, they said, were conservative. Their methods changed no faster than their technology—technology they had inherited or stolen, not developed. One ferosin, a pilot, never left his control pod. If the ship carried others, replacements for the Sons of Pharos, those would be in the first ship segment aft of the bridge. The rest of the ship would be cargo space open to the nonferosin crew. A thousand years earlier, the witches said, that crew would have been human slaves. Unless ferosin had found more tractable servants, they still would be. They might speak a variant of some ancient Earth language—Danish, English, and Dutch were common, because many early refugees had come from such low-lying lands. They might, though, speak an oriental tongue or a patois evolved among slaves. Yan couldn't count on communicating with them.

He shrugged and went below. The radio might be useful. Any information, any faint clue, could mean much for their desperate effort. Yan turned the vernier slowly, seeking along the scale of frequencies. The set was more powerful than his, or than the witches' small radio aboard *Shallah Maid*. As well as the clear signals from Roke and Jossity, Yan picked up others, from Innis or beyond. The signal from the ferosin ship was now identical to the Roke one, no longer distorted by the Doppler effect. Several times, amid the confusion of unknown messages, he heard the sequence of GF–DF–4–24. Once he heard GF–9I followed by two long strings of numbers. 9I? He glanced at the chronometer mounted on the bulkhead, mentally translating into ferosin time. That's now! he realized. They're confirming our time and position. The long strings represented *Greasy*'s position. A chill chased up his spine and down: Were they asking for confirmation?

Slowly, stiffly, he keyed a response: GF–9I–3 [query]–23 [query]. The "query" sign was whistle code, but he'd heard it among the indecipherable ship code, too. "Ferosin," he repeated to reassure himself, "are unoriginal. They use the materials and standards at hand, as do I."

Three-forty in the dull gray light of a Lannick afternoon. Nineteen minutes stood like iron fence pickets between Yan and the fate of his species. Nineteen minutes: a barrier he could not smash with muscle, madness, or chromium-plated war axe. He had to wait. He thought he would really go mad. His arms trembled; one hand grasped the foremast's starboard stay with such force that the heat and pressure softened its tarry sheath. If his axe haft had not been clear Pensana ash, it would have borne marks from his fingers. At three-forty-five Yan loosened his grip, flexing arms and stiff thighs. The next half hour would decide Earth's fate.

The first flare of false sunlight was right on time. It did nothing to soften the harsh set of his features. It shone in the southeast, where Orion would rise—first a glow, hardening to intense light too bright to look at, then, just as Yan thought it would set rigging afire with its passage, it plunged into the sea a half mile away. A gout of steam obscured the vessel. The sailing ship came alive as a high whistle tones signaled a course change. Massive yards shifted, sheets were let out or taken in, capstans groaned, and the motion of the deck underfoot inspired nausea as *Greasy* wallowed on fat, sleek swells.

The alien vessel moved toward them, out from its blanket of steam. The vessels would meet at exactly three-fifty-nine. Did such precision tell anything about ferosin? The bulbous "bridge" of the alien ship pushed a wave ahead, a green swelling unlike the splashing wake of an ocean vessel. For the second time in his life, Yan gazed upon a ship of space. It was like and unlike the Michan ship, he saw. No metal-mesh dragonfly wings projected from this black hull. It was smaller, too—only four flanges separated its modular cargo segments. As the dissimilar vessels' courses converged, the alien ship slowed, then stopped.

Whistles and shouts were drowned in the snap and flutter of backwinded sails as *Greasy* clumsily hove to. A fresh glow pierced the gloom as a hatch yawned wide. Red light like the ferosins' unimaginable sun cast bloody patterns on the water, on the white-clad humans within. They waved and motioned frantically and grabbed the swinging boarding plank that probed their hatchway. White-clad men and women grabbed lines cast their way and pulled them inside the hatch, which was so wide eight humans abreast could have walked through it.

Dark-clad Shallans mixed with white-shirted others, and a babble of unintelligible speech arose. One white-clad man crossed to *Greasy* and shouted at Yan a string of excited, incomprehensible syllables. "Un maître est libre," Yan heard. What language was that? Yan pronounced what he'd heard sound by sound: "Oon mayter ey leeber. Oon maiter . . . It's Bekwah!" he shouted. "Anyone speak Bekwah? Quickly!"

A sailor approached. "I do."

"Find out what he's saying. Hurry!" Shaking with impatience, Yan listened to the rapid babble of the strange, sharp tongue. He had the impression it was not going well—had the slaves' tongue diverged from that spoken in the north? Did the two men understand each other?

There was a racket somewhere in the depths of the huge metal vessel, the clatter of metal on metal and a high, rushing, chittering sound . . . ferosin! "What's he saying?" Yan interrupted to demand.

"He's talking about some . . . *shiffrah*? Code? Yes, some

code they heard. It was wrong. Did you send a code? How was it done?"

"Never mind that, now. Be quick!"

"They guessed that something had happened to *Greasy*, but the beasts, the pilot, didn't catch on."

"They knew? Then what have they done to help us? What's the situation on their ship now?"

"The Fronsays—that's what they are, not Bekwahs—shut the bulkhead doors, forward, and locked the bug things up," the interpreter replied, gray-faced. "They planned to escape on rafts, even if there had been no suspicions—but now a fero . . . fero . . . a bug's loose, forward. Unless we clear a path to the bridge, they can't stop the vessel from rising. He says we'll all be dumped out . . . in the sky."

Axe high in his grasp, Yan vaulted between the vessels in one great leap. "It's mine!" his demon shrieked, an inhuman howl. "Make way!" Before him, white- and dark-clad men and women moved aside. He heard the familiar insect sound before his eyes adjusted, and smelled dead insects and dry, rotted flesh. Immense and shiny, the ferosin rose up on spiky legs. Limbs thrashed and slashed the air as it advanced. It could not jump in those close quarters, Yan realized. Seizing his advantage, he moved just out of reach of the deadly serrated appendages. He swung, and felt his blade sink into substance dense as cold pitch. He pulled back—but his axe stuck. He couldn't pull it free, and he had no leverage, nowhere to place a foot to brace himself. Slowly, inexorably, he felt himself being drawn closer. Sharp-edged black arms reached for him; mandibles vibrated madly. The alien stink filled the air and burnt his eyes. He knew he had to let go of his weapon or be drawn into the ferosin's grasp.

No! Gripping the axe's haft in both hands, he twisted under it, pivoting, twisting, wrenching it free. Aided by momentum, he slashed through something black and thin that crackled like old bark. Above, a spiky arm flashed toward him. He had just time to raise his blade in a parry. The force of the blow drove him to his knees. He sensed men crowding behind him, felt their hatred and fear, their insensate urge to destroy the thing looming over him, and he drew strength from their presence. His axe was useless in such close quarters. As if in answer to his thought, he heard a sword slide and clatter on the metal deck. He snatched it and thrust upward with the full force of his legs. The blade skittered off chitin, then caught and punched through. Chittering as of a thousand crickets swelled, drowning human screams and the clank of steel. A gush of noxious fluid frothed down his blade and arm. He shook it off, again wrenching free of glutinous muscle, then dodged sideways to avoid the black, probing limbs. Suddenly only an empty corridor was before him.

Leaving the damaged ferosin for others, he stumbled forward. He had to get to the bridge. Under his feet metal vibrated as the ship prepared to lift, to dump rebellious slaves and wild human animals, to drown them in the blackness of space.

The bridge. He heard chittering ahead, and the scrape of chitinous feet on metal. Braced for battle, but with a sinking sensation, he pushed forward, knowing he was losing strength. The sounds came from a closed hatch—the second Son of Pharos was still trapped in its quarters. Yan ran on unsteadily as the deck lurched under him. A hatch ahead was open, and the red glow of ferosin light was bright as sunshine. The silhouette of the pilot pod loomed, a bulbous, shadowy mass of black metal. Inside, the ferosin pilot fought to raise its ship.

A trunk of massed cables ran aft from pod to bulkhead, then overhead on thick metal rings. Yan dashed toward the pod, took his axe in both hands, and brought it down on the cables, severing the whole bunched thickness of them with one well-placed blow. Electric fire raced up his arm, stunning him. His blade spat sparks. A blue thread of energy bridged the gap to Yan's hand even as he fell away and backward into the thick darkness of unconsciousness.

He awakened to the hammering of a steamship pushing close to the wind. He was in his cabin aboard *Shallah Maid*. How much time had passed? Brief panic passed as logic took hold. He was safe, so the Shallans had won free of the ferosin vessel. Had he been transferred to *Greasy* and then to *Maid*? Had the ferosin ship taken off? He had to know.

Mustaf Bakh was on the afterdeck, one eye on his ship's wake, the other on a hawser snaking aft. Sparks and gouts of black smoke swept back from the funnel, and the vibration of engines operating close to their limit made Yan's feet skitter on the sooty deck. The mizzenmast was unstepped, and Yan skirted stacked spars to get to Bakh. Sailors were sawing them into lengths.

"At the rate we're burning coal," Bakh explained without preliminaries, "we'll need everything but the bare hull for the firebox, to make port. *That* monstrous contraption was never meant to cut water." Yan peered aft along the thick cable. The black bulk, almost lost in coal smoke, was the ferosin ship, being towed like the corpse of an immense, ungainly whale.

"The monster's crew are aboard *Greasy*," Bakh said. "There's still one storm between us and Shallah. I know you want to study the black beasts, scholar, but for me, I won't regret it if their ugly vessel goes to the bottom, and them with it."

Yan was surprised by his own lack of concern. He did not want to "study" the ferosin, but to talk with them—but remembering his two encounters, he wondered if they could "talk" at all, as men thought of it. Perhaps the only way they could communicate with humans was to command—and that, he vowed, would not be. No one of Earth would take ferosin orders again. "Where's my axe?" he asked, grinning. "I'll cut the hawser for you."

Bakh shook his head. "I'll try to get the beast to port. Anyway, your axe is welded to the deck, where you left it."

CHAPTER TWENTY-SEVEN

There are many ways to manipulate history. Most involve emphasis—picking and choosing among events great and small until the written tale matches the unwritten agenda. It is much less complicated to create the events oneself, and to write them too large for clever revisionists to erase.

Y. B., 3851 CE, *Shallah*

The wing tower spread heavy-timbered legs across Ararat's common, stretching two hundred feet into the ice-gray dawn. Spattered wet snow lightened the north-facing square-hewn timbers and whitened the canvas over the launch platform. Morning mist and light drizzle had left crystalline sheaths on the twigs and branches below, and a chorus of icy squeals and crackles moved in sweeping arcs across the valley with every shift in the mild breeze. In hollows and on north slopes, surviving snow crusts sagged as their substance diminished in icy trickles. A dark line of deer crossed the far clearing, leaving their winter yards to seek scraps and tidbits left behind when snow had come. It had been a hard winter, but it was ending.

Yan Bando beat his fleece-lined gloves together to warm hands stiffened during the long skyward climb. His eyes followed the deer's progress until he lost sight of them behind intervening trees. Then his view swept to the ridge where low-hanging smoke marked Jasso's cliffside flying school. With his mind's eye, Yan scanned half-buried stone hutments and the "great hall," a barn disassembled in Ararat, then laboriously carted up steep switchbacks to the flight line. Even at this early hour the hall would be bustling with young fliers preparing for the day's activity.

Ararat was awakening. Shadowy figures, foreshortened by Yan's elevation, trudged between houses and along puddled streets to their day's occupations. Among them were molders, forgers, and machinists on their way to the engine manufactory. Smoke columns south of town told him that brewers and distillers were already at work making spirits, not for the throats of men but for the thirsty little motors that would soon pull the new generation of wings through even quiet air. The tower where he stood was not yet obsolete, but the day was near when wings would rise under their own power.

His eyes swept the cliff where the ancient tunnel hid his young wife, who labored and learned among the witches of Ararat, digging through records and reflections of a millennium for long-forgotten details of the universe beyond Earth. Illyssa was not unchanged by her sojourn among the old women, but her husband had little cause for complaint. If her training encompassed more than book-learning and document-chasing, she demonstrated it only in a more assured and self-confident manner. With each weekend reunion he experience an odd déjà vu brought on by new mannerisms and turns of phrase that were already oddly familiar to him. Several weeks had passed before he had realized the source of that familiarity: the gap between generations was narrowing, and though the elder Martina was gone from Ararat, her presence was still felt.

The ancient records contained much of value—more than the stuff salvaged from the ferosin ship before it had gone down twelve miles out from Shallah harbor. No lives had been lost there except for two ferosin, locked in a chamber and in the disconnected pilot pod. Among the records were coordinates for Foothold, a frozen world in the Oort cloud that orbited Earth's sun perhaps once in a million years. Concealed within its caves of ice and rock was Mankind's first—and only—independent settlement in space, built not by Earth men but by Illyssa's ancestors. Foothold's present fate was unknown. The surviving human crew of the ferosin ship, the Fronsays, knew nothing of it, even as legend. Perhaps it lay abandoned, its ships and facilities gathering dust; ship pilots had always been a rare breed, and only the hope that Earth, the fount of human diversity, might supply them had caused Foothold's erstwhile occupants to risk ship after ship returning to the mother planet. When Illyssa's ancestors had left the way station, there had been debate among those remaining on Foothold whether to send another ship to Earth if the mission never reported back. Perhaps there were no pilots left, and no hope but the witches of Earth. Much was to be seen.

The elders had allowed Illyssa to tell Yan what Others long dead had told her: the synergy of human minds linked, as Yan had experienced in Innis and Jossity, was a superior mechanism for starflight, far superior to the tenfold ferosin mind divided among its black segments. Ferosin ambition to control that uniquely human ability had kept Earth safe for a thousand years; ferosin fears might yet destroy it. But for now, there was time. The Fronsays believed theirs was the last vessel intended to visit *"La Terre"* until the new ferosin masters grew old. Only their belief that never again would another chance for freedom arise had led them to plan a desperate escape without hope of success; their frail rafts would never have survived the cold Lannick seas.

The Masters, they explained, could spare no resources to monitor Earth. Their aggressive natures and prolific breeding, products of evolution in an inconceivably hostile environment, demanded continual expansion; whole worlds were stripped, their enslaved populations moved or abandoned; new worlds were settled, and the ferosin sphere grew, and the distance the Masters had to travel grew also. Simple geometry defeated them, for they were like spots painted on an inflating balloon. Travel across chords of the sphere was prohibitive; ferosin on one side of the balloon could have no contact with those on the other. Earth lay not on the periphery of ferosin domination, but deep within sphere after concentric sphere of dead, abandoned worlds.

"If *les Maîtres* had harnessed human star pilots to zheir craft," explained Marie-Claire Ailloud, an escapee, "paihr'aps zhere would 'ave been a ferosin renaissance. But zhere are no weetches among my people, an' no male weetches at all."

Illyssa had agreed. The separation of her own people in slavery had dashed their hopes. Witches, she explained, held half the secret of star-piloting. The lost men were the key. Mental discipline could control fusion fires, and witches could speak mind-to-mind as one, but the *men* were vital to the star-pilot gestalt; they were the eyes and nerve trunk of the synthetic being.

The men's ability was rare, a holandric trait, carried only in the male line. Few men carrying it had left Earth as refugees, Illyssa said, and on Ararat, the witches' last home before Foothold and the Return, discovery of the male link had been a fluke; only on Earth was there hope of finding such men—and that had not happened.

Only on Earth, Yan thought, understanding now why the ferosin had spared his world. Only on dusty roads, in primitive cities, mountain villages, in yet-unexplored countries far north or across unmapped oceans, was the witches' key to be found, and the door to the stars opened; it was a monumental task—but now, free of ferosin intervention, it would be done. Surely one of the fliers going out to universities and cities across the continent would find the catalysts. Surely somewhere on the vast planet Earth those men—like the mutated hemp from planet Ararat that joined minds without lethargy or befuddlement—had taken root and grown. They would be found.

It was spring, and the slow pace of winter was over. Omer was arranging an expedition that would leave on the first spring winds. The Bolide ship might never lift again, but the ancient witches' menfolk had promised, in the Oath of Innis a millennium before, that they would leave messages there if they regained their freedom. Perhaps there would be a clue to the pilot gene.

Three ships were at anchor in Shallah's harbor. Yan could imagine Omer's energetic supervision of them. The old sailor had recovered well and had only a limp to show for his ordeal—that and his hair. The last streaks of color had left the fringe around his bald head, and only his mustache was yellow from pipe smoke.

Yan clapped mittened hands together to warm his fingers. He peered into the distance as if he could see beyond the hills, the Inland Sea, over the roofs of Wain and Nahbor to Nipigon, where the witches' ship lay frozen beneath winter ice. The night past and the coming day were of one length—the vernal equinox, a day when all Earth's promises were laid out before its denizens. The long winter was ended, and it was time for men to go into their furthest fields.

Yan felt the vibration of booted feet on the ladder below. He peered down at the anonymous, hooded climber, then reached to lend a mittened hand.

"I thought I'd find you here," Illyssa said.

"And I hoped you might, too, when you got tired of that musty cave. You'll be an elder yourself someday if you don't stop working so hard."

Her smile sparkled with mischief. "How do you know I'm not already?"

For a moment, Yan was tongue-tied. Elders were . . . old. Weren't they? Yes—just as "witches" were *witches*. But of course Illyssa insisted that Ararat's witches weren't really *witches* at all, and Yan knew that, too. So must "elders" be elderly?

The hot flush that accompanied a brief, intense memory of Martina answered his question. "*Are* you an—" He curtailed his query. Only a fool asked for answers. Elder or not, witch or not, she was . . . Illyssa. He pulled her close and buried his face in the snow-flecked fur of her hood.

"Are you still moping about losing the ferosin ship in the storm?"

Yan drew back with a sigh, smiled, and gestured to the clearing sky, where spring winds drove the last wintry clouds back toward the north. He shook his head. "Not at all. When we go out there, when we meet the bugs in space, it won't be in a clanking alien sewer pipe, bumbling and bumping through reefs of gravity and shoals of undefinable energy. We'll meet them in a ship of our own making, a *human* ship built right here, by our own hands. Ferosin will still consume decades crossing between one star system and the next, but we'll go out singing, a choir of mental voices raised in exultant song. We'll sing where others chittered, croaked, and bellowed, and dance between the stars where others crawled."

EPILOGUE

The ancient mind was suffused with silent laughter. *He doesn't know, does he?* It was the youngest old mind.

We *still don't know, for sure. How could* he? Sharp old thoughts, those, intolerant of laughter and comparative youth.

The signs are there, a third mind said, impatient. *Have the girl bring us his blood, and we'll know.*

One pilot? One man? Bah, we need many. Sharp, impatient thoughts, at odds with patient, ancient memories. *And he's not one of us. It would be . . . distasteful to share his thought.*

Old woman, old fool, the fresh young-old mind thought. *I'll share thought with him . . . and more.* You *didn't mind sharing him with* me, *did you?* And silent laughter echoed from dark stone arches, all the length of the Unending Cave.

DEL REY DISCOVERY

Experience the wonder of discovery
with Del Rey's newest authors!

. . . Because something new is
always worth the risk!

TURN THE PAGE FOR AN EXCERPT FROM THE
NEXT *DEL REY DISCOVERY*:

The Rising of the Moon
by Flynn Connolly

After fifteen years of self-imposed exile, Nuala Dennehy came home.

The walk from the landing bay to the center of the terminal wasn't a long one, but Nuala was in no hurry. She avoided the moving path and did her own walking, the strap of her carry-on bag clutched tightly in her hand. The fifteen-minute walk, added to the short hop over from Glasgow, gave her more than enough time to remember the day she had fled Ireland a decade and a half ago.

She had been twenty years old. Twenty going on fifty. It was two days before the graduation ceremony at Trinity, but she had already left campus, left Dublin, because there was no point in staying. They would not be granting her a history degree after all her hard work, because her thesis was not "acceptable" to the Jesuits who had taken over the Protestant university decades before. She had chosen the field of matricentered pre-Christian Ireland, knowing they—the Jesuits and the occasional nun who made up the faculty—wouldn't *like* it, but that there was a slim chance they would grant the degree anyway. It was usually just recent history, especially the last two centuries, that they were so strictly revisionist about. So she had gambled—and lost. It had saddened more than angered her—though she *was* angry—saddened her to see how quickly Ireland was changing. She had been in trouble many times in her life for speaking her mind—since she was six years old and had debated the existence of God with the parish priest, to the humiliation of her mother—but when a free exchange of ideas, a search for knowledge, for the truth, was not allowed even in a university, she knew it was time to leave.

Her sadness was tempered by bitterness: if the people could

not see or did not care that the Catholic Church was gaining control over every aspect of Irish society, including the government, then why should *she* care? But she did. Profoundly. Being forced to abandon her beloved country to seek education and opportunities elsewhere inflicted an angry wound that had never healed.

Belfast's travelport was crowded with tourists: because of the many traditional music festivals, August was a popular time for visiting Ireland. Most of the tourists were speaking English with a variety of accents, but Japanese, Welsh, German, and many other languages could be heard in the din; some Australian students were even attempting to converse in hesitant Tlatejoxan as they waited in line, practicing the clicks and laryngeal stops that were so difficult for human vocal tracts.

Nuala recognized a few of the Tlate phrases. EuroNet had a weekly program on Tlatejoxan culture, and she never missed it, being as curious as anyone else about the first extraterrestrials to make contact with Earth.

Nuala eased her way through the crowd, scanning the signs overhead until she found the one she was looking for: *Saoránaigh*, it read, and underneath, in slightly smaller letters, *Citizens*.

An exile though she was, she still carried Irish citizenship, so Nuala left the jabbering tourists behind and set off down the corridor under the *Saoránaigh* sign, her stomach roiling with bitter memories.

She fingered the tiny new ID chip she had been issued at the Irish office in Edinburgh. As she fidgeted with the shiny dog tag, she went over Máire's cryptic instructions in her mind for the hundredth time: don't attract attention, and say as little as possible to the *gardaí* or anyone in clerical garb. Máire would say no more over the 'phone, and her expression had been, as usual, unreadable, her eyes hooded.

Máire was frequently cryptic, often exasperating, but then she had been ever since Nuala had met her nearly twenty years ago. She wondered why they were friends—or if they really were—but then she always had to remind herself that Máire was the only person from her university days in Dublin who had bothered to keep in touch for the past fifteen years. She was never sure why Máire continued to write and occasionally 'phone, but never having had a surplus of friends, Nuala couldn't just abandon her. In some ways, Máire was one of the remaining tangible links she had with Ireland. And she did write intriguing—if enigmatic—letters about the situation back home. She and Nuala felt the same way about the state of their country, shared the same hopes for Ireland's future. So when Máire hinted strongly that it was time for Nuala to come back, well, she had to come see for herself what was really going on.

Nuala tried, yet again, to decipher Máire's unspoken warning about not attracting attention. What did she mean? Say as little as possible about what? But then she found herself at the end of the short corridor. She fell into the queue of people waiting to pass through the Eye.

"Cuir do thraipisí go léir ar an mbord agus siúil tríd an scanóir." The young female voice repeated in a bored monotone, this time in English, "Place all your personal belongings on the table and step through the scanner."

Those instructions had been a recording at the Edinburgh travelport, but in Ireland, where every man and every unmarried woman was guaranteed employment, unnecessary jobs were frequently invented.

As she came closer to the front of the queue, Nuala could see better what awaited her. There was the Eye, looking just like the one at the Glasgow travelport: a black rectangular box tall enough for humans to step through, narrow enough to admit only one at a time, and about a meter long. At its right side was a waist-high table with a smaller Eye for belongings to pass through, and beside it stood a bored customs assistant in her forest-green uniform. Beyond the box was another customs assistant, and, to Nuala's uneasy surprise, fanning out on either side were four armed *gardaí*: the young blue-uniformed officers held their Armalite plasfire rifles ready, but they looked just as bored as the customs assistants.

Even though she carried no weapons or "suspicious substances"—whatever they were—Nuala's stomach churned again at the thought of the rumors she had come home to investigate. She told herself to remain calm. She had broken no laws; she should have nothing to fear.

At the head of the queue, Nuala took a chain off and handed her ID chip to the customs assistant, watched her insert it into the side of the Eye, then placed her bag on the table and stepped into the box.

There was a flicker of light as the Eye activated, but Nuala couldn't see what it was reading; the screens were only visible to the customs assistants on the outside, not to the person in the Eye. She wondered if every scar, every dental restoration, maybe even her dozen or so gray hairs and the shape of her spleen were being noted and added to the sparse information on her new Irish ID disk. She fought off a wave of claustrophobia, and sighed in relief when the door slid open.

Stepping out of the box, she glanced at the *gardaí*, but they were chatting with each other and paying her no mind, so she reached for her bag as it came sliding out of the smaller Eye and placed its strap on her shoulder. The second customs assistant slapped the ID chip into her palm and waved her on her way, saying, *"Lean an riabh uaine."*

Green stripe? Oh, there, on the floor, a weathered plastiseal strip that led past the *gardaí* and on down another corridor.

"Follow the green stripe to the first free returning-citizens interviewer," the customs assistant prompted her, raising her voice at Nuala's hesitation.

"Interviewer?" Máire hadn't said anything about any interview.

"The first open door," the assistant said, her voice taking on an edge of annoyance as she waved toward the corridor a second time.

Nuala moved forward, toward the *gardaí* with their lethal Armalites. Although she didn't know much about weapons, she knew enough to recognize a plasfire gun when she saw it. The police in Scotland carried guns that could only stun; the Irish police carried the Armalites, which could be set on stun or set on plasfire, to kill. What were they so afraid of that they carried the plasfire weapons in a travelport? Were the IRA up to their old tricks? They were never mentioned on the news in Scotland—but then, *Ireland* was never mentioned on the news.

None of the four men glanced at her as she passed them. Nuala was relieved to leave them behind; she had made it past the first hurdle. She was beginning to wonder just how many more there would be.

Starting down this new corridor, Nuala unbuttoned her linen smock and plucked at her peach-colored, cotton T-shirt, pulling it away from damp skin. The first open door? They were all open, at least halfway. They were probably supposed to be closed for privacy, but it was obvious that the air-conditioning was malfunctioning. She almost smiled at that. When she had left Ireland fifteen years ago, the air-conditioning had been broken, too. No doubt it had been "fixed" countless times since then by the travelport maintenance men who never had to worry about being out of a job, because they never did that job too well.

Nuala continued down the corridor, looking for the first unoccupied returning-citizen interviewer. The lights flickered once and then again; apparently the air-conditioning wasn't the only system on the blink. As she walked, she caught snatches of polite, practiced instruction from the young, female customs assistants to their interviewees:

"Oh, no, ma'am, for a stay of less than six months, volunteer charity work is not compulsory. If your husband takes a job in Ireland, however, even a temporary one, that would, of course, change matters."

"You have thirty days to register at the church of your choice, sir. If you haven't decided on a church by then, the closest one in the parish will be chosen for you."

"I'm sorry, but I'm afraid the implant will have to be removed for the duration of your stay, ma'am. Contraceptives are, as you know, quite illegal. But I'm sure it'll be no trouble getting another when you return to England."

"In here, please. *Isteach anseo, le do thoil!*"

With a start, Nuala realized the words were directed at her. A weary young woman with wilted brunette hair waved at her through the wide-open door. "Close the door halfway, please, and take a seat."

Before Nuala had even taken her carry-on from her shoulder and sat down, the interviewer's hand was reaching across the circular metal desk. Dropping her bag, Nuala handed her the dog tag, then sat down on the uncomfortable fauxwood chair as the lights flickered once more.

"Welcome home . . . Miss Dennehy," the assistant recited as the 3-D computer screen on the corner of her desk lit up.

"Go raibh maith agat," Nuala thanked her politely, telling herself she had no reason to be nervous. She should have nothing to fear from an interview. But why the hell hadn't Máire told her what to say? She cleared her throat. "It's nice to be able to speak *Irish* Gaelic again, after so long in Scotland."

"Yes," the assistant murmured as she read what little data there was concerning Nuala Meabh Dennehy.

Seeing that the young woman was occupied with the computer, Nuala didn't interrupt. She looked around the cubicle. Just as she had expected, there was the Pope on one wall, an eight-by-ten 3-D glossy of himself in full gaudy splendor, and opposite on the other wall hung another eight-by-ten, this one of the current *Taoiseach*, the Prime Minister of United Ireland. The irreverent joke that declared the two men to be the same person had no truth to it—else how could they appear together in public every year when His Holiness visited Ireland? But there was a certain resemblance, Nuala thought, a sort of weaselish look about the nose and mouth. Perhaps the *Taoiseach* had Lithuanian relatives . . .

There was little else to see in the cubicle. No family holos on the meticulous desk, no other pictures, or a plant, or even a window. Nothing to break the monotony of dull celadon walls except those two pompous portraits. How dreadfully bored the poor thing must be to work in here full-time, six hours a day, four days a week. Would a friendly overture be the right approach. Máire's instructions had been so ambiguous, Nuala wasn't sure how to act. If she were taciturn, would that provoke suspicion? But suspicion of what? What was the purpose of this interview? Damn Máire for not explaining. Should she—

"I see that this is a new chip, as you've been gone from Ireland for quite some time, Miss Dennehy," the interviewer said, interrupting Nuala's racing and confused thoughts. "I suppose they weren't in use yet before you left. That means there's a great deal of information we'll have to add. Our conversation will be recorded, and the pertinent information will be added to your chip."

"Fine." Nuala glanced at her watch, sighing. It was well past teatime; she wouldn't be getting out of here before Máire got off work. Perhaps a friendly act *would* be her best bet. If only she knew what was expected of her.

Still engrossed in the screen, the interviewer began. "Now then, Miss Dennehy, in the past fifteen years, have you—"

"Who are you?" Nuala forced a phony smile.

The surprise question finally forced the interviewer's eyes from the screen. She blinked. "I beg your—"

"What's your name? You know mine." Nuala's smile felt strained as she pointed to the screen. "And some other things, none of which is anybody's business." No, that wasn't right. Hold the irritation in check. Keep smiling. "I was just wondering who I was speaking with."

"Oh . . . yes." The assistant flushed, straightening the already-straight lapel of her uniform jacket. "Noreen O'Mahony *is ainm dom.*"

"Ah, well then, Ms. O'Mahony—"

"*Miss* O'Mahony."

Nuala raised an eyebrow. "So, Noreen, do you like working here?"

"I—" She blinked in confusion again; the interviewer was not used to being interviewed. "Do I—"

"Well, is it a full-time job? I imagine the pay is pretty dismal, since you're a woman. I doubt *that*'s changed since I've been gone." Nuala glanced around the cubicle. "And you've nothing colorful in here to liven things up even a bit. Or do you hide holos or a novel or something in your desk?" Nuala smiled again; her cheeks were beginning to ache from the forced cheerfulness, and her nerves were already too taut from this tightrope walk between caution and false empathy. How much empathy was going too far? How much honesty was dangerous?

Noreen just stared at her, puzzled. "I think we should get back—"

"If you wish. I was just trying to be friendly. Interviews can be so cold. And so boring for the one asking the questions." She smiled yet again. "I've had bloody boring jobs myself, shopclerk, library tech, and such, so I know how it can be."

A half smile, but still a wary one, finally tugged at a corner of Noreen's mouth. "Yes, it—" She hesitated, glancing at the half-open door, then leaned forward and whispered in a sudden flurry of honesty that surprised Nuala. "If you really want to know, it *is* bloody boring, as well as uncomfortable, asking people questions they don't want to answer for a stranger. But it's all over soon; I'm to be married in three months' time. I'll never have to work again, thank God!"

"You mean for money?"

A startled recognition flitted over Noreen's face, then was gone. The returning-citizens interviewer took over again. "Now then, can we get back to this? The sooner we start—"

"The sooner we'll finish, right. Fire away."

"Now, then, Miss Dennehy—"

"Call me Nuala. I hate formalities."

"I'm afraid that's not allowed. Now, could we just stick to the questions, please? This will go faster."

"Sure. I don't want to cause you any trouble—or myself, either."

Finally Noreen gave her a genuine smile, though a brief and weary one. "In the past fifteen years, since leaving Ireland, you haven't married?"

"Whatever for?"

Noreen hesitated in surprise, her hands hovering over the keyboard.

Nuala shrugged sheepishly. "Sorry. Uh, no, I haven't."

Noreen typed, watching the screen as the computer added this information. She continued. "Your father is still your nearest male relative, then?"

"He is."

"And does he still reside in Falcarragh?"

"He does."

"And is he still employed by Donegal Renewable Resources, Limited?"

"He's not. He retired three years ago, for health reasons. He's not well."

Noreen frowned at this. "Well, if he's not employed, then who—" She stopped, glanced at the screen, then said, "I'm sorry about your father. I hope he's feeling better soon."

Surprised by the gesture, Nuala smiled, and this time the thanks wasn't forced. "*Go raibh maith agat, a Noreen*. That's nice of you."

Noreen nodded. "As your father is unemployed, who then is your nearest *employed* male relative?"

Nuala hesitated. "Haven't any."

Noreen stared at her as if she had said something obscene in church. "None?"

"None."

Noreen's frown deepened. "Then who's to be responsible for you while you're in Ireland?"

"I'm an adult, *well* past twenty-one," Nuala replied, an eyebrow raised. "I'm responsible for myself."

"Well, of course, but—" Noreen leaned forward and whispered. Nuala had to strain to hear her. "I have to put something down. You really don't have *any* male relatives."

"Just my father," Nuala whispered back.

"But he's not employed; I can't use him!"

"Then what shall we do?"

"Well, I—" Noreen was at a loss.

"What do you put down for women with no family at all? Do *they* get to be responsible for themselves?"

"Only as long as they're employed, after that the Church—"

"Why are we whispering?" Nuala interrupted. "Isn't this being recorded?"

Noreen blushed, to Nuala's surprise, and shot a glance at the half-open door. As if in answer to Nuala's question, the lights flickered again, went out completely for a few seconds, then came back on.

"It's not working?" Nuala guessed, suddenly understanding Noreen's previous burst of honesty.

Noreen shrugged, her expression a mixture of guilt and apology. "We're told to lie about it, to make you *think* you're being recorded. But you're right; the spy system's been down for days. They can't seem to get it fixed. *Nothing* works right around here."

Nuala saw Noreen's embarrassment at being caught in a lie she hadn't wanted to tell in the first place. "So I won't be dragged off to jail for saying the wrong thing in front of cameras?"

Noreen sighed; she suddenly looked exhausted. "You wouldn't have been arrested, but you might have been followed—and watched."

The two women stared at each other. Nuala wondered if Noreen was thinking the same thing she was: How much honesty can I risk?

"And now?" Nuala said. "Since this isn't being recorded?"

Noreen swallowed and sat up a bit straighter. "You don't have to worry about that from me. I give you my word. Some of us still believe in the right to our own opinions."

Nuala considered that for a moment, then nodded. "Shall we finish this, then?"

"Right." Noreen studied the screen. "Where were . . . Oh yes. Well, if you have no employed male relatives, are you going to be seeking employment yourself while in Ireland?"

"I hadn't planned to be here long." Nuala could see that wasn't the answer Noreen was looking for.

"Uh, well, perhaps you might consider that. What is your current occupation in—" She glanced back at the screen. "Edinburgh, is it?"

"It is. I've been living in Edinburgh these ten years past. I was in Aberdeen before that, doing postgraduate work."

"And you've been employed?"

"I have. I'm a professor at the university in Edinburgh, in the Celtic studies department."

Noreen's face fell. "But you're not—a nun."

"No." Nuala shrugged. "So I suppose I won't be seeking a teaching position in Ireland, will I?"

Noreen thought for a moment, then tried a new tactic. "Do you have any male *friends* in Ireland who could vouch—"

But Nuala was already shaking her head. "Not a one. It's been a long time."

"Perhaps some friend of your father's would be willing—"

"Is it really necessary?" Nuala's jaw clenched in irritation. Perhaps the usual tone of melodrama in Máire's letters hadn't been exaggeration, after all. And the other rumors?

"I'm afraid so. All females must be under the protection of a male relative, or some other suitable adult male, pursuant to the Mother and Child Act of—"

"Why?"

Noreen paused. She had every reason to be angry with Nuala for being difficult, but she didn't seem to be. "Well, it's—the law."

"So a female friend, even an employed one, couldn't vouch for my good name and character? Couldn't swear that I wouldn't rob a bank or try to assassinate the Pope or whatever?"

Noreen sighed, shaking her head. She pointed at the screen. "Your ID chip is a legal document, and women can't—That is, women aren't allowed to—"

"Things have really gone to hell in the time I've been gone." Nuala's glare of disgust took in first the *Taoiseach* and then the Pope. "How have the women of Ireland let things get so out of hand?"

Noreen's eyes widened, then she surprised Nuala with a smile that disappeared almost immediately. Noreen cleared her throat. "Uh, perhaps we could try a few of the other questions."

"We can try."

"Good. Then: Where are you planning to stay during your visit to Ireland?"

"I'll be going to Donegal, to Falcarragh, in a few days to see my father. I'll be staying with him."

"How nice. I'm sure he'll be able to think of someone to vouch for you, to fulfill the law . . . So you'll be celebrating Mass at St. Finian's, then, where your father is a member of the congregation?"

"Whatever f—" Nuala bit her tongue, then lied. "Of course."

Noreen's expression clearly said she recognized the lie, but she smiled anyway. "You *were* baptized at St. Finian's in Falcarragh—"

"Well that wasn't *my* fault, was it? I was just a baby at the time."

"There is a Presbyterian church in Letterkenny—"

"No. Not Protestant."

"I don't suppose you're Jewish?"

Nuala returned Noreen's smile. "Atheist, actually."

She knew she had gone too far when Noreen sighed and shook

her head. "You *have* been gone a long time, haven't you, Miss Dennehy?"

"Nuala. If we're not being recorded, then there's no need for formalities, right?"

"No. But I have to update your ID. If the *gardaí* stopped you and found you with incomplete or unacceptable records—"

"Why would they stop me if I don't break any laws?"

Noreen stared at her in disbelief. "The *gardaí* can stop anybody, at any time, and frequently do, especially a woman who is not accompanied by a man or a child."

"I can be harassed by the *gardaí* simply for being female?" Nuala forced the words out between clenched teeth.

Noreen shot a glance at the door as a couple passed by. Getting up from behind the desk, she crossed the cubicle and closed the door, then slowly walked back to her seat, frowning. Nuala watched her, cursing her own temper and big mouth. Noreen seemed to be open to honesty, but how far was too far? She was not under the "protection" of any man; she was an atheist; even her profession was unacceptable. If she held foreign citizenship, she might be deported as undesirable, but she was an Irish citizen. What kind of trouble could Noreen cause Nuala if she wished? Had she really meant it about the right to her own opinion? Or would she have her followed, as she had mentioned? Nuala would *have* to be more careful.

Noreen was staring back at her, studying her with a curious expression.

"I'm sorry your father isn't well, Miss—*Nuala*. But my advice to you is to go back to Edinburgh and have him visit you there when he's able. You don't belong in Ireland."